WITHDRAWN

TRUMPET OF JUBILEE

THE WORKS OF

LUDWIG LEWISOHN

Fiction

THE BROKEN SNARE
DON JUAN
THE CASE OF MR. CRUMP
ROMAN SUMMER
THE ISLAND WITHIN
STEPHEN ESCOTT
THE LAST DAYS OF SHYLOCK
THE GOLDEN VASE
THIS PEOPLE
AN ALTAR IN THE FIELDS
TRUMPET OF JUBILEE

Drama

ADAM: A DRAMATIC CHRONICLE

Trumpet of Jubilee

A NOVEL BY

LUDWIG LEWISOHN

*Then shalt thou cause the trumpet of the jubilee
to sound. In the day of atonement shall ye make
the trumpet sound.* LEVITICUS 25:9

PUBLISHERS

HARPER & BROTHERS

NEW YORK   MCMXXXVII   LONDON

TO THELMA

CONTENTS

❡ THE PROLOGUE

N'est-il pas surprenant que les peuples chrétiens seuls aient été capables de créer la civilisation la plus distante des préceptes de l'Évangile, la plus opposée à toute forme de vie chrétienne?

ANDRÉ GIDE

(Is it not amazing that the Christian peoples alone should have been capable of creating the civilization that is the remotest from the precepts of the Gospel, the most contrary to any form of Christian life?)

THE PROLOGUE

I

FROM earliest times men have told each other stories, and they have told them for both entertainment and truth. Never were the stories mere feigning. The very fantasies of fairy-lore amused men only as they were convincing, and we have lately learned that they did so because their wildest images correspond to dreams, to desires, even to cognitions anchored within the very structure of the human soul. If gods appeared in the stories, it was because neither teller nor hearer could conceive of a Godless and an empty world; the men and women in the stories had to have verisimility: they had to be like the hearers of the tale not only in their physical natures, not only in their dealing with hunger, shelter, love. They had to act according to motives and upon principles at least intelligible to the audience. No story was convincing and therefore true unless its creatures and its hearers stood on some common ground and had some common faith.

It follows that the teller of stories which were convincing because they were true had to be deeply rooted in the life first of his clan and folk, next of mankind itself. He had to know more than the ear heard or the eye perceived. He had to know more about his hearers than they themselves knew. He had to know more about man than man knows with his aware and waking mind. Hence his so-called omniscience was never, as has been foolishly asserted, the mere convention of

an art. For his creatures are both concretely and symbolically more real and more secure from time than beings of
mere flesh and blood. They are creatures—created things.
Not, to be sure, created out of nothing. Agonized observation,
pity that scorches the heart, aspiration that rends the sky,
identification of his own hunger, passion, frustration, prayer,
with those of his fellows—such are the elements out of which
the artist fashions his creatures. He knows their secretest
thoughts and has paid dearly enough for that knowledge.
He has, in truth, come by it so hard that he may well be
believed.

He is in a different case when he must delineate men he
has seen in the world with the eye of the body—God's creatures, not his own. He cannot, strive as he may, be within
them. They are opaque to him. A luminous outline hides a
core of darkness. He hears speech; he sees gesture; he listens
to legend. That is all. Yet there are three men that must be
told of in the story which follows who live and breathe, whom
I have seen and known, with whom I have held converse
in more than one city and, in fact, on more than one continent. How many times? Not many. Nor were any of the
three commonly given to quick intimacy or self-revelation.
Luckily and naturally I am not the only one who has known
Peter Lang and Jehuda Brenner and Andrew Saracen. People have spoken to me concerning them in Boston and Hamburg, in New York and in Constantine, in San Francisco
and Jerusalem. Thus I have been able to add glimpse to
glimpse and detail to detail. And all facts about these three
were pregnant with meaning. For no mind open to the
strangeness and terror of this day in history but knew at
once that these three men, though allied to immemorial
trends, could have been hammered into this shape by no
other age, by no other world save this twentieth-century
world which nevertheless each of them desired with an inveterate passion to shatter into dust and re-create after an
image that burned with an unfaltering flame within his heart.

II

PETER LANG gave himself away whenever his kind blue eyes were frightened into sternness. He liked pain and harsh struggle no more than a child. He was on many occasions like a very intelligent and very charming child. I have an image of him playing tennis on the court of friends in Cambridge, lithe and boyish in his white suit, poised on one foot with racket held aloft. A New England Hermes. Later around a fire kindled against the chill of autumn I first saw during an anecdote told by Professor Thwing, our host, concerning bleak suffering in a near-by industrial district that frightened look in Peter's eyes. What frightened him then and always was the defencelessness of the weak. He did not care to weigh issues; he shrank then and always from analysing any given situation of that kind. I watched his white, square, reliable hand holding his teacup. There were a purity and a singleness of mood and mind in him that felt subtlety like an affront. The weakness of the weak was a tragedy to his soul. It frightened him—that and the monstrous fact that men could bear to oppress the weak because they were so. And thus at once his eyes grew stern at the oppressors and at himself for not being even now beside those who were oppressed, for not already adding his own to their little strength and suffering with them need stripes, prison and contumely. . . . All this I f once, and this impression was confirm when, walking past the State H Boston, I saw Peter Lang across viously for the hundredth time, which Saint-Gaudens has commen   white

5

New England soul," Robert Gould Shaw leading his Negro troops into the battle of their own liberation.

Less secretive concerning his origin than Saracen, less indifferent than Brenner, Peter Lang spoke more than once of the many-columned early nineteenth-century house in Castleton, Vermont, in which he had been born. He was never either glib or eloquent. He conveyed to us, nevertheless, images of the cosmic starry tranquillity of white winters as well as of the sudden blossoming of May—that other whiteness of cherry and of apple trees in bloom tinged by the lilacs and by the lofty, faintly green arches formed by the interlacing elms. He made you see the strong rocks and serene birches by hidden lakes, the trees and waters of a good, grave, simple land. His father had been and continued until the other day to be the Congregational minister of the little town. To the Langs, as to not a few like them, faith had long been wholly stripped of doctrine. What they embraced with an entire ardour was the ethic of the Gospels. Follow that and the world will be saved. Thus Peter's father preached; on this principle Peter acted. And the first act of his youth's adherence to the literal Gospel nearly wrecked his life.

Coming home from Harvard at the end of his junior year (according to Mrs. Thwing, herself a Vermonter from Brattleboro), Peter found in his parents' house in Castleton a maidservant, a smooth-skinned, full-bosomed French Canadian girl of eighteen. Her bare arms brushed his hands, her red curved lips seemed to blossom toward his own. He had been rigidly pure and almost untempted. He was twenty and found himself suddenly bursting into an all but unendurable flame. He met the girl apparently by chance in a dark and sheltered garden and in a moment they were in each other's arms.

Next morning he heard his mother say quietly to his father that she was afraid the Boutilier girl would have to be discharged. She stayed out late every night and was sleepy and lazy and ill-tempered in the morning and probably up to no good. Peter went into his father's study. They came out together, the two men, white and grim and shaken, but in agreement. Libby Boutilier had to be coaxed and almost bribed to marry Peter. She had quite other ideas. Needless to say, her confessor agreed with the Langs. That broke her for a time. Peter took a job driving a motor-truck and settled down with his wife in a three-room cottage at the edge of the town. "You can imagine the boy," Mrs. Thwing said, "dizzy with passion of the body, dizzy with his soul's passion for righteousness, too, working for his bread with his hands, dreaming of combining this work some day with a ministry, however humble and obscure, of the Gospel." But Peter's mother had, of course, been quite right. Libby had no taste for high-minded poverty and the ethics of Jesus. Her notion of gaiety and triumph, in plain words being surrounded by men who were lusting after her, was the very breath of her nostrils. She went ostensibly to visit her parents in the northern part of Vermont, joined a discharged soldier from Fort Ethan Allen, and disappeared in the French quarters of Montreal.

Peter did not return to Harvard. His mother, sensible woman, sought to persuade her husband and him that he had been lucky enough and should now sue for a divorce. But her two followers of the Gospel shook their heads and tightened their lips. An irreparable sin had been committed against Libby. Undoubtedly, Mrs. Lang agreed, though the question was by whom and when and whether Libby hadn't gone to meet the sin more, oh, quite more than halfway. Her arguments did the poor lady no good. Her husband continued to give away his cloak when his coat was asked for. Peter went to Russia, where, according to him and his father and many others of their kind then and later, the poor and lowly had been lifted up, the proud oppressors had been overthrown, and the tears had been wiped away from all eyes.

It was in Moscow in 1923 that Jehuda Brenner met Peter Lang, ill almost to death, desperate to the very centre of his being, and nursed his body back to health and saw to it that a group of British Quakers employed him on the staff of their relief-workers in Central Europe. The meeting and the story of it burned in Jehuda Brenner's mind. He had come to love Peter Lang, whose life and fate and future seemed to him of an immense significance. Quietly but thoroughly, as was his wont, slighting no intricacies, he spoke of the matter on the dark deck of a small liner sailing from Marseilles to Algiers. "The boy was living in filth. With filthy brawling people, coarse and foul-mouthed. He could understand the the filth, since there were no waterpipes and those that were had been smashed or had burst when frozen, and since there was no soap in the land. What he could not understand, what scorched him was the brawling, the blasphemy, the raw and shameless copulation, the malice, hardness, cruelty. Were not these the poor and the oppressed who had been set free, free for equality, mercy, brotherhood, free for the very Kingdom of Heaven? And what he saw was the under dog having become upper dog with more than all the greed and ruthlessness of the old upper dogs and with a savage re- vengefulness to boot. Yet that aspect was not Peter's lowest depth. He could have reconciled himself to the suffering and degradation of the aristocrats and bureaucrats and officers and prelates of the Tsarist régime. But he saw few such. Many were dead; more had escaped. The desperate de- classed beggars whom he saw, these creatures tortured out of human semblance—who were they? Himself, so to speak, his father, his teachers, comrades, friends, the intellectuals and revolutionaries of the spirit and followers of an ethical command. They were dying, these people, and many thou- sands had already died, and many other thousands were in prisons or in prison camps, and terror and the fear of denunciation rose like a foul miasma from the earth. And what tortured Peter most deeply was this fact: that these many thousands would be forgotten or fade to a legend. For extermination works and the dead are silent. And therefore when this new polity became like all the other polities of man—oppressive, corrupt, cruel, seeking only its own ruthless goals—men would forget the reason, the dreadful reason which was that it, too, had been founded in murder and mortised with blood and tears, like all the other states and polities of earth, and forgetting the reason, men would remain untaught by this crucial experience of the ages and sink into a deeper and bleaker despair. Peter used to repeat that phrase of his, 'Extermination works!' " Brenner stroked his small, pointed black beard. His hands were slender and beautifully articulated, neither bony nor too padded. "The whole business nearly killed Peter. He couldn't then, he doesn't even now, accept life as tragic—inherently tragic, I mean. He wants miracles, ethical miracles—sudden salvations, the Messiah around the corner. What he 'discovered' in Russia some of us wouldn't even have had to go to ascertain. But he wants the Word to change and redeem the world on the instant. If it doesn't do so his soul sickens and there overcomes him the old, old despair of the Aryan-speaking peoples which you find in the Upanishads and subtly worked into the Gospels too, and above all in that Aryanising, upside down Jew, Paul. Life and the world have no true worth. The will to live is a corrupt will; it's a disease in an otherwise respectable planet. Didn't your American Mencken say that? He probably found it in Schopenhauer. Anyhow, if that is so, then Nirvana or the Second Coming or an entirely inhuman heaven must be the dream and the goal. To be delivered 'from the body of his death' because 'the time is short'; to hope that 'mortality might be swallowed up of life' because the Kingdom is not of this world—this defeatism has gnawed at the soul of the noblest Christians. Look at Pascal! Look at the *Imitation*! And that miserable neurotic Jew, Paul, played into the hands of this defeatism of life. He ought to have been sent to the Berggasse in Vienna to be told by our good Papa Freud that his livid terror of the eternal Eros was symptom and symbol of a death-wish for himself and all mankind." Jehuda Brenner lit a cigarette. It glowed red in the blackness. "Don't mistake me. I love Peter. In a sense I revere him. Our feet are set upon two paths. But the paths will meet. Meantime he is *my* Christian. We are brothers. *O si sic omnes.*"

Brenner and I parted next morning as the *Georges Clemenceau* floated into the blue Algerian bay and we saw that city which has the aspect of a dream out of the *Arabian Nights*. Since that day long intervals passed without direct messages to me from either him or Peter Lang. But credible rumour as well as small paragraphs in the papers now and then kept the image of Jehuda Brenner's Christian vivid enough in the minds of the few friends who loved him best. Peter carried relief by plane to starving isolated miners in the Middle West; he was reported living here and there in the Negro quarters of large cities at times of danger and crisis; he returned to Europe and risked his life again and again when the Socialists of Vienna were massacred by the Heimwehr troops under Dollfuss. After that we heard no more of him until the other day. But that last authentic piece of news was strangely great and led to an event that will be preserved for ages in the more vigilant hearts of men.

From Vienna Peter Lang returned to Germany, where he had lived and worked with the British Quakers years before. From April 1, 1933, the anti-Jewish boycott day on, he had lived among the German Jews—going from house to Jewish house, present at small trembling Jewish assemblies, eating with Jews, praying with Jews, bearing witness to them to the existence of a Christian world which did not consent to the insane outrage of their degradation and undeserved despair. By what means he escaped the hounding of the spies of the *Gestapo* we have not yet learned. But lately living in Hamburg he was so wrought upon by the matchless and perverse cruelties he was witnessing that he announced that he, an American Aryan Christian, would publicly embrace Judaism and henceforth live and suffer and die as a Jew in Germany in order to expiate by that small act in that small measure the unbearable sin and shame of Christendom. No sooner had he made that announcement than there came forward a German, a professor at the University of Hamburg, named Emil Genauer, and bade Peter Lang go home to his own land in peace, declaring that it was the duty and the right of a German to perform that act of symbolical expiation. Genauer and his wife and their seven sons and daughters embraced Judaism. Peter Lang, once more much broken in health by his terrifying experiences, sailed for England, where he was welcomed by his Quaker friends.

III

I T WAS in Warsaw in the dining-room of the Hotel Bristol. Small glasses of sharp colourless vodka stood before us. The waiters went about with great platters of cold fish. Each piece of fish on its separate plate was a triumph both gustatory and pictorial. Each was different from the other. Fish in jelly, in aspic; fish with tomatoes or capers or truffles; fish with the spices of the fabled East. We ate fish and drank vodka and smoked the abominable cigarettes of the Polish government monopoly. Jehuda Brenner was quietly merry and hummed the tune of a Yiddish ditty between portions of fish.

> *As der Rebbe Elimelech*
> *Is geworren sehr frehlich . . .*
> (Whenever Rabbi God's-my-King
> Waxed very, very merry . . .)

He swayed very gently back and forth. Dr. Grünfeld, the famous neurologist, whose guests we were, looked sharply at Brenner.

"You speak English like an American, and Yiddish like a Litvak, and German like a Viennese, and Hebrew like a born Palestinian, and Polish like a Pole, Brenner. Where do you come from, anyhow?"

Brenner smiled and wagged his head.

"Where I come from? What is the difference whether I say Minsk or Pinsk or Vilna or even Pressburg? Needless to say that I grew up in a *Yeshiva* [Talmudic School] and that I was a *Mathmid* [devout student], studying and praying night and day and seeing sun or rain through the bleared

windows of a hovel, and that I was undernourished and had
broken shoes and no warm coat for winter, and lived in my
imagination in the land of Israel with the kings and prophets
and sages of old. One fine day a film seemed to fade from
my eyes. I suddenly saw the misery and want round me.
It began with a tin spoon. We had only two. Two tin spoons.
And one was lost. And my mother covered her face and
wailed. When she took the shawl from her face I got up and
permitted myself at last to know awarely that she was old
before her time and soured in temper, and that my father
almost fainted daily under his peddler's pack on the long,
long Polish plain, and that my five surviving young brothers
and sisters had rickets because they had never had enough
to eat. So my old world crashed both within me and round
me. I studied Polish and German and joined the *Bund*
[Jewish Socialist Federation] and learned to be a carpenter."

Grünfeld shook his head.

"Astounding. I can see, of course, how your having been
a carpenter led to other developments. But I don't connect
the free-thinking variety of Socialism with you at all. You'd
certainly gotten over that phase long before I met you."

"Precisely," said Brenner. "It didn't even last long in
my case. It's not a bad phase for extreme youth. But to
be frozen, as it were, at that point is to skip from youth to
senility. That's one of the troubles of the world today.
There are so few mature people—people neither crude nor
senile. . . ."

I turned to Brenner now.

"I'd like to know what your attitude is today to your
early training. Here you sit eating *trefe* [ritually unclean]
and the last book we discussed coming in was Aldous Hux-
ley's *Brave New World*."

Brenner laughed. His low pronouncedly masculine laugh

had both a kindliness that warmed the heart and a pungency that braced the mind.

"I'll tell you a story," he said, "a story, by the way, that cuts deep and applies to the ways and works of many men in many lands—especially to all those who are proud of being 'modern,' 'up to date,' following *le dernier cri*. Listen. In the days of the *Haskalah*, the enlightenment, there was a youth in an old-fashioned Jewish village who wanted to be up to date too. And that meant then, as you know, being an *Epikoros*, a militant freethinker and breaker of the Law. But he had never in his whole life seen anyone but Jews who instinctively lived by the entire Law, and some Polish peasants. So he wondered how one went about being an *Epikoros*. A wag told him that in a village twenty versts away there lived a man who was known as Shmuel the *Epikoros*, Samuel the Freethinker, and advised our young man to address himself to *him*. Hours before dawn the youth started out on his ardent pursuit of unbelief. He came to that other village where a child pointed out to him the house of Reb Shmuel. He knocked at the door and was told by a young woman that her father, Reb Shmuel was, of course, in *Shul* at his morning prayers. Bewildered, the youth hurried to the synagogue and an instinct told him that the man he sought was a grave, handsome person of middle age who did not race through his prayers like the others, but pronounced the sentences of the liturgy as though he relished both their sense and sound. These two, when the tiny congregation scattered, faced each other in the morning sunlight.

" 'Reb Yid [Master Jew],' said the youth, 'are you he who is know as Shmuel the *Epikoros*?'

" 'I am,' answered the other.

" 'But you *daven* [recite prayers] with more fervour than the believers! And it was from you that I hoped to learn how to be an *Epikoros*, like all the great and enlightened people of our time.'

"Shmuel, a man of kindly countenance, stiffened. His eyes and lips were stern.

" 'How much *Chumesh* [Bible] have you learned?'

"In spite of himself the youth flushed.

" 'A little in *cheder* [Children's School] when I was a child.'

" 'And how much Talmud?'

" 'A paragraph here, a paragraph there . . .'

"Reb Shmuel uttered a brief laugh, severe and rebuking.

" 'And you want to be an *Epikoros*? What right have you to criticise the faith and wisdom of the ages which you do not even know? Go home and study for ten years. Then you will have to ask for no instruction. You will know of yourself—or not.' "

We were all silent for a space. Then I said:

"It's one of the best stories in the world. But few will take it to heart today."

Brenner turned to me and there was a deep glow in his eyes that were brown as the leaves of autumn.

"This is a dark age. It will grow darker still. There will be a great dying among men—first of the spirit, next of the body. But God will not leave us in darkness for ever."

He looked at his watch.

"You must pardon me now," he said and rose.

He gave each of us his strong small hand which really clasped our own.

"*Shalom* [Peace]," he said, and "*Shalom u'beracha* [Peace and benediction]," we answered, and both felt a pang as though life and the world were lonelier for us for his going. We looked after him as he walked toward the door.

Dr. Grünfeld filled our glasses and offered me his cigarette-case.

"I thought you'd known Brenner for a long time?" I said.

"Off and on for years. But never really intimately. When

I first came to Warsaw to practise—that's all but ten years ago now—Jehuda Brenner was an antiquary here."

"How very curious!" I exclaimed.

"Maybe," the Doctor assented. "His being a carpenter led to that. And he is the sort of person who would have strong æsthetic sensibilities. Anyhow, his shop was small but exquisite. His objects were all choice. The few Poles, magnates and industrialists, who had any taste all dealt with him. He closed his shop on the Sabbath; he served his customers in caftan and *yarmulke* [skull-cap]; he refused to chaffer. Each object had its price—no more, no less. Every June and July he closed his shop to travel in the west of Europe. Now one summer, while his shop was closed, I drove about the countryside in one of the first motor-cars about here, to visit the Chasidic wonder-rabbis and their followers. I'm from Danzig, as you know; I hadn't come in contact with that sort of thing, and now, both as a psychiatrist and as a Jew, I wanted a first-hand view. Toward the end of a hot day in July, after a long drive over the sun-drenched plain I came to a large village dominated by a Zaddik's house. The afterglow lay in crimson and orange ribands behind the shadowy white bars of the birches. The whir of my car, a rare enough sound in this region, brought one of the Rebbe's assistants out of the house. He was a both cunning- and fanatical-looking man whose greenish eyes and Slavic nose were scarcely visible through the thick tangles of his reddish brows and beard. 'You'd better drive on,' he said, abruptly. 'There's no place in the house and no place in the inn.' I made it clear that I had a letter to his Rebbe from the Chief Rabbi of Warsaw. 'Not before tomorrow,' he almost screamed at me. 'The Rebbe sees no one before tomorrow.' With some impatience I asked him where I was to pass the night. He pointed to a huge barn at the left of us. 'The Chasidim are in there; from near and far they've come to our Rebbe.' He turned and ran back to the house, the skirts of his caftan flying behind him. Luckily I had sandwiches with me and cocoa in a thermidor. I ate and drank slowly and lit a cigarette, and then strolled under a swiftly rising half-moon over to the barn. Its huge door gaped. On the straw-strewn floor lay in sleep or crouched in prayer the Chasidim, men of all ages, with beards and ear-locks, their boots and caftans on, their heads covered. The pallid moonlight flooded the nearer groups. It shone on many finely moulded faces and many rude and dull ones; shone on limbs in grotesque postures and in strange attitudes of prayer and supplication. Moans rose from sleepers in their comfortless places; sudden fragments of *niggun*, of prayer-tune, broke from the lips of those who were awake. An odour of hot unwashed bodies and stale clothes hung in the air. Then the dark figure of a man recumbent in the shadow of the barn wall stirred and slowly rose and came to the door, stepping over the forms of the sleepers. It was Jehuda Brenner. He had let his beard grow. Earth was on his shoes and cloak; earth stained his very hands. Silently he stepped out into the open and joined me. By the brighter light of the moon I could see, as he recognized me, a troubled look stealing into the peace of his countenance.

" 'Sorry you found me here,' he murmured.

" 'I thought you were in France or Italy.'

"My words sounded affected and foolish in this place—remote and unreal. Brenner looked about him. He too, I knew, saw the Louvre—and this; the Botticellis in the Pitti—and this.

" 'The benediction of the Holy One, blessed be He, is peace.' Slowly he uttered the sonorous Hebrew words. He brightened.

" 'Since you have come upon me I will explain the matter in confidence to you. All year long I touch things made with hands—things made to be beautiful in space. And then I go to the west and see museums and shops full of painted canvases and bronzes and brocades and images cunningly wrought, and my eyes grow blinded by the pagan beauty of things and my heart becomes surfeited and ill at ease. I come here each year to purge my eyes of sinful seeing and my heart of error. Here men do not know the difference between beauty and ugliness. If they see a tree they do not pause to say: how beautiful is this tree, for fear of forgetting during even that instant the Eternal and his Law.' "

Dr. Grünfeld paused. He looked at his hands contemplatively. He did not look up at all.

"In those days," he resumed, slowly, "I knew even less than I know now. Sterile materialism was in my very bones. I had come, as I knew retrospectively, to prove that the Chasidim were dupes and the wonder-rabbis rogues. I turned on Brenner sharply that night.

" 'You take this hocus-pocus seriously? These men are dirty and ignorant and superstitious.'

"He laid his hand on my shoulder.

" 'You speak of accidents. I am dealing with essences. I believe in the belief of these poor men in Israel. I believe that their belief brings them near to the central truth of things and of the universe and of God, and I pray for a time when the learned and the wise in the world's learning and wisdom will add *this* belief to their own. A day may come when you will suddenly remember these words of mine, not as *my* words, but as true words.' "

Dr. Grünfeld rather abruptly raised his hand and, summoning the waiter, asked for his bill. While the waiter stood beside him and he counted out the worn, soiled *zloty* notes he said, as though casually: "Brenner was right. The day came. Not once. Many times."

For some years I had again to rely on rumours and anecdotes concerning Brenner. I was all but sure that I saw him one day in a courtyard of the Jewish quarter of the Algerian city of Constantine, in converse with a girl who wore the conical embroidered cap used by the Jewish women of that place. But when I entered the courtyard to make certain, he was gone. The next year he was in America for a brief visit. I, however, was on the west coast and to my sorrow missed him. But Peter Lang happened to be at home, too, and upon my enquiring wrote:

I had good old Jehuda Brenner up home here in Castleton for a week. He and my father took to each other tremendously. At very first Dad was a bit shy at the idea of a foreign Jew who used phylacteries and a prayer-shawl and kept his head covered during meals after he had added a Hebrew blessing to Dad's grace. But when Brenner agreed with him that the precepts of the Gospels were to be obeyed literally without so-called adaptation and sophistication and matched every command and every beatitude of Jesus with exact parallels from Talmudic sources—why then Dad begged him to occupy his pulpit and they took long walks together, and Dad ended up by thanking me for bringing Jehuda here and said he had had the time of his life.

IV

THE origin of Andrew Saracen remains impenetrably obscure. He himself sneered at the notion that one's kin and country mattered. "Man is maw and phallus and sometimes a gleam of mind; all men are alike; most men are equal." "When he says that," Peter Lang commented, a rare flush of irritation and uncontrollable anger slowly suffusing his fair skin, "when he says that he is a liar on his own ground. At all events, I know three things about him; one is this, that he was in the Greek Intelligence Department during the Greco-Turkish War. An American war correspondent, a fine chap whom I've known since my Harvard days, met him on one of the Dodecanese Islands and strongly suspected him then of using his Greek job to cover up his spying for Italy. Secondly, he held a position of pretty high rank in the GayPayOO in Moscow directly under Djerzhinsky when I was there, because I saw him myself dragging a man away from his family in the middle of the night. He deliberately kicked the man's small children. The man who had been a merchant was accused of having hoarded bits of his former merchandise in order to exchange them for milk and bread for those children on the illegal markets. Thirdly, one of my Quaker friends who stuck it out in Germany year after year, saw him in Munich in a storm-trooper's uniform, coming out of the Brown House in 1928."

"Did you ever tax him with that information?" I asked.

Peter shook his head.

"Something about the man makes me go numb all over. The muscles of my throat seem to contract. I can't talk. But

I'm sure Jehuda Brenner is right in his conviction that Saracen's disguises are mere disguises and that he's a Communist of the extreme type. Only one thing that Brenner says isn't altogether clear to me, and that's this, that Saracen's temporary shifting from Moscow to Munich, from Marxism to Nazism, was a mere slight neglect of paper principles and was both tactically and temperamentally of a piece."

When Peter first said that to me I was not sure that I could quite clarify Brenner's observation to him. A very few years later I could and did.

Guesses in regard to Saracen's origin, on which, curiously enough, all kinds of people were fond of exercising their wits, came to me not long thereafter in Paris from a Levantine of some literary pretensions—a large, pale, softly fleshy youngish man whom none of us trusted very deeply. Jules Satije pretended to be a Syrian Christian. He wrote articles for *L'Action française* and for *La Croix*. I never believed in his account of himself nor in the sincerity of his writings. Sipping his third *pernod* on the *Coupole* terrace, he would suddenly half-whisper intimate and obscure details of Palestinian life. A renegade Jew, we decided, educated in one of the schools of the *Alliance Israélite Universelle*. Satije became voluble the first time anyone mentioned Andrew Saracen. He spoke with the unctuous pleasure and release of one who, having found another more treacherous of soul, more basely equivocal than himself, paints that other in the most lurid colours as an act of self-exculpation. And laughs softly and continuously while he does so.

"André? André Saracen? *C'est un sale type, vous savez!* I could show you the stinking alley in Tunis where his father, Ali ben Radjeb, kept a pastry-cook's shop. His mother was a reddish Berber woman from a mountain village near Michelet. Ha-ha! André was brought up on goat's milk amid fleas. At fifteen he ran away from the French government school and hung round the Place de la Kasbah to pick up work as bootblack or guide or pimp. He knew all the women in the so-called Rue des Artistes even then. *Éh bien,* a rich Rumanian homosexual picked him up and took him to Egypt, where André learned English, and finally to Bucharest. There he promptly blackmailed his Rumanian into giving him a couple of million *lei* and set up as a dealer in prostitutes, male and female. Later he transferred his business to Istamboul."

"How do you know all that?" I asked, coldly.

Satije laughed knowingly. He chuckled.

"They are great gossips in the *souks* of Tunis. They have long memories and get and keep their facts straight."

You dismissed such rumours when you saw Saracen, as I did again that very year at a party given by some excessively "advanced" people in an ultra-modern house—a machine to live in—on the Rue Mallet-Stevens. The glass and metal furniture gave me, as it always does, a perceptible feeling of nausea which was not eased by the belated affectation of a recital, piano, violin, and flute, of "atonal" music. Here decay masqueraded as progress. I watched Saracen. He looked compact but somehow top-heavy in his well-cut dinner jacket. His head was large and seemed to bulge over his collar in the back. Yet the face was small, or seemed so—squeezed just too much by the potter's hand between forehead and chin. He moved his lean jaws a little, as though ruminating. One felt that the music filled him with contempt. Not because it was bad, but because it was music. He did not move his body at all, but his black roundish eyes were not still for an instant. They glided from figure to figure and from face to face. They stripped the women and dissected the brains of the men. After the music a buffet supper was served. Saracen and I, plates in hand, found ourselves side by side against a wall of the library.

"These people are quite up your street, aren't they?"

He missed the American idiom.

"*Dans votre quartier*," I tried to explain.

"*Merde*," he said, ever so quietly. "They think they are so different from the rest of their kind and will so acquire merit, so that when the earth caves in and the black waters come—they hoping all the time it will not happen—they will swim and not sink. *C'est fort amusant.* There will be no differences when the dark flood comes."

"And you enjoy the prospect?" I asked.

"I do not enjoy." His English became stiffly foreign. "I do not grieve. I do not pity. I do not approve. Nothing of all that. I have just told you that the earth is caving in and the black waters are coming. The masses are like that. They sweep forward. The depths rise up and the hills crash. *Qu'est-ce que vous voulez?*"

"Isn't there any difference between man and the blind forces of nature?"

He looked at me, as I had known he would, with contempt. And this contempt was so complete that it needed not to be arrogant. I understood then what men had thought they meant by the diabolic pride of the mere intellect. Only, as those poor theologians hadn't dreamed, this was not pride of the intellect at all. Intellect had nothing to do with it. This apparently ice-cold ice-sharp thinking was a cloak and a rationalization, a trick and a deception that deceived the deceiver himself. What Andrew Saracen really wanted was revenge—revenge upon all mankind except those dark masses whom he conceived of as the instrument of his revenge. He wanted destruction; he wanted chaos. "Chaos and old Night." The fleeting remembrance of John Milton comforted me in that comfortless place.

A blonde, rather stupid-looking, young woman, her décolletage showing her plump body to the utmost limits of decency, came up to us.

"Let us go, André." She was conscious of him only.

"I'm not ready," he said.

"I'm dead tired," she pleaded, *"brisé de fatigue."* Her voice broke down into a hoarse whisper.

"Then go!"

"And will you come later?"

He shrugged his shoulders.

"It's possible."

She lingered droopingly a moment.

He turned to me. She had ceased to exist.

"It is a most curious bourgeois superstition," he said, "that we should be enslaved by the feelings of others. The source of that superstition is, of course, economic. If Coralie lived and therefore worked in a proletarian society and were economically secure, it would not occur to her that *I* should go because *she* is tired, nor that if she wants to go to bed with a man, I must be that man, whether I'm in the mood or not. Some one else would serve her purpose. As it is, she wants to dominate me and drag me to her bed and there complete what will be less an act of pleasure than a gesture of parasitism."

"Possible, of course," I admitted, grudgingly. "But there is another and more plausible explanation. She is probably both very tired and in her own way very fond of you."

Ever so quietly and unsmilingly he said again, *"Merde."*

Once and once only in those days did I see Peter Lang and Jehuda Brenner and Andrew Saracen together. There are good reasons why I mention neither the city nor the house in which that meeting took place. The *Gestapo,* the Nazi spy system, though stupid, is ubiquitous. On that day and in that place a group of people had come together to hear Andrew Saracen recount in private certain aspects of the proletarian revolution. It was a gathering of grave men and women concerned over the future of mankind, desirous of understanding the revolutionary process as such. Saracen spoke very quietly. He said that in order to establish a new

order, any new order, certain very deeply rooted notions and reactions of men would have to be eliminated.
But since these historic ideas and reactions were concretely embodied in people, in people too stupid and too
slothful to change, it was necessary to eliminate these people
themselves. By execution. By starvation. By exile to waste
places. By the destruction of morale and physical stamina
in labour camps. This, he said, had been and was the method
of the proletarian revolution and would necessarily be more
or less the method of any radical revolution in modern
times, whether this radicalism was "rightist" or "leftist."
The point, he explained, was that in either case the entire
historic civilization, especially in respect of its religious,
moral, and so-called idealistic aspects, would have to be
exterminated in the persons of its representatives, so that the
generations left would blend into the new ideology and its
complete integration with the state, be it a proletarian and
egalitarian state or not, without inner resistance, anti-social
longings, or confusing memories. Thus and thus only could
a new order, and the new state as the expression of that
order, be secure.

I had been watching Peter Lang and Jehuda Brenner.
Both had gradually grown pale. They sat, as it happened,
at opposite sides of the large rich room in which we were.
There was no communication by so much as a glance between
them. Peter, looking down, had clasped and unclasped his
hands, and now and then dried the cold sweat of agony
gathering on them with a kerchief. Jehuda had at first
plucked at his small beard, and later, disciplining himself,
had closed his eyes and leaned back his head, so that his
face became a pain-touched mask. When at last Saracen fell
silent, they rose slowly, but at the same unpremeditated instant, to their feet, Peter Lang and Jehuda Brenner, this
Christian and this Jew, and like sleep-walkers, unseeing

yet unerring, approached each other until they were face to face. Then at last they lifted their lids and looked into each other's eyes and clasped hands in silence and arm in arm, with no look backward, walked forth from that accursed place.

THE FIRST BOOK: BURNING WORLD

THE FIRST BOOK:
BURNING WORLD

I

THERE was a constant coming and going of people in the parlours of the Hotel Fürstenhof. From his office on the Kurfürstendamm Dr. Kurt Weiss had come here by taxi. He had had neither respite nor food since breakfast. He had broken away at four, faint and unnerved. There had been a lull. Neither the doorbell nor the telephone had shrilled for ten minutes. He had told Fräulein Scholz to close the office. "If by any chance," he had added with a touch of bitterness, "you see or hear anything of my esteemed partner, Dr. von Wegener, tell him that we have a rush of business. He'd better be at his desk in the morning." Meta Scholz's eyes, blue as the blue of a sharply dyed ribbon, had been determinedly expressionless. That's her subtly coy way of implying by denial, Kurt had reflected, that there's something between Hannes and herself. There isn't. Hannes is too lazy, too clever, and too proud.

The waiter came and Kurt ordered a sandwich of smoked ham and a glass of port. He put the palms of his hands for an instant over his eyes and heard more clearly the hum and stir and felt more sharply the agitation, about him. At least there were no storm-troopers, officers or men, either here or on the sidewalk in front of the hotel. They had probably been ordered to be less conspicuous where foreigners were apt to assemble. Kurt took his hands down and looked

29

round. There were, in fact, no foreigners here. The people
were people like himself who had been more or less driven
from their habitual gathering-places. A few days ago he
had ordered a sandwich and a glass of wine at the Café
Bristol. Four Brown Shirts at the next table, smelling of
sweat and leather, had dipped their buttered rolls into their
coffee. One of them, loudly munching, had pointed at him:
"That sort always has money for luxuries." The men had
roared: "*Haste Töne?* Can you beat that?"

He shivered. The waiter brought his order. He sipped his
wine. It did him good, tense as he had been since morning.
Old clients, new clients, people who could not strictly be
called clients, since they had no specific case or cause. They
wanted to know what they should do, how they were to live
if that man, that man—the name choked them, they could
not utter it—made good his threats? Had they better incorporate at once with Aryan dummies as officers of the
companies? Had they better sell out for what they could get?
In the end they hardly listened to him, of which he was
glad enough. What had he to tell them? They had wanted
to pour out their anxieties to him and to comfort themselves
by saying at last: "Of course all this is purely academic. This
is a civilized country. There will be progressive moderation.
The election the other day did not give *them* anything like a
clear majority. Where is your partner, Herr Doktor?"

It had become like a litany. It had always ended with the
question about his partner—his Aryan partner, as these people carefully did not say, Dr. Johannes von Wegener. He
himself had kept his head, used as he was by now to an
inner discipline of which he did not count the cost. He had
let the unanimous final assurances of these people reassure
himself. They were no fools. They were nearly all older men.
They had gone through war and inflation; they had been
good and loyal Germans; they and sometimes their sons had
fought for the fatherland; they had lost their fortunes rather

than export capital to Switzerland and Holland. They had struggled through. They ought to have a sound instinct for the land, the people, the length to which these new rulers could go. And then Komerzienrat Salomon Steinthaler, his dead father's friend, had suddenly walked in and sat down and stroked his long grey beard with both of his hands.

"This is an honour," Kurt had said.

The old gentleman smiled and stroked his beard again.

"I didn't come for legal advice, my boy. I came to give you advice. I'm seventy. My life is over. Erich, as you know, is buried somewhere in Flanders." The great head drooped and then lifted itself up again. "I want you to get passports while you can get them and liquidate what and how you can, and take Gina and your little Gabriel and go to Holland. I have connexions in Amsterdam."

Kurt could all but see himself as he had both paled and stiffened. "This is our country, Uncle Salomon. The present political constellation"—his cheeks now burned at the Prussian formality of tone and phrasing he had used—"is the result of Germany's defeat and humiliation. Demagogues have taken advantage of that to create cruel divisions between German and German on the soil of the fatherland. We must stand our ground. We must fight for our rights."

The Komerzienrat had gazed out of the window where a tree with its buds of late March stood against a pale-blue sky. "Pretty!" he had said. "Pretty how they taught your generation the lesson they wanted you to learn. Well, they don't want it any more. We were expelled from England in 1290. Yes. You probably don't know that. And from France over and over again. And from Spain in 1492. There were always reasons like Germany's defeat and humiliation. There were always reasons. The reasons never had anything to do with us. Never, you understand, anything. We'll be expelled again. But first, as usual, there will be pogroms. You've heard them crying right here on the Kurfürstendamm, have you or not: *'Blut muss fliessen!'* 'Blood must flow!' Have you or have you not?"

Kurt had bowed his head.

"Yes. Nevertheless, Uncle Salomon, this is the twentieth century."

"Nu, and supposing it is. If there is no moral difference between the twentieth century and the fifteenth, then fifteen and twenty just become two numbers without any significance."

With a slight groan the old man had risen. He had stretched out his arm with pointing, urgent hand.

"I say to you: Go! Go while you can. Take wife and child and go."

A whitish blankness had seeped into Kurt's brain. His faculties had frozen. Mechanically he had asked:

"And you, Uncle Salomon?"

Steinthaler leaned heavily on his stick. "My holdings will be gradually confiscated. The process is beginning. If I live another five years I shall probably die of hunger. They will leave me a corner in one of my houses so that my carrion doesn't litter their clean streets."

At that Kurt had cried out, "You're talking nonsense!"

The old man had murmured and mumbled to himself. Energy had suddenly forsaken him. He had turned and stumped out.

Famished as he had felt, Kurt couldn't finish his sandwich. A longing for Gina came over him. He pictured her standing perhaps at a window in that beautiful, proud, and dreamy way of hers, or sitting very still with a book in her lap and her head bent forward and the dark bell of her hair shadowing her face, or else with their little Gabriel, grave and wise for his seven years, at her knee and looking up at her. He knew, of course, why he hadn't gone straight home from the office. Gina either could not or would not permit herself to grasp what was happening in Germany. She had grown up in that incomparable villa in the Grunewald to which the Jacobys had transferred the portraits and porcelains and Biedermeyer cabinets and sofas which spoke so eloquently of their long and honourable habitation of this city. Frau Jacoby, Gina's mother, was a descendant of that Friedrich Hitzig who early in the nineteenth century had built the Berlin Bourse and the Institute of Technology in Charlotten-burg. Framed letters of Rahel Varnhagen and of Heine hung in Herr Jacoby's study. Greatuncles and greataunts on both sides of the house had intermarried with Prussians, and though as the years went slowly on there had been gradual alienation and a gradual chilling of the air between the Ja-cobys and the quarter or eighth Jewish Instettens and Trep-tows, yet especially in her childhood Gina had seen not a little of the young barons and baronesses of both families, nor had there ever, until two years ago, been a great party in the Jacoby villa which had not had its quota of the no-bility of Brandenburg.

No, this was not the first time that Kurt had tried to still his gnawing or crying agitation before going home. He always remembered an autumn day, to be exact the 7th of November, 1932, on which Gina and he had been slowly walking, after the accomplishment of some forgotten errand, along the Kaiserallee. Brown leaves slowly fluttered down-ward through the mild air; towering clouds disparted now and then, and freed blue fields of sky and glints of late bronze sunlight. Kurt had yielded to the gentle enchantment of hour and mood as he had not dared to do for long. In yesterday's elections the NSDAP had lost thirty-seven of its two hundred and thirty seats in the Reichstag. The Com-munist gains had not been serious. Good sense was slowly coming back to this troubled land. He took deep breaths. He was at home again with sky over his head and soil under his feet. He spoke of these things to Gina, and Gina suddenly stopped. She was almost never irritated. But at this moment an unwonted asperity was in her voice: "But, Kurt, can't we ever, ever get away from politics any more? It's getting to be repulsive." He had tried to explain to her that all they were and had had been menaced. She interrupted him. "But you yourself admit that yesterday's elections put an end to that vulgar clamour! Then why concern yourself with it any more?" He had buttoned his overcoat as though an icy current of air were searching out his breast. His ease was gone. He suddenly doubted the respite that had been granted. He suddenly saw as in prophetic vision monstrous and unheard-of things. Terror clawed at his vitals. He pleaded tiredness. They took a taxi home.

He looked at his watch. It was five-thirty. He told himself that it was too late to risk taking the Underground home, and knew that, like everyone else of his kind who could possibly afford it, he would have taken a taxi, no matter what the hour. All public conveyances were apt suddenly to be invaded by Brown shirts. Then one of them would catch sight of a darker face or a more curved nose and, nudging his fellows, would raise the cry, *"Juda verrecke!"* ("May the Jews die like dogs!") And the individual who had by his appearance aroused the cry would feel his neighbours draw away from him as from a thing contaminating and dreadful.

He made his way through the crowded lobby of the Fürstenhof. The doorman asked, courteously, "Does the gentleman desire a taxi?" and Kurt, ashamed of his gratitude for the use of this common formula, put his hand in his pocket, searching for a coin. His shame deepened as he gave the doorman, who was holding open the door of the taxi for him, a whole mark and murmured his address, "Eisenzahnstrasse 14."

The traffic was heavy. Especially on the Leipzigerplatz Kurt's taxi had first to wait and then to crawl for dragging minutes. He suffered with a formless suffering. Usually his well-disciplined mind pursued a steady method: first it analysed a given situation, next it sought for ways of solving the problem presented or, at least, of mitigating ills that could not be avoided. On this evening his whole self rebelled. It rebelled against having to put his intelligence to the uses required of it. Why should a sane human being have to battle with confessed madness and open crime? One of his clients that afternoon had told him that the Jewish Passover was coming early this year. He himself had all but forgotten that there was such a thing. And then the man, a man whom he had disliked both for his shabbiness, which was, he admitted, ignoble, but also for his common and faulty use of language, had said: "And I tell you, Herr Doktor, these swine are capable of publicly raising the cry of ritual murder!" And though he had sharply disagreed, he had known that the man was right. He, for instance, who had not heard of Passover since his childhood in Frankfort-an-der-Oder, nor seen unleavened bread since his tenth year, would be included in the accusation of using Christian blood for the baking of that bread. What was the use of struggling with a civilised mind in a world slipping back into the jungle? Oh, but jungle was not the right word at all. In the jungle there were hunger, heat, death. The struggle on its primal basis was fair. Each beast could use what strength or cunning it had. No species was set apart by hate and superstitious fears to be slowly and cruelly done to death. There was no human vice in the jungle. The beasts had neither risen nor fallen to the state of sin. Sin! what a word! Kurt thought he had better pull himself together. This day had evidently tried him beyond all endurance. He leaned back in the corner of his taxi and closed his eyes. In a few minutes now he would be home. He must try to rest at home and shut out both for Gina and himself the tumult of the world and thus gather strength for the morrow. The farther Kurfürstendamm was calm. His own street was deserted.

He rode up in the electric elevator and let himself into his apartment. In the hall Liese, the parlourmaid, brushed against him with a pleasant " '*n Abend, Herr Doktor!*" The tension of his nerves relaxed a little. He went straight, as was his wont, into the spacious bedroom, and prepared to shave and change his clothes. Such daily formality had been no part of his frugal youth. But he had seen enough of the Jacoby household and the Jacoby fastidiousness in the two years during which Gina had weighed, as on the most sensitive of scales, her feeling for him, to slip without friction into the pattern of her habits. Here in their bed- and bathroom, life seemed natural and reasonable again, both sane and sheltered. He entered the drawing-room with a spontaneous smile and natural tread.

Little Gabriel came running toward him with a cry of joy and almost passionately outstretched arms. Kurt caught him up and kissed him. Gina had risen and came forward.

"Not so wild, darling, not so wild!"

"Yes, but I want to tell Papa something. You know it."

"You promised me to let Papa eat his dinner first."

The child drooped. "I promised," he said as though to remind himself. He walked slowly toward a corner of the room where a picturebook of large format lay open on a chair.

Kurt remembered afterwards the impression of something sorrowful and crushed about his small son's back. Now Gina's face was near to his. He shut his eyes and pressed his lips long and close to hers. She smiled and in that dark and lonely voice of hers said, softly, "You are sweet." He took her hand and drew her to a sofa, on which they sat down side by side. He wanted to feel her nearness, to inhale her aroma, to re-establish for himself through all she was and represented a normal and a human world.

"Gabriel and I walked over to my parents' house this afternoon," Gina said. "We had tea with mother. Father wasn't home. And fancy, it was so mild that we could sit for a little while in the garden. The lilac bushes are full of buds. Spring is early this year."

Kurt put his hand on her shoulder.

"How is your mother?"

"She seemed well, Kurt. Although, now that you ask me, I think she was rather quiet." Again she smiled. "You know how mother likes to talk."

"Did you ask her why?"

Gina shook her head.

"We're not very inquisitive in our family, you know."

Liese came in and announced that dinner was served. Gina called Gabriel. They went into the rather huge dining-room, characteristic of the houses built in that quarter just before the World War, and took their accustomed places. Liese served the soup.

"I mustn't forget to tell you, Kurt. Just after Gabriel and I came home from mother's Fritz Kübler called up."

"Kübler?" Kurt had not seen even his closest Aryan friends for months and had deliberately repressed the fact from his consciousness or else interpreted it as due to his neglect and to his preoccupations. "And what did Fritz want?"

"He wanted quite simply to know how we were. And he seemed very glad to be told that we were all well and that life, as he rather curiously put it, was taking its normal course."

Liese was changing the plates. A throbbing started in Kurt's throat. He saw Gabriel's eyes upon him, large, intense, full of a strange innocent and yet unchildlike wisdom.

"Oh, yes," Gina resumed, "and not twenty minutes afterwards Pastor Heintzius telephoned and made in his own way the same enquiry. You know he has rather a thick, beery voice. I told him that everything was well with us, and I think he said that he was passing through a very difficult time. But isn't the whole thing curious?"

The throbbing went from Kurt's throat to his temples. He laid down the knife and fork that he had ceased using anyhow.

"Gina," he cried, "Gina, don't you know?"

As she lifted her wide eyes to his, Liese, the maid, came in again. With inconceivable swiftness an old, old dolorous memory raced through his mind. His father had told the anecdote, to illustrate the quaint manners of a more than half-forgotten age, how *his* grandfather had said in the corrupt dialect of that far day, *"Stike vor die Shikse!"* ("Silence in the presence of the Gentile servant"). He, Dr. Kurt Weiss, was hurled back into that age. He dared not speak before the maidservant in his house.

"Why do you cry out so?" Gina asked, the colour of her voice a shade darker than usual. "Why?"

"I beg your pardon, Gina," he said, slowly. "We'll talk later."

They finished their meal almost in silence.

"You must eat the little that's on your plate, Gabriel," Gina said, gently.

Large pure tear globules, beautifully formed as Kurt eerily observed, started from the child's eyes and slowly rolled down his cheeks.

"I can't, Mamma, I just can't."

Dessert was left untouched. Gina led the way back to the drawing-room. She sat down on a high-backed straight chair beside a reading-lamp, and the light made a glittering onyx surface of her half-bowed head. She stretched out her hand after a book on the table and in that tranquil gesture—the bell-shaped sleeve falling back from her beautifully moulded wrist—Kurt saw the symbol of Gina's remoteness from the world. He stood watching her, listlessly turning over the evening paper on the other end of the same table. He felt a pulling at his sleeve and knew at once that it was his little Gabriel, and turned and put his hands on the child's shoulders.

"You wanted to tell me something, Gabriel?"

The child's face worked; it twitched; those perfect tragic tear-globules became visible again.

"Papa, Papa, I can't go to school any more—never any more!"

The child fell to his knees and sobs shook his body like the cold twitchings of a convulsion. Kurt gathered him in his arms and pressed his head against his own shoulder and sat down with him.

"You needn't, my darling. I understand."

Gina had looked up.

"But, Kurt, that's unheard of. Naturally he must go to school. Why shouldn't he?"

Kurt was bitter. For the first time in their eight years together he was bitter and resentful.

"He needn't go to school again, my dear Gina, because they insult and humiliate him there. Because they wound his child's soul beyond measure and beyond relief. I envy you your indifference to the dreadful fate that is overtaking us. Do you hear nothing? Do you see nothing? They torment Gabriel because he is a Jewish child." ·

Gina put down her book.

"Jew, Christian—all that seems so quaint and trivial."

Kurt laughed.

"I suppose you haven't heard the handsome contemporary summing up of the matter:

> "What the Jew believes is all the same,
>   In the race resides the stinking shame!"

Gabriel, who had quieted down, began to sob again.

"He has heard it," Kurt resumed; "he has probably also

heard their Horst Wessel song to the effect that everything
will be well when the blood of Jews spurts from their
knives."

The child suddenly wailed. Kurt held him more closely
to his breast. His tone, when he spoke once more, was dry.

"You Jacobys are very elegant people. For several generations you've had the wealth and the social position to
keep yourselves in a kind of glass case guaranteed to keep
out both dust and worms. I remember one time how your
father tried to get round the Jewish aspect of even the
murder of Rathenau by saying sententiously that in all re-
publics since Rome itself unpopular consuls had been assassinated. And you yourself have been a sort of princess
in an enchanted castle. I've loved that in you, too—loved
that, how shall I put it, sense of something inviolable? Well,
by God! the spell is broken. You're the Jewish mother of
a Jewish child whom they've tortured because he is your
child and mine. You'd better wake up!"

Gina arose and stood for a moment quite straight and
still. Her eyes were wide and stricken over her hands in
which she had cupped her face.

"I think I am awake, Kurt." Tears were in her dark
voice. "I know why your friends called up. I know. I don't
understand. But I know."

She came over to her husband and child.

"Come, Gabrielchen, Mummie will put you to bed and
sing you to sleep tonight and you shall stay home with her
tomorrow."

The child stretched out his arms and with a sigh snuggled
against Gina's shoulder as she went out of the room with
him.

Kurt sank into an easy-chair and stroked his forehead
with both hands. Perhaps something like an iron band that
had seemed to be round it had snapped or at least eased
its pressure. Now from this night on he would at least be

able to communicate with Gina; he would be able to lay down burdens in his home; he would be able to take Gina into his arms without an invisible wall, a silent lie, a cruel pretence between her and him. He leaned back his head and closed his eyes and tasted of a repose and respite that he had not known for long.

He heard her softly re-enter the room. He opened his eyes. She came and leaned over him and kissed his forehead.

"Gabriel fell asleep instantly."

Kurt nodded. He watched Gina as she went to the bookshelves that lined the wall. She passed her hand delicately over the top of a row of books and drew out a slim volume. She tasted on her tongue the beautiful syllables of the poet's name, "Rainer Maria Rilke." She opened the book and turned to Kurt.

"We mustn't let ourselves be lost in horrors. Do you remember this? We used to read it together long ago!"

Slowly she pronounced the divinely liquid verses:

"Swift though the world change like wrack
    Of clouds dividing,
All that is perfect melts back
    In the abiding.

"Above the flowing of things
    Freer and higher,
Lasting thy music rings,
    God of the lyre.

"Ill are our sorrows known;
    Love we have not learned well;
    Death the inscrutable
Darkly conceals us;
Song o'er earth rising alone
Hallows and heals us."

Kurt had hidden his face in his hands. He let them fall.

" 'All that is perfect melts back in the abiding,' " he repeated, slowly. "A German poet wrote that not so long ago. And now!"

Hoarse, raving truculent voices rose from the near-by corner of the Kurfürstendamm and crashed upon the ears of Kurt and Gina:

"When blood of Jew spurts from each knife . . ."

They were in each others' arms. They clung together. Two against the world.

II

THE face of Johannes von Wegener was long and whitish. Though he was in his early thirties, there were incipient cheek-pouches above his lower jaw and tear-sacks under his eyes. His straw-blond hair was sparse. From time to time the lid of his left eye twitched. He hated that. It was a weakness which seemed to belie the witness of his solid bulk and great height. His mother, Frau Ernestine von Wegener, widow of a Prussian colonel who had fallen before Verdun, had her formula: "The boy was like a tree. But imagine: it was in the hunger years that he made his *abiturium* and began to study law. And later, during the inflation, what did people like ourselves have? What was a pension then? One whole winter Hannes had no overcoat. For years he didn't have enough to eat. *Certain* elements of the population seemed to have food even then. I shall say nothing against them, since Hannes was almost a daily guest at their table. Nevertheless . . ." Having said that, Frau von Wegener would invariably blow her nose with a gesture from which righteousness and injured innocence exuded.

Whenever Wegener heard this quite set formula he would say with a dry courtesy: "If you please, Mother." Yet in his very deprecation there was a shadow of assent. He was not sorry to have at least her know why he so often, even as at this very moment, sat listlessly in his office for hours on end and why he was convinced that, if a human body could be struck even as one strikes against a gong or metal vessel, his own would give forth a hollow and a dolorous sound.

Fräulein Scholz had just given him the message of Dr. Kurt Weiss, his partner, to which he had answered with the humorous use of Jewish expressions which Kurt and his kind never permitted themselves to use: "I'm here, at my desk, tell Dr. Weiss when he comes in. But today is *Shabbes* and there won't be many people." He had settled back in his chair and heavily raised his legs to lay them on his desk. They ached. Sinews and tendons were sore. How many miles had he walked last night? He had been overcome late in the afternoon by that insufferable sense of dulness which he knew so well—an anæsthesia of the body and the mind. A numbness crept on such occasions over the skin of his entire body until he felt like a creature in a leather sack. He used to know a woman who owned dog-whips. That had done no good, either. The smart had remained local.

At dark he had had a couple of whiskies at the Eden Hotel and had telephoned his mother that he would not be home for the evening meal. Then, sullenly, he had made his way to a once flaring establishment, now busier than ever, but hypocritically driven to drawn blinds and apparent furtiveness and had picked a very dark woman, a woman from the Slavic marches with high cheek bones and black coarse hair and swollen-looking lips. He had pinched and beaten her until she threatened to cry out, and the numbness had melted a little from his flesh.

He had come out of that place with three S. A. men in their brown uniforms, and they, somewhat in liquor and taking him for their own kind, had begun to talk freely to him, and he had gone on with them. They had insulted and molested passers-by; they drove people from the sidewalks. "There goes another Jew-swine! *Raus!* Out with him!" "That's one of those Communist sows! Smash his teeth down his gullet!" And Wegener with closed eyes had heard with both horror and relief the heavy brass knuckles' impact upon human flesh and bone. He hated these brown louts, yet he followed them. They took the Underground and still he followed, though they had almost forgotten him in their increasing drunkenness on their own licence. They came out into the night far in the north of the city into the midst of a workingmen's quarter and strolled through deserted streets. A dim lantern shone over an unpainted door. They crashed in. The split rotten door was left open, and so he followed here too. Dejected workingmen, unwashed, hollow-eyed, were sitting over mugs of thin beer and hunks of stale bread. The storm troopers rushed forward with suddenly drawn revolvers, and Wegener saw that he who was the leader held his revolver in his left hand, the right arm being withered and short. Quickly he gazed at the man's raised face. It was white as paper and twitched all over as his own lid twitched, and the irises of the man's eyes were as though flooded with blood. Tables crashed and mugs flew. The workingmen defended themselves. Arms, almost fleshless bones, worked up and down like flails. Then shots crackled. Again, again, again. Four men lay still. Wegener jumped backward from the thick rivulets of blood that seemed to be hurrying, hurrying along the slanting floor to his feet. He looked up. A back door gaped. No one was left but the dead men and the three storm-troopers who held, surrounding him, a lad, almost a child, a frail, pale gentle-faced boy. They grunted with each breath like animals. *"Nee, Ede,* you don't escape. Not you. We'll shoot you in the arse later. But first, first—" His shirt was ripped from his white body. Wegener beat his fists against his head and forced himself to flee.

Slowly, like an old man, he took his feet down from the desk. With closed eyes he had reënacted in his imagination the scenes of the night. His lid twitched. He made a gesture with his hand like that of a man who brushes away a whirring insect. Then he got up and, going slowly through the room between in which Meta Scholz, sitting at her typewriter, was busy plucking her eyebrows, he went straight, without knocking, into his partner's private office.

Kurt looked up from the pile of papers on his desk.

"Morning, Hannes."

"Morning, Kurt. Sorry I wasn't here yesterday. I felt rotten. I do now. Nothing doing here, of course, on Saturday."

Kurt shook his head.

"But next week will be a heavy week, Hannes. And you and I should have a consultation on what to advise certain people. There is a panic—a moral panic. I can't make up my mind how justifiable it is." Deliberately he turned his head and looked out of the window at that tree on the Kurfürstendamm. "You ought to be able to take a cooler and more objective view of the situation than I."

"Yes, that may be true. But whether it's true or not, I think we ought to stick to the facts. I'm afraid that the hounding of certain elements of the population is going to be relentless."

"I agree with you. All the more need for the sharpest legal support of those elements irrespective, mind you, Hannes, as far as this office goes, of their race or religion!"

"*Du,* Kurt, we've known each other, haven't we? since we were two little snut-nosed boys in the *sexta* of Schillman's establishment?"

Kurt leaned his elbows on his desk and folded his hands, and with a faint look of amusement regarded his partner.

"Since when do you indulge in sentimental reminiscences, Hannes?"

Wegener leaned forward.

"You're quite right. It isn't my way. I was trying to say this: I don't need, so to speak, to—er—legitimize myself with you."

"No."

"You know pretty much what I'm capable of doing and

what I'm *not* capable of doing. You know my moral possibilities."

Kurt nodded.

"Treachery of any kind may be eliminated from our calculations."

"Yes. Well, then, listen. My advice is that we close the office. We can't help our clients. We can't give them legal support, as you call it. There is no law left. All law is being abrogated. And the worst of it is this: no new law in the traditional sense will be promulgated. There will be, there is already, complete arbitrariness, complete chaos. I with my own eyes saw four men murdered last night, four German workingmen. And the thing ended right there. It has, as matters stand today in Germany, no more to do with law or justice or any such concepts than if starving wolves attack deer in the wilderness. No more. For God's sake, let's both, especially you, save our skins!"

Kurt got up. He stood before Wegener. He lifted his head.

"We're not at that point yet, my dear Hannes. If, for a time, justice is obscured and made difficult, all the more reason to fight for it ——"

"To the very foot of the gallows, eh? That's very noble and, if you'll forgive me, very Jewish. You've been used to looking at life, so to speak, from a high watch-tower. All over!" With one of his rare gestures Wegener lifted his arm and hand and let them drop limply. "Do you want to be placed under protective arrest? Don't you know what's going on in the concentration camps and in the cellars of the S.A. barracks and at a certain number of the Friedrichstrasse? Don't you know?"

Kurt blanched. He retreated to the window and leaned against the ledge.

"We've been accused of atrocities before."

Wegener laughed. It was a hard, dry, joyless laugh. When

he spoke again he lowered his voice. It became almost a hoarse whisper.

"Don't be a fool. Face it! We're in the midst of a terror. Hundreds of people are being tortured to death. I understand it, too, although I hope I'll have the guts to put a bullet through my head before I join it. Hunger and hate and frustration are unleashed. Murder has become an end. They torture and murder for the sake of torture and murder."

"I was afraid so, Hannes, only I was trying not to believe it." Kurt clasped his hands in front of him. "We've been so proud of our high civilization. And we German Jews have contributed to that just pride and lived in it and by it. Aside from any question of danger, all meaning is going out of life. What is there left me if I can't resist——"

"Well you can't, unless you want to be killed." Wegener raised his voice again and it rasped. "And as for your high civilization—our high civilization—we got magnificently far with it, didn't we? We got the exclusive war-guilt clause and the hunger blockade after the Armistice, and the Polish Corridor and various other handsome things. High civilization! When you come to me with that I'm for rearmament and the third Reich." Wegener's lid twitched furiously. He leaned forward, as though to hide it. Then he laughed that joyless laugh again. "And the bloodiest irony is this: You and your particular crowd of old Jewish families would agree to every word I've said and join the forces of the third Reich, too, if they'd let you—if only they'd let you. *Ach!* it's a filthy mess, I grant you."

He groaned. His legs still ached. He watched Kurt, whose hands had dropped, whose eyes seemed to study the carpet, whose pale face seemed to have relaxed like that of an unhappy child. Slowly, however, a normal tension came back into Kurt's body. He lifted his head. He spoke out of a concentrated bitterness of spirit, a bitterness so tangible that he tasted it like the bitterness of a decayed nut upon his tongue.

"Why don't you join them, then?"

Wegener yawned and stretched himself. "Can't be done. I've had that out with myself. If we had quietly rearmed and one fine day simply marched into the Polish Corridor or anywhere else, by God! I would have marched, too—officer or even private. But I can't stick the fight against the so-called internal enemy, this cheap war of extermination against a handful of Jews and liberals with a worse campaign of dirt and slander than ever we Germans even were subjected to and with *no* provocation, no resistance, no reason. No." He fell silent for a moment. Then he smiled. "There's another thing. I can't stick either these—these"—he seemed to choke and almost retch—"gentlemen who are now in control. You've heard Mother tell the story. We were just road-builders. But a certain Cornet Johannes Wegener was ennobled by the Great Elector himself on the battlefield of Fehrbelin in 1675. I *could* follow a Prussian king . . . *Na also*. That's how it is."

Kurt began to walk up and down. For some minutes neither of them spoke. Wegener lit a cigarette and began to blow rings. Kurt stopped abruptly in front of him.

"We won't close the office. Can I count on you?"

Wegener nodded.

"We'll try with the utmost prudence and within the framework of the present situation to serve our clients."

"Agreed."

"If I"—Kurt held up clenched fists—"if I should be prevented from continuing to practise, will you carry on?"

Wegener looked up.

"On one condition."

"Namely?"

"That you take that Franzen document which you have in the safe over there and send it by messenger to Reichsjustizkommissar Heinrich Franzen and insist upon a receipt signed by himself."

Kurt took one stride toward the safe and planted himself, as though to protect it squarely in front.

"Never!"

Wegener sank deeper into his chair. He lit another cigarette and blew more rings into the air.

"Very sorry, Kurt. In that case I'll have to clear out. I've got an old uncle in Pomerania, as you know. I could go on the farm and lie low and seduce a kitchen maid or two."

"You know perfectly well, Hannes ———"

"I know perfectly well all you have to say: Franzen is a thief. His father was disbarred for theft. I know. Franzen publicly insulted you in court and you brought an action against him before the Court of Honour of the *Anwalkskammer* and procured a certified copy of the disbarment proceedings against his father. That action is pending. Let us say, it *was* pending. For you are a Jew and have been declared with all other Jews as incapable of the very concept of honour, and so there *is* no case. What you may not know, but what I've made it my business to discover, is that the original records of the disbarment proceedings, together with all the protocols, have been destroyed and that Franzen, senior, is judge of the superior court in Stettin. Meanwhile, as you do know, Heinrich is Commissar of Justice and lectures at the university on the necessity of eliminating from the legal profession and the administration of law all "race-alien, un-German elements.""

Kurt left his protective station before the iron safe and wearily sat down. He bent forward dejectedly and let his hands hang down between his knees.

"And this is Germany." He drew himself up. "Hannes, granting the fact of a nationalist uprising as counter-pressure to the pressure upon Germany—why by thieves, by cheap perverts, by rancorously envious failures, by sadists, by the

very off-scourings of humanity? The country is turning into
a cross between a sty and a prison of the Inquisition. Must
that be so?"

Wegener's lid twitched. He closed his eyes. "I've got my
own dim notions on the reasons, Kurt. But I'm too God
damned tired and confused to try to straighten them out.
You always had a better head than I. Do it for yourself.
And don't get away from the point. Are you or are you not
going to send back to the Herr Reichsjustizkommissar Heinrich Franzen the only remaining evidence of his father's
swinishness?"

"I'll think it over."

"Don't think! Just do it Monday morning. Early!"

Meta Scholz came in.

"I knocked," she said, apologetically.

Kurt swung round to her.

"It's all right. We were talking. What is it?"

"Herr Dr. Kübler is here and ——"

"Fritz!"

Kurt sprang up. He took a step toward the open door behind Meta Scholz. But there, having heard voices, stood
Fritz Kübler, short, frail, with his wheat-blond small beard
tousled and dank with sweat, and his blue eyes feverish with
terror. He must have been running. Having now come to a
halt, he trembled, trembled all over like a driven horse.
Kurt pushed him gently into a chair and with a look and
slight upward movement of his head dismissed Meta Scholz,
who lingeringly closed the door behind her. Kübler whim-
pered. Wegener took out his large leather case and offered
him a cigarette.

"Calm down, old boy," he said, soothingly. "*Sachte, sachte,*
as the Berliner says. Go easy."

Kurt returned to his place by the window and leaned
against the ledge.

"Something has evidently happened to you, Fritz. What is it?"

Kübler had inhaled a few whiffs of smoke. He pulled himself together. He grasped his knees with his hands and leaned forward eagerly.

"I didn't intend to go to the office today. But about two hours ago Helene's mother—you know my secretary, Helene Schwarz—you know, you know . . ."

Kurt and Wegener made signs of assent.

"Helene's mother called me up in livid terror. Helene had gone to the office late last night to get something she'd forgotten and hadn't come home since. Hadn't come home all night." A sob shook him visibly. "So I rushed to the office. It had been raided. I don't know when. Everything smashed to splinters—every table, every chair, the typewriters. All our documents and records burned in the middle of the floor and the flame put out with urine. And Helene gone. Helene gone. But her bag, torn and foul, on the floor—on that floor where they had . . ."

He doubled himself over to ease the gnawing of grief and terror in his viscera. Wegener took out a new cigarette, put it between Kübler's lips, and lit it for him. He and Kurt exchanged a sombre glance. Kurt signalled to Wegener to speak.

Wegener shook his head in a kind of desperation.

"Why didn't you idiots, forsaken by God and sense, shut up shop promptly in January when this particular government came into power? 'International League of War Resisters!' The wonder is this thing didn't happen weeks ago. And in addition, with all due respect to Fräulein Schwarz, open 'race defilement' in addition. Why didn't you take your Helene and skip out?"

Fritz Kübler drew himself up. He was a little man and a stricken man. But now a spiritual dignity suffused his whole being. He took his hands from his knees and folded them before his breast.

"The time to defend a good cause is in time of danger, in time of adversity. I expected a raid; I expected to be taken into custody; I expected to be maltreated and perhaps killed. I was prepared—prepared to bear witness to the uttermost. I didn't think of anything happening to Helene—I didn't think of that—I couldn't imagine that—I couldn't—no, no, anything but that!"

"I don't blame you," Kurt said, dully. "I find it hard, too, even to imagine the things that are happening now. Hannes doesn't, evidently. He seems to have insights and sources of information that are inaccessible both to an Aryan like you and to a Jew like me. We seem to be living in a dream and he is awake. I don't say that, Hannes, in the way of re- proach, but of confirmation. And therefore, Fritz, Hannes may help you. I can't."

Wegener got up slowly. He seemed to be gathering his heavy limbs up one by one. *"Ech!"* he groaned. "I've more or less scraped acquaintance with a man high up in the *Schutzstaffel* crowd who isn't altogether happy. His mother's a Catholic. Let's see, Fritz, if we can dig him up and get him to get us some information. But I warn you, it won't be simple. Peace propaganda and race defilement—that's a combination!"

"Is there anything I can do?" Kurt asked.

Wegener shook his head.

"No, except this: don't forget bright and early on Monday morning to send back the document in question by personal messenger against the personal signature of the recipient. I don't feel like Pomerania. Moreover, as you see, I seem to be of more use here." He took Kübler by the arm. "Come on, old boy."

Kübler pressed Kurt's hand. Wegener nodded. Then those

two went out. Kurt sat down and pressed a button on his desk. Meta Scholz came in.

"Tell Emil to close up. You can go home, too, till Monday."

"Yes, Herr Doktor."

There was a curious caressing quality in the woman's voice that caused Kurt to look up. She leaned over and put her arms swiftly about him and kissed him full on the mouth. He shoved his chair violently backward. He frowned. He felt himself reddening with rage.

"Has anything I have ever done given you the slightest excuse for such an action, Fräulein Scholz?"

Coquettishly she rocked her head.

"Oh, I don't know."

"You are perfectly well aware of the fact that you are lying. You're engaged from the fifteenth to the fifteenth, aren't you?"

"Yes." Her voice was metallic now.

"Very well. I give you notice as of March fifteenth to become effective April fifteenth."

"You do, do you? Well, I guess maybe you'll change your mind."

She walked out straight and stiff.

Kurt's anger cooled and gave way to a little gnawing of fear in his very entrails. Did this miserably confusing and defiling thing have to happen, too? Idiotic to be frightened by it, though. There were other, graver things. The longing for Gina, which always came to him amid heat, confusion, turmoil, as a longing for beauty, sanity, tranquillity, flooded him now with its wave of healing. He would go home.

III

THAT Sunday late in March, 1933, was of an unusual
warmth. A presage of spring was in the air. Tight buds
were on the trees and bushes of the garden behind the
Jacoby villa and the evergreen tall pines that bordered it,
the Brandenburg Kiefern which were the special pride of
the Privy Councillor Hermann Jacoby stirred and swayed
in a mild and sun-filled breeze. The great glass doors of the
circular reception and music room were thrown open, and
so the room and the terrace and the garden formed a unit
of beautiful rhythm in space. The hour of serving tea was
approaching, that Sunday hour consecrated for so many
years in this house to the spontaneous gathering of friends.

Jacoby was alone and wandered uncertainly about both
room and terrace. He was a slightly corpulent man in his
late fifties, with a tall forehead, a lean nose, and the clipped
moustaches, now nearly white, of the Wilhelmian era. His
grey eyes were bloodshot. Taking now and then a deep
breath, he sought to regain what had evidently been an inborn erectness of both the body and the mind. He failed;
he crumpled. Long-unaccustomed tears gathered in his eyes.
He had once more reached the terrace, but turned abruptly
round and from the threshold surveyed the room. He
nodded. A noble room, full of noble memories. Yonder had
once stood and spoken the bold and great, the charming
and generous Albert Ballin, creator of the imperial merchant
fleets; there in that place had oftener appeared the urbane,
the troubled, the self-sacrificing servant of his country, her
truest and best ambassador to a hostile world, Walter
Rathenau. Jacoby wiped his eyes. Self-murdered the one,

55

slain in the streets the other. Thank God, he muttered, that they were in their graves and had not lived to see this day. Other scenes came to him now out of the irrecoverable past: at the Bechstein concert pianoforte the glowing figure of Feruccio Busoni playing his arrangements of Bach with a unique elevation and grandeur. Not far from him, devoutly listening, his dark head with the ardent poet's eyes bent forward, had sat the novelist Jacob Wassermann here on one of his yearly visits—Wassermann with that bearing as of a docile child which hid and yet in some half-mystic fashion revealed the vast and visionary worlds he carried in his soul. And Jacoby remembered how, when Busoni had finished playing, Wassermann had raised his head and with an inimitable fervour merely looked his gratitude and how the mobile Italo-German had put his arms round the shoulders of the friend who was later to commemorate him so magnanimously.

They had hardly remembered in those days that they were Jews. Nor had Busoni remembered it except in honour and gratitude nor Gerhardt Hauptmann, who had been here with his ever more consciously Goethean head and his ever intenser thirst for champagne. Jacoby felt a sudden pang of fear. He remembered a certain day on which he, book in hand, had quoted to an illustrious company a passage from the letters of Theodore Fontane, the inimitably characteristic novelist and poet of this province and of this city, in which the venerable writer had expressed his preference for the Jews to the "Wendo-Germanic" natives and declared that, despite his sincere admiration for the indigenous nobility of the province, all liberty and high culture had been, at least here in Berlin, implanted by the Jews. And that illustrious company had applauded. Today he felt that very memory to be no more a treasure, but a menace. He had the impulse to hide it deep, deep within him, that he and his had ever raised their heads in just pride and in the serene consciousness of their oneness with this people and this land. For from unimaginable depths there had arisen and screamed from every printed sheet and every hoarding, and roared in obscene voices in every street a cry of hate so mad, so foul, so treacherous, so lying, so furiously fantastic, that it had lost all contact with humanity—with human beings as they are, with any kind of human beings, with men and women and children of whatever kind that have the form and bear the lineaments of man.

He came forward into the room and dropped into an arm-chair and put his strong, unwrinkled hands over his face. He groaned. What an empty and what a bitter world! And what fools men were and what a fool he himself had been. Weak words. Words that should have been swords and were as blades of grass. He pressed his hands closer to his face. Nearly two years ago there had come to him men running and breathless and had told him that on the day before, which had been the Jewish New Year, motor-trucks packed with Brown Shirts had appeared at the doors of synagogues, even on the Kurfürstendamm, and the troopers had seized and beaten to the streaming of blood and to in-sensibility the worshippers coming out of their places of worship. And Jacoby remembered how, though ice had seemed suddenly to coagulate in his belly, he had said that a part of the German people had doubtless been crazed by hunger and humiliation and the preying upon it of impure Jewish elements from beyond the eastern borders, but that he had a faith in this people and its republic and its will to-ward *Kultur* that transcended the street brawls of a given day or year.

He dropped his hands and had a moment of dizziness, and in that moment beheld again the face of one of the messen-gers who had come to him. It had been the face of Moses Troesch, one of the oldest and wisest of the men in the banking-house of Jacoby Brothers. The face was pale, thin, elderly, unhandsomely elongated by a thin wispish greying beard. The whole face, dominated by that beard and two eyes as of dark brown flame above it, had been tilted toward Hermann Jacoby in an inimitable gesture of reproach. The dried, cracked, strangely red lips had moved.

"*Herr Geheimrat,* did you know any of the people who were hurt?"

Jacoby had shaken his head.

"Do you know anyone who goes to *Schul* on *Rosh hashanah?*"

Again, and this time with a to him inexplicable pang, the Privy Councillor had shaken his head.

The tilted face had drooped. "I shall not trouble you any longer," the cracked lips had said. "I shall merely permit myself the observation that we are on the eve of a return to the Middle Ages and that no Jew will be spared; whether he is from Posen or Breslau or whether his ancestors have been settled in Brandenburg since the days of Frederick the Great."

And those burning eyes had been lifted for an instant toward where stood on a shelf in the Councillor's study the immensely prized porcelain apes of the eighteenth century, the purchase of which had been enforced upon the Jews of that period to subsidize the Royal Porcelain Works and to add another and a comical burden to the too heavy burdens of their subjection and their shame.

Hermann Jacoby remembered that he had tried to laugh.

Faintly he heard from afar the trill of a doorbell. But even that familiar sound was no longer a reassuring one. He had tried desperately not to believe the whispered tales of sudden incursions of storm-troopers upon a thousand homes by night, nor of the beating and maiming of living men in bloodsprent torture-chambers, nor of the sealed coffins sent to wives and mothers. The press declared stridently that these reports were the fabrications of foreign Jews bent upon the

destruction of the German people. This stridency was so
hollow and so obviously devoid of shame that it would have
broken Jacoby's last faith in these rulers even if he had not
known his Jews. But he had met in better days the leaders
of these foreign Jewries. He had met them from Budapest
to London. And all or nearly all had an ancestral and cultural feeling of kindness for the German people and its land.

He rose with a sudden astonished pang of gladness. He
stretched out both hands. For into the great bright room
ambled, as round as, but far less rosy than, formerly, Pastor
Gerhardt Heintzius. He took the Privy Councillor's hands
and held them. He looked from side to side.

"Is the *gnädige Frau* not receiving? Am I disturbing you?"

"We're quite willing to receive," Jacoby said, with a sententiousness which he himself felt to be false, "if anyone is
willing to come."

He led Heintzius to a chair and sat down opposite.

"Gina and Kurt will certainly be here. My wife will come
down presently." He faltered. "We have not seen you in a
long time."

Heintzius sat very straight in his chair. His over-chubby
legs were spread apart under his black-clad belly. He had
placed his hands, thick with light reddish hair, on his knees.
Jacoby surveyed that ball-like head so blond as to seem hair-
less, those pale eyes, that beer-soaked body, and saw, almost
for the first time, what Kurt, who had known Heintzius
since at six they had entered prep school together, had
always maintained, that there was a strong moral earnestness, a kind of moral valour in the man that were wronged by
his body and its taste for Culmbacher.

Heintzius cleared his throat. *"Herr Geheimrat,"* he said,
with a formality that sat not ill upon him at this moment,
"Kurt and Gina, and through them your wife and you, are
the only Jewish friends that I have. I wanted to come to
tell you that I have been forbidden to pray or preach in

public because I have resisted the new pagan reaction. I don't think they'll send me to a concentration camp. But they will try to starve and boycott me into submission. I shall not yield. And I wanted to tell you that I am happy. When things go well and easily with us, all that is deepest in us and in life itself has a way of becoming formula and form. Now I know that the Gospel is worth living for and dying for. It is a great thing to have learned."

Expectantly he looked at Jacoby, whose eyes, however, were suddenly fixed beyond him. Kurt Weiss had quietly entered and had remained standing in the door. Heavily Heintzius turned.

"Aha, Kurt!" he cried.

Kurt's voice was hard and dry and desolate.

"Keep your seat, Gerhardt. I've just heard what you said to father and I perfectly understand the message of consolation and of community in suffering that you're trying to bring us. Ha! How shall I put it? Father doesn't know what you're talking about. I know. But it's no good to me at all. Your message might do some good in the Rosenthalerstrasse to the Jews with phylacteries and praying-shawls. We westernized German Jews have nothing comparable to your Gospel, nothing that transcends the State and the culture in which we live. We have identified ourselves completely with that. If you take that from us we have nothing left. Nothing at all."

He took a cigarette from a silver box on a near-by tea-table and lit it. He walked up and down. The Privy Councillor assumed that look of instructive importance that had once been nature but was now bad art.

"We have always tried to serve humanity," he said, slowly.

Kurt stopped in front of Heintzius.

"I know how hollow that sounds, Gerhardt, what Father has just said. Yet there is an element of truth in it. We German Jews have always had a rather special concern with

the interests of mankind as a whole. They now make that a
bitter reproach against us. But we nourished that interest
as Germans. If all Germans had done the same, many things
might have been different."

Heintzius shook his head.

"I know that, Kurt. I respect it. But that's not what I
mean. All that was part of the world the fashion of which
passeth away. It was part of the pagan world. And now
the pagans who are naturally the masters of that world have
thrust you and yours and me and mine out of it. They are
killing us and torturing us and persecuting us." He leaned
back in his chair and folded his hands. "Kurt, have you ever
heard of Karl Barth?"

"Faintly," Kurt said. "Isn't he the leader of the neo-
orthodox movement? Are you trying to be a Christian mis-
sionary here, old man?"

Heintzius grew very pink. "I'm not that kind of an idiot,
thank you. Please listen: Barth was here recently and met
with a group of pastors. He told us, and we agreed with
him, that the genuine followers of the Gospel might be driven
and should, if need were, let themselves be driven, into the
catacombs by this government even as they were under the
persecuting pagan emperors of Rome."

"Very fine," Kurt said. "I understand and appreciate
that."

Heintzius lowered his voice.

"When I was in Rome I saw not only Christian catacombs.
I saw Jewish catacombs."

Wearily Kurt dropped into a chair.

"You're damned good at homiletics, my dear Gerhardt.
But your psychology leaves much to be desired. The modern world said to us Jews: be modern men and all differences
will be forgotten. We accepted that bargain. We accepted
it honestly. I see now how honestly. We became Germans.
We gave up all we had had before. We forgot it. We no

longer know what it was. I didn't know there were Jewish
catacombs in Rome. We have nothing; we are nothing; if we
can no longer be Germans we are finished, we are destroyed;
we have lost all."

The three men arose. From the terrace and the garden
came in Gina Weiss and Frau Jacoby. Gina was half-sustain-
ing her mother, a small, moderately corpulent lady of middle
age with cheeks still rosy and hair white as though powdered
brought to a Victorian knot on top.

"Don't get up," Frau Jacoby said. "I'm not very well and
we're not very formal. I was just telling Gina: nothing is as
it used to be. I get tired so easily, so very easily."

She let Gina almost lead her to a chair. The men greeted
the two women. Kurt kissed Gina on the forehead.

"Ring for tea, if you please, Gina," Frau Jacoby said.
Then she looked up at Kurt. "I wish you and Gina and
Gabrielchen would give up your apartment and come and
live with us. It's cold and lonely here. I never knew until
recently how big this house could seem. It did not seem so
formerly. Everything seems to be falling silent about us and
dying about us. How do you explain that Herr Pastor?
Doesn't it belong to your calling to explain such things?"

Heintzius looked rueful. He looked like a fat boy caught
in mischief. "It's very difficult, *gnädige Frau*. I'm afraid the
world we were all accustomed to is dying off. I can't say that
I like the new one—if you can call it new."

Frau Jacoby sighed.

"We were so happy and prosperous under our emperor!"

Vigorously her husband nodded. "We were; we were."

Kurt began moving about again.

"It was façade. The foundations must have been rotten."

"No," Jacoby protested. "As a banker I can tell you that
the foundations were sound."

Heintzius shook his head.

"The foundations in morals and reason were rotten. Stupid and cruel men governed us."

It suddenly seemed to Kurt that all he was hearing and all he had said was babble, faint and far away and unreal. He looked at Gina. She preserved her grave stillness. Why? By what means? The fact irritated rather than soothed him. The butler had appeared with the tea-things and at Frau Jacoby's request placed them on a table in front of Gina. She served with fluid, unaffectedly beautiful gestures. Bell sleeves fell back from her arms. The broken conversation became neutral in tint and evasive of all that was smouldering in each consciousness. We are like people in a picture, Kurt thought. The picture hangs on the wall of a room high up in a house of which the foundations are burning. Our gestures are fair and frozen. But the moment will come in which a tongue of flame will pierce through the flooring and lick upward and the canvas will shrivel into ashes in the twinkling of an eye. He pressed his hands together. He could see that tongue of flame.

Heintzius eyed yearningly the large slice of cake on his plate. He desired it intensely and was afraid to eat it. He smiled his innocent, fat, awkward smile.

"At least there's one Jew present at every Christian meal," he said, mildly. "You remember the child's prayer, dear Gina?"

Gina nodded. Heintzius, plunging into the cake, repeated:

> "Come, Lord Jesus, be our guest;
> May thy gifts to us be blest!"

Kurt felt as though a sweetish lump of pain were growing in his belly. All that he had known, seen, heard in the past months crowded his consciousness at this moment, all— to Kübler's face and form and agony the day before; all—to the fate of Helene Schwarz which he darkly suspected. He stood up. It seemed to ease the pain in his viscera.

"Drop your God-damned sentimentalities, Gerhardt. The time for them is over. Why not face the truth? Civilization is a mask. The mask is off and the primordial brute is let loose. There are a few of us to whom civilization was more than a mask; to us it was a matter of heart and conscience. Well, the brutes hate us for that reason. They're going to annihilate us; they *are* annihilating us. I don't know why I don't take the advice that old man Steinthaler gave me yesterday—to take my wife and child and flee. I don't know why."

The Privy Councillor Jacoby drew himself up in his chair.

"You don't take Steinthaler's advice because every consideration of honour and loyalty forbids it. Steinthaler was never a German at heart. We must stand our ground. Tyrants and their Prætorians have wrought havoc in other lands and ages. That is no reason . . ."

He fell silent as by a single impulse all eyes turned to the door in which stood, as though he had sprung out of the ground, Johannes von Wegener. The eyes not only turned; they stared. Wegener's clothes looked as though they had wilted and shrunken on his large body. Shreds hung from his necktie; his trousers were like old sacks. One sleeve was ripped. His face was the colour of dirty flour. He stood still, immobile, until his eyelid began to twitch over and over again. Then he came slowly forward, slowly, heavily. He dropped into a chair.

"*Tag,*" he said, hoarsely.

No one answered. No one stirred. Doom and death exuded from him as sweat does from an over-driven horse. Laboriously, as though with his last scrap of strength, he took a cigarette from the box on the tea-table. He lit it and inhaled the smoke and then for an instant puckered up his face quaintly like a child that is about to cry. "*Ech!*" he groaned, gutturally. He passed his hands over his face as if to smooth a crumpled fabric.

"Did Kurt tell you what I've been doing?"

"No," Kurt said. "I've told no one."

Wegener groaned.

"They raided Kübler and the Pacifist outfit yesterday and got hold of Kübler's secretary and sweetheart, Helene Schwarz. I've been looking for her. I got hold of a man who's in with them, a sick strange man who murders and then runs to his priest and tries to get absolution. He doesn't get it and believes he's damned and wants to be damned more and more, and weeps with contrition as he swings the rubber truncheon. We went together, that man and I, from barracks to barracks and prison to prison, into cellars— cellars full of spider webs and stinking refuse and vomit and ordure and blood, blood, blood." He licked his lips like an animal. Exactly like an animal, with broad unconscious tongue. "They had her on a table in a cellar. Naked. They beat her belly with canes. In between they raped her. Four of them. They pretended they wanted her to give the names of accomplices. But they had the membership lists of the society. There was nothing she could tell them that they didn't know. Nothing. We had them called off by telephone. We got a physician. But she died at five o'clock this morning. Her mother will get a sealed coffin with a weight in it by and by. I went to break the news—you call it that, don't you—to Fritz Kübler. I'd told him to wait for me in a café in Moabit. But the fool went home. He's on his way to the concentration camp in Dachau." He spread out his hands in a strange, long gesture. "Funeral services *in absentia* of the corpse, Gerhardt; you'll have to go in for that from now on."

Kurt looked at Gina. She held her head in both hands and her white hands were beautiful upon her dark hair. And tears fell from her wide eyes and she did not know it. Then there was a small anguished cry and sob and gurgle. Frau Jacoby had fainted.

IV

K URT WEISS found that he had been wrong about the business in his office during that last week of March, 1933. The crowding of clients ceased as suddenly as, some months before, it had begun. The office was empty. Meta Scholz sat in the outer room at her typewriter in a state of queer alertness. Several times Kurt caught her gnawing her nails. Hannes von Wegener had not been seen since Sunday. The usually busy telephone did not ring. A kind of death throbbed feebly in the empty air. Kurt, formerly wedded to the use of what he thought was reason, perceived that reason was helpless before the changed world that confronted him. He perceived more: this apparently changed world was the real world, the permanent substratum of all the fragile vestitures of civilisation. He had believed in the civilisation of his time as other men had doubtless believed in that of their own. It was gone. Naked savagery had come back. Come back? It had always been there held in leash by reins of gossamer. Only the primordial brute was now immeasurably stronger than he had been of old; he had machines; he and not Zeus wielded the thunderbolt.

He read the papers, idling there in his office—the papers that had during the past few months been transformed from decently intelligent organs of opinion, of policy, of news into the megaphones and loudspeakers of a madness like the mass-madness of the flagellants of the Middle Ages, those innumerable brotherhoods of hysteromaniacs who had wandered from city to city, stripping the countryside between, in flight from that pestilence known as the Black Death, lacerating themselves for the sins which, as they had believed,

66

had brought down upon them the wrath of Heaven. But everywhere and always, beginning with those foul and dreadful proceedings in the town of Chillon, the flagellants had cast off their supposed sins upon the Jews. Self-laceration and the torture of a propitiatory sacrifice and scapegoat had been blended. A process as old as the world and as new as the year 1933. Men cannot bear the burden of their sins and sorrows. They must cast off that burden upon a chosen victim. *He* then is guilty, and not *they*. And to convince themselves of the truth of this lie they must torture the victim before the sacrifice is complete. When the nails are driven through his palms, when the nails are driven through his feet, when the bloody sweat gathers upon his innocent brow —then and not until then is the primordial brute convinced of his sinlessness and of the victim's sin; then and not until then and not otherwise except through that torture of the blameless can the immemorial savage sleep in peace, even as murderers after murder, and jungle creatures after gorging and coitus, sink into the death-like nothingness of the insentient world.

He saw it, saw it with immense clarity and immediately rebelled against his vision. For to accept it was to abandon hope. If this thing were so, if this analogy were exact, if this recurrence could not be arrested, then all the dreams of all dreamers of good from Joseph on, and all the laws of righteous lawgivers and all the visions of the philosophic mind and all the aspirations of good men and good women in all ages after justice, after peace, after brotherhood, were of no avail, of no avail at all in the face of that eternal incurrence of sin and refusal of self-purgation and the dread necessity of purgation through hate and war and persecution. Then, if all this were so, he had reached the bottomless and central hell of human life which by its very existence negated civilisation as more and other than a vain device and specious adornment; then not only should he take his

wife and child and flee—since loyalty, faith, honour, civilised
co-operation between man and man were mere tricks by
which the weak and innocent confirmed their weakness and
sealed their doom—no, it was a question whether one should
or could endure to live in such a world and should not
rather cast oneself into the pyre or upon the savage spears of
the brutes and with some last cry vindicate those ideals
which had no dwelling-place on earth except within one's own
defenceless breast. . . . Well, that is precisely what his remoter ancestors had done. They had often killed their wives
and children rather than have them fall into the hands of
the primordial brutes, as poor little Helene Schwarz had
fallen, and had then literally cast themselves upon the swords
and spears and cried with their last breath: Hear O Israel,
the Lord is our God, the Lord is One.

He didn't know whether to laugh or to cry at this ultimate
conclusion into which vague but certain memories had betrayed him. For him there was no people Israel and there
was no anthropomorphic God about whom unity or anything
else could be predicated. There was no great resistance that
he could oppose to fate. There were only little and partial
and practical resistances, and he had better, by God! address
himself to these. Even a whole skin was something in this
world which had turned into a jungle, and he who kept his
skin intact had at least a chance to see how things would
develop and take advantage of any conceivable turn for the
better. A living dog was better than a dead lion. . . . He
sprang up. No. Something surged in his heart. He could not
reconcile himself to that attitude. It was not, he knew with
complete assurance, that he would not. He could not. It was
not for him. He was sworn to defend law and justice and
equity in this land. Let others trample these concepts under-
foot. He would defend them. He would be damned, for instance, if he would supinely send back to Franzen the copy
of the proceedings incriminating his thievish father. He could

still see that scene before the *Kammergericht* of Charlottenburg. He had already at that time, together with Wegener and other friends, sent in the heavily documented accusations against Heinrich Franzen to the *Anwaltskammer*, the Bar Association of Berlin. But Franzen had evidently even then been certain of that shift of power which would destroy the administration of justice in Germany and concentrate all power in the hands of the henchmen of the terror. For erect, purple-faced, with a front devoid of shame, Franzen with insolently uplifted arm had shouted with such violence of rage that his voice had cracked, "I'll pay you out for this, Herr Doktor Weiss!" And the three robed judges on their dais—Waldmüller, Damaschke, and Cohn—had lowered their eyes and begun to scribble and pretended to have neither seen nor heard.

Kurt wondered why he didn't simply go home. But he knew that this inner question was not really sincere. To go home at this hour would be to acknowledge chaos, to relinquish order, to consent to the crashing of the very structure of life. Hannes' absence was less significant. Poor old Hannes had always been intermittent about everything in life. Nevertheless, Kurt telephoned. It was a small action. It might bring a momentary relief. The querulous, elderly, determinedly refined voice of Frau Ernestine von Wegener answered. "*Jawohl, Herr Doktor*, my son is here. He is not at all well and he is very tired and I doubt very much whether, under the peculiar circumstances, he should come to your office at all.". . . Kurt heard something like a leap and a grunt and then Hannes' voice:

"I beg of you, Mother; you'll have to leave these decisions to me." Then loud and definite: "Are you still there, Kurt?"

"Yes."

"Look here, old man, I'm frightfully sorry. I'll be right down. You know what a good-for-nothing I am at best. All this business, God knows, hasn't made me feel any better. Have you sent back the Franzen document?"

"No."

A deep groan came over the wire. *"Schafskop'"* ("idiot") —but there was no affront in the humorous, affectionate term of abuse—*"Schafskop'!* Luckily the Realmcomissar of Justice is just now rendering Munich unsafe by his presence. I'll come right down."

"Wait," Kurt said, slowly; "there's really no reason. There's not a soul here. I called you up to—to persuade myself—to—to . . ."

"Tja!" Wegener drew out the vocable until it slowly died away in his throat. "I didn't agree with you that we'd be busy. People came for advice as long as they had any hope. They've given up hope."

"What do you mean?"

"I mean what I'd rather not say by telephone. As you know privacy of mail, telegraph, and telephone have been abrogated. And although both you and I"—Wegener's tone and enunciation were suddenly of an extremely Prussian "correctness"—"consent unreservedly to the National Revolution, without necessarily being uncritical of the personal character of subordinates like Franzen, we should all the more guard the discretion so essential at this hour. *Auf wiedersehen!"* Silence. Dead silence. The receiver had been hung up.

Kurt was astonished to find himself wringing his hands. He was caught in that gesture by Meta Scholz. She held a card in her hand and gave it to him and tried in that act to insinuate as much touching of his flesh by hers as possible. He drew back and looked up and saw her trying to work a pathetic and longing look into her metallic eyes. He shrugged his shoulders and looked at the card. It was that of a colleague and friend from Frankfurt-am-Main, a fellow-student of his and a distant kinsman of Gina's, Dr. Ernst Simon.

Ah, the world was not stagnant and dead. A strange rush of
hope impelled him to run almost into the outer office and
clasp the hand of his friend. Desperately he tried not at once
to take in the pallor of Ernst's face, the subtle cracks of that
once almost too elegant surface.

"Ernst, how fine to see you! How long are you staying?
We must let Gina know."

Silently Simon followed him into the inner office.

"Is the door well closed, Kurt?"

"But of course."

The dark eyes rested curiously and lingeringly upon him.

"You're not among those who still refuse to see, are you?"

Kurt shook his head. The false and foolish hopefulness was
gone.

"No. I do see. I've already vicariously witnessed horrors.
Sometimes for moments my mind refuses to grasp, to believe, to know."

Ernst Simon clenched his fist and beat slow rhythmic beats
upon the arm of his chair. He spoke in a hard staccato voice.

"I'm staying indefinitely. I am sent by the leaders of the
Frankfurt community to confer with the gentlemen of leading positions both in and out of the Central-Verein, with
chief Jewish personalities within and without Jewish organi-
sations. We must prepare to emigrate—if possible not family
by family nor individual by individual, but as a group, a
mass, a people."

Kurt jumped up.

"Impossible, both morally and physically!"

"No more impossible than what has happened. And this
is only the beginning. The boycott for day after tomorrow is
determined on. We German Jews will be pilloried and put
to shame before Germany and the world. We shall be
stamped as outcasts and as filth. Having done so, these people must do everything in their power to *make* us what they
have *declared* us. And it can be done. By excluding us from

both the social and the economic structure, by reducing us gradually to the status of hucksters and beggars and cleaners of ordure, by robbing us of all educational opportunities, we can be reduced—as any human group can be—within a single generation to the moral condition of outcasts. There is no alternative between that and flight."

"I had heard," Kurt said, feebly, "that very rich and influential personalities had reached some of the chiefs of the NSPD."

"Quite true. And they were ready to make immense sacrifices—both moral and pecuniary sacrifices. But the whole thing was both silly and futile. Since all Jewish wealth is going to be expropriated anyhow, the offer to part with any of it voluntarily was a bad joke. I'm credibly informed that the offer was received with ribald laughter. But that isn't all. The boycott is absolutely necessary to this régime. It has leaked out into the world that this Brown Terror in Germany is the most brutal and filthy and unmotivated in all history. There was no resistance. There is no resistance. Hence murder and torture are being practised as orgy and substitute orgasm. Now the only way that face can be saved within the country, as well as without, is to declare the Brown Terror a vile invention of foreign Jewry and to prove that accusation the Jews within Germany have to be tortured and degraded *as though* they were guilty of the enormities imputed to them. Do you see it, Kurt? Is it quite clear to you?"

"Quite clear," Kurt answered.

"Very well," Ernst Simon's words clicked with his intellectual clarity and incisiveness like a machine. "One more point: If all these goings-on were not the filthiest of hypocrisies and the murkiest of smoke screens—if, that is to say, even this madness were a sincere madness, this government would do all in its power to help the Jews of Germany to emigrate. Instead you have confiscation of property and passport difficulties. They want to keep us imprisoned; they want to torture and degrade us in order to prove to themselves that we *ought* to be tortured and degraded. They dare not, so far as they can help, let the world know us as we are. More, they will spend millions to slander us to that world in order to justify their brutishness and their lies."

Kurt drooped in his chair.

"And that's the German fatherland."

Ernst relaxed and took a cigar out of his pocket. Carefully he lit it and began to smoke.

"No, I wouldn't put it quite that way. There are millions of Germans who are very unhappy about this. But other millions are in a diseased condition. Unluckily, the disease is catching and even those who can't be infected will, after all, not sell out their fatherland for any abstract reasons or to save the skin of a few hundred thousand Jews. I can even understand that. You see it *is* their fatherland. It *isn't* ours."

"I thought it was!" Kurt bowed his head. "I built my life on that."

"We didn't so completely down in Frankfurt. That is to say, we never so completely merged ourselves. Remember, my people are orthodox."

"You aren't."

"I drifted, Kurt, and drifted with the current of the world. But whenever I came into my father's house I knew that I was coming home. And during the last two years I have come home to stay."

Kurt got up.

"Let's go out and have some luncheon, if you have time. Where are you staying, by the way?"

"At the Eden Hotel."

"Don't you want to see Gina?"

"Of course I do. Naturally."

It was refreshing to walk along the Kurfürstendamm. The

earlier part of the day was always freer from brutal turmoil. It was toward dark that the Brown Shirts came out to insult and persecute and murder.

"What you said to me a moment ago, Ernst—I wish I could understand it; I wish I could feel it. I don't; I can't."

"How about Gina?"

"She's completely bewildered, of course. You know the family as well as I."

"Yes. You see one of her greataunts married my grandfather. In Berlin that generation was already highly assimilated. In Frankfurt they were less so. At all events they remained faithful to the Law. We have our reward now."

"Exactly how?"

"We know *why* we suffer. We are not completely bewildered."

"Because you don't eat butter with your meat?"

"No, Kurt, because we know that we belong primarily to the eternal family of Israel which has suffered in these ways before and has survived and will survive again."

"To what end? To what purpose?"

"The meaning of history, Kurt, must be sought in its processes. We don't know ultimates. The manifest unconscious will of Israel to survive and live and function is its own justification. Did it ever occur to you to doubt that the will of the German people to live and be strong and victorious needed any excuse?"

"No, it never did."

"Well then?"

"The Jews, my dear man, are not a people."

Ernst Simon laughed.

"You say that in order to get out from under the iron fact. No one else is of that opinion, neither our many enemies nor our few friends."

They had been walking slowly through the mild air of noon. They came to a bookshop of a man named Sachs,

where Kurt and Gina had often bought books. Kurt stopped
in front of the large plate-glass window and surveyed the
beautiful display: the Insel editions of Goethe and Kant
and Rilke, the thin-paper edition of Thomas Mann's *Zauber-
berg*, which he had long coveted and forgotten to get; the
re-issue of Will Vesper's *Die Ernte*, an incomparable anthol-
ogy of lyrics from the twelfth to the twentieth century. He
knew the book. He could visualise it almost page by page
as Gina, who had a more spontaneous love of poetry than
he, had read it to and with him. And behind these books,
high up in the tall display, were a number of albums of
music, among them the selected songs of Brahms, and into
Kurt's heart stole measures of the divinest of these songs,
the divinest of all songs, it seemed to him, ever heard by
mortal ears, ever uttered by mortal lips, the song *"Von
ewiger Liebe"* ("Concerning Love Immortal"). He heard,
as though it were being sung to him by a living voice
over the ripple and murmur of the accompaniment, that
utterly earnest yet never solemn air, its unaffected exaltation, its pure curbed passion, its declaration of faith
in the eternity of love too deep to need the pomp of
crescendo, too high to borrow a romantic modulation, too
still and hushed to sing out that faith to any but its own
soul. . . . His lids burned. "Ernst," he began, but his voice
broke. He regarded his friend and saw a white, still, austere
face; he saw thin lips and eyes withdrawn toward an inner
vision. Then he saw a hand raised in a solemn monitory
gesture and heard the hard voice of his friend.

"I have already said farewell to all that. You will too,
Kurt."

"Never, never. Rather a grave in German earth."

They swung round as a yell arose behind them:
"Deutschland erwache! Juda verrecke!" ("Germany awaken!
Let Jews die like dogs!"). Not Brown Shirts, as they had
known from the high treble of the yell, only urchins who

were already scampering down the street. Nevertheless, they stood like men transfixed.

"There," Ernst Simon said, slowly, "there is your Germany of the next fifty years. That Germany won't know anything about Goethe or Kant or Brahms or Rilke. Not a damned thing. You might answer: All right. Then I'll save the real, the eternal Germany. They'll spatter you with their filth as you say it. They'll make the thing impossible for you. They'll defile your will toward their salvation. Oh no. We're human, too, and have the right and duty to be independently human. I quite agree with you that it's like a surgical operation. But operations do save lives, you know."

He hailed a taxi. They drove to the Eden Hotel. Ernst Simon ate his luncheon with a semblance of appetite. Kurt felt choked. It did not escape him that despite his handsome analyses of the situation he had in his own person and inwardness not yet begun to face either conflict or renunciation. He had been loitering at the brink of the abyss. He had known that the abyss existed. He had not looked down. He had somehow, in the most secret chambers of his mind, held on to the reservation that some, a few, himself, might fly across that monstrous chasm. And even now, even at this hour he felt a sudden enmity toward Simon which he was honest enough to interpret as the last resistance of a false and lying hope within himself.

"When shall we see you, Ernst?"

"I'll be in conferences all day tomorrow. On April first all hell will break loose. I doubt whether any of us had better go out at all on that day. There's no use directly provoking pogroms, though it might help us with the world."

Kurt drove home. The maid told him that Gina and Gabriel had gone over to the Jacoby villa to see how Frau Jacoby was feeling. He walked round vaguely in the apartment from room to room. He touched objects. He was surprised that his hand encountered solid surfaces, that all things had not turned into wraiths. Then suddenly a sharp anxiety for his wife and child assailed him. He telephoned to the Jacoby house. "Yes," the butler said, "Frau Dr. Weiss and Gabriel were with the *Herrschaften* on the terrace." The message, though expected, eased not only this incidental tension in Kurt, but the deeper and sharper tension under which he was. He yawned; he seemed to be about to collapse from sheer weariness. He lay down on the chaise-longue in the library and fell into a deep lethargic slumber.

V

IN THE streets about the Rosenthaler Gate, where two centuries and a half ago had stood the first inn to shelter the Jews at long last readmitted to Brandenburg from the south and the east, men got up early from their beds on the 1st of April, 1933, and washed their hands and put on their phylacteries and praying-shawls. Some, more intrepid than their fellows, went forth from their houses and gathered in the synagogues on the Oranienburgerstrasse and on the Fasanenstrasse and on the Lindenstrasse and in other and humbler houses of study and of prayer. These men knew that another *Geserah*, or persecution, henceforth to be known as the *Geserath Ashkenaz*, the German persecution, was about to be added to the intermittent persecutions and expulsions of the centuries. They knew that on this day they were to be pilloried in their shops and offices as their fathers had been aforetime, and in order to draw strength for the coming day and the coming days they went to the same eternal source to which their fathers had gone.

Their faith was not so strong as their fathers' had been. Perhaps that was because their sorrows and troubles had not been so sore. Yet neither under the King of Prussia, nor under the three emperors from 1870 to 1918, nor even during the brief and stormy existence of the Weimar Republic had these men and their wives and children forgotten or been permitted to forget who and what they were. A penurious paper equality before the law had been theirs. In the practice of life, in school, in the army, in business, in the pursuit of their varied callings they had been subjected to well-regulated slights, to brutal or coarsely humorous insult,

to private isolation and public obloquy. Yet they had not
until now complained nor thought they had much cause to
complain. There had been no pogroms within the memory
of men; there had been, until these last few mad hectic
years, no blood-accusation; one lived, therefore, upon the
whole in better times; now and then one's sons, despite all
obstacles, rose high. What more could a Jew ask? Oh, they
had been seemly subjects and citizens. They had fought for
king and fatherland; few of them had followed the open
Gentile example of exporting capital to neutral countries
during the World War; sedulously most of them had avoided
the political implications of Zionism. But they had never
given up a last reserve and doubt and distrust and by the
same token had never sacrificed to the pagan world an ultimate pride and stubborness and self-affirmation. Always
some bearded grandfather in their midst had muttered:
"Lamah rag'shu goyim?" ("Why do the heathen rage?").
Always when a child brought home from school some tale
of hurt or undeserved shame there had been a mother or
grandmother to gather it into her arms and curse, even
though husband or father said: "Hush, hush!" the hard
hearts of the pagans.

Now to these men this 1st of April, 1933, was a bitter day.
Many of them had already been broken and bankrupted by
both sly and open persecution. Gaining a meagre livelihood
for their wives and children had been for a long time a
struggle so harsh and relentless that any human beings but
Jews would have lapsed into despair and drunkenness. And
now, it was clear enough, even these superhuman efforts
would no longer be permitted to avail. But they laughed
with a bitter inward laughter when they heard and read
the screaming slogans that the Jews had sucked the economic life blood of the German people. It was certainly not
they and their kind. It was also not, as they knew with
precise shrewdness, the small group of second-rate bankers

or the half-dozen first-rate department-store men in Berlin,
West. It was—in this knowledge lay their strength—none of
these things. Old reasons, new reasons. Bad faith, bad race,
bad this, bad that. Here was a new *Geserah*, a new persecution like those of old. Therefore, though many had become
slack enough, God knows, even to the eating of forbidden
foods at Kempinski's in other and more prosperous years,
they now put on their phylacteries and wrapped themselves
on this brilliant morning of a northern spring in their praying-shawls and intoned as their fathers had done during the
innumerable generations: *"V'hu Eli"* ("And He is my God")
"v'chai goali" ("and living is my Redeemer") *"v'zur chebli
b'eth zarah"* ("and a rock in my travail in time of distress").
Thus they prayed and trembled and wept. But they also
knew a lifting of the heart in the midst of their terror and
their wretchedness when, as never before in all their lives,
they poured their whole souls into the supplication: *"Theka
b'shofar gadol l'cheruthenu"* (Sound the great trumpet for
our freedom! Lift up the ensign to gather our exiles and
gather us from the four corners of the earth! Blessed art
thou, O Lord, who gatherest the banished of thy people
Israel").

Not at all after this fashion did the 1st of April, 1933, come
to the West End of Berlin—to the people in the Tauenzien-
strasse and the Kurfürstendamm and its cross-streets and
around the Olivaerplatz and in the Grunewald section. No
one had slept that night, though husband pretended to wife
and parents to children and everyone to the German servants
who brought the breakfasts into those handsome, spacious
dining-rooms and took them out again untasted. Here furtiveness was in every eye, however clear and candid through
all the previous years of life; here pallor was on every cheek;
here there was a strange paralysis and a stranger powerless
rebellion, a vague speechless searching and questioning of
things inexplicable, inscrutable, monstrous. It was the ele-

ment of the monstrous that shook these people to the founda-
tion of their being. They were like people who had always
been greatly concerned, as indeed they had been, over the
health and cleanliness of their bodies and knew themselves
by every evidence of soul and sense to be straight and hale
and clean, without infirmity or blemish. And now the world,
their whole world in which they had always lived and without which they knew not how to live, arose and on this
day declared for all to hear that they were crippled lepers,
contorted, splotched, withered, stricken with boils and sore-
ness, oozing poison, contaminating the very winds of earth.
The worst of it was that they had always believed this world
of theirs and the voices of that world and defended the truth
uttered by these voices in good days and ill, in peace and
war. Now they peered at their straight limbs and smooth
skins and wondered with a stricken wonder whether it was
only that they had no eyes to see and blindness were added
to the other infirmities imputed to them. And there were
those, nor were these few, who almost hoped to find upon
themselves crookedness or blot, since, though full of trembling and tears, they would rather have condemned themselves than lose all faith in all they had all their lives believed, and be robbed of all love of that which all their lives
they had loved supremely. From among these came the
many who in the ensuing months took their own lives, and
from among these came that desperate and shameful group
who insisted until they were destroyed that they be permitted to make common cause with their enemies against
their flesh and blood, with an unfathomable but unconscious
treachery feigning to themselves that in them and in them
alone that flesh and blood and spirit had undergone a subtle transformation which left them clean, while their
brethren did indeed bear all the stigmata of the leper and
the outcast. . . .

In better case were those who interpreted this monstrous

thing in a more impersonal fashion. Clamour and hideous tumult were already sounding from afar when Gina and Kurt faced each other at the breakfast table. Liese had brought in fruit and rolls and coffee. She lingered a moment.

"There were no papers at the door, *Herr Doktor*."

Kurt did not look up.

"I got them; I woke early."

Gabriel at his end of the table was trying to build a triangular structure of knife and fork and spoon. Gina laid a calm hand on his small ones.

"Don't, darling."

Kurt looked up and now their eyes met. He had been afraid to meet her eyes. They were tranquil. He let his arms drop beside him and took a deep breath.

"*Die Tiefen haben sich aufgetan.*" ("The depths have opened"). Gina's voice was steady.

"Are you just saying that as a formula?" he asked.

She shook her head.

"Not at all. There is evidently more evil in the world than we thought. It's been gathering as in a reservoir. Now it's spilling over."

"When did you begin to think about it in this way?"

She put her hands to the sides of her head in her favourite gesture.

"I didn't tell you, dear, and I asked Gabriel not to worry you with it. But I sent him back to school for several days after you told him he need go no more."

"Yes, yes."

"He was openly called *Judensau* in the classroom and the teacher did not forbid it. He was forced to sing the Horst Wessel song. He was isolated with four other little Jewish boys on a bench in the rear of the classroom. I went to the school and saw it. I looked at the teacher and I looked at the German children. They were all like people who had been poisoned. And so it is: their souls are poisoned with evil. You had only to look at Gabriel and his four little companions to see the difference. Look at him now. He is your child as much as mine. Could anyone who is not dominated by evil be cruel to him?"

Kurt stretched out his hands across the table and Gina laid her own into them.

"And what do you think we ought to do, Gina?"

"I think we ought to go away. I asked Papa yesterday how much money he could give us. He told me that he had heavy interests in Jewish-owned banks in both Strassburg and Paris, and that he would gladly assign these holdings to us."

Kurt found himself spontaneously smiling for the first time in many days.

"Clever man! Weren't you surprised?"

"Of course I was astonished. I didn't say so. But Papa saw it and told me that these people were descended from an old Mannheim family, friends and correspondents for a century. He had been a silent partner in their Strassburg house when Strassburg was German. Well, when the war was over the Seckelsohns didn't consider *him* a conquered enemy."

"I see," Kurt spoke slowly. The old, old friendly brotherliness of Jewry. Something about it made him glad. Yet again a sharp pang of vicarious remorse went through him. Then some of the milder reproaches had a background of fact? No, no. Only Jews were less rancorous. At all events, this matter had no bearing on the poisonous ravings that had shaken him in his morning paper, that inconceivably stupid, brutal, and illiterate proclamation of the Women's Section of the National-Socialist Party: "This is the same Jewish atrocity propaganda that was responsible for our loss of the war, for our two million dead, for our starved old men, women, and children, for Versailles, Dawes and Young. . . . Don't underestimate the frightful seriousness of this decisive battle. The Jew wants to wage it to the point of the annihilation of the German people. . . ." He thought of poor little Helene Schwarz. His throat contracted. He started as from a heavy dream.

"Yes, Gina."

She had been busy with Gabriel. She looked up.

"When France seemed to be threatened with inflation in twenty-six the Seckelsohns appealed to Papa and he invested again."

Gabriel looked up brightly at his parents.

"Are we going away from here? Oh, how nice. Let's go right away!"

He bobbed up and down happily on his chair. "Please, please, right away." Then he burst into tears, those large luminous tears that always broke Kurt's heart.

Gina and Kurt looked into each other's eyes. Gabriel slipped from his seat and wandered over to the window and drew the curtain aside. Shrill cries arose from the street: "*Jude Itzig!* See Jew Izzy! See Jew Izzy!" The children of all the janitors of the block were having a holiday. Gabriel came back into the room. He was pale as a waxen flower. "*Are* we going away from here?" he asked.

Gina put her arms around him.

"Yes, my darling."

"When, Mamma, when?"

She soothed him against her breast. "Soon, Gabrielchen, soon. . . ."

"I'm going out," Kurt said.

Gina looked at him earnestly above the child's head.

"Do you think . . ."

"Violence has been forbidden," he said, grimly.

"Violence, violence." Slowly she repeated the words after him.

He went downstairs. The children on the Eisenzahnstrasse had run into the empty building-lots opposite. But in a moment he was on the Kurfürstendamm and saw on the window of the corner pharmacy the first fiercely yellow poster with the Star of David and in huge Gothic letters the word, *"Jude."* He shook his head. He hadn't known that the Strelitzes were Jews. He hadn't even known.

Out here in this almost suburban neighbourhood there were few people. But the storm-troopers must have come early. The posters glared in the sunlight. "Of the cash the sheenies stole, foreign slanderers got their dole." "Feed the Jew not in his sty; German should of German buy." "Every Mark in Jewish hand leaves the German fatherland." His eyes seemed to ache with a physical ache. Where should he turn them? Slowly he walked along. Slowly at first. Then the shops began to increase in number and here, in this quarter, many, of course, were owned by Jews. And on each shop window was the poster and the badge, and as the street grew more populous and busy the posters increased not only in number but in size and virulence. And small crowds gathered before these shops and before the posters on frames with their brief biting injunctions: "Shun Jewish physicians and lawyers." And suddenly a motor-truck filled with storm-troopers with the Swastika flag streaming high thundered past: "Germans, defend yourselves. Buy not of Jews!" The crowd stopped. Hundreds of hands were raised and hundreds of voices cried: "Heil Hitler!" Something within him had torn upwards Kurt's hand, too. He had uttered no sound. But his hand was up. He looked at it as though it were a foreign object. It dropped.

He pressed his hat down over his forehead. He knew that he was hunching up his shoulders. Thus had the Jews of old, as innocent—he knew it now—as himself, walked the bitter ways of earth. On he trudged. Now the region of offices began. He looked up, and on the second and third and even fourth story windows were the yellow posters. He saw them on the windows of great medical specialists and of counsellors-at-law of pre-eminent learning and high repute. None were spared. And so it was without a pang that he saw the poster pasted to the window of his own office, "Jew!" For the first time in his life he saw the Star of David, the hexagram, with anything but the indifference with which his kind and generation regarded all vestiges of the superstitions of the past. Had not his father spoken of it—faint and far was the memory—as the *Mogen Dovid* (the shield of David)? A shield? It had been turned into a mark of shame! Not his shame. Nor the shame of any Jew he had known. Oh yes, there had been certain Jewish criminals. There had been, as he knew from papers and legal periodicals, dishonest speculators, fraudulent bankrupts, evaders of commercial regulations. There had been no Jews like the men who had tortured Helene Schwarz to death. None. Thank God. Was that he who was saying "Thank God"? Was that he who was murmuring to himself that he would take that shield of David and make a shield of it once more against an evil world in whose evil he and his had no part?

He had reached the Gedächtniskirche. On the great triangular space the crowds were dense and festive. Banners streamed. High flew the Swastika. Glad cries of release throbbed. From the direction of the Zoological Gardens approached in the middle of the otherwise trafficless street a solemn single file of storm-troopers. Grave or sullen faces between cap and chin strap. Faces neither evil nor contorted. Not these. Faces of simple men doing a not too agreeable job that had been assigned them by superiors whose words they believed. A little dogged their expression; a little dogged their enforcedly waddling march. For each carried by a string around his neck a huge stiff pasteboard placard which covered him almost from shoulder to puttee. And these huge, ponderous placards also bore the legend: "Germans! Defend yourselves! Buy not of Jews."

A sudden core of heat began to glow in Kurt's brain. The

material boycott was a lie and a subterfuge. Had it been
sincere, it would have sufficed to order all Jewish shops to
be closed. The Jews, on the contrary, had been ordered to
open their shops, to spread out their usual window displays.
The apparently economic weapon was in fact a moral
weapon. The whole manœuvre from beginning to end was a
lie and a trick and the vile device of evil and guilt-racked
and perverse men. A sudden pogrom with looting hoodlums
would have been a decenter thing. . . . The sun of spring
rode high over that strange and accursed city and the holiday throngs grew denser. Kurt let the crowd carry him onward, and with that incandescence in his brain heard the
guffaws and now and then the screaming laughter as, nearer
the center of the city, more virulent signs—signs evidently
prompted by local rancour, had been affixed to Jewish shops.
"I am a dirty Jew!" he read. "I am the Jew Isidor. Look at
my nose!" And again and again there had been added to the
name of individual or firm the word "Judas." And Kurt
raised his face and his eyes to peer into the faces and into
the eyes of the people on these festive streets on which bands
blared and vendors cried their wares of *swastika* flags and
relief plaques of Hitler for the hearts and sausages for the
stomachs of the Berliners. He peered and peered and saw
not one look of deprecation or of sorrow, not one of uncertainty or compassion—not one, not one. Oh, he saw Jews
who like himself had for some reason braved this scene. His
glance seemed on this day to have acquired a preternatural
acuteness to recognize them. And some walked with eyes on
the pavement and hunched shoulders and pale or burning
cheeks. But others raised their heads in defiance and had a
flame in their glance, and some even—and his heart lifted
at the sight of these few—looked upon this madness and
sordidness of man with a cold and remote and immemorial
contemptuousness. He knew what word was in their consciousness—a word freighted with the bestialities and lies

of a thousand years: *goyim* (heathens)—a word which he, a German of the Germans, had never used nor approved, but had held to be the mark of those who had not yet, to their own hurt and shame, wholly identified themselves with this people and this land and its memories and its glories and loyalties and triumphs and defeats. *Goyim!* He raised his head. He clenched his teeth. . . . A girl, blonde as wheat, with eyes of the traditional cornflower blue, cried in his ear: "Now more than ever: Out with the Jews!" and thrust into his hand a vilely printed pamphlet bearing the words she had cried. He gave her, looking straight into her candid, joyous, stupid face, the ten-pfennig piece she demanded. He hid the pamphlet in his pockets as she called, ignorant of what he was, into his ear: "The Jews are planning to assassinate our beloved *Führer*. . . ." He laughed a bitter laugh to himself. One of his clients, an astute and humorous man, had said to him weeks ago: "We'd better pray for Haman-Hitler. If anything happens to that *rasha*, that man of evil, no matter by whose hand, they will slaughter us. . . ."

He realized that he was at the corner of the Leipziger-strasse and the Spittelmarkt. No wonder he was tired. His legs ached. His ears ached at the blare and crying. His eyes could no longer endure the sights they had to see. He was grateful for a single taxi left at the corner stand. He jumped in and gave his address. The driver gave him one swift glance and started. Then without turning round the man said: "There's worse'n this, Mister. They're butcherin' our comrades like cattle in pens. They're givin' 'em castor oil and makin' 'em stand up and say 'I'm a Communist sow' and beatin' 'em to death. And *that* won't stop the revolution. Nothin' will."

"And when the revolution comes, what will you and your comrades do?" Kurt asked.

The man bent over his wheel with a gesture of ineffable determination. He stepped with dangerous force on the gas.

"We'll rip the God-damn skin off of the backs of the God-damn sons o' bitches. We'll boil 'em in oil. We'll— Never mind. But we'll do nothin' to the Jews. No, Mister, we don't know no race an' no creed. . . ."

Now and only now an utter desolation came over Kurt. There were those in his very own group who had openly said that they would have preferred a Communist to a National-Socialist revolution. And doubtless no Jews would have been tortured and killed as such, as Jews. But in this man he saw a chaos as dark and gloomy as the chaos that had actually opened at the feet of men. Gina was right. The depths were open. The earth had been split asunder. Primordial madness and ferocity had come back. The jungle was invading the world. Tooth and claw and poisoned fang alone were left. . . . He reached his door. The taxi-driver took his fare and tip in silence. His car rattled off.

He found Gina and Gabriel sitting side by side. Gina had been reading to the child, whose eyes shone and whose cheeks were flushed from his absorption in the tale. He now jumped up.

"Papa! Mamma's been worrying." Suddenly he had become aware of that.

Kurt kissed Gabriel and then sat down beside Gina and put his arms about her.

"There was no need. I saw what, I suppose, it was best to see if we have to flee."

She bowed her head in assent. "It will be hard enough."

Kurt took from his pocket the ill-printed pamphlet which the blonde girl had sold him. He opened it and turned the pages for Gina to see with him. The heavy captions of the paragraphs sufficed: "Freemasonry in the Service of Juda," "Freemasonry and Marxism," "The Fifth kabbalistic Sanhedrin," "The Protocols of the Elders of Zion According to the Basel Congress of 1907." Gina shivered.

"You remember my telling you, Gina, how I found volumes of old, old magazines in the attic when I was eleven or twelve, full of old-fashioned mystery and horror stories. This stuff is exactly like those stories: conspirators meeting in graveyards by night, solemn conclaves of mysterious criminals with pseudo-Masonic hocus-pocus, men in the shape of vampires sucking innocent blood, strangers of unearthly origin bedevilling the pure and trusting. The products of a fancy both feverish and vulgar—the fancy of a scared servant-girl who has been to see a fortune-teller in Moabit. It's literally subhuman, as *they* are fond of saying, and it's the official doctrine of this government."

Gina clung to him. "And yet we shall be so lonely and lost elsewhere."

"But you were so certain this morning that we should go."

"I am still. But I see now what it will be like."

Kurt leaned his head on his hands.

"Yes, we are quite homeless."

"Even with each other," Gina said, in a level tone. "Do you feel that, Kurt?"

"We mustn't," he protested, feebly.

She spoke like one in a trance.

"All human relations exist within some atmosphere, some system. I'm not clever enough to make it clear. We speak to each other in German, don't we? We love each other in German. If we can't speak German any more we're stricken dumb. If we can't express what we feel any more, the feelings wither."

She wept.

Gabriel had been vaguely wandering about the room. Neither Kurt nor Gina had observed that he had finally stopped in front of the radio and had begun to manipulate the knobs. He gave a little cry of terror as there burst in upon the quiet room a voice—a crude, dragging, menacing voice, the voice of a male but also the voice of a virago, bringing the image of a crone with long sparse hairs growing from a withered chin, a crone virulent with fancied wrongs and rancid self-pity. The voice shrilled to a scream of rage; words raced with hectic speed and madness— words monotonous, common, dull, words carried beyond themselves by that half-male and half-virago scream with its underlying whine—beyond themselves to a tearing open of a womb in which had lain and from which now leaped forth all the hidden shames and fleshly perversities and dark impulses of sick and savage men, and flung their nakedness in a wild triumph of public orgy out into the world to whip up and to sting and to tear off the rags of obscene lust, until all secret sharers of those passions and perversities could whirl within the rage and gross self-pity and frantic exhibitionism of that monstrous voice.

VI

THE authorities of the new government had announced
that the boycott action would be repeated if world-
Jewry did not cease its campaign of slander against the
German people and its national uprising. Although the
Jews of Germany, and together with them very many thousands of liberals and republicans, were completely cowed by
the Brown Terror, no one quite believed that there would be
a repetition of what had happened on the 1st of April.
Enough foreign newspapers, especially those of German
Switzerland, made their way into the country and were more
or less surreptitiously seen by enough people to create the
definite impression that the civilized world had been horri-
fied by what had taken place. And it was tacitly understood
that behind the raging triumvirate of new rulers—the virago
in male form, the failure-maddened scribbler with the club
foot, the obese opium-eating hysteromaniac changing his
thirty uniforms in his nightmarish villa—there stood the
army chiefs and the industrialists who had less stomach for
making Germany an outcast nation and a stench in the nostrils of mankind for the second time within a single generation.

On a day early in April Dr. Simon brought to Kurt's
office, where he was dully reading the papers, a youngish
American, Mr. Peter Lang, who had been taken deeply
into the confidence and councils of the Central Association
of German Jews. In quite foreign but fairly fluent German
Peter Lang explained what seemed to him the reaction of
world opinion toward these recent happenings in Germany.
A sharp look of pain stole into his blue eyes as he began

by saying that, though he himself entertained quite the contrary feeling, the horror of certain sections of mankind was less evoked by the sufferings of the German Jews as such than by the bleak impression that certain quite fundamental, even though silent, compacts of Western civilization had been suddenly and spectacularly smashed. If, he explained, any class or race or religious communion—any group of men as a group—could suddenly be expelled from participation in a civilization which they had demonstrably helped to build, what man or group of men could any more be sure that tomorrow he or his group would not be rendered outcast, pariah, untouchable by sudden fiat. In brief, the discomfort, uncertainty, and hidden fears that had already been lurking at the core of contemporary society had been rendered more immediate and acute. He paused. "The worst of it is that this fear and distrust will make it easier for other Fascist groups in other countries." He clasped his hands. "Fear is the enemy! Scared men are feeble. That gives the ruffians their opening."

Ernst Simon shrugged his shoulders.

"That's perfectly true. And I saw how you winced at the proclamation of the Central Association. Don't think I didn't observe that. But we are a weak and small group. We are being destroyed. Now I don't agree with the C.A. leaders. My solution is emigration. But I don't blame these men for trying to stand their ground. After all, that takes courage, too, as things are today."

Peter Lang turned to Kurt.

"What's your idea, Dr. Weiss?"

"I shouldn't say I have any idea that can be defined. Until ten days ago I refused, foolishly, no doubt, to see and to believe. It's a case of the incredible and impossible suddenly becoming stark fact and facing one. As a practical measure my wife and I have agreed that we would take our child and leave the country. But we're afraid it's a plunge into nothingness."

Peter Lang took a paper from his inner pocket. He unfolded it carefully.

"Don't you read the *Jüdische Rundschau?*"

Kurt shook his head.

"The organ of the Zionists," Ernst Simon said in a flat voice.

Lang held the paper up and pointed to the heavy headline on the front page: "WEAR IT WITH PRIDE, THE YELLOW BADGE!"

Kurt was bitter.

"Very handsome. Unluckily it's beside the point as far as I am concerned. You condemn me for a crime of the very existence of which I was ignorant and then tell me to consent to the imputation as a method of the moral reaffirmation of my being. No. That's nothing for me."

Peter Lang clasped his hands.

"But you *are* Jews."

Kurt felt an immense irritation gnawing at him.

"I have never denied it. And it has often seemed to me that not denying it was a grosser lie than denying it would have been. You can tear open my breast and my brain and you will find nothing that is specifically Jewish, that is specifically different—generically different—from other men. Now you ask me suddenly to make a new content of life of something that is a figment."

"I don't agree with Weiss," Ernst Simon said, slowly, "though I am far from going the length of the Zionists."

Peter Lang slowly folded up the paper and put it back in his pocket. "I wish my friend Jehuda Brenner were here. I asked him to come. But he said that he was not needed here. He said the German Jews would find their Jewishness in their souls and learn to be Jews again without any help, just as certain Christians in Germany were learning to be

Christians again and were gladly taking upon themselves
the Cross of Christ."

"Who is this friend of yours?" Ernst Simon asked.

"He is a great Jew and a great human being," Peter Lang
answered, very simply. "He rarely theorizes, but he has
taught me by what he is what a great and precious thing
it is to be a Jew."

Kurt turned sharply.

"Why are you here, Mr. Lang?"

Peter laughed a candid, boyish laugh.

"I don't believe in persecution for conscience' sake. A
great many Americans don't. It makes them furious. I
know a good many English people who feel that way, too.
So I thought I might be of some use. Of course one man can
do less than nothing. What ought to have happened is this:
thousands and thousands of Christians should have come to
Germany and lived with the persecuted Jews and the persecuted liberals and pacifists and Christians. Wherever the
Nazis turned and whatever they did they should have been
met with the intolerable rebuke of Christians from all over
the world. Wherever they attacked a Jew they should have
found a Christian by his side to offer to share his suffering.
The trouble is, Dr. Weiss, that the Christianity of most
Christians is as dead or dormant in their hearts as your
Judaism is in yours. It's an unredeemed world and it's quite
literally going to the devil."

Kurt felt almost surly.

"Do you really think that religion and religious motives
can still be effective in this age?"

Peter Lang sighed.

"Look at National-Socialism! Look at orthodox Communism! There you have religions—evil religions. Religions
with angels and devils and saviours." He smiled a winning
smile. "It's still as true as ever that you can drive out the
devil only by the help of God."

"You mean that symbolically, of course?"

Peter Lang got up.

"If you like. But it's a pretty concrete fact, isn't it?" He looked at his watch. "We've got to go, Simon. We can walk to Meineckestrasse from here, can't we?"

"Easily."

Peter Lang turned in farewell to Kurt. "That's the address of Zionist headquarters." He smiled his infinitely winning smile again. "I'm only a *goy* and a foreigner, but I'm trying to get all you Jews to pull together."

Kurt found that this meeting and the words that had been spoken dwelt continuously in his mind. Yet nothing germinated. The seed, if it was seed, had been sown in a sterile place. Dull and dour were the creeping days of this detestable April. If there was sunlight, it struck him like an artifice, like stage illumination. In the morning he read the now monstrous papers and bent his back and bared his breast to the blows they brought. "Civil servants of non-Aryan descent are to be immediately retired." "Quota system introduced without friction in the slaughter-houses and cattle-markets of Cologne." "Compositions and records of the Messrs. Toscanini, Bodansky, Harold Bauer, and Gabrilowitch no longer admissible in German concert-halls or radio diffusion." "Special commission II sequestrates in a local bank the credit balance of Professor Albert Einstein amounting to 30,000 marks." "In the interest of discipline Herr Klemperer's concert at the State Opera House is deferred. Storm troops are needed for graver purposes than to protect Jewish bankrupts in art from just indignation." "Quota system introduced for notaries." "Only a very limited number of Jewish attorneys will be admitted to court practice hereafter. According to the Bar Association this number for Berlin will be thirty-five. The names will be announced later." "Visit to the largest concentration camp on the Heuberg. Under protective arrest there are to be found all prominent personalities having any 'leftist' affiliations." "Jewish cattle-dealers placed under protective arrest." "Every student at the universities is to cleanse his private library of all un-German matter and to contribute to the purification of the public libraries." "All books tending to the disintegration of the German spirit are to be collected and on the 10th of May given over to the flames." "We must accustom ourselves to learn how to punish again and how to be hard." "The excitement of our people over the presumptuous behaviour of Jewish lawyers and physicians has reached such proportions that we must reckon with self-defensive measures on the part of our people. Hence all Jewish judges are warned to resign at once."

Thus the days began. There was, of course, Kurt was drily aware, an element of cosmic farcicality about it all—the stentorian self-stultification of a great and cultured people could easily—he remembered his Heine—arouse the mirth of some heavenly Aristophanes. The tone of all the announcements of this government and its individual functionaries was so evidently, so blatantly the tone of the ill-bred, the ill-taught, the rancorous failures, the envious mediocrities, the thirsters and hungerers for revenge—revenge against others, better taught, better born, better bred, out in the sunlight of the world's rewards of either virtue or talent—for *their* miseries and failures and vices. The depths, as Gina had said, were opened. And out of these depths climbed noisome creatures, cripples of the soul and of the body, and announced themselves the very lords of life and enforced their announced lordship with concentration camps and rubber truncheons. But one could not laugh because of these rubber truncheons and these bullets in the back of the head of so many of the good, the brave, the kind, the intelligent, who had been "shot while trying to escape." Thus, according to Johannes von Wegener, had Fritz Kübler already met his end. To this end were destined, as the days crept on, so many more whom Kurt knew personally or by their good repute.

There was a great dying in the dark, and these deaths, as Kurt now knew, were never easy deaths, but deaths by long slow torture, deaths in filth and degradation, deaths by such devices as deeply diseased men imagine in half-bloody, half-lustful daydreams for those whom they have injured and whom they therefore hate with an implacable and self-torturing hate.

Thus the days began. Thereafter they were empty. Yet Kurt was strangely ashamed not to go daily to his office where Meta Scholz still sat and polished her long pointed nails. Wegener rarely appeared, and then looked wind-torn, as it were, and pain-racked. He still advised Kurt to send back to the Kommissar Franzen the document incriminating the man's father. But he did this, as everything now, without emphasis or energy. He explained that he was being torn to pieces. All his kinsmen were passionately National-Socialist. They lived in a perpetual fever of exaltation over the rebirth and awakening of Germany. And here was he inactive, still the partner of a Jew. He was betraying his people. A moment might come when they could, according to them, protect him no longer. Kurt assured him that he would dissolve the partnership at once and bear him no ill-will if he joined his kinsmen. "I'll be God-damned if I will." Wegener's eyelid twitched. With shaking hand he took out a kerchief and wiped his quivering mouth. "My mother's brother, poor old man, had to kick that Bruno Scheuermann out of the house. He was his oldest son, too. The fellow stole; when he was sixteen he lured little boys into the woods and used them sexually and tortured them. Now he's a *Gau-führer* and fellow saviour of his country. I was always held up to him as the decent and studious member of the younger generation—me, Kurt, *me*! Note the humour of that! So now he threatens to denounce me."

Kurt regarded him seriously.

"Such things are happening, Hannes. We might as well part."

Wegener began to weep in a wretched, weak way.

"Hannes!" Kurt cried. It was a shocking sight. The man seemed to be disintegrating, deliquescing, rotting away in some strange manner before his eyes. Suddenly, biting his lips, he stopped his quivering. He laughed harshly.

"You know my nerves. The whole business is too much for me. I'm a pretty degenerate specimen myself. You see, Kurt, you see——"

"Out with it, Hannes!"

"I'd like—I'd like—not a rubber truncheon. No. I'd like a whip. A long sharp whip that leaves a scarlet line on white flesh. Only, only, Kurt, they're doing it to the wrong people from my point of view, and so I have to go famished." He got up. "They gorge and I'm famished. So what do you suppose I'm full of?"

"What?"

"Morphine, my boy, morphine. Now do you understand?"

"I understand," Kurt said.

He himself, as he had not told Hannes Wegener, seemed afflicted with a massive lethargy, a paralysis of the will. Once or twice Gina had asked him whether they should not begin to make some preparations if they were going to leave the country. Little Gabriel was not going to school; he had few playmates; his temper was being spoiled. Each time Kurt had answered with a show of energy that they must indeed begin their preparations. And had done nothing. Meanwhile, to his amazement, the Jacobys, on the pretext of spending their summer, which was far off, at Scheveningen, had closed their villa and in their big Isotta-Fraschini had crossed the frontier into Holland. He had not asked Gina for details. All she had ventured was that her mother had been threatened with a nervous breakdown and that their old friend and family physician Geheimer Sanitätsrat Sonderling had

insisted on this move. He discovered later that Jacoby knew
he was to be forced to resign from his various directorships
and that the banking-house of Jacoby Brothers was being
"coördinated" by the passing of a majority of the stock into
Aryan hands. No wonder the Privy Councillor preferred not
to have to witness this process, nor that the authorities did
not prevent his flight.

Thus Kurt and Gina were isolated. Their Aryan friends,
between whom and themselves, as they admitted now, the
bonds had never been very strong, had quite simply disappeared. The Jewish group that had been theirs had begun to
break up many months ago. For these Jews had never embodied their Jewishness in any of the forms of their lives.
They belonged to no Jewish club or society or religious
organization. They feigned to themselves to be wholly German and their being Jews had no witness save for this vague
gregariousness with others of their kind. And even this slight
and ultimate bond was created solely by the negative circumstance of their certainty of being, among themselves,
free from the danger of affront. Now under the thunder and
poison, the deafening thunder and subtle poison, of public
and universal Jew-baiting, these Jews had grown afraid of
meeting other Jews. They trembled alone in their houses.
They drew the blinds down over their windows. They lit
their lights late and extinguished them early. Parents and
children, brothers and sisters, communicated with each other
guardedly by telephone. Blight and silence and loneliness
were their present portion. Blow after blow had fallen upon
them. Prayerless and blind, bowed and stricken, unsustained
by that guiltlessness and guilelessness of theirs which rendered but more incomprehensibly monstrous their present
plight, they waited with bowed heads for the next blow to
fall.

In this strange hollowness of existence Kurt clung to Gina
with a silent and absorbed tenacity. They had never ceased

being lovers. In her unreasoned but secure fastidiousness
she had chosen him, poor and without distinction of birth,
from among the suitors in her father's house who had included a Mendelssohn-Bartholdy, a Bleichröder, and a Richt-
hofen. He pleased her intimately. To Kurt his love had long
seemed hopeless. Thus he had never wholly lost the sense
of wonder in possessing her. The magic of her yielding had
never been tarnished by the film of custom and he now held
her nightly as though he would never let her go in his
impassioned and devoted arms. They had, these two, like
all their little group, no father image left—no State, people,
God, no refuge, nothing on which to lean. Unsustained they
were, and utterly alone in the universe. So more than ever
to Kurt Weiss his beloved became, though without ugly
awareness, that eternal mother-womb into which man desires
to return through the annihilation of the ecstasy of love. And
Gina, equally unaware, gathered her chosen man to her
bosom and shared with him the minutes during which a
hostile and a homeless world sank into complete oblivion.

He rarely went to his office now. The lease was expiring
within the year. A few clients still drifted in now and then.
But not only was he not among the few Jewish attorneys
still admitted to practice before the courts, but judicial tone,
temper, and decision made it more obvious from day to day
that not only could no Jewish litigant receive any longer an
equitable hearing, but that the last chance of such a hearing
was lost if he was represented by an attorney of Jewish birth.
Luckily, Gina, much at the time against Kurt's will, had
taken the dowry habitually given in her circles, and they had
now this money, greatly diminished though it was, to draw
upon. From this store they also contributed to those "funds
for help" which energetic Jewish men and women were now
quietly but sternly gathering for those daily increasing hundreds and indeed thousands among the German Jews who,
having never had more than their honest daily toil to supply

their daily needs, were now brutally and suddenly deprived of work and therefore of bread.

Once more by special appointment now old Salomon Steinthaler, feebler and perceptibly whiter, came to Kurt's office.

"Have you gained a little sense now? Are you going?"

"We're planning to go to France."

"That's better. Why planning? Why aren't you gone?"

Kurt grasped his head.

"It isn't so easy, Uncle Salomon. Do you realize how desolate it will be? Gina and I do. But we're going, we're going."

"I begged your father thirty years ago in Frankfurt-an-der-Oder to give you a Jewish education. Oh no, that wasn't the 'advanced' thing to do. And the 'advanced' thing was the 'loyal' thing. And the Jacobys have been at that game a hundred years. Now you and your wife are desolate. In the old days, the better days—yes, better—when Jews were expelled they got in touch with their Jewish brethren in another country and joined *them*." The old man laughed bitterly into his beard. "If you are going to France to be Frenchmen and to bring up Gabriel as a Frenchman, you might just as well stay here. You may be safer there. Your problem and your misery will remain the same."

"I think you've touched our wound," Kurt said, slowly, "though my terms would be different. No, I can't imagine us French. That's why we cling to the weeks, days, hours of still being, after some fashion, German."

"*Stuss!* You're not German and you're not French. You're Jews. When will you learn that lesson?"

Kurt shook his head.

"I'm afraid we've forgotten too deeply to relearn that."

The old man leaned forward and took both of Kurt's hands into his own.

"You're wrong about that. I won't argue. I want nothing but that you remember me and my words. And promise me one thing—tell Gabriel that he is a Jew."

"They left him in no doubt about that," Kurt said.

Steinthaler nodded emphatically and tremulously.

"But if you and Gina had told him first and in the right way! You see the force of that?"

"I see it."

"That is enough. Everything will grow from that."

The old man went. He had come late in the afternoon and it was now dusk. Kurt sat at his desk and lit no light. Fancies and images rather than thoughts floated through his mind: a playing-field of his childhood in autumn beside the broad and slothful Oder River. He could see himself and his fellow urchins race about that field during an hour of dusk. Then he saw, as though it were here and now, two of them with whitish faces close together whispering and turning their eyes, suddenly no longer the beautiful eyes of childhood, but old, malignant, treacherous eyes, toward him. . . . He saw a brown shabby but lovable college classroom— he was already a *primaner*, a senior—and saw the small group of his classmates about him and saw the teacher, a tall blond man with a great blond beard, of which he was proud, and heard that half-forgotten ironically didactic voice: "Our Kurt Weiss here will probably not understand why we Germans cannot regard the activities of Karl the Great with undivided pride. . . ." He saw other scenes, heard other voices—were they dream or reality? What of this day's and hour's intimate quality? The real had a way of turning into fantasy, nightmare, monstrous and unbelievable legend. . . . He heard the door softly opening. He turned. Meta Scholz, more than half stripped of clothing, slipped in and flung herself upon him. He felt her breasts against his own; her cold lips were mangling his. He fought her, fought her all the more desperately because the feeling and the scent of her flesh began to affect him. But she was a powerful woman and clawed her hands into his shoulders and lay across him who was leaning back under her weight. He pressed his hands against her to push her off. But something eerie and unnerving in that struggle in the dusk confused him. Then he heard a voice that crashed in upon him with the echo of doom, although it was a hoarse, vulgar, stupid voice. The door which the Scholz woman had left ajar was kicked open by a hard boot. "Caught! *Ertappt!* The Jew swine! Can't keep your filthy paws off of German girls, eh? We'll teach you!"

Meta Scholz let go of Kurt and stood up. The action had been curiously deliberate. Three storm-troopers stood in the room. The faint light of a street lamp glimmering through the window shone feebly on the steel and polished leather of their belts. "Get up, Jew swine!" roared he who was the leader.

Kurt Weiss got up and faced them.

AT THE beginning of that first evening of Kurt's unusual absence Gina, clenching her hands in a fashion
she had never done before, told herself, carefully articulat-
ing the words so as to grasp their import, that in the present
panic, this deep and silent and ominous panic, people were
giving a disastrous interpretation to every small delay or
accident; that, secondly, she had heard definitely of scattered cases of men being taken into "protective custody" and
released after weeks or even days. If by any chance Kurt had
been arrested she reasoned, from all she knew, that he
would necessarily be among the latter group, since he had
never been politically active or in any way exposed to
the raging controversies of the time. These inner defences
she carefully built up before, the dinner hour of seven having
arrived, she telephoned to her husband's office and found
that no one answered.

She directed the maid to serve Gabriel. She herself would
wait until the Herr Doktor returned. She sat down at table
with the child, however, in order to encourage him. This was
difficult enough. She discovered to her own amazement that
the sight of the food on his plate caused a constriction in
the muscles of her throat and a spasm in some region just
below that led almost to retching. She coughed voluntarily
and that eased the sensation. Gabriel looked up at her.
He frowned a grave childish frown.

"I wish Papa would come home. I don't like to eat alone."

He didn't, in fact, eat more than a few morsels.

"Please, please, darling," Gina said, and did not hear

the terror in the beseeching of her voice, "do at least drink your milk!"

Obediently he drank the glass of cool milk. His face began to twitch. Quietly he was crying. At that a fever seemed to invade her—a driving fever, a fever to make one run headlong forward, without reason or direction, only forward, onward, until one dropped, dropped. She caught with both hands at the wooden frame of the chair on which she was sitting. She controlled herself and seemed to see herself in that act of self-control and knew on the instant that one can learn how to bear pain and fear and sorrow because pain and fear and sorrow are native to the human heart. The banal but biting phrase raced through her mind: "If anyone had told me, told me only a few months ago . . ."

"Gabrielchen," she said, quietly, "it's possible that Papa may have to stay out late. You mustn't cry. You just go to bed. I know you're tired."

Gabriel lifted his eyes.

"But I want to wait for Papa. Why can't I?"

"Because it would be too late. Then you'd fall asleep in a chair and be cross." She closed her eyes for an instant. Then words came to her which seemed to hurt and heal her at once. "You know, darling, that this is a hard time for us Jews. You must be good and patient."

The child's clear treble rose. "Why are we Jews, Mamma, and why does everybody hate us?"

Instinctively Gina glanced at the door, hoping the maid had not heard. She clasped her hands on her lap. That fever, that flying fever caught her again as with a hot searing wind.

"Are we bad?"

Gabriel's voice seemed even shriller.

"No, no, no!"

"Then the others are bad!"

She wanted to cry out, "Yes!" and forced herself to say: "No one is all bad and no one is all good. I'm not clever enough to explain it to you and you're too little to understand, Gabriel." Then for a moment her control gave way. "Please let me put you to bed, Gabriel, please, please!"

He looked up at her in sorrowful astonishment.

Liese, the maid, came in. "I'll take Gabriel, Frau Doktor, and tell him a story. Then he can go to bed. Wouldn't you like that, Gabriel?"

The child looked with a mature look from his mother to the maid. Then he got up and walked over to Gina and held up his face. "Good-night, Mummie." She kissed him and noticed that his lips were cold. He went out with Liese, and Gina laid her head on the table before her in a sudden access of agony.

The telephone. The telephone. She knew what shred of hope had kept her erect at all. She flew into the library and called the Eden Hotel. Unbelievable words formed themselves in her mind: "God, God, God, let him be there and let him *know*!" She heard the answer to her question. Dr. Ernst Simon was in the building, but not in his room. He would be paged. How can a heart hammer like mine, she thought, and not burst one's breast? Her head swam. The whole world must hear her heart. At last, at last— Ernst Simon's voice. "Yes, Gina." She told him the simple ominous facts. She heard his gasp. Then in a level voice he said: "I'll get into communication at once with the son of your grandfather's partner. Do you understand?" Oh yes, she understood that Simon meant the eminent non-Aryan, that is to say, half-Jewish financier, who was rumoured to have been hitherto exempt from direct persecution and to be using his exemption in favour of his father's people. "But can you? Can you?" she asked. "Yes, I saw him this afternoon. I know he will be home tonight. So, *Kopf hoch*, courage, Gina! Meanwhile Kurt may come home."

She felt very weak; she felt small like a child beaten and lost in the wilderness of the world. All her life she had been protected and everyone had showed her respect and tenderness, and now she was out in a wilderness. The house and the walls seemed less than no protection. All the evil winds of the world were blowing through. She shivered as though her fancy were a fact. She cried and she talked to herself, and this, too, was a thing she had never done before. "If anything happens to Kurt I shall kill myself. I have no one but him and I couldn't live in a world that let anything happen to him. But, no, I can't even do that. I mustn't do that. I must live to take care of Gabriel and to bring him up. But what is the use of letting Gabriel grow up in such a world? What is the use? If Kurt isn't safe— O God, he must be safe!—what is the use?" She was appalled at her own hot whispering. She raised her head. She trembled. Yes, yes. There was one other thing she could do. Her hand was on the telephone. She called up the Wegener apartment and heard the precise voice of Frau Ernestine von Wegener. She asked if Hannes were at home. The answer came with a both sorrowful and rebuking rasp in the voice. "No, he's not. And I don't even know where to reach him." Somehow Gina felt that she dared tell this German woman concerning her bitter anxiety. She did so. For a moment there was silence. Then in her old-fashioned way Frau von Wegener said: "What you tell me, *gnädige Frau,* cuts me to the very soul. I have been a patriotic German woman all my life and both my husband and his father gave their lives for king and fatherland. But the things that are happening now I do not understand. No, *verehrte gnädige Frau,* I do not understand them, although I am sorry that Hannes seems quite so untouched by the National Awakening. I will tell him what you have told me so soon as I see him. Good night."

Slowly Gina put the apparatus back on its table-stand. Now she faced the night. It was only eight-twenty. The night? Oh yes, the night. For Kurt had never in all their years together failed to apprise her of the slightest delay, nor she, thank God, him. They had not lived in chains, as some couples do. But they had sought by a tacit agreement to save each other irritation, fret, embarrassment. It was the night she faced, the night. She put her hands on the sides of her head in her favourite gesture. The situation was one—she saw that clearly—of pure disaster and of pure horror. Nothing could mitigate it. Nothing. There was no trace of guilt or even of unwisdom or of carelessness or of the disregard of alien sensibilities that could be tortured into any explanation, far less, of course, into any excuse, for such things happening as were happening to herself and her husband and to others more or less like them. If the world had been dark and its processes opaque before this thing had come to be, that darkness and that opaqueness were as nothing to the chaos in which human life was now plunged. Men had gone mad—mad in ways she had once read of in a severe and yet horrible book. She remembered the case histories in that book which sullied and stained the soul and which she had tried to put resolutely out of her mind. The world had turned into a place filled with such people. And her man was at the mercy of such. . . .

Toward three o'clock she fell asleep on the sofa of the library. She had not dared enter their bedroom. But every few minutes she was shaken into sullen wakefulness by fantasmal dreams. At dawn she brewed herself some coffee in the kitchen and drank a cupful. More she could not swallow. Then she wrote out a guarded telegram to her father. And again there was for her the writhing hollowness of mere waiting. At seven the telephone rang. Her hand trembled so that she dropped the receiver and had to pick it up again. It was Ernst Simon. His tone was measurelessly weary and discouraged. The eminent non-Aryan financier had been able to find out that Kurt was in protective custody and was getting in touch this morning with a very high member of the Nazi government to plead Kurt's entire political harmlessness and the unpleasant impression it would create of the National Awakening of the German people if the innocent were confounded with the guilty. . . . "What hope is there?" she found herself asking in a strangely steady voice. The answer came, each word wrenched from Ernst Simon's soul as rocks are hewn from a cliff, "I do not know, Gina." Silence. Slowly she put the apparatus back.

Gina never, in the years that followed, quite reconstructed for herself the fantasmagoria of the next two days. She supposed that the fantasmal quality—things and people seeming to lose their concrete reality and being like wraiths —was created by her from within so that she might live. But she had during those days the sensation that, if she only willed it, she could walk through the walls and presences of the fantasmal world in which she moved out into another world, a world of goodness and health and reality in which she and Kurt would meet as of old. She had but to wait for the magical moment.

She sent the telegram to her father and received the answer that he was returning at once. She tried to get in touch with Pastor Haintzius and was told that he had gone to Danzig. Messages came to her, stealthy messages, from friends and acquaintances and from colleagues of Kurt, messages of enquiry and of sympathy, and these messages, even when the people tried to give her hope, were in their tone and stealthiness, in the hidden fear and repressed trembling, themselves devoid of hope. Old Salomon Steinthaler came to her in person and said: "As soon as Kurt is released, you must flee. I besought him to flee. In the meantime, my child, you must pray." She had sobbed for the only time during those two days and had answered, "I don't know how to pray." The old man's voice had been hard: "I suppose you know the German classics by heart. Well, you will all learn how to pray again."

Perhaps her most dreadful agony was the agony of facing her child and the servant Liese, to guard for Gabriel some peace of soul and to guard herself from Liese's sympathy. For Gabriel went about with sorrowful eyes, subdued and saddened, and clung to her, and evidently did not believe her promises and reassurances, and Liese, the maid, went about with a red nose and suppressed weeping, and Gina knew that the girl wanted to weep openly over her and Gabriel, and felt that she must avoid such a scene at any cost and yet dared not warn the girl. This strain was eased when toward noon of the second day of her agony her father walked in. Luckily, Liese had taken Gabriel for a walk and father and daughter could be open with each other. Yet they were not entirely so. Jacoby said that of course Kurt would be released, that those who had not been, were, as a rule, though he deprecated the methods used, elements of an undesirable sort. And suddenly Gina knew that her father was lying both to himself and to her and would have to go on lying this lie in order to live at all and that if he were himself to be taken to a concentration camp he would still try to say that miscarriages of justice were common under all governments. So in a flash there came to her the unfathomable falseness of the talk she had heard during recent years in her father's house, with its wretched refrain that the rising horror of madness and of evil in this land had been caused by a handful of Polish Jews, or by a still smaller handful of Zionists, or by the few conspicuous Jews in radical movements. In the great clearness of her agony she saw how her poor father's whole being was one web of inextricable self-deceptions and pitiful escapings from the iron truth. He wanted her and the child to come home with him. But she insisted that the place of her waiting and her vigil was here. He said next that he had had to leave her mother in Holland and had not been in good health himself. She looked at him as she had not done before, her vision being turned inward. He was old now. He was crinkled and crumpled. All moral forces that had sustained him had withered in his soul. He was a wilting shell. And that shell was empty. Gina wept and wept, not over herself or her husband, but over her father, old, frightened, selfish, dishonoured by a defensive lie after a long life of generosity and rectitude.

That evening a little unexpected spring of hope seemed to bubble briefly within her and she told Gabriel that when Papa came home they would all three go away, quite far away, to a beautiful and peaceful city where they would be happy again as they had been before.

"Will we be Jews there, too?" he asked.

"Yes, my son," she said, slowly, in an immense wonder at herself and at the strength the words gave her, "we will always be Jews. Wicked men cannot soil that."

She had been speaking to herself as much as to the child.

"Then they won't hate us there?" Gabriel asked.

"No, they won't hate us there."

She took sleeping-tablets that night with a half-mystical inner assurance that on the next day, which was the third, Kurt would come back. There is nothing against him, nothing —she repeated the words in her drowsiness. Even *they* can find nothing against him—even they.

The third day came. An empty hell opened its iron jaws, a hell from which all but naked pain was gone. Gina walked unseeing. The faint hope of the night before was unimaginable now. She went through the gestures of life in a solid, impenetrable blackness, waiting for the final blow to fall. When, toward the very late afternoon, the doorbell rang, she knew that the moment had come. Again she had sent Gabriel out walking with Liese. She went to the door. Silently she admitted Johannes von Wegener. Silently she led him into the library. Without looking at each other the two sat down. The over-curtains had been drawn to against the sunlight of the earlier day. The room lay in dusk. She heard a nervous grinding of teeth. Even now she did not look up. Even now she did not speak. She heard the hoarse voice of the man before her breaking into a sob.

"He will not come back, Gina."

The sweetish sickish agony in her vitals was so violent that she bent her lithe form over and, resting her forearms on her knees, hid her face in her hands. She made no sound. She listened.

"I told him, I begged him to send back his copy of the document incriminating Franzen's father. That was it. Simon's friend traced him. He was in the hands of Franzen's special henchmen. They telephoned to Franzen. Franzen answered: 'That one belongs to me.'"

He stopped. She heard something like a whine—the whine of an animal. Then there was silence again. She spoke through her hands, "Go on."

"Our stenographer, Meta Scholz, was a spy and a hired plotter. I wanted Kurt to engage a Jewish girl in these times. He was afraid. Meta Scholz made advances to Kurt which disgusted him. That infuriated her, even though she was a cold hireling. She called the Franzen troopers and had them find her half-naked and apparently in Kurt's arms."

A trembling came over Gina like the trembling of a cold fever. She muttered, "Judas!"

She heard a despairing cry. "No, Gina, no. I beg you for God's sake not to think that. Don't believe that! No . . . no . . ."

"Then why do you know so much? How can I be sure?"

"My cousin, Bruno Scheuermann, is a *Gauführer*. I told him I would join the party if he saved Kurt. He answered, 'You have no choice unless you want to join him in a concentration camp.' Out of spite he dug up the details—spite against me."

Again the silence fell and the dusk between them deepened.

"They wanted," he went hoarsely on, "the ostensible

charge of blood-defilement against him in case of an investigation. The storm-troopers were to have a cause for feeling their German sensibilities so outraged that they could go to any lengths."

She stopped trembling. Close, close she pressed her hands against her face. If only tears had come. But in this hour she had no tears.

"Of course, the first thing they did was to force him to open his safe and give them the copy of the document that proved old Franzen to be a liar and a thief and his son the Commissar no less. Then they dragged him with them and put him in an auto and took him to a certain house in the Friedrichstrasse and into the cellar of that house. There *Reichsjustizkommissar* Franzen was waiting in person. He and two others."

Gina moaned. She had not meant to do so. But an icy unhuman shadow fell suddenly upon her soul, such as falls upon the soul in agonizing nightmares, only a thousand times icier and eerier. And she was awake. She was terribly awake. She could not raise herself up nor look at the face of the man before her.

"They killed him."

She heard the stony words. She knew that she would be nailed all her life upon the cross of those mysterious words unless she was told more, told all.

"How?" Her tone was quite expressionless.

She listened sharply and heard for a time only Wegener's tight, hoarse breathing. She repeated the word:

"How?"

"They stripped him and beat him with their rubber cudgels. They beat him a long, long time."

Wegener sobbed without tears. His sobs were more like hiccoughs. He fought the spasm down for a moment.

"They took a knife and gelded him and he screamed."

Gina did not move. For an instant she lost consciousness.

Then she felt herself slipping toward the floor. Automatically she pulled herself back.

"Then they shot him twice in the back of the head, so that they could say he was shot while trying to escape."

Gina raised herself up and took her hands from her face. For the first time she looked at Wegener. Was it the deep dusk in the room that made his features look like those of an idiot—blank, staring, pasty, empty of soul and sense?

"You are sure he is dead?"

The man nodded.

To her amazement she heard herself crying out loud, loud and shrill:

"They are not torturing him any more?"

"No," he said. "Thank God."

She had risen during her loud crying and he had risen, too, and now they stood facing each other in the gloom.

"I do not expect you ever to think of me without horror and loathing," he said now, in a low, natural, humble voice. "But I want you to remember this: I shall join them. Yes. But I shall betray them wherever and whenever I can. They have killed our German honour. If that is ever to know a resurrection they must be destroyed."

She looked at him once more. She could barely distinguish his features. Darkness, darkness forever now, and at the core of that darkness a fiery, inextinguishable point of pain.

He lowered his head.

"Good-bye, Gina. God protect you and Kurt's child."

At last tears came. At last she wept. A low strange wailing burst from her bosom to give a little ease.

Wegener stood regarding her a moment. Then he turned and gently left the room. On tiptoe he walked through the hall, opened the door of the apartment and closed it behind him as softly as though he were afraid of waking a child.

VIII

THE chestnut trees were in bloom in the Champs-Elysées. The Punch-and-Judy shows were giving performance after performance to children and their nurses in the little roped-off squares. The sun shone as brilliantly as it ever does in Paris—that is to say, as though from behind a thin white cambric veil. In that whitish rather than golden light the Arc de Triomphe glittered mildly at the end of one vista, the Obelisk on the Place de la Concorde at the end of another. The polished cars flashed by with an air of well-bred eagerness and the people on the broad sidewalks under the trees loitered as though there were nothing to do in the world except enjoy with cultivated sensibilities the day, the city, and the scene.

On a bench within sight of the beautiful and vivid fountain on the Avenue Montaigne side of the Rond-Point des Champs-Elysées sat Gina Weiss with her small son beside her. Her spring frock was of midnight blue with small chic hat and shoes to match; Gabriel had on a sailor suit of the same unobtrusive colour. Mother and son, but for their foreign speech, might have been taken for the wife and child of some reasonably prosperous indigenous advocate or business man or politician living in one of those vast and slightly sombre and slightly pretentious apartments to be found in the older houses of the Étoile quarter. Gabriel said: "It's lovely here, isn't it, Mummie?"

And Gina, with grave, drawn face, answered, "Yes, it's very lovely here."

"Didn't we see Punch-and-Judy shows over there?" Gabriel's voice was hushed, as though he knew he shouldn't have asked but couldn't help it.

"Yes, darling. We can watch one later or tomorrow. But it's all in French, you know."

He smiled for a moment his old, blithe smile that Gina had not seen in many weeks. He rubbed his head with a quaint little gesture against her arm. "Let's go, anyhow."

There was only one thing in the world about which Gina, all alone, with no advice and no guidance, had come to a conclusion. At the risk of a desperate shadow over his childhood and his youth Gabriel must not be permitted to forget. To forget would mean to be, like Kurt and herself, unwarned and therefore unarmed. Unwarned of the fact that this great fair world, this world of the Pariser Platz and the Champs-Elysées, this world of thought and music and books and plays, of art and industry and politics in the old sense, was but the thinnest of veils over unfathomable bestiality, over a chaos in which there was no justice, no mercy, no wisdom—nothing, nothing but fang and lash and maw and bludgeon and phallus and knife. And she could see as in a vision in this hour and at this moment these noble streets and squares suddenly sink into the earth and the space in which they stood over-run by naked wolf-like creatures in human form with low foreheads and bloody knives clamped between the yellow fangs of their huge jaws. Gabriel must know. For, she reasoned, I'm not a bit hysterical; I'm perfectly cool and sane; this thing is so and I, who had not the faintest suspicion of it, know it to be so because of what happened to me and mine. And all those who pretend that it is not so are liars. And it was perhaps this conclusion and this rigidity of complete despair, a super-personal despair too deep for either anger or grief, that had kept Gina from collapse, madness, suicide since that day eight weeks ago on which Wegener had come to her.

She had from the first refused all consolation. Heintzius

had written her a long letter about the equal fate of Jews
and Christians under the persecutions of Rome. She had
shrugged her shoulders and thrown the letter away. All her
life she had been lied to about "progress" and "high civilization"—*hohe Kultur*—and now the poor fool babbled about
the second century. When, according to the traditions of Berlin Jewry, an unmeaning, large, square, black-bordered announcement of Kurt's death— ". . . sudden passing of our
infinitely beloved and mourned husband, father, son-in-law
. . ."—had appeared in the *Vossische Zeitung*, and fifty colleagues of the Berlin bar, both German and Jewish, had each
cut out the notice and written across its face: "*Your* murder, *Reichsjustizkommissar* Franzen!" and mailed the clip-
ping to the man—when this had happened and had been
told her in the way of consolation, she had looked up with a
bitter calmness and had said: "Now they protest from hiding
—now? How funny!" And that night she had had one of
those crises of agony in which she saw as in palpable presence
the scene of Kurt's torment and death. She did not have them
often, these crises of vision and vicarious martyrdom. Not
that she consciously avoided them; at least she hoped not.
Her waking mind feigned to itself to welcome them as part
of an expiation which she owed. Expiation for what? For
having been, she would have replied, duped all her life by
men and by the world, for not having earlier awakened to
the supreme horror and danger of the situation in Germany,
for not having insisted to Kurt that they flee at once and if
need be without a change of garment when first Gabriel had
brought back from school the hints of the moral torment
he was made to suffer there.

He tugged at her sleeve now and awakened her from staring into the lawn-like veil of spray of the beautiful fountain.

"Let's go, Mummie!"

"Where?"

He looked at her gravely and critically. She knew he was wondering whether he dared ask her to go to the Punch-and-Judy show. He evidently decided that he had better not. Her heart ached over that. Poor darling! But she couldn't quite bear the thought of herself there among those bright French children and their nurses with blue veils and all the greenery and twitter and thin merriment of the scene. So she repeated her question, "Where?"

A little sadly he said, "Oh, just for a little walk, Mummie, if you're not too tired."

He had at times his wild and naughty and even stubborn spells. But he was mostly as now, gentle and highly perceptive for his age of mood and circumstance. She took his hand warmly in her own.

"Very well, darling. We'll walk back to the bank to see if there's any mail. And we'll go on the other side of the street and stop and look at the windows of the big toy-shop."

The Seckelsohns of Strassburg, whose silent partner her father had been for years, had handed her over, as it were, to the Lévy-Blochs of Lévy-Bloch Frères et Cie. of Paris. These private bankers had in turn established a credit for her at the Crédit Commercial de France on the Champs-Elysées, partly, at least, Gina suspected, because they did not relish the thought of Jewish fugitives from Germany openly crowding their counting-houses and offices. They had done more—these in their own conceit admirable and, above all, proper people. They had hired for her and Gabriel a tiny snug pseudo-elegant service flat on the Rue St.-Didier not too far from their own rather portentous *hôtel particulier* on the Avenue Kléber. So much they apparently felt they owed to the house of Jacoby of Berlin. In addition Mme. Lévy-Bloch, Sr. had called. The small, thin, fussily-dressed elderly lady had kissed Gabriel on both cheeks and cried out: "*Oh, comme il est mignon!*" To Gina she had exclaimed in a noticeably harder voice: "*Vous-êtes tout-à-fait*

*bien ici, n'est-ce pas? Est-ce qu'on trouve le confort moderne
à Berlin?"* Gina had been in no mood to defend the universal
confort moderne of her native city. But though her own
French was halting enough, she could have sworn that this
woman spoke with a heavy German or Alsatian accent. So
if the woman wanted to be kind, why didn't she speak German? As Mme. Lévy-Bloch continued her carefully Parisian
exclamations the purpose of the comedy came flamingly to
Gina. These rich French Jews were now taking the same line
in regard to the German Jews which the rich and cultivated German Jews had taken until just the other day toward the Russian and Polish and Rumanian Jews: inferior
people living among barbarians whose fate could in no wise
be conceived of as having any bearing upon their own. Objects of charity and commiseration. One did what one could
for them. One even—in very special cases such as this—took
a personal interest. One called. One tried, of course, to keep
the call on a civilized level. One chatted—*on bavardait*—
a little. Gina had summoned her utmost French, such as it
was, in an obvious and uncomfortable pause of Mme. Lévy-
Bloch's laborious *bavardage* and had said slowly: *"Madame,
est-ce que vous savez par hasard ce qui se passe à present en
Allemagne? Est-ce qu'on vous a raconté le sort de mon mari?"*
The woman's thin, dry, heavily jewelled hands had gone
up in a sort of palsied flutter. *"Si, Madame, si! Ah c'est
affreux! C'est incroyable! Mais les Boches! Qu'est-ce que
vous voulez? Les Boches! Vous n'ignorez pas, Madame,
comme nôtre pauvre France a souffert!"* Gina regretted later
that she had not laughed in the woman's face. She could hear
as in a dream the accusing, darkly prophetic, rebuking laughter that might have interrupted that effrontery of callous self-
deceit. Instead she had fallen stonily silent and had let Mme.
Lévy-Bloch caw laborious inutilities until, with an apologetic
glance at an obviously placed clock, the woman had ex-

claimed with not quite well-bred relief: "*Ah, chère Madame, il faut que je m'en aille. J'ai encore des courses à faire.*"

They had reached the windows of the toy-shop. Bright and gay with many colours were the dolls and games and mechanical toys and seemed to Gina to form a quaint, self-contained little world, so close to the heart, so exquisitely remote from reality, that for the first time in days her eyes grew moist at the light, bright pathos of this children's dream. She looked at Gabriel. He was gazing earnestly. His eyes were almost solemn.

"Do you see anything you'd really like to have?" she asked him.

He looked up at her.

"I don't know, Mummie. If we could go in."

"Do you want to go in now?"

A little sadly she thought he shook his head. Yet he lingered on a minute or two. Then he brightend. "Surprise me some day, Mummie." He hung himself with both hands unto her arm. They crossed the street at the next safety aisle to drop in at the bank. The only letter was one from her mother. She was still in Holland, where her husband had joined her after Gina's departure. She said that she sorely missed her daughter and little grandson and that she and her husband both missed their home. She asked, as though unaware of anything, whether Gina intended to remain in Paris very long. She spoke inconsequentially of a trip to Paris that she and her husband had taken a number of years ago at the end of Germany's isolation through the war. "It was very agreeable there, but at bottom entirely strange." Gina folded the letter and put it into her bag. She took Gabriel by the hand and with him left the stately building in which the bank was housed.

"We are all alone in the world, you and I, Gabriel," she said. "Do you understand that?"

"Yes," the child said, "I think I do."

Clouds had floated over the milky whiteness of the sun. The faint brilliance had been sucked out of the scene. The pearl-grey sky and atmosphere were almost a relief to Gina.

They walked back to their house in its narrow street. Luncheon was waiting for them there, served on a folding-table in the tiny salon of the flat. M. Lévy-Bloch had with great nicety made arrangements for Gina and her child according to her present means. The capital which in his time Privy Councillor Jacoby had invested in the Seckelsohn bank had amounted to little more than 400,000 gold Marks. This sum had been made over to Gina. The Seckelsohns through the Lévy-Blochs paid Gina four per cent. Her income was therefore precisely 96,000 francs, which was, as M. Lévy-Bloch had with thick uplifted forefinger explained to her during their single business interview, *grande aisance* for a widow with one child. It was, in fact, wealth if she would keep house with a single *bonne-à-tout-faire*. Of course she would need furnishings, for which an advance—a reasonable advance—on her income was always at her service. She had had the feeling that the man, after her departure, had nourished a rich fatuous conviction that he had done a good deed, had ministered to the widow and the fatherless, because he had advised her how best to spend the money given her by her father. Gina often wondered nowadays how it came about that she perceived at once and with precision the moral qualities and moral gestures of people. Perhaps because she saw them on a lower plane than formerly, the plane of reality.

The too-loquacious valet came to take out the dishes and the table. Gina detested his servile affability. *"J'espère que Madame a bien déjeuné? Et le petit? Faut bien manger, mon petit; ça fait pousser!"* She had the strength not to reply. She nodded. Gabriel did not understand the man's chatter. A little surlily and noisily he went out.

Gabriel retired to a corner by the window with his thick volume of the mystical and heroic legends of Musæus, of which he never seemed to tire. All that Gina had brought, except their clothes, was a box of books: all of Gabriel's favourites, a handful of thin-paper volumes of Goethe and Heine, of Rilke and Thomas Mann for herself and the same thin-paper edition of the works of Kant, a deeply treasured possession of Kurt's since his student days, which she had never read.

She sat down in a cramped little *fauteuil* beside the other of their two windows that gave on the dingy Rue St.-Didier. Her hands were in her lap, her slender strong hands, one laid across the other. And she looked at her hands and it came to her that her hands had never been tired. She could not bear the thought of reading. Her eloquent favourite books were here, and surely, surely neither Goethe nor Rilke had had or could have had any part in the foulness and filth into which their people had fallen. But the beautiful German language, the only one she really knew or would ever truly know, was bitter, bitter on her tongue. Bitter, bitter, she repeated the word in her mind, and wondered how it would be to live not by words, but by work, by the expression of the hands, by work of the hands, by something fashioned by the hands. Almost now her hands became a mystery and a hope to her. For this there was another reason. Her hands could live or could be called to life without horror and disloyalty. The rest of her was dead. Her body was dead. Her woman's body could not and dared not ever come to life again. It must remain forever with Kurt where he, mutilated, crucified, mouldered in his grave in the cemetery of Weissensee. It must retain forevermore the stamp and impress of those last desperate, beautiful embraces of his before they took him from her. Yes, her body was dead and the speech of her mind and of her heart died, even as it was uttered, upon her tongue, and her father and her mother were separated from her by a wall impalpable as gossamer, impenetrable as brass, and so there were only two things that kept her moving in space and having the semblance of life—her child, her man child who by gesture, expression, by little tricks of speech and taste, by the very posture in which he composed himself to sleep, was symbol, commemoration, life beyond death of her husband, and by the miserable self-preservative functioning of her organism which could evidently go on when all its higher qualities and activities were dead to live no more.

So in her hands she saw a faint hope. She could not sit here day after day or merely wander these bright and yet somehow melancholy avenues and boulevards. How would it be if she took an empty flat and furnished it and dispensed even with the maid-of-all-work of whom M. Lévy-Bloch had so sententiously spoken, and cooked and scoured and washed for Gabriel and herself? For her hands were unskilled hands and the best she could hope was that they would learn to do very humble tasks. She wondered how exactly she had spent all her time in her old home, in her old life. Her activities and tasks had been few enough. Ah, it came to her so clearly: hope and anticipation fill life; it is they, too, that bring tranquillity. And they can exist only where life has a pervasive meaning that quickens all activities, however small, and lends import and direction even to daydreaming, and reading books, and playing music, and hours in gardens and tasks of shopping, and meal-time and rest-time and love itself. All these things, so long as her and Kurt's old existence seemed intact, had been done within a framework of a civilization to which each act and each thing, whether consciously or not, directly referred. The centre of reference was gone—not only because Kurt was dead. His world and hers was dead. That world had been murdered. And she could not bring herself to take even the first step toward entering another world. Mme. Lévy-Bloch had asked whether Gabriel

attended school and had rather foolishly extolled the schools
of France in quite the same manner in which, as Gina had
acridly noted, her old group in Berlin had been accustomed to
declare the German schools the best in the world. She had
evaded the question. She looked up at Gabriel. A sudden
fright came over her. His cheeks were glowing in his absorption in his book. It was a German book, brimming with
that German romanticism which had ultimately—the conclusion flashed cruelly on Gina—led to the horrors and
crimes and expulsions of this day. Gabriel was feeding his
sensitive child's soul on the sweet, subtle, stinging poison
that had been brewed to destroy him and his kind. Yet with
what word, what gesture, what excuse or explanation was
she to tear the book from the child's hand? For she had
nothing to give him in its stead. He was happy enough not
to go to school. He would go, of course, whenever she made
the decision for him. She had not been able to bring herself to make it. Why? Did she fear an alienation of her
child from herself? Doubtless he would learn French rapidly
and take on the notions and tastes, superficially at least, of
his fellow pupils. Was it that? Yes, it was that, too. But it
was more than that; it was a deeper fear which she could not
define to herself. Was it a lingering anti-French feeling which
her German self still harboured? Still? A little. Yes, a little
that too—shameful and foolish as that now was. But there
was a fear beneath that fear and an edge of further and
more nameless horror.

She felt very tired and very helpless, and wondered if
there were anyone who could help her a little, if only by a
word, if only by hearing of these perplexities of hers which
could not be hers alone, for she knew, isolated as she was,
that Jews were fleeing from Germany week by week and day
by day, and that many, if not indeed the majority, of these
fugitives were coming to Paris. Where were they, these
fellow victims, these sharers of the fate of herself and her

son? Was it not monstrous that she should not know, that she and her child should be sitting here in the stillness of this strange house, utterly alone and uncompanioned? Were they not human? Was there not some human fellowship for them? As of old Gina put her hands on the sides of her head with fingers lightly on her temples. She was seeking something in her consciousness which she had forced herself to forget. Now it came to her. Very soon after her arrival in Paris she had received a letter, written laboriously by an aged trembling hand. It had been from that friend of Kurt's father, Salomon Steinthaler, whom she had not seen more than half a dozen times in her life and whom her father in the old days had always spoken of with humorous deprecation. She had wanted, she knew not why, to forget that last time when he had come to her during the agony of her waiting for Kurt, and so she had also thrust into the bottom of her bag his letter and had then thrown it into a drawer of the small rickety desk in this room. She observed now that she had, in spite of the denial implicit in these gestures, defensively retained one sharp detail—that he had written about her to certain friends of his, friends whom he had known for fifty years, friends of his childhood and youth in the provinces of East and West Prussia, and that she was to communicate with these friends when she needed consolation and counsel.

Slowly she rose and went the few steps to the desk and found the letter in the drawer and drew it forth and opened it and found at once the lines she had remembered: *"Geh also zu Meyerheims, mein Kind, wenn Du Trost und Rath brauchst—und Du wirst sie brauchen"* ("And so go to the Meyerheims, my child, when you need consolation and advice—and you will need both"). Now she knew, too, why she had tried to put the whole matter from her. She had said to herself at the very beginning: there is no consolation to be found in a world in which such things can hap-

pen. It is an insult to one's intelligence and moral judgement even to think so. One must be hard; one must hug
to one's bosom desolateness and horror. One must despise
oneself for living at all. But if one has not the courage to
die, or has a duty, like mine to Gabriel, which would make
of one's voluntary death an act of treachery, then at least
one can be decent enough not to sentimentalize the situation
or pretend to oneself that this filthy world is other than it
is. And all that is true—most true, she said to herself now.
Only, only—it is terrible to be so alone; it is terrible for
Gabriel. She sat down at the desk with Steinthaler's letter,
which contained both address and telephone number of his
friends, before her and lifted up the telephone and laboriously gave the number in French to the operator. A servant
answered. With a quick pang of discouragement Gina asked
him to tell his mistress that Madame Gina Weiss *de Berlin
est à l'appareil*. Almost at once Gina heard a kind, cultivated, aged voice speaking in German: "We have been ex-
pecting to hear from you. We've been tempted to look you
up, but we didn't want to disturb you. Won't you come
for tea on Sunday and bring your dear little boy with you?"
Gina thanked Mme. Meyerheim and promised to come, and
put the telephone back on its stand and felt as though a
faint ray of sun had fallen upon the ice that was her heart.
And immediately despised herself for that softness and
went into the bedroom and threw herself on her bed and
stared with angry tear-filled eyes at the silly cupids on
the ceiling.

There Gabriel, having suddenly missed her, came to find
her.

"Mummie, Mummie!"

"Yes, darling."

"Let's go out, Mummie; let's do *some*thing!"

The pathos of that cry cut her and awakened her thoroughly. She got up.

"I'll get ready, dear, in a few minutes. We must see some of the famous places in Paris. We've seen nothing so far. Then on Sunday we'll go to see some very nice people, and by and by we'll see about your going to school and having some little friends. Wouldn't you like that?"

He smiled his blithest smile.

"Yes, Mummie, I would."

Kurt and she had often tenderly laughed at this little precise way of making his affirmations that he had had since his babyhood. She choked.

"All right. Let's hurry now!"

Gina had a little guide-book and she and Gabriel saw many beautiful and astonishing things in the succeeding days. They had hitherto not really gone into the Tuileries Gardens, nor into the courts of the Louvre; only from afar had they seen the Place Vendôme, and with a perceptible flush of shame Gina found herself glancing at the displays of the jewellers on the Place Vendôme and the Rue de la Paix. But her sharpest experience came to her when she and Gabriel, on a long mild afternoon, walked on and on after having crossed a bridge to the left bank of the Seine and found themselves suddenly in front of the cathedral. The truncated towers of Nôtre Dame seemed, despite their bluntness, to have direct commerce with the bright blue-grey skies and the myriad-moulded sculptures of the gates and walls and towers to rush forward to Gina—those kings and saints and beasts and demons, creatures innumerable, wild, dark, grotesque and even in their ascetic attitudes and frozen gestures strong and self-consciously victorious.

Gina bowed her head. Like all the young men and women of her generation she had had her yearnings toward a mystical and poetic Christianity and had read Rilke's book Concerning the Life of Monks and had read those resonant verses in which Ernst Lissauer had chanted the glory of Luther and Bach and Bruckner. In her early girlhood she had seen the Cathedral of Cologne, and Christendom and German art and German verses—verses that partook both of the sun and of the thunder—had all blended in her soul, and she had gone alone one day into the cathedral and had knelt there and felt herself at one at least, oh, at the very least, with all that the cathedral meant of human beauty and of human aspiration. She clenched her hands now. There was a crucified again. Oh yes. Kurt Weiss was his name. Jew was his name. This church and every church was Golgotha—every Christian church in the world. The whole world was one Golgotha. On the cross hung a man. On the cross hung a Jew. His face was the face of Kurt. Her clenched hands shook.

"What's the matter, Mummie?"

"Nothing, darling." She grasped his warm little hand. "At least nothing you could understand now. I'll tell you some day."

"Soon?" he asked, with his most solemn look in his wide eyes.

"As soon as possible, my son. Just as soon as possible."

He squeezed her hand in childish gratitude for this assurance, and with a sweet gravity walked beside her across the square.

IX

SUNDAY arrived in a soft blur of rain. Gina almost prayed that it would not pour. For she knew she would go to the Meyerheims whatever the weather. Yet to go in a downpour would show an eagerness from the display of which she sharply shrank. Is it not very strange, she reflected, that one who has seen and suffered what I have should be so bound by these impalpable inner bonds of conventionally proper behaviour? A ceremonious and unruffled society would be very well in a secure and peaceful world. But in this disguised jungle, were it not better that men and women should cry out and raise their voices in accusation that rends the world and its unscorched veils asunder? Is not this well-bred silence playing into the very hands of the brutes in human form? It is not a noble stoicism, this silent perishing of the so-called civilized; it is a betrayal of humanity.

For all that, she knew that she would behave conventionally at the Meyerheims that she would introduce her perplexities, if at all, in an almost casual tone; that she might even refrain from going if it stormed. Luckily, afternoon brought bluish-grey patches into a windless sky and several careful, palpitating minutes after the appointed hour Gina and Gabriel stood at the door of the house in the Rue Pommereux.

They were ushered into a large and beautiful drawing-room in which there were ten or twelve people separated for the moment into small groups. Mme. Meyerheim, a tall erect lady of seventy, white-haired, with wrinkles as of translucent porcelain, welcomed Gina and Gabriel with a beautiful un-

obtrusive warmth. "We have long wanted you to come!"
She took them first to her venerable husband, a heavy, large
man in his eighties who rose despite his age, interrupting
his conversation, which had been in French, with a dark
sparsely bearded clerical-looking man beside him, and taking Gina's hand, as if he did not want to let it go again, while
he placed his own left hand as though in blessing upon
Gabriel's head. Gina trembled a little inwardly while she
caught the name of the clerical person who had also risen
pronounced by Mme. Meyerheim—"M. le Grand Rabbin
Marcel Melamède." She felt a sudden strange, faint, sweet-
ness in the scene, the atmosphere, the moment, something
she had never known but recognized at once, something for
which—so slight was it in actual being—a nostalgia arose
within her. She had no time to nurse this feeling. Old Meyerheim growled benevolently in German: "Why did you not
come before? Steinthaler wrote again and again. Now we
won't let you go any more." She could almost feel his kind
grey old eyes following her as Mme. Meyerheim introduced
her to the other people in the room. She barely caught
names. She saw faces with immense vividness: the grey riven
face of a middle-aged man with stubborn, parched, embittered mouth; the elegant mournful one of a slightly younger
man, and that, like a dark glowing flower, of his young
daughter. Next came a couple, swarthy, with luminous black
eyes—the young man deprecating with self-ironic smile the
world, himself, his fate; his wife stilled and quenched by
suffering. Then came an enormously stout, eager, intellec-
tually-bustling woman of forty-five, who alone of all these
used the French formula, *"Enchantée."* Last she saw a
slim man, neither old nor young, a very white, very tall
forehead, eyes brown as autumn leaves, a glint of teeth
through a small black beard, and felt the pressure of a
strong and speaking hand. She caught the name too as Mme.
Meyerheim smilingly spoke it: "And this, Frau Weiss, is

our dear friend Herr Jehuda Brenner. Where shall I say you are from, Jehuda?"

"Say I'm from the East, Aunt Bianca, from Misrach. I am and we ought all to be. Just look about you, Frau Weiss."

She lifted her eyes again. Yes, she saw as in old days she had not seen, or perhaps not permitted herself to see, that the people in this room were people of one kind. "You are right," she said to Brenner. She wanted to ask him if he knew in what this oneness in kind consisted. But Mme. Meyerheim said that they must make little Gabriel comfortable with another little boy who was already there and was lonely. So Gina and Gabriel followed their hostess into the dining-room, where milk and cake were being set for two, a very dark little boy, Erich Gauss, the child of the swarthy young couple. Softly, as the children were being settled at the table and regarding each other with friendly shyness, Mme. Meyerheim explained to Gina. Gauss was a young musician from Berlin. He had had to flee by night across the Dutch frontier. A Nazi wanted his job at a radio station. He would have been murdered, as several of his colleagues were two days later. His wife and child followed. They were almost penniless. Yet they would accept no help. "I'd like to speak to Frau Gauss," Gina said. "I don't know what to do with Gabriel." She faltered.

Presently she was sitting beside Frau Gauss and listening, listening with an attention of her whole being.

"We sent Erich to school here. Everyone was very kind to him. The teacher told his pupils that he was a victim of Boche barbarism. He learnt French very fast and would hardly speak German to us any more. Do you see what that meant, Frau Weiss?"

Again Gina felt that strange nostalgia for she knew not what.

"Explain that to me exactly."

"Well, we had all been trying to be Germans for a century. We tried so hard and so honestly. My husband can't resign himself yet to not being permitted to be a German. And is there any use in trying now to be French—in starting the process all over again?"

Gina bowed her head.

"But wasn't it for your little boy a choice between the two?"

Frau Gauss shook her head.

"No. It mustn't be. Of course we can't speak Hebrew yet, though I'm studying hard. But in German we told Erich all about our people and its history and faith, and taught him to be a Jew. When he was asked: 'What are you?' he answered, 'I am a Jew.' But after three months in that very nice French school, when he was asked his question he turned on me belligerently, with a quaint childish fierceness and said, '*Je suis Français, tu sais, Maman, et j'en suis fier.*' Then even my husband saw that we must go to Palestine. It wouldn't be fair to let our children and *their* children tread that long road again, would it?"

Gina was conscious of an evasion as she asked, "What will you do in Palestine?"

"We hope to go to a new village called Ramath Hashavim and learn poultry husbandry."

"But isn't your husband a musician?"

Frau Gauss gave Gina an astonished and faintly contemptuous look. "We've left all those questions far behind us. You can't be a musician or anything else like that in the void and out of the void. We have to recover the meaning of life for ourselves again by earning our bread in *Eretz Yisrael*. If music comes to Alfred again out of that life and its meaning—then, perhaps, he can be a musician again."

"What was that expression you used?" Gina asked.

The little woman smiled. "It is the Hebrew name of the land of Israel."

Gina fell silent. She had a slight feeling of having been rebuked. She remembered vaguely now arguments she had heard, but not closely listened to, in her parents' house during the past two years. Bitter attacks had been made on people called Zionists. None of these people had themselves ever been present. But she did recall now that about eighteen months ago Ernst Simon, then as later on a visit in Berlin, had said very earnestly: "I do not share the Zionist ideology myself, but all that has been said here is thoroughly unjust and, if you'll forgive me, rancorously stupid. People whose lives have been robbed of all meaning through no fault of their own are doing no ignoble thing when they try to recover meaning for their lives by an appeal to their spiritual heritage and a return to their ancestral land." How well she recalled the words and saw in recollection suddenly illuminated how Ernst Simon had first, sitting in a corner beside the concert-grand piano, fidgeted in mounting impatience at all that was being said, and had then suddenly arisen and stepped forward into the middle of the room and uttered the words which, strangely enough, her memory had so precisely retained. And she remembered, too, now how a hubbub of voices had confusedly arisen and saw here in this Parisian drawing-room, with the eerie detached clearness of a dream, the speaking round-mouthed faces of her father and of Kurt. Kurt. Her soul plunged into a mist of pain. She wanted to take her child and go. She wanted to be alone with her familiar sorrow and her familiar loneliness, as though this sorrow and this loneliness were now become a home and a refuge to her. But an inertia held her where she was. And she noted presently that the conversation had become general with the merging of the small groups in this room into one, and so voices clove through that mist of pain to her ear.

It was the elegant Herr Lenz of Essen who was speaking concerning his daughter, who had seemed to Gina like a dark and glowing flower. "I am going back," he said, "to see the gradual destruction of the factory and the business my father and I built up. I can definitely see the end of the process when we shall be completely impoverished. I want to save my child. Today I can still raise some money. I'll leave her here with that money. But I want her to save it and to go to Palestine and join a girls' *kvutzah* [commune] and learn to work with her hands."

The friendly aged growl of Meyerheim arose. "But if you do that and go back to Essen and it is known, and others do likewise and it is known, will not that harm the Jews who must remain in Germany?"

The grey middle-aged man with the terribly embittered mouth said, hoarsely: "You cannot harm the Jews of Germany any more. They are beyond harm; they are beyond help."

The hubbub that arose now reminded Gina of that remembered hubbub of voices with which the words of Ernst Simon had been received in her father's house. It was the Rabbi Marcel Melamède who protested most vigorously in French and whose voice finally rose above the other voices. The German Jews, he declared, should do nothing that might look like a voluntary renunciation of their rights as Germans. For they were Germans of the Jewish faith and must insist on their standing as such until the beginning of a better time. *"Moi,"* he ended, so far as Gina understood, *"je suis de Varsovie et néansmoins je suis Français, cent pour cent comme disent les Américains!"* And to this the stout middle-aged spinster who was, it appeared, an *institutrice*, a teacher of French literature, and of Alsatian origin, added in exquisite, though slightly vociferous, French that if a fate similar to that of the Jews of Germany were to overtake the Jews of France, utterly impossible as such a supposition needless to say was, she for her part would become a laundress or a scrubber of floors in the eternal *patrie française* and wait for a better and juster day, whether it came in her lifetime or in the time of another generation.

Mme. Meyerheim now rose and begged her guests to come into the dining-room where tea would be served. Stragglingly they followed her. Gina found Gabriel and little Erich Gauss at their small table, evidently pleased with each other. Gabriel, seeing Gina near him, said eagerly, with glowing cheeks, "Mummie, you must let me go and see Erich!" At that the two mothers, separated by the broad table, nodded and smiled agreement and assent to the children and to each other.

They took their places at the table informally. Tea was here a bounteous and elaborate meal and Gina found herself between Jehuda Brenner and Mme. Meyerheim. The latter was busy seeing to it that her guests were served. Brenner turned to Gina.

"Did you meet my American friend, Peter Lang, in Berlin?"

"No. I heard of him once or twice."

On this, as on other occasions, she avoided a direct mention of Kurt, who had told her of the American. She did not want to plunge too often into that mist of pain.

Brenner spoke again, this time very softly, "How do you live?"

She was tempted to pretend defensively that he meant had she money enough. She caught sight of his grave profile beside her and answered.

"I hardly know. I'm trying for the moment to find out what I ought to do with my small son."

"Did anything you heard here this afternoon help you to decide?"

"I don't know yet. I'll have to reflect. I'm going to see Frau Gauss again." She turned fully and looked at him now and added. "You didn't say anything all afternoon."

"No. You are right. I was listening. In addition, nothing

can be done by arguing or by debating. The way must be communicated from heart to heart and must be found through experience."

Gina raised her head.

"You speak as though there were one way and only one. Do you mean that?"

He looked at her fully for the first time and let his eyes rest on hers, and said, very simply, "Yes, there is only one way for us Jews, though there are many fashions of explaining what it is and many avenues that lead to it."

She had the impulse to ask him for his definition of that one way, and then checked that impulse, she knew not why, and asked instead whether he thought that any of the people here, round this table, had found the one way. The noise of general conversation gave them privacy enough both for her question and for his answer.

"Our dear host and hostess," he said, "belong to a generation which despite many shortcomings had never lost the way and had never consequently to seek it. Of the others I think your little Frau Gauss has her feet firmly set on it."

"Because she's going to Palestine?"

"No. She's going because for her and hers that's the surest method for staying on the way."

"But it's not the only method?"

"No. There are many in exile who follow the way. But exile does make traitors." He lowered his voice. "That unspeakable Melamède, for instance. But we mustn't continue that discussion here, though there is no secret. *He* knows that I know that he knows that I know."

And Jehuda Brenner laughed, and for the first time in so many, many weeks Gina felt a human warmth, a presage of hope in her tried and tired heart.

In a pause of the conversation old Meyerheim said across the table to Brenner: "Jehuda, you've been absorbed in your pretty neighbour at table. Everybody has been saying the

most gloomy things and nothing else. I'm eighty-six. I need
a little cheer to keep me alive, not that it matters. Are you
slumping into the general misery, too?"

Brenner looked up. "Not quite, Uncle Theodore. I don't
believe you are, either. I don't say the situation isn't dreadful. But as long as the Jewish people exists—there is hope,
however far off, both for it and for the world."

The grey man with the bitter mouth let his thick parched
lips writhe with contempt.

"What is there about the Jewish people and its existence
to give us hope? We're not as brutal as the Germans or the
Poles; we're a little maturer, individual for individual; we
are more moral, that is to say, more circumspect, but that is
because we are weak and in constant danger. Otherwise!"
He flung out his hands in a gesture denoting emptiness and
negation.

Jehuda Brenner looked intensely grave. His small, strong,
beautifully-articulated hand toyed with a spoon. He seemed
for a moment or two to be interested only in his hand and
the spoon. Then he raised his eyes.

"Some of you," he said, slowly, "have heard of the Rabbi
Levi Yitzchok of Berditchev. Certainly you, Uncle Theodore
and you, M. le Grand Rabbin."

Vigorously old Meyerheim nodded; Melamède looked half
non-committal, half disapproving. Mme. Meyerheim folded
her fine white wrinkled hands.

"He was," Brenner resumed, "a rabbi of the Chasidic sect
who lived in the second half of the eighteenth century in
Galicia. The Berditchever, as he was known from the town
of his residence and ministry, was a man of fiery spirit, and
the sufferings of the people Israel often so wrought upon
him that he, though in his own person the humblest of men,
called God as it were, before a human judgment seat. It follows that he was jealous of Israel's honour and righteousness
even though he made the plea to God that it were a diviner

mercy to forgive his wicked and disobedient children than such as sedulously kept His law. Revolving these thoughts, he took a long walk in the fields of spring, since it was Passover time. On the edge of the woods he came upon a group of Russians encamped there who, not knowing him but seeing he was a Jew, offered him smuggled silk for sale. Now the laws against smuggling silk out of Russia were severe and the frontier guards had orders to shoot smugglers on sight. He asked the men how much silk they had for sale. They answered, many hundreds of ells and that, if what they had did not suffice, they would bring him as much more as he wanted. 'Do you not know,' he asked them, 'that your Tsar has forbidden this traffic and is ready to enforce his law with all his power of soldiers and policemen and armed guards?' For answer they laughed him to scorn and offered him vodka to drink and called him a cowardly Jew. A fear of human carelessness and depravity burned in the Berditchever's heart. What of his own people at this Passover time? He hastened back to the little town and went from Jewish house to Jewish house, enquiring of each householder whether he had obeyed the command to cleanse his house of *chometz*, of leaven, before the coming of the Pesach feast. And the people were astonished at his question and answered that of course and in very truth they had cleansed their houses of leaven as they had done all their lives and as their fathers had done before them. Whereupon the Rabbi Levi Yitzchok went to the synagogue and prostrated himself before God and prayed for the redemption of Israel, saying: 'Behold, Adonai, how the world's peoples do not obey the laws of their rulers, though the penalty be instant death. But Thy people obey Thy Law which Thou gavest them three thousand years ago and on the infraction of which there is set no penalty. Redeem, therefore, thy people Israel in this generation and in this day."

Gina felt the sting of tears in the corners of her eyelids.

The bitter-mouthed attorney from Cologne said, hoarsely and with a smothered yet not wholly desolate laugh:

"The vast majority of men and women of my generation in Germany no longer know the word *chometz*."

"Precisely," said Jehuda Brenner.

The lovely Lenz girl from Essen, flushing more than ever in the likeness of a dark flower, raised a soft, trembling, but insistent voice:

"You don't mean, Herr Brenner, that we are literally to return to those old customs?"

Jehuda Brenner leaned forward. Gina saw that he wanted to give himself wholly in his answer, to pour out his best at the feet of youth.

"I used the matter as a symbol—a symbol of a double obedience: obedience to the law of our being, obedience to the Law of God. For Jews these two obediences are one. There are higher and greater ways of practising that double obedience than by removing leaven from our houses at Passover. Do you think the Jews of our time practised those higher and those greater ways?"

The girl shook her head.

"We threw ourselves away; we threw ourselves under the feet of any who chose to trample on us; we invited them to trample."

"You have answered your own question excellently," Brenner said. "The Jews who cleansed their houses of leaven, West or East, never quite did that. They clung to at least a symbol of their own law, their own being, their own self-respect. They said to the world at least what Moses said to Pharaoh: '*Ivri anochi*'—I am a Jew. They are less desolate and less defeated than the others today."

M. le Grand Rabbin Marcel Melamède arose. Bristling with evident disapproval, he flung a *très joli* at Brenner, declared that it was unhappily getting late, and made his way toward his hostess. The party broke up at once. Gina and

Frau Gauss, each afraid that her child had overeaten of the rich cake, rapidly made an appointment for Tuesday. Mme. Meyerheim assured Gina that she would be heard from.

In the soft dusk of the street Gina found herself walking to the corner with Gabriel between herself and Jehuda Brenner, who had, she knew not how deliberately, taken the child's hand. She felt protected for the moment and dreaded the desolateness that was ahead of her. In the privacy of the darkness of the narrow ill-lit street she had the courage to say:

"What are we to do, Herr Brenner, Gabriel and I? Do you know our story?"

"I know it," he answered, very simply. "I think—and I'm not alone in that opinion—that for most of our people from Germany the *étappe* Paris was an accident and an error. I am not criticising the French people. They have done very well under these circumstances. There is no place for us here, neither for the majority who must work to live nor for the very, very few like yourself who are still safe from hunger."

"You asked me there at table how I lived." Gina stared straight into the hollow of the street. "In a sort of vacuum, which you've now defined. There is no place here. Where is there a place for my child and me—above all for my child."

"I don't think you are ready for Palestine, nor is Palestine ready for you." His words were very slow and very deliberate. "I think, in fact I'm sure that you and your child could go to America. There are Jewish masses in America; there is a Jewish future in America—there, at least, if anywhere in *Golus*." [Exile.]

"That is your definite advice?" she asked.

"Quite definite."

They had turned several corners and were now on the

Avenue des Champs-Elysées. Brenner stooped and kissed Gabriel's forehead.

"Here I must leave you. I'm leaving France, too. There is nothing to do here. Nothing to hope; nothing to fear. We must feed our fugitives till they can go elsewhere."

Gina looked up. Though in a sombre fashion, her heart was uplifted as it had been in old and better days upon reading certain verses or hearing Bach.

"Who are you, Jehuda Brenner? What are you? You are the only human being I have heard speak for years who isn't wandering in a fog."

He took her hand in both of his.

"I am a simple Jew. A Jew from Poland."

"And what is your work in the world?"

"I try to serve our people."

When he was gone his final words echoed and reëchoed in her as articulately as when he had uttered them: (*unserem Volke zu dienen*) "to serve our people." It was that word "our," that was it—that was the word that had pierced her heart which she had thought congealed into utter desolateness for evermore. His people and hers and Gabriel's—above all, Gabriel's, and the people of Kurt who had died upon a cross because that people was his people, too. She had not wept for long. Now the tears streamed down her face.

"Why do you cry, Mummie?"

Passionately Gabriel clasped her hand and arm.

"Because it seems to me, darling, that there is some hope in the world where I thought there was no more at all. Do you understand that?"

"I *think* I do," he said, with a quaint little emphasis.

When they got back to their flat and Gina had helped Gabriel undress and go to bed, she sat down at the rickety desk in the small salon and wrote a long letter to her father. She told him that, though she expected nothing more from life for herself, it was her duty to think of Gabriel and his future and that she could not see any reasonable future for him in France. He might indeed grow up here and become more or less of a Frenchman and make his way in a worldly sense, provided nothing happened to the little fortune she now possessed. But she had come to the conclusion that making one's way after a fashion in the world was not enough and, above all, not enough for a Jew. Her husband had been a gifted and able young man who had made his way in the world, too, even before they were married. She had been advised to take her child and go to America, to the United States, and that had vividly reminded her of the fact that her great-granduncle, Bernhard Jacoby, the friend and fellow revolutionary of the poet Gottfried Kinkel and also of Carl Schurz, had fled to the United States in 1848, and that she had heard her father say that the descendants of his uncle were still living and prospering in some populous Western city. And so she begged her father to make the necessary enquiries concerning these relations, and whether and how she and Gabriel could gain entrance into the United States, and whether and how she could transfer her money thither.

She read the letter through and sealed it and addressed the envelope, and sat there another hour before she could compose herself sufficiently to hope for sleep. And for the first time since that tragic day on which Wegener had come to her she felt that she was a living being in a living world.

X

TO GINA WEISS, who was now thirty-two, and also to Gabriel, whose eighth birth anniversary they spent on board the *Rochambeau*, Paris became the city of a purging, a revelation, and a dream. That visionary quality came over the city for Gina even while they were still there. So soon as she discovered that the migration to America was possible she knew that in this flight to another world lay more in symbol and in fact than a renewal of hope for her tragic life or the expectation of a reasonable future for her son. She saw decay touch these towers and palaces and gardens, though not one stone was crumbling nor one flower less than perfect in the courts of the Louvre.

Knowing that her time here was measured and her liberation sure, she took long walks with Gabriel, exploring this city which, she was certain, she would never see again. From the square of the Church of St.-Sulpice they walked toward the Seine, crossing the Boulevard St.-Germain by the square and Church of St.-Germain-des-Près. They entered the Rue Bonaparte with its book and art and antique shops, passed the École des Beaux Arts, glimpsed for a moment the small immemorial empty Rue des Beaux Arts and came out on the Quai with its busy traffic and crossed to where, overlooking the river, the vendors of books with their boxes stood or sat on camp stools, patient and somnolent.

A vanishing world, a perishing, mouldering world! Gina was sure of it, sure with an impersonal ache and strange nostalgia. The German barbarians had been able to attack the very heart of Europe because that heart was already broken. It was defenceless as a broken heart must be. The friends of mankind and lovers of freedom had gone down in Germany, like Fritz Kübler, like her own husband, isolated and without a struggle. She seemed to read the meaning of that disaster here in this proud and superficially still valiant city. The heart of Europe was a sick heart. Unguarded were the gates of civilization. The barbarians who added astuteness to ferocity knew it well.

This perception was sharpened for her when one day Frau Gauss, who lived with her husband and child in a small hotel not far from there, took her to that new old Ghetto that lies behind the Hôtel de Ville and guided her through crooked alleys on cobblestones, as in a mediæval city, to the crazily winding Rue des Rosiers—the street, ironically enough, of the rose bushes—where poverty and dirt are stark and the rickety tenements seem palsied and about to crash. Men and women and children in the street, shabby, in shawls and tatters, speaking a dialect brought from the East and North, weary, undernourished, buying, as Gina saw when Frau Gauss took her into a huge baker's shop, a piece of a black loaf with copper centime pieces carefully hoarded, and brought forth by women out of many wrappings. A scene of utmost poverty; a scene of exile, of driven strangers in a strange land who had fled hither from cruelty and oppression and knew not when they would have to flee again. And alive. Palpitating with life—with some indomitable hope, with some unconquerable onward impulse. Toward what? She asked her question in simple terms, and Frau Gauss stopped in the middle of the Rue des Rosiers and turned to Gina and replied: "I think I know. Toward peace, toward justice, toward some land or age where peace and justice will dwell. Our people cannot bring itself to consent to the triumph of evil and the death of the world."

But worlds can die. On the last Sunday before she and Gabriel were to leave, Mme. Meyerheim insisted that she must see at least one of those spots that had for so many years endeared France to herself and her husband who could now no longer see them but had to content himself with a daily walk and drive in the Bois de Boulogne. So, starting quite early, they drove to Ermenonville and ate their *déjeuner* in the garden of the Hostellerie Jean-Jacques Rousseau and thereafter loitered for two dreamy hours in the park of the château of the Rochefoucaults who had befriended the ageing Jean-Jacques. The park, though shaggy and not too far removed from nature, bore in its groves and on its hills and beside the margin of its lovely waters memorials of the age when it had been a living scene. There was a half-ruined little Temple of Reason, of which the inscriptions bore witness to the aspirations of the men of that age. There were spots marked for revery; in a tangled grove there was the half-hidden grave of a painter from Strassburg who had served the family in the château, and though Alsace had then been an integral part of the French Kingdom the patron who had buried the man in his domain had caused to be inscribed on his headstone a legend in his servitor's native tongue, saying of him, with the restraint of that age no more than that he had been *ein aufrechter Mann und ein geschickter Mahler* (an upright man and an accomplished painter). Tears came into Gina's eyes. That age had aspired after humanity and freedom and tolerance. Small as her knowledge was, she remembered Rousseau's notion of society as based on the free consent of its members; she remembered the young Goethe and his friends; strains of Mozart arose fragmentarily in her inner ear. Gone, perished for evermore those principles and aspirations which had echoed even in the days of her girlhood. And in that perishing, Europe was perishing too. She did not wish to sadden her aged companion. But she said, "This was a beautiful world."

She was surprised when Mme. Meyerheim said, quietly: "Yes, and there is a sense in which it lasted until 1914. We are in a dark age now. I shall not be sorry to leave the world when my dear husband has left it and my last duty is done."

Gina put her arm lightly about the old lady. "You had no children?"

"I had one son. We lost him many, many years ago. Even for that I am less sorry now."

All that, those scenes and visions and words, though luminous enough in memory, lay infinitely far behind her now. Even while she was still there and saw and heard, flight was in her soul so throbbingly that at times she felt as though she were a winged creature, though still unfledged. The journey from Paris to Cherbourg had raced past her with sharp green rain-drenched fields, and so had the brief stop in the drizzle of Cherbourg itself, and the lighter that carried Gabriel and her to the *Rochambeau* and the days of sunlit but tumultuous summer seas. For but half a day she had glimpsed the pinnacles of New York, white unimaginable shafts piercing a sky that, after the faint heavens of Europe, burned with a scarce endurable flame of blue. It had, in fact, been hot and humid and Gina and even Gabriel had felt listless and also bewildered by a sense of speed in the very air and by the clamour of unintelligible speech. For though Gina, like most of the members of her generation, had studied English in addition to French and had actually read selections from Galsworthy under a philologically well-trained teacher, what she heard here seemed to correspond to nothing she had learned. After immense but not unfriendly turmoil mother and child had been sucked up into the funnel, as it seemed to Gina, of a Pullman car. Here, too, it was hot despite the whir of the electric fans, but all the circumstances surrounding her slaked that sharp thirst for flight that had come to Gina in Paris, flight from Europe, flight, therefore, from its cruelty and madness, flight, though she knew it not, from the too piercing stab of her man's agony.

Now they were in Ozark City. Gina had inquired after the name of a not too expensive hotel there. But Albert Jacoby, grandson of that Bernhard Jacoby who had fled to America in forty-eight, was at the train with a spacious Packard car and Negro chauffeur and declared in fluent enough but amusingly Anglicized German that first of all Gina and Gabriel were to come to his house, where he and his wife were already entertaining a first cousin of the latter. Gina had regarded Albert Jacoby, a man of her father's age, with amazement. He looked more German, in a rather common way, than the German Jacobys. Round-headed, now bald but originally blond, almost snubnosed, there was nothing about him in his easy well-made American clothes to mark him as Jewish. He asked Gina no questions concerning herself or the kinsmen in Germany, although his actions had, from her father's first letter of inquiry concerning herself and Gabriel, showed so active and sagacious a loyalty. He had gone personally to Washington to arrange for her entering the country; he had caused her money to be transferred to an Ozark City bank of which he was a director; he had sent her a typewritten sheet of directions and had wired at the proper moment to a lawyer in New York to facilitate her dealings with the immigration authorities. For all this Gina tried now to express her gratitude. He waved all that aside. *"Kleinigkeiten!"* ("Trifles!") Evidently it raised him in his own esteem to belittle what he had done. Mere nothings for a man of his importance. He was—so much was clear at once—a new type in Gina's experience. With chubby hand covered by reddish fuzz he pointed out to her meticulously on that first drive the public buildings as well as the chief banks and office buildings of Ozark City, directing the chauffeur twice to make detours for that purpose.

"This was a village when my grandfather came here. Just a village in the prairie. He opened a drug store." (He said

Drogengeschaft instead of *Apotheke*, but Gina had been informed that that great-granduncle had been a pharmacist.) "He made some money. Quite a little for those days. But my father founded the business in the 'eighties and branched out in many directions as the city grew. We have many varied interests now. But of course we have a population of over three hundred thousand and, would you believe it? our population hasn't decreased even during the worst of the depression!"

Gina found it difficult to make any reply to these observations. But Albert Jacoby seemed to expect none. He turned with a genuine kindliness to Gabriel.

"Well, little man, how do you like America?"

Gabriel, who had been told all the details by Gina since she had no other confidant, replied in his best-behaved manner, "I like it very, very much, Herr Jacoby."

At which Jacoby laughed heartily and said, "You must call me Uncle Albert."

From the city proper they had driven along very straight streets, very broad, lined by young recently planted trees. On either side stood private houses on unfenced lawns— "villas" Gina called them to herself—of every style of architecture or pseudo-architecture known to man, many of them undeniably charming, a few here and there exquisite, all in a state of immaculateness and perfect repair that seemed to make them glitter in the overwhelming American sunlight. Gina had seen villas as lovely, perhaps lovelier. And nearly all that she had seen had stood in shadier gardens, more private, more secluded from both traffic and observation. Did these people, she asked herself at once, not mind living, so to speak, in public? But she admitted that she had never seen so many, when Albert Jacoby, who knew Europe well, proudly asked her that question. She wondered, in fact, whether there were as many in all Europe.

"How many rich people there must be here," she said.

Jacoby smiled a subtly superior smile.

"These are middle-class homes."

He did not say, "Wait till you see my house!" He might as well have done so. Gina winced. No German Jacoby she had ever known would have been capable of this subtle vulgarity.

The car turned left and entered scrubby woodlands. It followed a very curving gravelled road that finally led up a gentle rise of ground.

The pudgy red-fuzzed hand rose and waved.

"The only hill in this part of the state. My father bought all this land for a few thousand dollars in 'eighty-nine."

The house came in sight. Some one had seen a château and also a huge peasant house in Normandy, with a pattern of criss-crossed lathes over rubble or stone walls, and out of these glimpses had built an immense, rambling, many-gabled house which had doubtless been much uglier once, but which now, shaded by handsome evergreens and covered by vines and creepers dotted with crimson flowers, gave Gina a strong feeling of coolness and home and refuge. Sincerely she could say, as the car stopped under a half-rustic *porte-cochère*, "How beautiful!" And she was near to tears when, stepping out of the car, she felt herself taken at once into the arms of a dark, sallow, eager-looking woman, and kissed and patted and bidden welcome, and, above all, when Mrs. Jacoby put her arms around Gabriel and kissed him, and giving one of her hands to each of them led them into the house.

She and Gabriel were taken by Mrs. Jacoby to their room—spacious and light, over-furnished with very new-looking, very nondescript but emphatic "period" furniture, but wonderfully comfortable and adjoined by a marble bath-room of immense size. Mrs. Jacoby stood in the middle of the room while the chauffeur brought up small bags and valises. Her German was scrappy and incorrect. But she managed nervously and with a punctuation of little hoarse laughs to tell Gina that the trunks were being sent for, that luncheon would be in an hour, and that she hoped her son, the doctor, would come for dinner that evening. Gina thanked her and added that soon she must find some place for Gabriel and herself and try to build up a new life. At that Mrs. Jacoby's longish nose seemed to grow both thinner and longer. "Don't think of that, please! This house is so big. There are eight bedrooms and our son, the doctor, has to live in town near the college and the hospital." In spite of the heat of the day she seemed to shiver. "Now I'll leave you. If you need anything, just ring. You speak a little English, don't you?"

This house and these people were new and strange to Gina. For weeks she walked as in a thin fog. Even the other fugitives from Germany who were the Jacobys' guests seemed already to have undergone a subtle change from what they had once been. These were Mrs. Jacoby's first cousin, Dr. Georg Hellmann, and his wife. With sudden fury they had been driven from a small Franconian city in which the Hellmanns had lived for at least ten generations. The doctor had had the largest practice in the town, because the people trusted not only him but his name. It was the faith in the probity and humanity of an old Jewish family which the Nazis desired, as contrary to what they wanted believed to be possible and normal, to destroy and stamp out. Georg Hellmann, except to closest scrutiny, looked German in a rather faded way, and his wife was an Aryan German or as, to Gina's surprise Julia Jacoby dubbed her, a *shikse*. [Gentile woman.] She was, in fact, this Jetchen, as everyone called her, the type that Gina and the friends of her girlhood had described as *kartoffelhaft* (potatoish), with skin of the dead whitishness of the inside of a raw potato, with nose round as a small potato, with lightless blond hair gathered in a knot at the nape of the neck the size of slightly larger potato.

The history of the Hellmanns Gina got neither from them nor from Albert Jacoby. It was Julia who would suddenly knock at her door and slip in with a half-furtive gesture and gossip volubly as though in relief, and also, though with a sincere solicitude, try to draw Gina out. It was as though Julia suffered from the reserve that governed the common meetings, at meals and at other times, of the people in this house. They all sedulously spoke English, though the English of the Hellmanns was still very broken and though Gina had often to ask for an explanation of what was being said. The Hellmanns, though in America only a little over three months, never mentioned the past. If at any moment a reference to the persecution of the Jews in Germany seemed in danger of being made, Jettchen nipped it or smothered it with her unvarying observation: "Ziss iss not ze reel Tchermany. Zet vill come beck!" To which there was always vociferous agreement, and which at dinner, when everyone felt leisurely, would lead Albert to tell anecdotes of various trips to Germany in the past, during which he and his wife and son had been treated with exemplary courtesy and had indeed been accorded special favours by everyone. The implication was that there had been merely a stupid interruption of this state of affairs, an interruption that was bound to end. Once and once only Gina had said, bitterly: "A rich American might stop at the Adlon Hotel now and not see the martyrdom of his entire people." A hush that was both empty and surly had fallen on the company. Frantically, thereupon, Julia had babbled that they must hurry through dinner in order to get on time to the movie they had been planning to see.

It was Albert Jacoby who puzzled Gina most. He was, at whatever remove, her kinsman. They had a common ancestor. He was within a month of her father's age; he was,

like her father—or at least as her father had once been—
a man of substance and of influence in his city and in his
land. He represented the third generation of his family in
the United States and the second generation to be born on
American soil. And he was, in fact, an immensely contented
and sincerely patriotic American. Though beyond the age of
military service at the time of the American declaration of
war against Germany, he had evidently been heartily in
favour of it. He had been a dollar-a-year man in the government's service; he had liquidated important holdings in
order to buy a fortune's worth of Liberty bonds; he had
seemed to himself inspired not only by the zeal of a born
American, but by the spirit of his grandfather who had first
resisted and then fled from imperialist tyranny in Germany.
Nor was this all. For the benefit of the Hellmanns and of
herself he extolled American liberty, tolerance, the friendli-
ness of the American way of life. He said that he was happy
in the thought that little Gabriel would be an American and
accompanied Gina and Gabriel to the school in the neighbourhood, a not unhandsome building in a fine garden, which
Gabriel was now attending. From the principal's attitude to
both Albert and herself Gina had been deeply contented for
Gabriel. He would be in a friendly world. She was grateful
for that; she was grateful for everything.

What was it that puzzled her? What was it she missed and
began to long for? "There is an emptiness," she said articulately to herself, "a great emptiness. Albert has been an
alderman of Ozark City; he is one of the directors of the
Symphony Society; he is on the board of the Fine Arts Center and Museum; he is also a trustee of both the St. Vincent
Hospital and of the Jewish Home for Incurables." Her father
had never been so variously and officially engaged. It was
all admirable. Wholly admirable. Yet it all seemed to her
like the gyrations of a force about a centre of nothing in a
void. It seemed to her that she must go out from this house

and from among these people and especially away from Albert Jacoby, to seek and find America if she was ever to come to know America. For there was no light to be gotten from the friends of Albert and Julia Jacoby who came to this house and to whose houses Gina was invited and who lived, in fact, in a higher state of merry and continuous gregariousness than she had ever known any group of people to do. They were all extremely like Albert and Julia despite an hundred variations in age and looks and individual temperament. Everywhere she found, after penetrating to a certain point, that same gyration about no centre.

One evening fairly late, coming home from a dinner party which Gina had found dull, Albert, chatting desultorily, drifted into her room. He saw her bookshelf and went up to it. He put on his glasses.

"Goethe? You actually still read Goethe?" He did not wait for her answer. "Rilke? Never heard of him. Thomas Mann? Oh yes, they tell me he's very fine. Julia has a book of his in English translation, I believe. Well, well, well! Do *you* read Kant?"

He swung round and took off his glasses.

"It was Kurt's edition," she said, in a hard, dull voice.

Albert's face assumed the gravity he thought appropriate to the mention of the dead.

"He must have had a most unusual mind, for a young lawyer."

"I cannot truthfully say that," Gina replied. "At least all his friends, whether Jewish or Gentile, read philosophy and tried to find a *Weltanschauung* of their own."

Albert Jacoby laughed. It was a superior laugh that did not believe in its own superiority. It was, for a man of his age and importance in the world, a singularly immature laugh.

"In this country," he said, "they wouldn't have had the time. Especially if they were bright and successful."

Gina knew at once that she had now come upon the answer to her puzzled question.

"What do you believe in, Albert? What does anybody believe in among the nice people I've met through you and Julia? Tell me!"

He stared. He winced. He laughed that immature laugh again. Then he parried by asking: "What does your father believe in?"

"Nothing now. And it's killing him that he has nothing left to believe in. He *used* to believe in the power of German civilisation to raise the universal level of civilisation and in the high and noble part which his group of Jews had played in raising Germany to that distinction."

Albert looked grave, but there was something comic about his gravity. It was so official and assumed.

"Well, that's the same thing here. I've told you what my grandfather and my father, and I, too, contributed to Ozark City and indirectly to the state and the nation. And we certainly believe in America. Why, even now isn't it the freest and the richest country in the world?"

Gina gave a little gasp. She had almost said: Your contribution has been manufacturing paper boxes and buying real estate low and selling it high? Instead she said, colourlessly, "Yes, Albert."

He stood before her a little flushed now, doubtful, evidently, of the quality of her assent.

"And I'll tell you one thing, Gina. Our employés, over six hundred, are the best treated in the Middle West. We co-operated with their becoming unionized. We never had a strike. We didn't fire a worker even in 'thirty-two and 'thirty-three. Sociologists come to study the conditions in our factory and our welfare arrangements. I could be a much richer man than I am if I hadn't practically shared with my men and their families."

"Yes," Gina said, "that's admirable. But that *is welt-anschaulich* from a Jewish point of view."

He bristled. He was almost crimson now.

"Not at all! Not in the least! It's both humanity and good sense. It's good Americanism. That's what it is!"

Julia came in in her dressing-gown.

"I hope you two aren't quarrelling. I heard you shouting, Albert."

He laughed. The tension was broken. He had slipped back into the sheath of his accustomed inner comforts.

"I wouldn't quarrel with Gina. She's much too nice. But she'd better get rid of some of her highfalutin European notions."

They bade her good-night. Julia kissed her. Along the hall and even from beyond the door of their bedroom Gina could hear the rumble of Albert's voice.

She was sorry. The Jacobys were endlessly good to her. Again and again they had insisted she mustn't look for an apartment yet; she must stay with them. And how handsome of Albert not to have boasted of his generous support of music and of art and of the hospitals of the city. Or was it that he had forgotten? That these things seemed trivial to him? That he had done what he had done as a matter of family tradition—a tradition which in his father's time had still been a living force, but which in him had become merely a handsome habit? Wasn't it a fact that everything was or seemed outside of him and nothing within him? Where was his inner world from which his actions sprang?

Four days later there was a cocktail party at the Country Club. The far-flung pseudo-rustic building stood in an endless expanse of marvellously-kept lawns. The party was given in an enormous raftered hall with a fireplace at each end. Along one whole side ran the bar. Opposite were tables equally long, loaded with salads, lobster and chicken and crab, with a whole smoked salmon, with little barrels of

caviar. Gina had already learned to take a cocktail or two
and to experience the relief and release from memory and
spiritual pain. She knew a good many of the people here.
A Dr. Hollander, a tall thin old gentleman with an ironic
and yet friendly mask, himself born in Germany, was fond
of chatting in German with her whenever they met. He was
a pediatrician and hence she had once consulted him about
a small ailment of Gabriel. She said to herself that some
day she would ask Dr. Hollander her troubling questions.
But the doctor had already had two whisky-and-sodas and
had insisted on taking a third with her, and was now leading
her to the buffet tables to be sure, as he put it, that she ate
enough, because, according to him, she would be even lovelier
if she put on about ten pounds.

There at the buffet they met a swarthy, heavy, tousled
man in his early forties who said to Gina, speaking with a
thick foreign accent, his vivid golden-brown eyes humorously
on Dr. Hollander: "I'm going to introduce myself, Mrs.
Weiss. My name is Ezekiel Frosch and the German-Jewish
aristocracy frowns on me. If it weren't for the depression and
the drop in membership, they might even have black-balled
me. But they'll take their thousand-dollar initiation fee even
from a mere Litvak [Lithuanian] like me now."

Dr. Hollander's expression was sweetish and sour, too.

"Of course you misrepresent the situation, Ezekiel. But
why did you join?"

Exaggeratedly, Frosch, twinkling at Gina, lifted his shoulders.

"My wife, poor darling, thought it would do me good to
play golf, and the junk business is a good business. All right.
So I joined and we came to a party—a party, Mrs. Weiss,
just like this. And when my wife, who is a *bekovete Yiddene*,
a respectable Jewess, you understand, from a fine rabbinical
family, saw the wife of the reform rabbi drinking cocktails

here and saw all this *trefe* [ritually unclean] food—well, she got sick and went home."

Dr. Hollander squeezed Gina's arm.

"Don't take everything Frosch tells you seriously. He has a reputation for ironic wit to sustain."

Deliberately the doctor turned and let himself be drawn away by a very golden-haired woman with a not entirely steady glass in her hand. Gina looked back at Ezekiel Frosch. His eyes were serious, almost melancholy, now. His jocund air had given way to dignity.

"Irony," he said, "is either a mask or else it is a matter of courtesy. I cannot tell these charming people what's the matter with them, seriously. Anyhow, it would do no good."

Gina laid her hand on his sleeve.

"What *is* the matter with them?"

"You want to know? Aha! Now I understand why you have already the reputation of being highbrow?"

Gina smiled.

"Yes, Julia teases me with that and explained the expression to me. I assure you I wasn't considered especially cultured in Berlin."

Now he glowed and almost sparkled again.

"These people are empty; therefore they are always in a hurry. Empty people who were not born to be empty are always in a hurry. They read the latest pretty good novels; occasionally they read a pseudo-serious book. But they don't relate any of that to their lives."

"Yes, yes. Go on!" Gina was a little breathless.

"There isn't yet any spiritual American culture that soaks into everybody, as there is a German and a French and even a Russian. And these people here—look at them: Jewish people in a hundred-per-cent Jewish club—have abandoned their Jewish culture, both religious and secular, and so— well, so they are what they are. Jews simply can't substitute golf for *Gemore* [Talmudic lore and learning] in the broader sense. They become stupid and silly. Just plain silly. Of course, when Hitler came into power they had a few pretty bad weeks. They were scared as hell. They sent for their *mishpocheh* [kinsmen]—you're a living example of that. Now they've settled down again. They've readjusted their blinkers. They'll wear them, God forbid, to the gates of the concentration camp."

He was sombre now. She had taken his arm, which he had half offered. They were walking in a half-deserted corner of the vast hall.

"Yes," Gina said again. "Yes. And you? And you?"

He laughed.

"I'm a Litvak, a Lithuanian, from a village near Kovno. I'm an *Ostjude.* You know *that* word. Here they call us ignorant foreigners. Specifically, I'm secretary of the local Zionist district and president of the Conservative *shul* and a subscriber to the three big Yiddish dailies. And I bet you I know Emerson more intimately than either Albert Jacoby or Gustave Hollander. I'm an ignorant foreigner and talk English with an accent. Privately, I could talk with less of an accent. I won't. *Dafke!* I'll be damned if I will. Do you understand?"

She laughed. She had not really laughed for long.

"How well! How well! You remind me of people I saw, of things I heard, in Paris. Have you ever heard of Jehuda Brenner?"

"Oh yes," he said, very simply. "A great spirit. I know him. He was here some years ago."

A little to her own surprise she now heard herself saying: "I'm determined, in spite of Albert and Julia, to find a little home for my child and me. Then we could be friends, couldn't we—your wife and you and I?"

"You must come to us even before that," he said, warmly. "I really have a regard for the older Jacobys. But now that I know you a little I'll be glad to have you get away from the orbit, so to speak, of Julian." He mimicked Mrs. Jacoby, "Our son, the doctor."

They turned and saw Julia coming at almost a little run toward them. She nodded to Frosch. "I've been looking for you everywhere, Gina dear. It's getting late. And you know Julian is coming for dinner." She almost whined and barely permitted Gina to press the hand of Frosch. Later in the car on the way home she was half plaintive and half acrid. "I can't imagine what place people like Frosch have in our club. It's that kind that pull us down and give us a bad name. Why wasn't he black-balled, Albert? A junkman who can hardly speak English. I noticed when we gave our banquet for the mayor how disgustingly he pushed himself forward. Why, then, if people think we're all like that——"

Albert, sitting with the chauffeur, turned around and interrupted.

"That's not fair, Julia. The mayor and Frosch have been personal friends for years. There was no pushing."

"Oh, you admire him too, Albert? And Gina seems to have spent the afternoon with him. Well, I can't say that I share your taste. I consider him a menace. And all like him. I'm ashamed every time I pass that Polish *shul* of his. No wonder Julian hates all Jews and will hardly come to the house of his own parents when they associate with people like Ezekiel Frosch. No wonder. But I mustn't wear myself out. We have barely time to dress for dinner, Gina. But please, please avoid those terrible people."

Gina shivered at the woman's servile fright. She saw Albert frown in a heavily puzzled way. He shared his wife's sentiments. But her expression of them troubled and subtly outraged him. Carefully he avoided Gina's eyes. In silence they drove home.

XI

THIS dinner party was by very far not the first occasion
on which Gina had met Dr. Julian Jacoby. He had not
appeared, as his parents had hoped, on the evening of her
arrival in Ozark City. He had telephoned that he could not
come. A surgeon is socially beyond control. One has to take
his word. Nearly a week had gone by before he had suddenly dashed in during the forenoon and gazed at Gina in
coldly insolent appraisal. Communication had been slow.
He knew or pretended to know no German. He was tall,
slender, thirty-five. His eyes were black and studiously impersonal, his clothes and car untarnished and precise, his
gestures few and measured. Over his forehead his hair was
very thin; over his temples very grey. This gave him a worn
look which his mother attributed to the immense drain of
his profession. The most intricate operations in general practice and at St. Vincent's hospital were turned over to him.
He was associate professor in the medical school of the state
university. He was, moreover, on the governing board of
the Century Club and of the Lakewood Golf Club; he belonged to the ultra-exclusive Saturday Circle. All these details
his mother had communicated to Gina. After a heavy dinner
party where, from cocktails to dessert champagne, the drinking had been constant, she had added the whispered detail,
"He's the only Jew in any of these clubs."

After that first time he had dropped in at the oddest hours
—for breakfast, at eleven at night. His mother had been
both delighted and disturbed. His absence and remoteness in his bachelor flat with his Filipino manservant were
her constant sorrow. She treasured every hour he spent under

the paternal roof. These hours were now more frequent. But since he came with quietly brutal frankness to see Gina, Julia Jacoby's feelings were tangled and much nearer pain than joy. After he had lingered on one occasion till beyond midnight, his mother, with the attitude of one at bay, said to Gina: "You can imagine that we'd like Julian to get married. But he won't; he just won't. We hoped at one time he'd marry Yvonne Hollander. They're lovely people and the doctor is rich and it would have been so suitable. Albert urged it on him once, and one word led to another, and when Julian does once fly into a rage he stops at nothing. And do you know what he said?" Gina, tingling with vicarious shame, shook her head. "He said, 'If ever I do marry, it'll be a white girl.'" Gina winced and Mrs. Jacoby whispered, "He meant a *shikse*."

"Well," Gina asked, "would you mind?"

"Not exactly. There's no real reason. Of course his children wouldn't belong to us much."

Gina did not know what to reply to that. Nothing of all that she had learned in the past six months would have reached Julia's mind. Out of a silence Julia finally said, both plaintively and accusingly.

"He's never shown so much interest in any woman as in you, Gina. But that ——"

Quietly Gina interrupted her.

"You need have no fear, Julia. I ought not to have to explain that."

"He's very handsome and distinguished!"

Only her heavy burden of obligation to the Jacobys kept Gina from saying: "You too stop at nothing, quite like your son. You want me to reassure you on the basis of my unworthiness." Instead she said:

"I've begged you to let me find a home for Gabriel and myself."

"Oh, he'll come there!"

Gina got up.

"All I can tell you, Julia, is that I won't marry again and that I'm not a light woman. Is that enough?"

Julia had kissed her and apologized. She must have reported the conversation to her husband. For a day or two later Albert had said to Gina:

"I want you to know that I'd be happy and proud if you and Julian would get married." He smiled a melancholy smile. "I'm afraid there's no such luck. You're lovely and cultured and you're a Jacoby. I don't know what's the matter with Julia or with him."

Gina smiled back at the poor puzzled man. She knew he was fond of her; she knew, in addition, that he had never analysed or faced a single interior situation.

"I'm too old and sorrowful to marry any one, Albert. But I want you to take me to look at those apartments you were talking about. I feel the need of being alone, and alone with Gabriel, more."

He nodded and patted her hand.

"I'll miss you and the child."

Neither he nor his wife was fully aware, in fact, of what had from time to time happened between Gina and Julian. They had had hours alone together. Occasionally he had taken her driving in his glittering car on still, sultry September nights. He had talked to her in a kind of torrent of words, as though speech had been pent up in him. He never drove less than sixty miles an hour, which made answers or comments from her almost unnecessary. He had begun by diatribes against Ozark City.

"This is a lousy provincial town. You ought to see that. I've gotten almost as far as one can get here. What am I to do with the rest of my life? They don't even run to interesting cases here. Appendicitis, gastric ulcers, hernia, cancer. I hate golf and play twice a week. I play bridge and I play a hell of a good game, and I hate that. I go to parties and I know what they say behind my back."

He stepped on the gas.

"What? Please don't drive so fast. I'm a mother."

"They say that for a kike I'm a good egg."

"Why do you go where they say that?"

"Where the hell else am I to go? With Rabbi and Mrs. Fidelman, or with the Hollanders or the Littauers or the Blocks or the Ezekiel Frosches or the Cohns or the Levys?"

"Why not? Just precisely why not?"

"Because they take it for granted, God damn them for a bunch of fools, that there's a special bond and a special likeness and a special obligation between them and me and that I belong to them. It isn't true. It's on a level with Christian Science. There are no races. Environment and social forms are the determining factors. I haven't anything in common with the people in Fidelman's temple or in the Country Club."

"But you don't like golf and bridge, either, or your American parties."

"That's a question of individual variation. If I'm anything I'm an American. That's not a racial or religious classification, anyhow. First of all I'm myself."

"Then why haven't you married an American girl?"

Once more the speedometer shot up and once more Gina protested. He slowed down to forty miles an hour.

"Because the lousy Jews, by their self-segregation, have poisoned the whole situation. If I marry an American girl below my social or cultural or economic level I ruin myself by the tacit admission that that's the best a kike can do. If I marry an American girl in my own class—I was engaged to one once and I know—all her relations, including my best men friends, are openly doubtful or condescending and all my relations have an ancestral colic of the worst kind."

Gina pondered. Sidewise she looked at Julian. He could hardly keep himself from speeding up again. Between the fingers of his right hand on the wheel he held his eternal cigarette. She almost yielded to the illusion that his whole head was elongated by his mad forward impulse of speed and flight.

"In my great-great-grandfather's time the German Jacobys intermarried with the Prussian nobility. I have a drove of distant cousins among them now. And my child and I are fugitives. Do you think Jewish self-segregation explains it all? My husband, too, was very German and so were all his friends and mine. Much more German than you are American!"

Rage seemed to shake him.

"I'm sick of hearing about Germany and Poland. With all due respect to you, Gina. I'm unable to estimate what happened there, and all reports are partisan and false. In Soviet Russia, where self-segregation is impossible and anti-Semitism a crime, the Jews are disappearing. And that is in a large measure possible here, too."

"You do trust the reports from Soviet Russia, then?"

"They're not messed up by racial or religious nonsense."

"And you want the Jews to disappear?"

A liberating cry broke from him.

"I most certainly do. By God! I do. No such luck in my time!"

Gina felt a pang of forlornness. Did that feeling seep into her consciousness from his or was it the answer of her inner self to his negation of their people? She did not know. What she did know was that the entire conversation had been a mask for this man's desire for her. Sitting close together in the small swift car, their bodies had been touching. Now and then, steering with his left hand only on the wheel, he had thrown his right arm almost about her and had thus increased the surfaces that touched. And to her shame and misery, her body which had, as a body of flesh and blood, died with Kurt and had been dead to this very hour, flickered with a faint response of pleasure and excitement. Faint, remote, germinal, but unmistakable. Now the forlornness which rose in her from his last observation caused that flickering to die. She felt hot in spite of the speed of the car. The heat from the motor seemed suddenly to rise toward her. She begged him to return home. At the entrance of the Jacoby house he deliberately turned before opening the door of the car, took her by both shoulders with his long strong surgeon's hands, and kissed her roughly on the mouth. He drew back and looked at her in the dimness.

"Means nothing to you, eh?"

Slowly she shook her head.

"All right. Of course you've pretty deliberately shut off the gas. We'll see. Good-night."

Thereafter he disappeared for a period. She, on the other hand, was not unhappily preoccupied. Albert had found an apartment for her in a house owned by a friend. There were five friendly rooms overlooking a garden on one side, a public park on the other. Gabriel was intensely delighted. He said: "It's so nice, Mummie, for you and me to have our own home again." He spoke English. He said "home." Gina felt herself blanch. She put her hand against the wall and for a moment leaned her forehead against it. She sank into that mist of pain from which for weeks, almost for months, she had fled, from which she had been able to flee because, since she and Gabriel had boarded the train at the Gare St.-Lazare for Cherbourg, she had been, as it were, continuously on the wing. She had fled from memory; she had fled from herself. Often in the dead middle of the night she had awakened to an intolerable moment of entire recollection. But daylight and the day had carried her onward and out of herself again and the constant soft impact of this easy, frictionless American life with its apparently smooth surfaces had helped her to repress, what her whole being had wanted to repress, intolerable disaster and unbearable grief and that early resolve never any more to be taken in by the world, never more to be the dupe of any hope.

"What's the matter, Mummie?"

Gabriel's clear voice seemed to come from far away. She sat down. He came to her and she clasped him in her arms.

"Do you remember Berlin?"

"Oh yes, I do," he said, softly.

"Do you remember Papa?"

He hid his head against her breast. She felt his nod.

"Do you know what happened to him?"

Again she felt that nod, and then his tears against her throat. His little body shook with sobs. She could not weep. But though she held him still closer, desolateness swept over her, wave after wave, desolateness and nameless terror, while through the window streamed the deep golden sunlight of an American autumn day.

She let him go and rose. It had been cruel of her so to assault the feelings of the child. A touch of remorse was added to her desolateness. But she could not unsay her words nor bid Gabriel forget. For she, it was clear to her with a fierce and burning clearness, would never forget again. Flight had come to an end in this apartment in Ozark City; autumn was here—autumn with such a blaze of gold and old gold and tobacco brown and scarlet of sere foliage as her eyes, accustomed to the dim and sombre misty season of Europe, had never seen before—autumn with a strange sort of triumph in its aspect, as of a mild but dazzling conqueror that dreaded neither snow nor frost nor the decline to barrenness and winter.

That afternoon she walked in the park. Gabriel had been invited to visit the children of Ezekiel Frosch, who lived not far from here. She wished that she were old and walking through some immemorial autumn of Europe, full of the presage of decay and death, presage for the world, presage for herself, so that she might weep and dream of the tranquillity of extinction. Instead she was in a scene of splendour. The cries of bugles seemed to be in the still golden air. Colours had become as sounds to her. Yet there was silence— deep padded silence not only here, but (as in a flash she knew it) silence in this whole American life by which she was surrounded, a silence that now in the stoppage of her flight, in the ceasing, as it were, of the whirring of the wings of flight, would be for evermore like thunder to her ears.

It was a silence about Kurt. It was a silence about that crucifixion which she had seen when she stood before Nôtre Dame de Paris. Kurt had been murdered. Others had been murdered. Life and honour and hope had been foully destroyed. No one spoke out. No one cared. The world, this world, went on in its accustomed easy way. They ate and drank and slept and copulated, these people, as though nothing had happened. No one cried aloud. No one threw himself into any arena. Tacitly they planned to spend their future summers elsewhere than in Germany; a little less tacitly they avoided buying German merchandise. No one cared. Not Jew, though the Jews were secretly frightened. Not Christian. The American papers were slightly deprecating. Worlds were perishing in blood and torment. Doom was on the horizon of earth. And cocktails were drunk and flirtations carried on at the Country Club. In the huge falsely solemn Reform Temple she had heard Rabbi Fidelman preach on the iniquity of the Germans and the barbarism of the Poles and on the contrasted glory of American freedom and tolerance. And though blunt pang after pang had come to her during the sermon, it had not broken that lethargy in which she had been sheathed. Nothing had broken it; nothing had been there to break it. At first there had been those other fugitives, the Hellmanns. But these, lisping their broken English, had evidently been determined to join with all their might that great conspiracy of silence and forgetfulness. A group of villages had been found in the extreme southern part of the state that needed a physician. No one had said, there are no Jews—not a single family—in Martindale County. It was a fact. Hellmann would not be recognized; his wife was Gentile. They had dived deep. The waters had gone over them. Half-frightened at the enormity of the thing, Julia Jacoby had somewhat shrilly rejoiced. Albert had withheld all comment. He had a way of treating many things in a debonaire way as nonexistent.

Gina sat down on a bench under a flaming maple. What am I to do? she asked herself, forming the words almost audibly. What am I to do? I'm not the crusading type of woman. I don't even know enough. Father writes me that conditions have slightly improved. I know he lies or lies to himself. He means he still has enough to live on and that he and mother can sit alone in their house and shut their minds and ears to what is happening because they still have food and shelter. Dreadful rumours come to me and I know they are true. Father, I can see, is afraid to answer questions. He is afraid to have me ask them. But what am I to do? If I ask Fidelman I know what he'll say: American Jewry is raising money for relief. And that's true and it's fine. But it doesn't break the silence or the daily and hourly indifference. It changes nothing. It changes nothing at all. It leaves the doom and the blood and the torture untouched now and for the future. But what do I want? Do I want revenge for Kurt? No, I don't even know what that could or would mean. I want people to see to it that it doesn't go on or, at least, that it doesn't happen any more or, at the very least—and maybe that least would be best—I want the whole world to know and to grieve.

Clouds had been gathering while Gina sat under the maple. She looked up. She looked about. The scene was stern. A wind blew from the north. She rose and walked

against the wind. Northward against the wind. She bowed
her head and clenched her hands. That was it: if the whole
world knew, if the whole world grieved, if the whole world
were filled with sorrow, and if the cry of that sorrow, if the
cry of that shame over the cruelty and madness of men,
rose and rose and gathered force—not loud, not shrill, not
eager, but swelling in volume like the music of an organ and
rolling slowly, solemnly like the thunder of an organ over
sea and land until it reached all ears and all hearts, would
not then knife and whip and faggot drop from the murderer's
hand and the murderer himself sink to the earth in contrition and in woe?

She began to smell rain in the wind. Drops dashed against
her face. Gabriel had no raincoat with him. She changed her
direction and hurried now with a small warm pang in her
heart. She was grateful for that pang. At least she had
Gabriel. She hoped she would reach the Frosch house on
the other side of the park before Gabriel had started home.
She ran the last few blocks. It was dusk now and the bright
windows drew her on. She rang and Sara Frosch herself
came to the door.

"How nice to see you! Gabriel is playing with Gershon
and Ge' ulah on the back porch. Come in. Do come in."

"Oh!" Gina's exclamation was one of relief. "I'm so glad
he's still here, so glad."

She choked a little and did not see Mrs. Frosch's dark
eyes penetratingly on her.

"It's going to rain. Why don't you and Gabriel stay for
dinner? Ezekiel will be here any minute. If it's bad later he'll
drive you home."

They had gone into the living-room. The furnishings were
modern and ugly. But the crammed bookshelves reached the
ceiling.

"I mustn't," Gina said. "I have no right to be a bother."

"A bother! Such nonsense! The *shikse* does all the hard

work. I like to cook. But my cooking is done and the girl
will serve. Will you stay?"

Gina looked into those immensely intelligent and kindly
eyes.

"I'd love to. I don't deny that."

"Fine," Sara Frosch cried. "You see, Mrs. Weiss, we
could have a cook. But I like to be sure, myself, that everything is *kosher*, and it's homelike so and Ge' ulah is twelve
and already helps a little."

"Ge' ulah," Gina repeated. "What a strange and beautiful
name!"

"It is the Hebrew word for redemption—the redemption
of our land and the redemption of our people."

Gina felt her lids grow wet.

"Oh, if I could believe in that, Mrs. Frosch! No one needs
some belief and hope like that more than I."

"That's what Ezekiel said the other day. Well, if you'll forgive me you'll not get it from the German-Jewish crowd at
the Country Club or in Fidelman's *shul*, granting a few ex-
ceptions. Ezekiel is fond of saying they're neither *milchig*
nor *fleishig*, neither milky nor meaty. They're *parve*, neither
the one thing nor the other. And that's bad." She laughed.
"He's also fond of using a Christian saying about them to
the effect that they live without God or hope in the world."

Gina folded her hands.

"And you have a hope, Mrs. Frosch?"

Their eyes met.

"Yes, in good days and in evil, thank God, we have a hope,
a work, a cause. Ezekiel and I give a good fourth of our income and all the time we can. And we believe that that's
a better heritage for our children than if we hoarded a few
dollars."

The children came in glowing from their talk and play.
Gershon was a year old than Gabriel, Ge' ulah was slowly
blossoming out of childhood. Gabriel with a cry of joy rushed

to Gina and flung his arms about her. She had never seen him so handsome and tense with life.

"Mummie, Mummie," he said, "I've had such a good time. Gershon and Ge' ulah can speak Hebrew. They've already taught me some words. May I go to the same school to which they go? May I, Mummie? Please, please!"

Gina pressed her lips to his warm hair. Then she lifted her head. The eyes of the two mothers met.

"Yes, darling," she answered, "you may. You may indeed."

XII

IN HER small drawing-room, on the opposite side of the grate fire of natural gas which Gina rather hated, sat Dr. Julian Jacoby. A bottle of Scotch which he had brought stood unopened beside him on the green tiles. Gina had told him that if he opened it he would have to go or else she would lock herself in her bedroom. It was not, she had explained, that she was in the least afraid of him. But to the sober the drunken are disgusting. And she had seen him drunk. He had to content himself with cigarettes. An ashtray heaped with stubs stood on the little table at his elbow. This was by very far not the first time that he had sat here through long evenings. Except at certain quite rare moments of a boyish, almost pathetic, ingenuousness, Gina disliked him. Then why did she let him come? From her girlhood in the ultra-modern atmosphere of the Weimar Republic, soaked with psychoanalysis and expressionist literature, she had carried over a definite realism of the interior life. She was a woman. She was under thirty-five. She was widowed. She was eternally widowed. It nourished her womanhood to be desired once more.

Ah, if she could have said loved! And in fact she knew that Julian loved her. But she disdained to use a term that he himself repudiated. Love, she was quite clear about that too, was associated in his mind with permanent elements of human life, with sanctities which, both as a scientist and as a man, he repudiated. This repudiation had to be total. For anything less than total repudiation would have led him back to the question of his Jewishness. And that he had to avoid like fire or poison. For it infuriated him so that he lost his

173

head. He raved; he stuttered; he babbled; sounds unintelligible like the cries in nightmares came from his lips. It drove him quite literally to the refuge of drink. And so he dared not say he loved her. He dared not say it and she would not. She might have broken the stubbornness of his heart with her insistence on this point. But since she did not want his love, since there was nothing in the world she could do with it, she did not dare, merely for her own barren comfort, to press the point.

He had been absent from Ozark City for two weeks. He had been the local delegate to an association of American surgeons that had had its annual meeting in New York; he had, in addition, visited a number of clinics in other Eastern cities. He had been back only four days. He had telephoned Gina on each of those days. When he had come in at nine o'clock on this evening he had caught her by the shoulders and he had strained her to him and had kissed her and had pressed his teeth against her nether lip. For a fleeting instant weakness attacked her as of a hot ichor rolling down her spine and her taut lips threatened to relax. But in that embrace their eyes met and his were cold and flickered with mere lechery, and also bloodshot with recent drunkenness. She froze again and disengaged herself. But he, having observed that swift moment of yielding, was well content and settled down in his now almost accustomed place to talk himself out.

"I used to think, Gina, that I'd like to live in New York. Well, I'm through with that. It's not an American city. It stinks with foreigners. I never noticed it as much as this time."

Gina smiled ironically.

"The French call that xenophobia, a pathological dislike of foreigners. Not a very enlightened sentiment. How about myself, by the way?"

"Don't talk nonsense and shift the issue." He frowned.

"What you mean, I suspect, Julian, is not foreigners at all. You mean Jews. Since you hate the Jew in yourself you hate all Jews."

He flushed. He lit a new cigarette.

"Never mind that nonsense of yours, Gina. You'll drop it by and by. I heard a man speak at Cooper Union. His name was Andrew Saracen. He spoke of the new life in Russia. He admitted that not all the proposed ends had been realized, especially as regards the production and distribution of consumers' goods. But he did make it clear that the personal and intimate life of people was being sanely and rationally based. Religion and racial superstitions are practically exterminated; the family is gradually being eliminated; children are largely cared for by the State. There is immense freedom and immense flexibility. Human happiness is the goal, not methods of self-torture."

She did not reply at once.

"Didn't you listen?" he asked, sharply.

"I heard every word, Julian. We went through all that in Germany several years ago. There was even the argument that fewer people were going insane in Soviet Russia ——"

"Well, it's a God damned good argument, as I ought to know."

"No, we came to the conclusion that it wasn't so very good. I heard a very great physician explain the matter in my father's house. If impulse and instinct have no obstacle the morons won't go to the wall. That's very true. But then for their sakes you're destroying the forms of life in which normal people need to work out their happiness."

"You don't really believe in freedom."

Gina laughed.

"We used to hear that, too. And we knew the answer. Freedom means picking your path and your goal. It doesn't mean having neither the one nor the other; it doesn't mean wandering in the wilderness."

"You don't understand. The ideal in Russia is social."

"It's not enough. Mass ideals are always dangerous, too. Look at Germany and Italy. But I won't argue. It's futile and tiresome. It just amused me for a moment to hear you say the things that I heard when I was twenty. But as Ezekiel says, America always discovers ideologies fifteen years too late. It discovers them at the moment of their decline."

He flared strangely. He sprang up and faced her.

"Ezekiel! I suppose you mean that Frosch person. Frosch! Mother is an awful fool. But she was right enough evidently when she told me that you'd fallen disgustingly under the influence of those people. Are you in love with that fat imbecile?"

She rose, too.

"Julian!"

He frowned and turned aside.

"Of course I didn't mean that. Don't be a fool. You knew I didn't. But those people are taking you away from me."

"From you? What do you mean?"

"I want you! You must know that."

She looked at him. His face was taut and pale and desperate. She sat down again. She stretched out her hands to the fire.

"Poor Julian! I've found a little peace; you grudge me that. There's nothing I can be to you or do for you."

He fidgeted. He let himself drop back into his seat. He leaned forward. His eyes were now insistent.

"What do you call a little peace? Into what have those people fooled you? Tell me that."

She watched the blue-and-orange tongues of flame. They were too regular, too artificial. They gave more warmth than cheer.

"I'll tell you. I'll try."

"Very well. Let's hear."

He was forcing himself to use an ironical tone.

Slowly Gina spoke.

"I'm just an ordinary human being who had to meet and face a dreadful fate. There are things we all expect. People are sick. People die. But I and the others like me—well, we were attacked by something. . . . You ought to be able to explain it better than I. None of us believe in ghosts, do we?"

He shook his head.

"Suppose a ghost appeared and throttled your dearest before your eyes. Wouldn't you have to revise all your notions?"

"It's a nonsensical supposition. But for the sake of the argument . . ."

"It's not nonsensical," she cried. "It *is* like that. The deeps *did* open at our feet. Monstrous things *did* happen."

"Have it your own way." His voice was dry. "Go on."

"I was lost. I was a lost soul. There was no place for me. There was no place for my little boy. Now we've both found a place. We've found our little corner in the world that is ours. Ours. Our own."

Julian laughed harshly.

"Mother tells me you embroider mottoes."

"I've always had a knack for such things. But they seemed useless. But these Sabbath cloths we embroider are sold and the money goes to help the medical service of our people in Palestine."

Again he laughed.

"I once knew a girl who sewed clothes for the missionaries to give to the heathen babies."

"I don't think I should ever have laughed at that. But I wouldn't have quite understood it. Now I do. The world is stupid and evil. Terribly stupid and terribly evil. There are great persons who can resist the evil in the world in a great way. But for ordinary people like me small things must be enough. Yet if all the ordinary people will do some small humble useful unselfish thing every day—don't you think it might help? You see, Julian——"

She hesitated. He looked up with a sombre look in his black eyes.

"Go on, go on!"

"You've never encountered evil or suffered from evil yourself in your own person."

"Haven't I? Oh, haven't I, just? Do I look or act very radiant?"

"No. I didn't say that. Yet you have so much!"

For a moment he threw up his hands. He let them drop. He reassumed his studied impassivity of gesture. But his eyes smouldered.

"It's dust and ashes. It's like grit between my teeth. It had to be bought and paid for bit by bit, and the price was too high for the article. I took both my arts and my medical degrees *summa cum laude*. Hell! That was easy enough. I've got the surgeon's eye and hand. Moreover, I've got a hunch in diagnosis. I can smell it out! And yet I tell you that they would have ditched me if my father had been less wealthy and less foolishly generous—if indirectly he hadn't bought me the little I got before I had a chance even to deserve it."

He stopped to light a cigarette.

"That was more or less so in Germany even in the best days," Gina said. "I realized that, of course, recently and late."

"That doesn't help me. I don't see how it helps you. I don't see how talk like that helps anybody. The fact is you go through life like somebody with a hideous birth mark. You've seen them: half of the face a smudge of filthy reddish brown. You pay and pay to have the mark forgotten, to have it overlooked. It isn't—not ever. They say by implication or *look* by implication: Don't worry! You haven't got it, not *you*. And the more they say it and the harder they

look it, the more you see that they believe in its existence."
He laughed. "And the cosmic howling joke is that it isn't
there, it doesn't exist, that it's unadulterated superstition."

Slowly Gina shook her head.

"What do you mean," he cried, "by shaking your beautiful stupid head?"

"The birth mark is there. Only it isn't ugly and it isn't
disfiguring. It's noble and tragic. Stupid and vicious people
pretend that it's ugly for reasons that haven't a thing to do
with it or us. I have come to be glad that I bear that great
mark; my little Gabriel, thank God, is already glad."

"Jesus Christ! what unscientific drivel! How do you get
that way?"

She put her hands to either side of her head. A pang
stabbed her. Kurt had loved that gesture of hers. Her voice
was soft.

"You must love the Jewish people, its martyrs and its
leaders and its humblest too."

He blanched and then reddened with anger and disgust.

"Love! I've loved no one. Mother is a fool and a hypo-
crite. Father? I don't know what he is. I've never known.
He was alderman of Ozark City two terms. That's what he
is—an alderman. He's cleaned out of his innards everything
but the alderman. That's his way of hoping the birth
mark will be forgotten."

Again Gina shook her head.

"Not quite like that. His kindness to me proves it, too."

Julian half closed his eyes.

"I'm glad you're here. But his sudden accesses of Jewish
sentimentality sicken me. Anyhow, I've loved no one. I've
liked no one. The Jewish crowd disgusts me—the self-conscious Americanized crowd, and the other with its filthy
Ghetto yearnings even more."

"How about your Gentile friends? You have so many?"

He looked at her with dolorous eyes.

"They try not to peer at the birth mark. They're jolly and friendly in a superficial way. Professionally most of my colleagues are white men. But they stay in their shells as far as I'm concerned. I don't know them and they don't know me. I'm isolated, caked in ice."

"How is it that Ezekiel and Sara Frosch have Christian friends, real friends who open their hearts to them?"

"Who the hell are they?"

"A couple of professors and their wives from Western Ozark University, a Universalist minister and his wife who love to dine with them on Friday nights when Ezekiel makes *Kiddush* ——"

He jumped up and faced her.

"This is the twentieth century, Gina. Let's cut the hocus-pocus. It doesn't surprise me that the rear-guard of super-stition closes its ranks—Christian and Jew. That makes no place for me. That couldn't break the caked ice round me. That can't fill the horrible emptiness or quench the hatred I feel for such a world as this and for myself be-cause I'm a part of such a world. The whole structure is rotten, rotten, rotten! It ought to be destroyed; it ought to go up in flames. Only a universal conflagration can burn it clean. I'd like to fling the first torch. But in addition to everything else I'm a coward and I want to keep my job and position and security, although I loathe and despise the whole business so that I get sick, deathly sick, at the very thought of it. And nothing eases me and blunts the misery—neither liquor nor whores nor even the hypodermic any longer ——"

"Hypodermic?"

He tore open the cuff of his shirt. He drew up with a quick gesture the sleeves of both his coat and his shirt. His arm was splotched and dotted.

"You're killing yourself, Julian."

He leaned forward and laid his hands heavily on her shoulders.

"I believe that you could help me. I have a thirst for you— for your mouth and breasts and thighs. You're the only thing I've wanted for years. I want . . . I want . . . I want to sink into your womb . . . deep, deep. . . ."

His fingers seemed to divide her flesh. With both hands on his wrists she pushed them back. He made no resistance. He drew himself up slowly, feebly, like an old man.

She got up, too, and once more erect, they faced each other. A cold horror-stricken pity assailed her. She understood him dimly but powerfully. She was to be to him substitute and victim, her womb the mother-womb of his folk which he needed and hated, her blood the blood for which he thirsted and yet repudiated. He wanted to use her. Then he would torture her and not know why he had to torture her, and betray her because he needed to betray even the unconscious symbol of his deepest need.

"There's no use and no sense in this, Julian. You don't even love me."

"What does that mean? I want you. I know that. I may even want to hurt you. What of it? If you want me to marry you I'll marry you. Hell! That's a simple matter."

"Have you ever thought of me as a human being or of the fact that I have a child?"

He turned aside. He seemed to shrink. His face seemed to shrink into a strange contemptuous and yet uncertain smile.

"Have it your own way. Babble irrelevancies. Use sentimental verbiage. Be a fool and a liar like all the rest. I thought you were rather superior. You aren't. I'm tired. I'll go home. I'll take a hypo. I've got to have some sleep. I've got an important operation in the morning."

Slowly he walked to the door. She followed him. In the small entrance hall he picked up his hat and coat.

"If you change your mind, Gina, you can let me know."

"Sorry, Julian. There's nothing about which to change my mind."

"All right, you little fool. Good-night."

She turned and re-entered the living-room. In the middle of it stood Gabriel in bare feet and pyjamas, his face pale and sorrowful and anxious.

"Did we wake you, darling?"

She went to him and knelt down and put her arms about his sweet, slender, sturdy little body.

"Mummie!"

"Yes, my sweet."

"I think Uncle Julian is a wicked man."

"He's very unhappy, Gabriel. Maybe it's fairer to say that."

He shook his head. His eyes were solemn with the pure, untroubled, undoubting earnestness of childhood.

"He's wicked, Mummie, he's wicked. You won't let him come to see you any more, will you?"

"I don't think," she said slowly, "that he will come any more."

"Ever?"

"Ever."

A tension seemed to relax in the child. He nestled his head against her shoulder.

She took him and tucked him into bed in his little bed-room. Then she undressed and went to bed herself, and knew, as she reposed her body, that she was utterly exhausted and needed a long, long sleep.

THE SECOND BOOK:
APOCALYPSE

THE SECOND BOOK: APOCALYPSE

I

THE soul of Gabriel Weiss was a tranquil soul. How deeply the storms that had shaken his childhood had affected it he did not know. But that childhood had become as a legend to him, remoter than the time that separated it from him now, softer but also more significant than reality. On its visual side it had a preternatural clarity. He could summon its scenes before his inner eye as one turns the pages of a book of pictures. There was the garden of his grand-parents in the Grunewald, with its border of tall Scotch firs and the bushes of white lilacs; there was the apartment of his father and mother on the Eisenzahnstrasse in which he could see each piece of furniture and its place in each room; there was the school, grey stone and brown wood, filled with faces fixed for ever in expressions of fear and hate and the stealthy imitation of fear and hate; there were fountains and squares and streets in Paris, and last there was the dazzling turbulence of a summer ocean.

He could summon these images at will. Or they would come, unsummoned, at the fragrance of lilac or of fresh-baked rolls or at the acrid scent of ink. A way trees had of waving which he could never capture in words brought back Paris in that single spring of his eighth year. At first the perceptions that roused these memory pictures brought with them a touch of nostalgia. Later, only a little later, when his mind began to grasp the world, the accompanying emotion changed. He now occasionally cultivated his memory pictures in order to enjoy the relief and release of turning from them to the security and order of his accustomed world, even as one who has had a bright and colourful but troubling and disturbing dream opens his eyes to the familiar objects in the peace of his chamber and is thankful that the dream was but a dream.

He had never asked his mother to tell him in so many words the details of their last months in Germany or of his father's death. Nevertheless, he knew them. He knew them from chance remarks; he knew them from the papers that continued through the years to describe the sufferings of the rapidly diminishing community of Jews in Germany; he knew them because he knew the character of the iron age in which his childhood and his youth had fallen. He had shared his mother's moderate grief when in his early adolescence Ernst Simon had broken to her from Amsterdam at short intervals the news of her father's and her mother's death. Nevertheless, he thought of his father, whom he remembered with great exactness, far oftener than even his mother knew. In the quietude of his mind he made of him, freed so long ago now from the pangs of mortality, an heroic figure which obligated him to definite loyalties and duties.

He did not find these loyalties difficult to entertain, nor these duties difficult to practise, in the America of his day. It was a divided America; but it was divided on definite and intelligible grounds. Even before the Black Legion insurrection of 1940 the lines had been drawn. But when it was discovered that the fomenters of this insurrection, as well as the mobs responsible for the epidemic of lynchings in the South, had been the openly paid mercenaries of the munition manufacturers, even Americans who through obscure envy and obscurer fears had opposed the re-election of Franklin Roosevelt in 1936 took fright. The stubborn American romanticism concerning the oligarchs, which derived from the old frontier hope that each man or his son might become one, perished at last. It was seen that a small group of men no better than others, and probably originally no worse, had been willing, for the mere preservation of their power, which did not even add to their human happiness, to plunge the nation into bloody civil war, to break with every instinct and tradition of kindliness and freedom, to establish a cruel dictatorship and to sell out America to the hordes of Fascist barbarians who were even then butchering their path through the Ukraine.

And so it came about that from 1940 on there developed a growing movement of solidarity among all liberal and libertarian parties, the Roosevelt Democrats, the Progressives, the Farmer-Labor people. These in turn formed strong alliances with the rapidly extending co-operatives of all kinds, the Farmers' Co-operatives, the Consumers' Co-operatives, the Small Manufacturer's Co-operative Union, the Householders' Protective League, and the Freeman's Educational Units Association. These interlocking movements and mutually implicated influences had arisen gradually but spontaneously among the American masses. Hence they were no longer, as politics and economics had once been, preoccupations of either a season or a crisis, but definite expressions of the total will of American men and women toward a freer and a better way of human life. They provided, as it were, the medium within which society lived and functioned.

Nor could this great grouping of people ever become slothful or inattentive to its rights and needs. Its majority position was never certain or secure. Again and again reactionary leaders roused immense sections of the backward masses to opposition. Since the benefits of the economic technique of co-operation could not be denied, these leaders and their henchmen had recourse to the old rituals of evil myth, asserting that the neo-liberals were chiefly led by Jews or, which was far truer, did not discriminate against Negroes or were secretly plotting to involve the United States in those sporadic but bloody conflicts by which Europe was gradually preparing the second world war. Men not uneducated and otherwise sane were found in the ranks of the sullen reactionaries in every town, in every city. Gabriel never forgot an observation which he had heard Ezekiel Frosch make at a modest little party which his mother gave on the occasion of his becoming *Bar Mitzvah* a Son of the good deed or command [Confirmation] in 1939. Some one asked Frosch, who was an untiring worker in the Jewish Section of the Freemen's Educational Units Association, why a group of the alumni of Western Ozark University was suddenly calling for the formation of groups of armed vigilantes. "Man," Frosch had said with humorous sententiousness—"man does not live by bread alone; certain varieties of the species need their daily cup of poison." Later in the psychology classes conducted by Dr. Schoenfeld in the graduate department of the Jewish Unit of the Freeman's Association Gabriel had learned that that daily cup of poison is in reality an antidote against the ravaging of other and more corroding poisons that certain men—unlucky creatures!—brew, unaware of them, within their hearts.

Yet all these circumstances, both the positive and the negative circumstances, tended to make the adolescence and early youth of Gabriel and his contemporaries—the boys and girls born around 1925—much more coherent in aim and unified in spirit and endeavour than the preceding American generations had been. Hence they were in essence happier. The hectic and artificial flirting with Russian folk-bolshevism, always a defence against aimlessness and an escape from an unguided reality, had died down very rapidly after the middle nineteen-thirties. The anti-Roosevelt campaign of 1936 had been a danger signal which none could refuse to see. Its irrational bitterness and foul unfounded accusations, its

frenzy against Franklin Roosevelt and his advisers born of
the very fact that these were men of culture, peace, moderation, good-will, had alarmed and aroused all who were not
willing to see America gradually sink into the tribal stupe-
faction, with sadism and blood as opiates, which had been
creeping like a leprosy over nation after nation. Men and
women in their middle years sent forth a ringing call. The
first neo-liberal groups were founded. The youth of the land
that was not quite blinded by drunken doctrine saw suddenly that its job and its duty were here at home, here and
now, and that the equal brutalities of Berlin and Moscow and
the equal brutalities of the Spanish civil war had nothing
whatsoever to do with that job and that duty. It rallied
and came home. Instead of staring at the paper promises of
the Communist Manifesto it went to work. As early as 1938,
it will be remembered, there were founded the first of those
Youth Colonies of the internal colonization movement which
borrowed their technique (though the admission of this was
often inhibited) from the co-operative freehold villages of the
Jewish resettlement in Palestine. At this time, too, came the
liberating common-sense answers to those problems that had
been so unendurably complicated and sophisticated. If cen-
tralization and mechanization are either destroying us or
leading to the servile state, whether called Fascist or Communist, then in God's name, let us decentralize and let us
curb mechanization. As early as this began here and there
that voluntary abstention from traffic with chain-stores, from
the indiscriminate purchase of articles only because national
advertising vulgarized and dizzied, which was in later years
seen as perhaps the chief measure which saved American
economy during the isolation of the second world war. In
industry, in commerce, in education, the small unit system
came into vogue and use. Gradually, therefore, property was
redistributed. Men were amazed to see a spontaneous rebirth
of high religion and an equally amazing support of sound art

as hundreds of thousands substituted the aim of independence for the aims of wealth and power, and so began to conceive of themselves again as the pillars and creators, not the slaves and objects, of their state and their society. It belonged to them; therefore they loved it again. They made it; therefore they cherished it. Patriotism, which had been for ages the first refuge of the power-brute or the common sadist, because once more part of the normal sanctities of life.

During Gabriel's early youth these principles and movements, the flowering of which he was to watch amid tempests that shook the world, were slowly but powerfully germinating. He and his contemporaries watered the ground; they tended the faint green shoots that broke the crumbling earth. They were filled with purposes that gave form to their lives—that form which had been sought in vain. They knew suddenly what had been so long forgotten, that only form means freedom; that freedom consists in choosing the form of your life; that he who has not chosen a form is not exercising liberty but is being a slave of chaos or of some brutal Moloch of monstrous form, whether oligarch or totalitarian state.

In 1941, when Gabriel was only fifteen and attending the recently founded Jewish Junior College Unit, Dr. Julian Jacoby had finally to be placed permanently in an asylum for the insane. The case puzzled his colleagues. He had kept his drug-addiction within definite limits. They had observed no specific paranoiac symptoms. He had grown more morose. Then had come periodic outbreaks of great violence. He had roared that he was King of Africa and that his bidding must be done. Next he had shown bitten stigmata on his wrists, declaring that these were the marks of the chains of a galley-slave. Gina, though in these later years she had seen him but rarely, had always kept a wistful pitying tenderness for him. After all, he had offered her all he had had to offer. She had accepted autumn as the longest season of her life; in retrospect she cherished the image of that last blaze of summer which Julian might have brought her. Though she was barely forty now and her face had only a few faint lines, she had grown grey rapidly though irregularly. Strands of pure white alternated with black in her thick hair, which, as of old, swayed forward like a bell when she inclined her head.

"Poor, poor Julian," she said. "Albert is so feeble, feebler than his years. He won't survive it."

She was sitting opposite Gabriel in the small sun parlour that served as a dining-room. He was almost as tall as she. Despite his intellectual ripeness for his years, he still had, especially with her, many childlike moods. Now, however, she watched an almost stern expression come over his face.

"Yes, Mummie. But Aunt Julia will do worse. She'll invent funny excuses."

"Can you blame her, after all?" Gina asked.

"No. But what did any of you expect?"

"I've noticed before," Gina said, sadly, "that you children of today are all hard."

"I don't think we are, Mummie. But think of Julian! You know the story best. He didn't want to be anything he was; he didn't want to feel anything he felt. According to his notion of scientific fact he wasn't what he was and had no business to feel or want what he actually felt or wanted. And everything and everybody round made him feel that it was just grand to take that attitude. So he devoured himself and went crazy."

Gina laughed.

"Gabrielchen, that's too clever even for you. Where did you get it?"

He laughed too.

"Lecture on the psychology of culture groups by Dr. Schoenfeld at the Unit. But honestly I understood it almost before he'd said it because it's so obviously true."

"Yes," Gina said, slowly, "it's obviously true. How lucky

you children are to find it so! We had to fight so bitterly
hard for that truth. So very, very hard!"

She looked at her son. There was still something exquisitely
childlike in the pure contours of his face. No hard hand of
fate had yet made harsh the lines. But the forehead was
even now the thinker's forehead, and the unconscious gesture
with which he brushed aside a dark lock that had a way of
falling forward was also the gesture of man pondering and
so helping to shape the nature of things. She experienced a
lifting of the heart. At least it had been given to her and
Kurt to bring into being one who was higher than they, one
who was—how well she remembered Kurt quoting to another
purpose the phrase of Nietzsche—an arrow of yearning toward a farther shore.

"Psychology is a new interest with you, darling, isn't it?"

"Maybe. But I'm going to stick to it. You know what a
dumb-bell I am when it comes to science? Well, this is science, too. But it means something."

He hurried off. The Young Judeans were that afternoon
acting as hosts to the Youth Units of the Unitarians and Neo-
Anglicans. Since Gabriel's own section of the Young Judeans
was Conservative in religion with Neo-Chasidic leanings, he
and his friends and the young Neo-Anglicans understood
each other very well. They all agreed religion to be so inevitable an expression of the soul that its central assumptions
could be set and fixed in a realm of truth over which non-
creative processes of proof simply had no control. To this
the young Unitarians occasionally objected. They criticized
the self-limitation of the reason. Today, however, as Gabriel
knew, such questions would not be touched. It would be a
political meeting. Unannounced and unprovoked the German
air fleets had just made a mass attack on England. They
had come like a cloud of locusts darkening the sky. They
had belched flame and poison. Streamers of fire had by some
new and secret device unfurled from them and scorched paths

of destruction through the land. Nearly a thousand civilians had been killed; several million pounds' worth of property had been destroyed. Nevertheless the British War Office had been able to issue the announcement that, such an attack having been not wholly unexpected for years, this particular one had been repulsed by anti-aircraft devices, that the British air fleet had barely gone into action and sustained only insignificant losses, while three-hundred and nineteen enemy planes had been brought down.

So far, so good, thought Gabriel as he walked across the park to the Jewish Junior College Unit Building. He had not, except by a few words at breakfast, discussed this burning matter with his mother. She had been preoccupied by the tragedy of Julian Jacoby; she winced inwardly, he knew, at any mention of the Germans and the German menace in the world, although she still loved and read the poetry books of her youth and had taught him to love them. He knew, too, and with the inner tranquillity native to him, understood well the peace she had found and in which she had clothed herself more and more, as the years had gone on, as with a garment. He looked up at the brightness, already a little too intense on this Mid-Western plain, of the sky of spring. He stopped in the park here and there to contemplate for a moment uncurling leaf and early blossom.

So far, so good. Only latest Associated Press bulletins had revealed the fact that, under cover of that air attack on England which, had it been more successful, would without doubt have been repeated at once, five German divisions, stealthily concentrated on the eastern frontier of the Reich had, unresisted, crossed over into Poland and that, at the same time, an equal Italian army had passed through Innsbruck. The long delayed Fascist attack on the world had begun. Would France strike? That was the question that seared every liberal heart in the world. Could France strike? Or would the French reactionaries rise and seek to overthrow the Socialist

Republic the moment a French soldier left the line of impregnable fortifications along the frontier of the Reich? And men asked also: would the Czechs strike? Or would they in turn be paralyzed by the nazified Germans in Egerland? The worst of all was that America seethed with the unconscious and misled slaves of the munition trusts and the financial oligarchs, who, desiring as of old to fatten on blood, had never let die down the slogan that Communism was the enemy and that the Germans and Italians, whatever the faults of their internal régimes—such lip service to American tradition these people still paid—were the crusaders for property and civilization against the Red Terror.

Now every child had known for years that there was no Red Terror any more in the revolutionary and therefore flamelike and incandescent sense. The Soviets had settled down to a placid, hard-working, poverty-stricken state-capitalism with pseudo-democratic trimmings. It was precisely as though some super-Morgan-Dupont Trust had swallowed all the wealth of the nation and paid all expenses out of its own pocket and reinvested all surplus capital. Favoured classes of the government trust were given, so to speak, better rations—housing, clothes, food, even trips abroad. The vast majority of the Russian millions toiled as the masses toiled everywhere for bare subsistence. There was as yet no unemployment partly because the mechanization and industrialization of Russia was far from complete and also because capital surplus could constantly be reinvested in works that provided labour and in an army of ever vaster size. There was little liberty and less creativity within the people. Life had become unendurably dull. Innumerable small sharp revolts sprang up. But these did not shake the gigantic state-trust, for they were religious revolts, outbreaks of deathly impatience with the endless, the cruel, the unexampled monotony and aridity of Soviet life. Spontaneously here and there men turned from their machines and their barracks and

their shops and their state-controlled sports and amusements
and went into the woods and fields and mountains to practise primitive and orgiastic rites. They heard voices and saw
visions and danced naked by moonlight round images of
which the symbolism was immemorial, nameless, and dark.

Oh yes, the American liberals and their children knew
concerning all this. The Jews knew best of all. For to them
came the cry of their Russian brethren not, as from Germany
and Poland and Rumania, for bread and garments, but for
machsorim, books of liturgy and prayer and for Hebrew
Bibles and Hebrew books of a secular character, too, which
were all forbidden to be printed in the Soviet Union, but were
now smuggled without much difficulty from Sweden on across
the Finnish frontier and distributed from Leningrad. The
Russian Jews, grateful enough for their comparative physical
security, their mass settlements in the Crimea and in Biro-
Bidjan, and the permission granted them to speak Yiddish,
had returned to the essential faith of their fathers and knew
that they were in exile in the Soviet Union, too. They had
in the early days been misled by the Trotzkyist pseudo-mes-
sianic, pseudo-Jewish prophetic dream of world revolution
and of a messianic age on earth. They had now long known
that Russia had taken a foreign theory and turned it into a
Russian national movement and civilizatory structure which
was an enormously reformed replica of the Tsarist régime.
They knew that the comparative toleration of themselves and
other national minorities was due to the recognition that the
old autocracy had heaped up useless hatred against itself.
They no longer identified Russia with a better world to
come; it was simply in this age an easier exile than many of
the other exiles on earth.

With the pure unsullied flame of indignation which extreme youth knows Gabriel determined to present this knowledge of his at the meeting of the Youth Units, especially for
the benefit of the Neo-Anglican section, whose members were

still sometimes troubled by the blare of the reactionary
papers that America should join the universal crusade against
the Red Terror of Communism. There had, Heaven knows,
been a Red Terror—he had read a few books—twenty and
even fifteen years ago. Today, he would tell his Christian
friends once more, today in 1941 there was only one Terror
and that was the Fascist Terror, one and one only and the
implacable foe of humanity itself and of them all. And for a
moment he saw himself standing before his young friends
and comrades and the three leaders who would be there, per-
suasive, eloquent, ardent. But at once shame at this vision
overcame him and he could literally feel his cheeks burn and
tingle. What lack of humility! What ignoble substitution of
the self for the cause! He ought now to penalize himself by
not speaking at all. Moreover, most of the boys and girls in
the Units were older than himself. And also, at bottom, there
were things he cared so much more about, if only in this
dark and catastrophic age one could dare to withdraw oneself.

He lingered still a little in the park. There was a tree—he
knew that tree personally, so to speak—which had rosy buds
and leaves of the same hue. It seemed to be both exotic and
at home. The very form of its branches was subtly other
than the forms of the branches of any tree there. Of that tree
and its blending of foreignness, of otherness, with healthy
earth-rootedness here in this park in Ozark City he had written verses. He had known that tree season after season. Each
spring it had raised the banner, as it were, of its distant and
unfamiliar beauty. For long he had merely seen it with the
outer eye. Gradually seeing had become vision. Vision had
grasped that tree creatively. Sitting up late one night at his
small desk in his small room while his mother slept he had
written the verses concerning that tree. He knew the verses
were not very good. He was fifteen. How could they be?
His training had been sound enough to make him see that.

Both at school and at junior college the modernistic slip-shodness of the earlier twentieth century had been abandoned. Playfulness was no longer called creative impulse nor any kind of showing off spontaneity of expression. Understanding reverence for the masters and one's own humility before them had been taught. Gabriel had already studied both five plays of Shakespeare and three books of *Paradise Lost* as well as Vergil, on the one hand, and both Jehuda Halevi and Bialik on the other in the original Latin and Hebrew. At home he had read his mother's few German poetry books over and over again—the poems of Goethe, the poems of Rainer Maria Rilke—that tranquil rich and subtle voice of a Europe, of a humanity seeking to save itself and having the wisdom and the vision and not the strength—that voice of the three mingled strains of blood that were the poet's: German and Slavic and Jewish. Already it seemed to Gabriel, already—and here on this day of spring under this faintly exotic tree it came all over him again—that in certain verses of this poet which he knew by heart and had so learned not by any effort but by poring over them again and again, there lay the great secret, *his* great secret, the solution of a central mystery, the mystery that he must know and live in order to be at all. They floated into his mind—those verses, they spoke out of his soul:

> What we o'ercome is the diurnal.
> Even our successes make us small.
> The unaccustomed and Eternal
> Will not bow down to us at all.
> It is that Angel who contended
> With warriors in old histories,
> Who felt their adversary straining
> With sinews that, like metal, gaining
> Tautness, beneath his hands extended
> To harp-strings of deep melodies.

Whom this great Angel overcame
That oft the humbler foe rejected,
In light and righteousness erected
From that stern hand goes forth his frame
By moulding as of God completed.
No victories can make him free.
His triumph is: to be defeated
By ever loftier powers than he.

The boy under the tree in the park murmured: "No victories can make him free." Jacob had wrestled with the Angel. Because he had been defeated he had been called Israel. To wrestle with the Angel and to be defeated, that was to be an Israelite. That, too, was to be a poet. . . . By a sudden impulse he looked at his watch. He laughed at himself. It was past the time for the meeting to start. He had hurried forth so bravely and ardently. He had stopped to dream by the wayside. Luckily Dr. Aaronson, the Young Judean leader for the Ozark City district, understood him. He had been late at the last single Unit meeting and Aaronson had laughed and quoted: *Hineh, ba'al ha-chalomoth!* ("Look, the master of dreams!"). He had asked if they had not better call Gabriel Joseph hereafter. So Gabriel ran.

II

ONCE more the Germans had dreamed of a short and merry war. The insane violence of their need to overcompensate an inferiority feeling of gigantic depth had made them see themselves once more as the swift dictators of the world. They had counted, not wholly without apparent cause, on Britain's decay and senescence. From the middle thirties of the century on Britain had repeatedly submitted to humiliation or had, as in the Palestine disorders of '36, forborne to strike until irreparable and preventable damage had been done. What the German camarilla sitting under a huge swastika in the Wilhelmstrasse, stiff with braid and decorations, shaven of head, brutal of jaw, could not understand was the sincere hesitancy of all classes in England to plunge the world into war. It had come over England that war was stupid and violence barren. She wanted something better, other, more.

By 1941 this hope was seen to be dead. Nor had it needed the air attack of that spring to teach the lesson of hopelessness. Britain had slowly and carefully made her preparations. She did not, as the Germans had expected, return the air attack. Instead, a highly mechanized army, long prepared, sailed in transports from Haifa and from the restored Cyprian port of Famagusta. It landed on the Greek mainland opposite the island of Thrasos. Greece had been uncertain for years on which side of the coming war her profit would lie. There was not a soldier in sight. Bulgaria had been quietly bought with both gold and promises. In less than a month the British forces had completely demolished the Rumanian oil-wells, destroyed the railroads,

blasted the factories, smashed all machinery, left the Rumanians nothing but their lives and the corn of their fields.
Then the British withdrew. They had had a few skirmishes
with Hungarian troops who reluctantly came to the rescue
of the effeminate Rumanians. That was all. The German
armies could not march without Rumanian oil.

The French armies had been massed in Normandy. But
that had been a feint. The government knew that the armies
were loyal to the Republic. France declared a state of emer-
gency, cut off all communication with the outside world,
and suspended all civilian travel. At the end of two weeks
the cables spoke again. Thousands of Fascists, the entire
moral leadership of the *Croix de Feu* organizations, were
on their way to French West Africa, there to be guarded
by a few Algerian regiments. The chief military forces of
the Republic were switched south and were pouring over
the passes of the maritime Alps in Lombardy. Sharp fighting
took place. But the Italians, who during the first World War
fled even before the Austrians at Caporetto and who, once
a free people, had now been stupefied and corrupted by many
years of dictatorship, were nowhere a match for the brilliant
valour and intellectual energy of the French. Turin and
Milan fell. As the British had done in Rumania, so the
French destroyed thoroughly and scientifically the industries of Northern Italy. Then, contrary to all the old usages
of war, the French armies, protecting their rear by swarming planes, withdrew to the shelter of their Alpine fortresses.
Meanwhile the combined British and French fleets block-
aded both Germany and Italy. The cables flashed the news
of one Germany victory after another over the Soviet armies
at the Russo-Polish frontier; Mussolini announced with his
bad rhetoric which had grown worse year by year, that
his ever victorious armies, swollen by all loyal Austrians,
would soon stand before Vienna, shatter the hesitant and
divided Czechs at Bratislava, and join the equally invincible

German hosts at Cracow. The Western democracies waited in apparent inaction. Their only moves were to choke, to destroy if necessary, any source whence coal or iron, petroleum or cotton, chemicals or machinery or machine parts, could even trickle into the territories of the dictatorships.

From this circumstance arose the troubles in America. The industrial oligarchs said that the United States must join the crusade against the Red Terror. They meant that they wanted to sell war supplies, defeat all liberal opposition in America, and teach the French Socialists and the British Labourites what they considered a needed lesson. They would not have objected to selling to both sides, although they hoped that the dictatorships would win. But since they did not quite dare plead business, they inaugurated what they called a crusade against the Progressive administration which had been elected in 1940 and had a solid majority in Congress. Sharp laws against selling war material to either group of belligerents had been passed. All the new Unit groups and organizations of the land were privately and publicly, despite their passionate sympathy with the Western powers, vigilant to see that these laws were enforced. Private motor-yachts and speedboats made themselves the willing auxiliaries of the Coast Guard service. Thousands of manufacturers, Christian and Jewish, pledged themselves to investigate the ultimate source of every order. In reply the Liberty Leaguers deliberately sabotaged certain industries, suddenly increased the masses of the unemployed, hired strikebreakers and other hoodlums to organize these dazed breadless men into cohorts of the Black Legion, and thus provoked the insurrection of October, 1941, in which hundreds of Negroes as well as eleven Jews and eighteen liberal leaders of New England lineage were assassinated. When at the end of a month the insurrection had been stamped out, the Liberty League press bureaus announced that nearly 800 Americans had been butchered in order that Communist world conquest might march on. A Congressional committee at once undertook a very public investigation of these charges. The povocative plot of the Liberty Leaguers was exposed in glaring detail. Even Old Guard Republicans of the 1936 vintage hid their heads in shame and remembered that they were Americans.

Thus by Christmas, 1941, America was comparatively at peace. The first dream of both the Italians and the Germans of a gallant war of movement, of armies sweeping onward like those of Attila and Tamerlane of old, had come to a muddy and dolorous end. Two lines of deep fortified trenches stretched from the Dniester River to Vitebsk and Polotsk. The German and Italian press bureaus announced that all immediate objectives had been gained. In spring Japan would strike in the East and before summer the great armies of the new empires would stand at Odessa and command the Black Sea. Fleets of Turkish transports would then set out from Istamboul and all Asia Minor would lie at the foot of the conquerors. The net of Turkish railroads had long been completed. Division after division of the united Fascist legions would be transported over Angora and Aleppo to Damascus and it would not be long before the proclaimers and heralds and prophets of the new heroic age would enter and symbolically make level with the earth that miserable city of Jerusalem whence had issued those twin slave religions and moralities of Judaism and Christianity to corrode and corrupt century after century the hard refulgent splendour of the peoples of the North.

"*Nu,*" said Ezekiel Frosch to a group of young men and women whom he had gathered at his house, as once or twice a month he loved to do, "*nu,* they're not so far yet. At present they're stuck in the mud and the Soviet army is big and well equipped. The Japanese attack in spring will be a separate war. It won't relieve the Ukrainian front. The Russians counted on both wars. They had the man power to do so. In addition, thank God, there are three British divisions in Palestine and Transjordania and two French divisions in Syria, and our *Yishub* in *Eretz Yisrael*, as you children well known, now counts over a million souls. We hate fighting and loathe it and don't believe in it ever. It's strictly a *goyim-naches*, a Gentile pleasure. But you know and I know that we will defend Britain and the British occupation and *Yerushalayim* as the Holy City of all human decency and of all Western civilization to the last man." The young people cheered him. "Wait," he said, "listen! The danger is at home in our own country. We must fight for the Units, political, economic, and cultural, and for the co-operation of the Units to sustain strong libertarian and neutral administrations. If the Liberty Leaguers and the Black Legions get hold of the country and begin exporting foodstuffs and war supplies and help the Fascists to realize only a portion of their dreams, then"—he laughed a little—"then we can all kiss ourselves good-bye, all of us, Jews, Christians, agnostic democrats and libertarians— everybody who isn't a crook, a brute, or a slave. So, as they used to say in the first World War that seems ancient history to you: Keep the home fires burning. Buy your gas and oil and shoes and cutlery and groceries of Unit merchants. See to it that your unit merchants buy their merchandise from Unit manufacturers. See to it in every department of life that property keeps widely distributed. A free property-owning man will want to remain the citizen of a free state. A corporation slave won't even notice a change of masters. Trust today, Fascist state tomorrow. He won't know the difference till it's too late."

These matters Gabriel, like nearly all the young people he knew, kept warm and living in his faithful heart. And he learned from his mother how lucky he was, though this was, of course, very hard for him to realize. She told him how in her youth no one had been free happily to be what he needed or wanted to be; everyone, not only the Jews, had felt it necessary to conform to standards of thought and feeling imposed by social and political pressure; therefore nearly every one, if only he dug deep enough into his inner realities, had been desperate and in the end aimless. Now in America within their circles and their groups Jews could be Jews again and Christians Christians, and each group wanted the other to be what it needed to be in conformity to its ultimate nature, and these groups, recognizing and respecting their complementary differences, were co-operating toward the ends which were the common denominators of their varying faiths and inheritances: peace, freedom, release from slavery to the machine, the redistribution of property, the protection of the workers, the more intelligent grounding of those central sanctities which stamp man as human.

But the greater part of Gabriel's life was not now or in the years that followed very constantly preoccupied with these matters, deeply as he believed in them and adhered to them. Rhythm had quivered in him early and words had been incantations to him as far back as he could remember. It was not until he was sixteen that he knew that he wanted to be a poet. Or, at least, he had not uttered what seemed to him the presumptuous word. A teacher at the junior college did that for him, not, as it happened, the teacher of English, but of Hebrew literature. For Gabriel seemed the only student in the class who could grasp the immensely intricate technique of the poems of Jehuda Halevi. He alone heard at once all those answering bells of rhyme. He translated one of the simpler of the poems, the *Khochbei Thebel* ("Stars of Earth") and repeated over and over to himself *Khochab mizrach ba la-ma'rav* ("Star of the East hath westward come"), and wrote on that theme with that line as motto, a longish poem which, so soon as it was finished, he rejected as being jewelled and sonorous in the manner

of Elinor Wylie, that American poet of a previous generation whose legend still spoke, though with an almost archaic
accent, to the hearts of youth, but whose verses had yielded
very little to the tarnishing of time.

It was not easy in those years from 1941 to 1944 when
Gabriel was to leave the Jewish Junior Unit College and
enter the University of the Western Ozarks for a young poet
to find his way. His contemporaries, few enough in number,
failed him and it was hard to be without immediate en-
thusiasms. The opaque pseudo-communists of the late 'twen-
ties and 'thirties had faded from the scene. The aged T. S.
Eliot and his few remaining grey-haired followers droned
still to Fascist *cénacles* in London. It had been discovered
suddenly a few years before Gabriel's time that it was quite
legitimate for a poet to be difficult, provided that, like the
poets from whom this notion had been originally derived,
Mallarmé and Valéry, you were difficult about something
discoverable, the discovery of which, like that of the full
meaning of Valéry's *Le Cimitière Marin*, was infinitely re-
warding. But Gabriel did not know French. He and Gershon
Frosch had one day raided the Carnegie Library for the
volumes of the dark-browed poets from Ezra Pound's
"Cantos" to the opuscula of Spender and Tate, and had,
by special permission, taken an armful of them all. Beginning to read them to and at each other after dinner in
Gabriel's small room, they had awakened Gina after midnight by the sounds of their inextinguishable laughter. She
had slipped into a dressing-gown and come in. They had read
choice bits to her. But she had never ceased to be hesitant
about her judgement concerning things in English.

"Listen, boys, there are passages in Rilke, too, that I
couldn't quite explain."

Gabriel was serious now.

"I've thought out the difference, Mummie. Rilke always

gives you his special kind of beauty—like a Grecian vase. These johnnies give you nothing."

"Did you keep a copy of your parody of the over-stuffed sausage?" Gershon asked Gabriel.

Now the boys giggled again.

"That's what I call the group of Eliot's dense poems," Gabriel said. "But they're like Rilke in the sense that they do convey something."

"Oh, do get out your parody!" cried Gershon. "Didn't you ever show it to Aunt Gina?"

Gina smiled at her son.

"You know, Gershon, how shy he is about such things."

"It's no good," Gabriel said. "Gershon thought it did sound a lot like the sausage-poems. I can repeat it, if you like.

"The dark convolvuluses drowse
   And leave no impact on the eye,
The unmitigated crows carouse
   Under the arches of the sky.

"The trees are made of adamant;
   The brindled cat has eyes like grapes.
A nigger dreams of Charlie's Aunt
   Eerily chuckling at his japes."

"I think there's a weird beauty about that," said Gina, "in spite of the fun."

Gabriel frowned.

"You see that's why I don't show much to Mummie. She thinks it's all right because I did it. I don't want that."

Gina got up and passed her hand over Gabriel's hair.

"That's not half as true as you think, dear. But we'll let it go at that. Meantime you boys had better think about bed."

No new or striking poet, at all events, had arisen in recent years, so far as Gabriel knew, in any language. Exquisite cries of despair, like those of Edna Millay, had arisen after the first World War. But in spite of bitterer war abroad and difficult conflicts at home Gabriel's generation could make nothing of that kind of despair. That generation had, to begin with, recovered religion for itself, not as dogma nor as rigid rite and practice, but as a method of apprehending the only realities that count, the only realities that make for life, the only realities that must be conquered, whatever happens to the others, if human existence is to have either meaning or quality. It had, among other things, witnessed the gradual revolt of the scientists against the brutal and destructive misuse of their discoveries; it had glowed and mourned over the beheading of Ferdinand von Hoff in Berlin because he had refused to pursue researches which might have placed in the hands of the Nazi government a new explosive of unexampled power; it knew that several Russian chemists had been exiled for similar reasons; it had on its shelves a small book in which the bearers of venerated names, including that of Albert Einstein, had declared that it were better, save for matters of pure theory, to desist for a decade or two from all research and all invention unless a moral regeneration and an emergence of economics from the pre-scientific stage, could first assure mankind that discovery in the laboratory would not lead to insaner butchery and that ever more intricate machines would not, by robbing men of work, drive them through desperation into the battlefields.

Thus, for instance, when old-fashioned people were heard by Gabriel or Gershon Frosch or their friends, Allen Jones of the Unitarian Unit or Bertrand Sanders of the Neo-Anglican Unit, to say that the account of man's origin in Genesis was not true, the boys simply laughed in his face. For to them the most tremendous of facts—a fact literally to make one tremble—was this: that somehow, somewhere, on some day of eternity, man had been torn out of the realm of animal nature and had come to the knowledge of a thing called good and a thing called evil and to the dreadful and sublime necessities of choice and guilt. And he was still choosing—mostly evil; and he was still incurring guilt, and the unadmitted guilt was still driving him to further evil. All history, the whole present, every hour in every man's and every woman's life, cried out this central, this overwhelming reality.

When Peter Lang, now grey and somewhat crinkly of skin as fair men are apt to get, came to Ozark City in 1943 to gain new adherents for the World League of War Resisters, especially among students, he was heckled by a group of elderly men who could not forget the teaching of their earlier years to the effect that Darwin and the theory of Evolution had definitely negated the Scripture and the paradoxes of the moral life. They babbled of religion and science and of the survival of the fittest. Peter Lang heard them with tranquil countenance. Then, smiling at Gina and Gabriel in front seats, he said: "Look, when I say that the square of the hypothenuse of a right-angled triangle is equal to the sum of the squares of the other two sides, that is true. For this earth and for man it is true. When Jesus of Nazareth said that a man in order to gain his life must be willing to lose it, that is also true. It cannot be proved by a merely intellectual process like the first truth, but all human experience, East and West, Jewish, Christian, and even pagan, bears it out. All right. The two truths don't conflict. They don't even touch each other. But there is this difference between them, and all so-called modern history confirms this difference, that men can know the first truth thoroughly and yet be murderers of the body and of the spirit and in the end of themselves and of civilization, and so destroy all so-called truth which has value to man only as part of human civilization. But men who thoroughly know and understand the second truth and all the allied truths will be and do none of these things; they will preserve that humane civilization within which alone truths of a mathematical and scientific order have meaning and function. Now the past century and a half have proved up to the hilt that the over-zealous and all but exclusive devotion to scientific truths has led very nearly to the destruction of man and of civilization. We have enough weapons and enough machines. We have, in fact, too many. What we need is men and women who can use what we have to preserve the race and not to destroy it. Therefore today and for ever truth for truth—unless we learn the second truth the first is useless; it is destructive; it leads, unguided by the second, to death and hell. That is the answer."

Gina had told Gabriel long ago of Peter Lang. He again had heard from Jehuda Brenner of her living in Ozark City. So he had called her up and after his address and the long question-and-answer period that followed, he joined Gina and Gabriel, and they walked over to a little college inn not far from the hall. Peter Lang put his arm over Gabriel's shoulder.

"I suppose you can bear now to be told that I was one of the last people to see your father?"

"Yes."

"You are being all he would have become had he lived. I thought you would like to know that."

Gina had winced. The edge of that old mist of blind and hopeless pain could still touch her.

"Tell me about Jehuda Brenner," she said, softly.

Peter Lang sighed.

"I haven't seen him in a long, long time. He lives in Palestine; he travels much less than he used to. You see, no one is needed in Europe now except the relief and immigration agents for the Jewish people. There isn't a Jew in

Europe today who doesn't want to go to Palestine, except those in England and France and Scandinavia, and the people in these countries are all Zionists, too. History has done Jehuda's old job for him. I hear from him once in a long while."

"You've been in Europe recently, haven't you, Mr. Lang?" Gabriel asked.

They were settled at their table in the inn now.

Peter spoke slowly; he leaned his head on his hand; his blue eyes had in them that old look of stern and astonished pain.

"Yes. Conditions are very bad. Worse than you gather from our papers. The Soviet armies are tired; there's been any amount of typically Russian mismanagement in the last two years. And they did, after all, divert troops to Siberia instead of letting the Japanese march in and get bogged. England made another foray on Rumania. But either it was less effective or the Germans are at last manufacturing a satisfactory substitute for gas. There's intermittent civil war in Czechoslovakia, as you know. The Poles are starving. The Germans shoot them if they don't die quietly. Bullets are cheap, comparatively."

"How do the Germans feed themselves?" Gina asked.

"There's blockade-running from both North and South America. Then they just march in and steal whole harvests. They did it in Slovakia. That started the civil war. The Czechs and Slovaks accused the German Bohemians of letting the Nazi robbers through. You see, Europe is reduced to absolute barbarism. Armies, especially the German armies, live on the enemy country and simply let the native populations starve."

"Do you understand," Gabriel asked, "how we still get some of our people out of Poland, then?"

"Don't you know? Well, it's not generally known. The

Jewish Agency simply ransoms them from Poland for money and supplies. The Germans close an eye because they take the stuff away from the Poles who are always hoping they can keep some. England connives at the practice because she wants more man power in Palestine and Transjordania. It's ghastly. You'll see, the Germans will get near Moscow this summer. They, too, don't really want to fight any more. But they live on it now. If they didn't fight and steal and rob and maraud and live on added bits of conquered territory, they wouldn't know what to do."

"And France?" Gina asked.

Peter Lang sighed. "They have had to deal with vast obscure rebellions in Africa. The Socialists are for abandoning the colonial empire. A majority of Frenchmen say, not without reason, that then the Italians, now, like the Germans, on a level of primitive barbarism, will swarm in. Africa to the Equator would be lost to civilization." He turned to Gabriel. "What do you do specifically?"

To Gina's slight astonishment Gabriel answered at once, "I write—mostly verse."

The older man and the youth looked into each other's eyes.

"Poets are needed," said Peter Lang. "There are few. Is any of your stuff mature enough to be heard?"

"I doubt it," Gabriel answered. "It's not my own yet. But I've translated some Rilke, Mummie's favourite poet, to show the trend. He died many years ago. People loved his poems but didn't listen to their meaning. He prophesied all the new meanings."

Peter Lang leaned forward, but lowered his eyes. "May I hear?"

The room was still. Only a few quiet people dotted it here and there. Gabriel spoke simply but with definite marking of rhythm and rhyme:

"We in this whirl are caught.
    The whirring of time's wing,
    Hold it a little thing
In that which changes not.

"All that on speed is bent
    Shall fall from its estate;
    Only the permanent
Doth consecrate.

"Youths, O be brave no more.
    For swiftness of the way
    Nor flying spend your power.

"Repose dwells at the core
    Of darkness and of day,
    Of book and flower."

"You are right, Gabriel," Peter Lang said. "But in my youth, when these verses were probably written, nearly all people were drunken with the drunkenness of the mechanical. Lindbergh flew and the world went mad with a strange ecstasy. No one asked, to what end? Nor to what end will others fly? And now it is the battle and bombing planes that threaten to make war endless and therefore suicidal."

"Many of my generation know the answer and the meaning now," Gabriel said.

Peter Lang nodded.

"Even in my generation some did. They were too few. I pray God that you and your comrades are not too late."

III

IN 1944, having, as now was usual, taken his first degree at the Jewish Junior Unit College, Gabriel matriculated for two years of advanced studies, to be followed by whatever professional course he would choose, at the University of the Western Ozarks. He had played with the idea of going to the Jewish National University near Washington. His mother had not sought to dissuade him. Hers had been from the beginning a nature without sharp or immoderate desires. As the years went on and her knowledge of her people was increased by reading and by conversation, she had become accustomed to saying that she understood those Jewish women of another day who by either inherited means or personal activity had supported learned husbands whose studies were quite without worldly value, wholly *l'shmo*, that is, for the glory of the Ineffable Name.

It was Gabriel himself who determined to stay. Here were his friends, his mother, and his home. He was not very adventurous by nature, nor socially ambitious. Two other motives he did not so clearly admit to himself. Here in Ozark City there was already a slight belief in him. It was known that he was a poet. At this notion of his being a poet he frankly laughed. But the belief and hope of his teachers and his friends might help him to become a poet. And there was another motive which at first he chose to believe was the same. He had already met Elizabeth Warner. She shimmered in his mind. She throbbed in him like remembered music. He did not speak of her to anyone. When others spoke of her he feigned not to have heard. He was in his nineteenth year. There was a lonely altar to her in his heart.

She was, so far as that was possible in Ozark City, a great lady. She had a house, handsomer, more modern, more elaborate than Albert Jacoby's in that same park-like neighbourhood and on the only other knoll. Julia Jacoby said, "The woman will never see forty again." It was not true. Elizabeth Warner had been born in 1908 and was now thirty-six. Julia did not take the trouble to say, "And her maiden name was Kohn," since Mrs. Warner, far from wishing to conceal the fact, made it perfectly plain to all fitting hearers that her father had been a German Jew of the extremest assimilatory type who had never consorted with his fellow Jews and who, able and successful in America almost from the day of his landing, had forty years ago married a Christian girl very much as a matter of course. She and his only child and later heiress had been brought up in the Episcopal communion. No one had thought of Betty Kohn as Jewish. At twenty she had married Stanley Warner of what was considered in the Middle West an old family. Nine years later the handsome young attorney whose passion for aeronautics had dazzled her youth crashed down in his private plane and was instantly killed.

The young widow had closed the house in Ozark City and spent several years abroad. She had had a flat in London and gone for the winters to Cannes. Now she had been back home for some time, though she went to Europe every summer. And she seemed to have changed. Her old set found her no longer keen about anything they cared for. She was no longer a Republican; she played no games; she read books; she made a gift to the Jewish Junior College Unit and a smaller one to the Neo-Anglican Junior College Unit. It was at one time rumoured that she was going to marry Dr. Aaronson of the former institution. Gradually the rumour died. But she continued to open her house to the literary clubs of the units and seemed to enjoy with a vibrant glee the company of the boys and girls whom their leaders brought to her.

Delicately and with a light touch she had singled out Gabriel almost from his first shy appearance. Then one evening he had been permitted to read some verses, both original and translated; another youth from another unit had also done so. She had been gracious enough to that other whose verses were neat but unexciting. Nor had she publicly been profuse in her praise of Gabriel. Late in the evening, when the young people were beginning to drift away, she had taken Gabriel by the hand and drawn him into the dining-room. Between the emptied silver platters there were pools of strange light in the burnished mahogany of the table; the prisms of the chandeliers overhead had a magic glitter; the flowers on the sideboards were beginning to droop and to exhale a sharper and a wearier fragrance. She stood beside him there with her hair as bronze as autumn leaves, and her fair, still unblemished skin and her green eyes—not leaf green, but sea green, swift, gleeful electric eyes—and she cupped his young head in her two hands and kissed him on the mouth. "Dear poet!" Of course he had melted; of course he had glowed. Of course he carried the image and the moment in his heart. Of course upon that altar in his heart he laid his daily taciturn offerings of verse, music, memory, adoration. When others spoke of her he would not speak. Even when others praised her he was silent. He and his inviolable secret stood apart.

The opening weeks of the university were confused and noisy. There was a great hurrying to and fro across the great flat campus. A good deal of it seemed unnecessary to Gabriel and a remnant from other days. For in his time the young men and women who were definitely encouraged by the Junior Unit Colleges to pursue their studies further were those whose gifts and tastes, visible and developed with

some precision, ensured both the character and the usefulness of their higher studies. No one any longer wondered
what to "take." Gabriel, knowing that he would have to
earn his bread by teaching in a Jewish Junior College,
"majored" in English and "minored" in philosophy and
Hebrew literature. Gershon Frosch had long determined to
go in for agricultural chemistry in order to join one of the
Jewish colonies of the internal colonization movement; their
Christian friends were equally certain of their tastes and
goals: Allen Jones was taking the pre-theological and Bertrand Sanders the pre-legal courses, both quite sharply outlined. Here, too, old-fashioned "modernistic" slip-shodness
had long been abandoned; the colleges had become sieves
rather than cornucopias; registration had enormously declined in the universities; they gave higher degrees to men
and women fit for leadership by character and intelligence.

The trees on the campus were beginning to turn tobacco
brown and faintly gold and red, and a wind with a touch of
autumnal keenness was blowing and leaves flew. And then
again would come days of a perfect stillness, days of vast
blue and gold and russet, in which the season and the year
seemed to stand silent and motionless, poised and waiting.
On such days Gabriel was tempted to loiter and to wait,
poised too with the waiting year, and to stretch out his
arms toward the miracle of life, whose farthest wing had
lightly brushed his youthful burning cheek. For though he
and the boys and girls of his period had escaped through
the immediate bitter teachings of the historic process an
hundred follies and fallacies that had warped and falsified
the lives of their parents and grandparents, there was one
thing concerning which they knew no more than the men and
women of old; there was one flame that seared them still
as it had always done. They no longer called it sex. At least
not often and not very seriously. Because it was so immensely obvious now when the scientific affectations were as

dead as the earlier pseudo-spiritual affectations that sex was sex, but that it was in man sex plus infinity. Birth control devices, both mechanical and chemical, could be had in every pharmacy for half a dollar. It was nevertheless a matter of common knowledge that in the Junior Unit Colleges all over the country, though they were mostly coeducational, chastity was the rule. Occasionally there flamed up, of course, irresistible passions between two young people. These commonly ended in either betrothal or renunciation. There were no casual affairs, because it was understood that affairs were, especially for the girls, never casual, since this particular experience transformed for good or ill the entire personality. It was understood that you cannot play checkers with bits of white-hot coal nor wash your hands in molten steel.

Talk was frank and discussion even in the class-rooms open, and that helped the boys to sublimate. They also read voraciously from time to time all books concerning this central and formidable matter from Plato's Banquet to the works of D. H. Lawrence. It was Allen Jones, who had found it on his father's shelves, who had lent *Lady Chatterley's Lover* to Gabriel and Gershon Frosch. The boys had read it separately and had then met and talked about it and laughed almost as they had laughed over the dark-brow poets of the nineteen-twenties and early 'thirties. Here, they reasoned, was a woman with a crippled impotent husband who was disagreeable to boot. So she takes a lover. Not a very fortunate situation but as conventional as a Christmas card. That the lover is her husband's gamekeeper tinges the tale with a sort of Victorian horse-hair romance. But what could be more respectable than the ending? The lady and the gamekeeper get married and have a baby and go to live on a farm. What then, the boys asked themselves, had seemed to make the book significant? The vicarious exhibitionism evidently of seeing in print words long tabooed. Over these words they frankly giggled, and from the angle of 1944, saw no point in being solemn about so trivial a matter.

For all their good sense the boys had their many secret hours of suffering and sorrow, of conflict and even rebellion over the tragic discrepancy between their ripeness for love and the impossibility of fulfilment within their tradition and society. Yet when Bert Sanders dug out of the library Malinowski's account of the complete pre-marital sexual freedom among the Trobriand Islanders, they were surer than ever that the acceptance of their tragic conflict must be part of their fundamental religion, since the practice of the Trobrianders, though it might ease their immediate pangs, would irremediably destroy their future. Bert, though he had been rather triumphant about finding the book and bringing it to the attention of his friends, had been the first at one of their confidential meetings to declare its uselessness. "It's all part of the pseudo-scientific racket that went on in our parents' time. It's interesting and it's fascinatingly mysterious how those girls never got pregnant till they wanted to. But it has no bearing. You can't argue from the primitive to us. It's silly. You can't even argue that Richard Roe will do a thing because John Doe within the same culture has done it. All these analogies and inferences from origin or supposed origin were plain foolish. I don't believe our ancestors, no matter how far back you go, ever did this sort of thing. Neither yours, Gabriel, nor mine." Gabriel had, of course, agreed. He had given a little desperate shrug of the shoulders. "It's all part of the same thing. It's like form in literature. It's like form in verse. If you don't aim after definite form you have no resistance to overcome, and instead of poetry you produce porridge. Did you ever read the free-verse stuff of the first World War period? Those people by all accounts slept round and spilt words round and shirked all the resistances that make for form. They got what they played for, more or less. Must have been fun for a while, though." He had sighed. A grey depression had come over him. That afternoon he had slipped into the synagogue for *Mincha* prayer. He knew what he needed—to reaffirm the fate of such a being as he was in such a universe as this; to re-embrace his *kind* of humanity; to be strengthened against the temptation of sloth and flight. He sought to concentrate all the forces of his young and troubled being and chanted not without a tear gathering under his lid yet not falling, *"Emeth v'emunah khol-soth v-kayam alenu* . . . Truth and faith is all this and established for us. . . ." *Emunah*—that which is trustworthy, that which does not change and on which the soul can lean, that which is so *alenu*—for us. He was tranquil when he came home for dinner. His mother, who was sensitive to him, did nothing to disturb his mood. He worked solidly that evening and slept at peace that night.

Yet it was magical to loiter under the autumnal trees and dream of Elizabeth Warner. He had seen her again just the other day and she had said in her gay, clear, decisive alto voice: "You must come to see me, Gabriel. Just you." She meant it, of course. But how was it to be done? One had, he knew, to pass the butler at her door and to be ushered into the long drawing-room and wait there for Elizabeth. Perhaps, too, she would not be at home. And to telephone for an appointment would only stiffen still further the ceremoniousness which would erect so intangible but real a barrier between them. Ah, Gabriel thought, if they could have met in fields or woods and by a sudden impulse raced each other through some glade and she had slipped on the too smooth needles of the pine which carpeted the glade and he could come upon her so and put his arms about her and lift her up. He recognized the symbolism of his revery and wrote it into one of his few sonnets, since it was so dreamily clear that the rhythm of the race through the glade was the octave of the sonnet and her faltering and slipping and his coming upon her and lifting her up, her face for that instant under his, was destined to be the sestet. So instead of attempting to see her he dreamed and wrote verses as youths and young men have done under such circumstances since the beginning of time.

As October advanced a sterner preoccupation came upon Gabriel and his world. The German armies in a last desperate effort before the setting in of winter had broken through the Russian lines. That was not the worst. Italian speed-torpedo boats had made a sudden attack, beaten off with difficulty and serious losses, upon the British Mediterranean fleets and at the same time the Arabs of the desert kingdoms had marched to the very banks of the Jordan. British airplanes manned by Jewish pilots harassed the Arabs. But the Arabs had tanks. All these things pointed to a wide-spread breaking of the British blockade of the German and Italian coasts, to the feebleness of French co-operation which had for years suffered the strain of having to keep armies on three fronts—the German, the Italian, and the Spanish, even though the Spanish anti-Fascists had never wholly given in, but carried on a continuous guerilla warfare, feebly enough helped thereto by like-minded groups in Mexico and the Argentine.

In the United States it was election year. The reactionaries represented themselves as the parties of peace and of the freedom of trade. Why should America be impoverished by not trading with half the world because the British Labor party and the French Socialists choose not to see the inevitable trend of history toward the totalitarian hieratic state? If once America gave up her craven neutrality the war would soon be fought to a finish. There would be peace, recovery, swarming international trade routes. It would mean order; it would mean money earned by promoting peace in the pocket of every American. The arguments were well and subtly calculated to ensnare both the mob and the men of mere business. The oligarchs poured unheard-of sums into the election coffers and once more threatened sabotage of industry and hunger-revolts and a march upon those colonies of the inner colonization movement which had saved the working youth of the country both physically and morally. Wild preachers of obscure and orgiastic sects went from village to village. Christ wanted peace, they said. But the Godless people in England and France and Russia would not give the world peace. Was America to continue to thrust the spear into the side of the bleeding Saviour? There was a great rolling in the dust at camp meetings; there was a great consuming of corn-whisky; the Jews had crucified Christ once before; the Jews of the world were trying to crucify him again. Was it an accident that there were no Jews in power in Germany and in Italy and in Spain and that all Jews everywhere were on the side of the Godless and Christless English and French and Russians, and that the very pivotal point of the British Empire, which ought to be the Holy Land of Christendom, was held and defended for that empire by Jewish legions?

Wealthy elderly gentlemen sat in luxurious clubs and said to each other that they hardly liked these arguments and agitations. But their sons had abandoned all scruples. The land roared. And the liberals of all parties, the Democrats and Americans of all strains, felt a terrible sinking of the heart. For they knew the mind of man and of the mob-man to be so constituted that reason and justice and freedom have little power over it. Dark passion and the accumulation of even normal frustration cause the small island of the aware consciousness to be submerged by the fierce primitive seas of the raging and formless subconscious, and to sink to those depths where lurk the frightened but untamed primordial hungers for destruction and self-destruction and death. Oh yes, the liberal leaders knew the facts by now. Danger had taught them and broken down their initial resistances.

Depth analysis was no more the plaything of maladjusted ladies. It had become the instrument of statesmen. The liberal leaders knew that the *id* was sucking in the feeble *ego* of average men as, under a neo-barbarous alternation of attack and release, it had done in Germany for many years now and thereafter in country after country. Pamphlet reprints of the terrifying third chapter of Sigmund Freud's New Introductory Lectures on the "anatomy of the mental personality." were in all hands. Free men and good men wondered as they saw the coöperatives threatening to crumble again and even merchants and small unit manufacturers selling out needlessly to the trusts and becoming the wage slaves and the political slaves of those trusts, how the *ego* was to be rescued from the *id* and some shadow of a *super-ego* to be established.

A council of all Democrats and Progressives was held. Summonses were sent out over the land to impress on men and women the crucial character of the hour in human history. Volunteers were called for of both sexes, of all occupations, of all ranks; to go from place to place, from village to village, from house to house, to plead the cause of freedom and goodness and light. Families volunteered everywhere to house and feed these emissaries; universities gave their students leave of absence and credit for dedicating themselves to the campaign work; members of youth unit organizations pledged themselves to go out among the young people of the reactionary parties, whether they were of voting age or no, to persuade them not to abandon the few gains that mankind had made through the slow and difficult ages, and to urge them to preserve themselves from the labour camps and the military servitude that had devoured successively the youth of all the Fascist countries.

Gabriel volunteered for this work. Insane though it seemed, there were small groups of Jews here and there, even in Ozark City, who hesitated, who faltered, who wondered whether they had not better swim with the stream and run with the reactionary mob, who went to the shameful length of disassociating themselves from the Palestinian people as a bulwark of British policy. And in Ozark City, as everywhere, there were men and women of mature years and of means who undertook to support and finance this movement of the young campaign volunteers. Thus it came about that Elizabeth Warner telephoned to Gabriel and asked him to be at her house on a definite day and hour and that he glowed through every vein with a double ardour. He had his insight into the workings of the eternal Eros which is generative of peace and of art and of man himself. He was its servant now. He was among its hierophants, though young and of the least. He was of those who here and in other lands were opposing that dark and immemorial aggressiveness and wish for Doom and Death which had so often brought to ruin the towers and pinnacles of some City of God.

He stood before Elizabeth now at the appointed hour, lithe and erect and as tall as she, feeling flame-tipped, as it were, knowing no cleavage between his great cause and modest mission and the bright, natural red of her lips, the lift of her breathing bosom, the whiteness of her arms that was revealed by the slashed sleeves of her frock of sea green, fashioned of that hue to match and render luminous her eyes. At once she took his hand and led him to the sofa that flanked the tall fireplace. They sat down there and she, turning to him, leaned forward and folded her hands upon her lap.

"Have you exact instructions, Gabriel?"

"I'm first to work here in the city among the Jewish groups that have no Jewish affiliations. They're frightened in the wrong way. So frightened that they forget that balloting is secret."

"Yes, yes," Elizabeth assented. "My poor dear father

used to go to all kinds of lengths to show that, though he was a Jew, there was nothing in his life that was Jewishly motivated. He would tell people things that were none of their business, that they didn't expect him to tell. Oh yes."

"And next," Gabriel said, "I'm to go for ten days to the small towns in the state and see the young people in the Units there to be sure that all who can vote do so and are not intimidated, and also that they try to give courage to their parents."

Elizabeth reached over and took his hand in both of hers.

"It's wonderful for you, Gabriel, in spite of all the horrors in the world. It's a new kind of knighthood, isn't it? In my youth we were so stupid and so purposeless!"

His throat throbbed with an exquisite small fever.

"You could never have been that," he said.

"Oh you darling!" Her cry was soft. "I was, quite desperately so. I was until poor Stanley was killed and I found that I couldn't grieve except in an impersonal kind of way. Gradually it became so clear to me how empty my life had been—how ghastly."

He looked at her and their eyes met and came to an understanding which Gabriel dared not accept.

"I had no chance," she said, slowly, "to give anyone anything. There was nothing really deep that anyone needed of me. Stanley wasn't even interested in children. He was interested in speed. I know now that speed is flight and substitution—naked speed. He wasn't using speed to save anyone. All the people in that crowd were playing a game. So to me—I think now it was to the Jew in me—there seemed no difference between winning and losing, since there was nothing worth gaining and nothing worth regretting."

Gabriel bowed his head. Beyond her words he heard another meaning. What was it? Her low clear voice had been so vibrant; her hands had not let his hand go. He felt her leaning a little nearer to him; a faint strange perfume that she always used seemed to tingle in his face.

"Gabriel!"

"Yes."

"Dare I give you a gift—a pure gift with no return and no obligation and no claim, but a gift you need to have given you?"

She drew him gently toward her. Their lips met and clung. He felt with wonder her smooth arm under his young and unaccustomed touch. He trembled. His eyes grew moist.

Her hands now on his shoulders thrust him gently back.

"I am to be a dream to you, Gabriel, a dream of youth. Nothing but that. It will not matter whether later you remember that dream or not."

"I shall always remember," he said.

She laughed a little earnest laugh.

"You may. But it doesn't matter. What is important is that it is a pleasant dream and that you do all the things you are doing more freely and more beautifully because of it. If it drugs you—you must awaken from it."

"It won't." He felt like swearing a great vow that it wouldn't, that he would gain strength and ripeness and firmness of purpose from this enchantment. "It won't," he repeated and at last he dared to breathe her name.

On that first day she did not keep him long. She had his schedule; she would be, as often as it was fitting, where he was. They would meet, too, in one or two of the smaller towns to which he was sent. These meetings were to be assured. She wanted for a period to be to him a source of strength and joy, never of anxiety and vain longing. It was from these that she hoped to set him free. She had meditated on all these matters, on all that concerned any kind of a profound relation between a man and a woman, however curious, however uncommon that relation might be.

And she had concluded that what made so many such relations spiritually barren was a lack of serenity and of balance and of measure. Lure and unreasoned withdrawal were as evil as slackness and satiety. She wanted to sustain her poet, as laughingly she called him, and be to him a bridge over a difficult and decisive period.

With that she had dismissed him. He came out into the dusk of the late afternoon and in that wooded neighbourhood in which she lived the leaves of October were thick upon the paths. A wind had arisen and the leaves danced and flew and whirled and raced, and in the West the early afterglow beyond the trees laid its orange and crimson bars, edged by mauve clouds, across the sky. One of the clouds had the form of a wing—the precise form of the pinion of some great unimaginable angel hovering over the Western edge of earth. Gabriel stood still and clasped his hands. He lifted up his face to the sunset beyond the trees. Out of the exaltation of this hour of his youth he spoke the words of the Psalmist to himself: "I shall not die but live and declare the works of the Eternal."

IV

BY A very narrow margin of electoral votes Leonidas Whyte, the candidate of the American United Liberal Parties—Democrats, Progressives, Farmer-Laborites, Neo-Liberals, Socialists—was elected to the Presidency in November, 1944. It was evident, however, that he would not command a majority even in the Lower House and that the Senate would be definitely hostile. A wave of suppressed turbulence seemed to be rolling through the land. The discipline of democracy was crumbling in America, too. There was talk of a march on Washington, of an impeachment, of a seizure of power by a furious demagogue named Gunther Hicks. A number of circumstances combined to preserve apparent peace and equilibrium; the armies in Europe dug themselves in for the winter; both the mark and the lira simply stopped being quoted as having any value that anyone could rationally assign to them in exchange for either money or goods; Britain and France, Holland and the Scandinavian countries, on the other hand, sustained their credits and their currencies. Despite the rigid censorships, it was known that the cities of Germany and Italy and Spain were decaying and that millions of people in those lands were beyond the edge of both nakedness and hunger and had to be driven to their toil by task-masters—*Zuchtmeister,* as the Germans called them—with whips. Thus reactionary turbulence in America was held in ultimate leash by certain fears. It was also an open secret that the Liberty League itself would have to send its thugs against Hicks, the illiterate Mississippian, who swore that he would not only stamp out unbelievers, Catholics, Niggers, and Jews and deprive all naturalized citizens of the franchise, but that he would lead his cohorts into the corrupt cities, especially New York, and drive out the Babylonian whoremasters and their minions from the "gilded saloons" of Fifth Avenue and Park Avenue and bring about the day when simple, strong, native Protestant whites would spit the juice of their honest home-grown plug-tobacco in the place defiled by the stinking perfumes of foreign brew.

The liberal parties, hoping for four years of comparative freedom, desisted from all political work. They had learned the lesson that democracy in its permanent nature must be grounded in a society of a certain kind. They defined this as a society in which most men had some property and the pride of that property, and in which, furthermore, by virtue of an entire metaphysical liberty, men were enabled to make this property, both property held individually and property held corporately by their group, the concrete symbol of their tastes, their aspirations, and their sanctities. For property so conceived and so held, for this house and garden, shop or farm, share in church or synagogue, school and college, where the lore of their tradition was taught, for —symbolically speaking—the ashes of their fathers and the temples of their gods—for these they would fight to the laying down of their lives. For these which constituted the instruments of freedom. Not for stocks and bonds. Not for invisible property. No; by the ownership of invisible property they were, on the contrary, sold into slavery to the remote uncontrollable forces that managed such property and paid interest and dividend. And those remote managers of invisible property were precisely the oligarchs who threatened to bring the new Dark Age of Europe to these shores.

So all the efforts of the liberal parties from 1944 to 1948 were directed to strengthening the Unit merchants' and manufacturers' movements and the unit home movements and the coöperatives by which merchants and small manufacturers' and farmers protected their individual liberties and enterprises against the ruthlessness and icy efficiency of the great corporations. It became among great groups of the people a point of honour not to work for an employer whom you could not see, with whom you could not sustain a human relationship, who was not allied to them by a knowledge and love of the craft—be it preparing drugs or weaving silk or moulding metal—which master and man both practised. Among the powerful slogans that arose was this: Own no property you cannot see! And many people did what Gina Weiss had done. She withdrew her small capital from the investments that Albert Jacoby had made for her. She caused to be built a group of model cottages about a garden with a fountain; she rented these to families for the least she could, each family having the option of buying the cottage with no profit to the owner but the five-per-cent interest on the original outlay that Gina and Gabriel needed to live on. She collected the rents herself; she learned to supervise repairs; her tenants were her friends. The change of investment cut down her income to a bare three thousand dollars a year. But both she and Gabriel felt happier and freer. Many thousands of people did similar things during this period. For it was by now thoroughly understood by the clear-minded that the enslavement of men in dictatorships, whether Fascist or Communist, came from the concentration of power, that is of capital, in too few hands and not from the holding of private property which was a necessary function of the race of man.

Later, much later, amid the sombre storms of a darkening world, Gabriel looked back upon these years as golden years. Love had been his such as first youth needs—love that is creative not yet of biological immortality, but of the hope of the escape from death through art; passionate coöperation had been his with other men in his time and country in a great battle against the evils that threatened to overwhelm the world; the adversary had met him, the adversary whom he needed both as man and poet, but also the confirmation of great voices rising from time but not its fools or slaves, and therefore sure of their resurgence on a tomorrow however far away. He had been mature for his years at every stage; now he grew rapidly into a manhood no less firm in intellectual grasp and ethical certainty for all the glow and magic of its moulding.

Elizabeth and he surveyed the world from her house in the woods near Ozark City. At first there had been a shadow. The shadow of Gina's jealousy. It came upon her suddenly that her man child was no longer wholly hers, that he who had come out of her womb and had now for so many years been her only vindication and her only triumph was seeking for himself the womb of woman. She was too intelligent to hope to halt the cycle. She had built rationalizations about her feeling drawn from the specific circumstances. Tensely she had watched Gabriel's comings and goings. One night she had sat up for him very late and out of her sufferings flung at him, when he returned, an accusation not against him but against Elizabeth.

"It's unscrupulous in a woman of her age to seduce a boy."

Gabriel had looked at his mother wide-eyed. He saw that she was suffering. He did not then understand the processes out of which those words had come. He made, of course, no denial. He could not think of any defence, for the attack was dark to him. Very simply he said:

"Elizabeth thinks her age is an advantage. It makes it so clear that she wants only to give and not to take. She's beautifully unselfish with me, Mummie. She never even asks me, when will you come? She leaves everything to my mood and impulse. I am very grateful to her."

There was a little break in his voice.

"Why shouldn't she do that?" Gina asked, with some acerbity. "It's the only way she can hold you."

Gabriel bowed his head. He reflected. Never before had he heard his mother make an observation of that character. He spoke very slowly.

"Aren't there only two ways in every human relation— the way of tenacity and the way of freedom?"

Gina looked up at her son.

"I suppose so."

"Then isn't it better to use the second way than the first? Isn't that the best that anyone can do, given the relation?"

"Given the relation," Gina repeated, bitterly. As of old she put her slender hands upon her temples.

"Does it make you very happy?" she asked, after a silence.

He nodded. His throat was tight and fevered. He wanted to explain how happy it made him and why. But something told him that his mother would be disturbed by that. He said, very simply:

"I am helped. Helped so deeply. My friends have no such help."

First she was sombre. Then she smiled wryly.

"You still love Mummie?"

He put his arms about her.

"Look, Gabriel, I don't mean to be a too possessive mother. But the circumstances are peculiar. I suppose if your father had lived . . . As it is, you and I . . ."

For the first time in years he saw her weep. His very soul seemed to dissolve and yet he dimly recognized the injustice to him of those tears. He stood up. He clenched his hands. He succeeded in making his voice sound final.

"Nothing has changed between you and me, Mummie— nothing, nor ever can. That is enough."

She too arose.

"It is enough. And even if it isn't quite true, I must be satisfied."

She held on to that little note and gesture of unwilling stoicism until one day Gabriel and Elizabeth conspired, on an afternoon on which Gabriel was necessarily at the university, to bring her to Elizabeth's house. Gabriel rather quivered at his table in the central library. He trusted in Elizabeth's tact and what seemed to him her immense winningness. And he found his mother that evening serene and almost merry and freed from the darkness that had been clouding her inner life.

Elizabeth reported to him several days later. They were upstairs in her small private sitting-room. Now it was winter and logs were burning in the grate. Outside was dusk, and through the window-panes they saw the patterns of the shapely black trees against a dim sky. There was no light in the room save that of the fire and Gabriel saw only Elizabeth's hair and eyes and white hands.

"I didn't try to generalize," she said. "That's so false, anyhow. I told Gina that you—you as you are—should be saved the ordinary sordid sufferings. Because they are sordid. Of course she asked me why I cared."

Gabriel went to her and took her hands and kissed them. "Why do you?"

"Most people would say, Gabriel, that it was the sensuality of the dangerous age. Gina had the grace not to say that. I think you know better. I do, I do love your young love. Why should I deny it? But truly I didn't *see* you more than I did the others till you read your poetry. You may not know how that is. But when one has lived here and there and met many people, one ceases to see them except quite superficially."

"So it was only my verses?" Gabriel asked, half sadly.

Elizabeth laughed softly.

"That's crude for you. There's no cleavage between your work and you. I saw *you*. And seeing you I also saw myself and my dreadful poverty. I was so poor, Gabriel, because I

was not giving myself entirely to anyone. There was no
one. There never has been anyone to whom I could give
anything that mattered. No one wanted anything of me—
neither child nor work. So I thought that *if* you needed me
I could have for a time and then later know that I *had*
had—both."

He flung his arms about her. He left her late. He was
of those—as he learned during these years—to whom love
and creation are one. There are the others who, in order to
create, withdraw into a naked asceticism and return to life,
as it were, when the work is done. Not so he. From her embraces he drew ardour for his work, and all that winter and
especially that spring he completed the first draft of the
poem which was much later to be the earliest of his works.
It was the "Moses in Egypt"—that modern reshaping of
the first mythic story of the Jews that symbolized not only
the history and fate of Israel, but also Israel's function in
the world and the nature of the nations' necessary resistance
to Israel whenever they desired to rebel against God and
raise once more the dark banners of the pagan forests of
the wild primordial world.

To him as to the poets of his own and the preceding age
the great difficulty seemed to be that of form. But this he
knew was only seeming. A great meaning would once more
beget a great form. He was sure he had the great meaning. History had given it into his hand. The peoples who
had been persecuting the Jews so bitterly since the beginning
of the fourth decade of the century were sinking into a
savagery made more ominous by the machines they could
still construct. The armies of those peoples with tanks and
planes and poison gases might still wrest territory from a
neighbour and let the inhabitants die of hunger while they
stole crops and mines and wells. But the light of humanity
had been extinguished among them. They had become
mechanized hordes literally at last like those Huns of old

who swept over Europe and left a desert where they had passed. The oppression and exile of the Jews had been the first lurid symptom and symbol of their degradation. Leaders had led the Jews forth. The myth of Moses had been reenacted, was being reënacted year by year. Its meaning was there for all the world to see.

So his great Jewish meaning, Gabriel told himself, was also a universal meaning. Only, would that meaning create a form for itself through him in the English language on this unstoried Middle Western earth under these yet unanimated skies? He wanted a form that was plastic; he wanted a form that was dense. But he wanted that dense and vibrant and plastic form to be not art, but message and thought in great humbleness, yet with often a sudden incandescence in his heart of that last nameless prophet who called himself *maleach* (messenger) or *maleachi* (my messenger), and also of those unrivalled verses of his old favourite Rilke in which that modern poet, though in a happier and more hopeful age, had prayed that he might be the dancer before a new Ark of the Covenant, the herald and the baptist of a new Messiah.

The long second summer of his and Elizabeth's love brought him his first decisive revelations. She had rented a cottage near a small New England beach. Gina had by now not only accepted the situation, but had regained her old tranquillity. And so Gabriel could go East and he and Elizabeth could be alone between sea and sky, living simply, living beautifully the life of the body which was for him at least also the life of the soul. The breakers came, truly like the long-haired daughters of Nereus, and dashed over them in fierce and joyous embraces. Or else they would sit on the dune and Gabriel, who had not seen the ocean since his childhood and had known the nostalgia of the inland-bound for the shores of earth, lost himself in visionary absorption in the waters which in unbroken expanse joined, however far away, the farther waters of the Midland Sea, so that the small waves which washed his feet seemed direct messengers from the cities and shores of the land of Israel.

He learned from the rhythm of the tides; beneath wild glee or wilder tempestuousness they conformed to a severe and calculable order. God's works have rhythmic form. He learned from Elizabeth's body and his own. He saw her freely here in their sun-flooded isolated cottage as he had not done during their sharp sweet half-furtive meetings in her big house at home. Here he watched the light on the planes of her naked body and saw in that body an hundred rhythmic similitudes, from the cæsura of her pointed breasts to the circle of her womb, and absorbed the curves of thigh and shoulder. Here he was aware of the rhythm and climax of their embraces. There was nothing in the universe without the order of rhythmic form. He freed himself from the last tinge of the folly that verse, however personal, could be free except with the freedom of rise and fall, of beat and resurgence which it had borrowed from sea and moon, from star and snow, from love and death. . . . He began to write down verses now toward "Moses in Egypt" and some of these verses, of a classical rhythmic order but of intensely personal variation with a sharp tang of diction and something of the cry and call of the initial verbs of Hebrew word-order, were embodied without revision in the later final form.

A stretch of cloudy weather came to the Maine coast. It veiled all emotion; it halted all impulse. Dreamily Elizabeth and Gabriel strolled across the windy beach. Suddenly she looked up.

"You have the letters to people in New York that Aaronson and the others gave you?"

She had a way of all at once lifting her head and opening her eyes wide that softly commanded complete attention.

"Yes. Why?"

"We've got to go home in a very few weeks. You should see New York and people in New York."

"I hate to leave you, Elizabeth."

"Not so much as you think you think." She had a small self-ironic smile. "You're a darling, Gabriel. There's not a shadow of reproach in what I say. Look, I shall miss you more than you will miss me, and yet I shall not be altogether unhappy for being alone awhile."

He frowned.

"I don't like that."

Frankly she laughed now.

"Of course you don't. We all like the objects of our affections to suffer more from absence than we do ourselves. It feeds our self-esteem; it gives us a feeling of security."

"You're not usually pretending to be hard-boiled, Elizabeth."

"No, I've left that folly far behind me. But what I've said to you is the simple truth. However, you need not lose your feeling of security. In any deep sense you are my first love and you'll certainly be my last. You have no rival and will assuredly have no successor. When autumn comes the ripe fruit will drop with a little thud. That's all. And you will go on to your spring and summer."

"And what is this and what has this been?"

"Presage of spring, darling. You know your Hofmannsthal better than I.

> "There blows a spring-like wind
> Through the leafless trees,
> Magical presage runs
> Through its melodies. . . ."

They were both moved, but Elizabeth had insisted on a light touch.

"Pack your two bags. Write to your Mummie that you're

staying in New York alone for two weeks. It will make her feel better."

"Elizabeth!" he protested.

"I want you to be more realistic about people and more tolerant. You think I blame Gina for feeling a touch of irrational discomfort? I don't. In her place, and I'm quite old enough to imagine myself in it, I'd feel as she does. When are you going?"

He threw back the dark lock that was always falling across his forehead.

"Monday. Tomorrow is *Shabbath*. No use going anywhere on Sunday."

He threw his arm about her shoulder. They were approaching their cottage.

"Elizabeth!"

"Yes, my sweet?"

"You will be in Ozark City? You're not escaping from me?"

"Not yet, Gabriel. But the day is not far off. I'm forty, though I pretend, transparently enough, to be thirty-nine. I want you to bless and not to curse me in the years to come."

A small sharp trembling of expectancy arose in Gabriel. He held Elizabeth close but in that very closeness he felt a prelude to some farewell. He had never been alone in a great city. He had had a longing for New York which he had half repressed and half evaded. The last decade had witnessed a decline of the cult of the great cities; it had especially witnessed a determined effort toward what was known by the ugly word of deurbanization among American Jews. The Jewish units of the inner colonization movement, commonly co-operative freehold villages founded on American-Jewish National Fund land, had absorbed a very great part of the younger generations. Contiguous groups of these villages had their own junior colleges; there was place in them for engineers, physicians, pharmacists. Thus the Jewish population of New York had declined, as the city's total population had remained stationary. And yet even now for every writer, and also for every Jew, New York was a centre and a point of concentration which long tradition and constant literary reference had turned into one of the few American legends that could touch the imagination of youth.

Gabriel arrived at the Pennsylvania station late on that August Monday. The heat did not trouble him even though he came from the sea. Two things, not unexpected, he felt at once from the city as he drove to the little hotel near Columbus Circle that had been pointed out to him, two things—an enlargement of the mind, the strong though subtle sense of cerebration, of people thinking, reasoning, debating here in great numbers, of myriads of people with a high awareness of the world and its hard rock-like questions. He felt that, whether through the inference from previous knowledge or not, whether by contrast with his Middle Western city or not. And the second thing he felt at once was that this city, though so huge and peopled by men and women of so many strains and cultures, had a density and oneness of psychical atmosphere that reminded him suddenly, strangely, to the point of a catch in his throat, of the Berlin and the Paris of his childhood. It flashed upon him at once how this city, if his impressions were true, illustrated the newer teachings of the psycho-sociologists, that strong peaceful self-conscious cultures can live side by side co-operatively if each, while retaining its own character, granted an equivalence of value to every other for the group that had produced it and lived within it. . . . Ozark City looked and felt fairly homogeneous, too. But that was, except for a few not too conspicuous groups like the Jewish, because of an absence of saliency, form, edge, and resistance. New York, if his reasoning was correct, was like a highly complicated organism. A thousand elements functioned in unity. Ozark City was like a sack of corn—one and at one through a mere lack of differentiation.

The lights bloomed toward him along Eighth Avenue, even Eighth Avenue, as he told himself later; Columbus Circle showed only its sweep and not its tawdriness at this hour. A little while later from the window of his small room he saw across the Park the soaring towers about the Plaza with their innumerable golden lights. And though all training and all reasoning and all experience had convinced him, as they had convinced all the thinking members of his generation, of the tragic insufficiency of skill in shaping matter into ever more complicated forms, whether as building or machine, whether as under-sea tunnel or the chaining of rivers unless that skill was the skill of men whose moral purposes were those of justice and of peace, yet here in these towers and pinnacles of New York Gabriel felt the energy of a creative imagination that had sought, whether consciously or not, to aspire toward the eternal Eros, the principle of life and peace and to save an abiding monument from time and death.

V

EVERYBODY whom Gabriel had hoped to meet was snatching a last week or prolonged week-end in the country. Through friends of Ezekiel Frosch's, themselves on the point of a delayed vacation, he fell into the hands of Max Kantor, who had a small stuffy law office in the East Forties. There was something dusty and old and yet casual about the two office rooms, as though Kantor moved frequently but never had his books or files or desks dusted. In the outer room sat a girl named Sonya, who seemed to have no other name or wanted no other. She had very black bold eyes and greasy short black hair and crow's-feet that somewhat belied the age she affected with her nondescript skirt and unchanging pseudo-proletarian sweater tight over her large conspicuously-nippled breasts.

Kantor, a man in his late forties, had once tried a case in Ozark City. He had defended workers dangerously stripped of their minimum rights by arbitrary injunctions and set upon by paid thugs. The period of this trial had been the early nineteen-thirties and at that period the mind of Kantor, who could not now have been older than forty-six or seven, had evidently become rigid. He feigned to himself not to have witnessed the new redistribution of property or the internal colonization movements nor the unit movements. He waved all these things aside as not worth talking about. Since, according to strict Marxian theory, they could not or should not have happened, he said they were passing surface attempts to save American capitalism, which was not yet quite ripe for the last-stand defence of out and out Fascism. He ignored the development of Russia toward an intensely nationalistic state-capitalism. Russia was more sorely beset by counter-revolutionary war and invasion than ever. And that was true. This summer again the Germans had penetrated deeper into the Ukraine. But when Gabriel did not assent at once to these almost geometrical simplifications of history, Kantor looked both hurt and puzzled. He had an inimitable way of doing that. His pursed puzzled mouth, his hurt astonished brown eyes reminded Gabriel of the mouth and eyes of a lank man from a Methodist Unit Group who had once talked before a gathering of students in Ozark City and had been told during the period of debate that, though no one desired to speak disrespectfully of his beliefs, the particular panaceas which he offered—faith in the Incarnation and strict prohibition of alcohol—seemed grotesquely irrelevant. Kantor shared the Methodist leader's total inability to understand how anyone could differ from him. If anyone did, the Methodist attributed it to sin hardening the heart. Kantor attributed the same phenomenon to being a slave of the profit motive. Neither admitted the possibility of a free and disinterested activity of the mind.

He had now asked Gabriel to dine with him. Gabriel was a little astonished. But about Max Kantor there seemed to hang a cloud of isolation. He was like a creature that had been forgotten. Gabriel reminded him of Ozark City and that, in turn, seemed to remind him of years in which he and all he stood for were alive and vibrant somehow, and counted in the spiritual economy of American life. They sat at a little table in a crowded restaurant. The faded decorations were of the old-style Russian kind—colours at once gaily yet sharply contrasted, paintings on the wall of Russo-Byzantine steeples like onions set on top of each other. Kantor praised the indifferent *borsht*. Everything Russian, no matter of what period, was involved with his convictions, his past, his poor remnant of vitality and self-importance. He put a lump of sugar in his mouth and noisily sucked hot strong tea from a glass through it. He had been in Moscow on an Intourist trip in 1933. His revised memories were his Utopia, dream, ideal republic. There tea had been thus drunk. He looked at Gabriel sorrowfully.

"I hate to see anyone as young and bright as you among the reactionaries."

Gabriel laughed.

"You use the word in a sense that's new to me. All my friends and I think we're fighting Fascism in America with all our might."

Kantor grinned.

"They've got you fooled. By dragging out the life of capitalism a little longer you give the Fascists a chance to gather their forces. Wait a little longer. Wait till 1948. Even now what can President Whyte do? All your co-operatives and unit movements and second-rate social-security schemes will be swept away by armed bandits."

"We're aware of the danger," Gabriel said, slowly. "We try to keep it before us. Of course, we wouldn't admit your terms or reasons. But we fight the good fight inch by inch. Munition shipments to Italy were definitely stopped again the other day and 60,000 of our people have already entered Palestine this year. Both on the American and the Jewish front we carry on."

Max Kantor snickered.

"And if you fail in spite of all that—as you will, as you will? Look at the French Republic. It's selling out step by step. I'm surprised they held out that long. What do you say?"

"There are several answers to your question. One is this: other civilizations have failed and returned to barbarism. Your generation believed firmly that ours could not. My generation has had to face the possibility. My father was murdered by the Nazis in thirty-three when I was a child of

eight. If in spite of all our efforts we go the way of Babylon—
well, there's no more to say."

Kantor half lifted hands that trembled more than at his
age was to be expected.

"Why not turn to the Revolution? Why not *act* while it's
still possible?"

"If you mean the Russian Revolution as a prototype—it
isn't, if you'll forgive me, good enough. I don't say that I,
as a Jew, wouldn't rather be in Russia than in Germany
with this proviso—that they let some of us go from Germany to Palestine and that in Russia we're permanently
locked up and Jewishly silenced, and that I might in Germany be one of the lucky ones to get to the land of Israel."

Kantor sneered an old, old sneer. It was a withered sneer.
He had used it so many years.

"Palestine is a promontory of British imperialism. The
waves will go over it."

"If they do, that's the end of all things. We're facing that,
as I told you before. Meanwhile to talk of British imperialism
has no meaning. Britain is fighting the fight of civilization."

Kantor shook his head. He looked more hurt than ever.
Gabriel thought for a moment that the man was going to
weep.

"Don't you believe in humanity?" he asked. There was a
whine in his voice.

Gabriel looked at his plate. There were a thousand answers to that hollow question and there was none.

"Don't you believe in progress and in the ascent of man?"
Kantor went on. "Don't you?"

"There hasn't been much evidence of progress recently
unless the American and West European liberal coalitions
win out. And you don't think they will."

"But the Revolution," Kantor cried. "It has come in one
country; in spite of all it will spread. It must."

"I haven't heard that very often," Gabriel said. "But I

understand that it was a common point of view when I was a child. It seems to me and to all the thinking people I know that the Russian Revolution didn't change society as a whole in any way that would do us any good. We're afraid of the state. We're afraid of concentration of power. We want decentralization. Didn't Stalin years ago have even all the old Bolsheviks shot? We don't want a society in which the answer to criticism is a firing-squad. It's just that that we're fighting, isn't it? Rule by the use of naked force and murder! Just that."

Sorrowfully Kantor shook his head. Then he looked up.

"There comes Sonya."

Gabriel turned a little. Sonya in her too tight skirt and sweater, with her conspicuous breasts shaking, strode rather mannishly toward them. She sat down at their table and looked at Kantor with a mingling of possessiveness and hate. He smiled his woeful smile.

"Well, Comrade?"

She spoke surlily:

"I've been busy with arrangements for the protest mass meeting."

"Against what?" Gabriel asked.

She brightened as she turned to him and almost smiled.

"England's official consent to prolong the agreement that the Jews in Palestine need not employ Arab labour."

The murky lights of the restaurant danced before Gabriel's eyes.

"What do you mean? Aren't you a Jewess? Isn't Mr. Kantor a Jew? Don't you know that we must get the last 100,000 of our people out of Germany before they starve to death and also out of eastern Europe? And don't you know that our example has made the Arab worker the best paid in all Asia, although we must find place first for our own? Don't you know all that?"

Sonya put her hand on Gabriel's arm.

"That's what they tell you. But even if it's true it's no good because it breaks the proletarian will to revolution. We want the Arab masses to fight British imperialism."

"Even at our expense?"

It was Kantor who answered.

"We don't believe in race or religion, you see. That's all over and done with. We're on the side of the proletarians."

"Unless," Gabriel said, "they are Jews. You have got a bad case of self-hatred."

Kantor and Sonya both laughed. This laughter was the strangest laughter that Gabriel had ever heard. It was not laughter that had arisen here and now. It was an old, old used-up laughter, a laughter that had been laughed until it was a weary echo of itself. It filled Gabriel with a kind of horror.

"You say you don't believe in race and religion. Well, race isn't a good word. There's only one race, and that's the human race. But within that race there are groups with their specific character and their particular religion. They exist. You might as well say you don't believe in desert and mountain. They exist and are different and are yet part of the earth."

Sonya was fierce.

"We want to break down those differences. We must. We must."

"So that you don't have to be Jews any more. Is that it? No members of other groups are so eager about self-immolation!"

Kantor and Sonya looked at each other. Kantor said:

"It's pretty bad. When I was your age young people were ashamed of being as reactionary as that. Next you will tell me that you believe in the Jewish religion?"

"I do," Gabriel said, gravely. "It is my path to God just as my people is my road to humanity."

Again that withered laughter sounded. Sonya took Gabriel's hand and stroked it. He was irritated.

"Where have you people been keeping yourselves? The great majority of young Jews think and feel as I do today. Otherwise how do you account for our unit membership of 800,000 and for our chain of colonies from Vermont to Texas and from British Columbia on the Queen Charlotte Islands down to Lower California?"

Max Kantor waved a feeble hand. "Passing phases. Social Fascist substitutes. The Revolution will sweep all that away."

"Let's go upstairs," Sonya said.

Kantor explained to Gabriel:

"A group of us meets upstairs usually once or twice a week." He smiled his wilted smile. "All kinds of people. Reactionaries, too."

They climbed the straight steep inner stair at the back of the restaurant and reached a room where people were reading newspapers and a few were bent over chess-board. Near the centre of the room stood two large circular tables and to one of these Kantor and Sonya guided Gabriel. He was introduced to several people who were sitting there already; an elderly American spinster with skin like crinkled leather who called the others Comrade but whom they addressed as Miss Bradley; a very tall, very thin man, also an Anglo-American who had once evidently been blond and lithe and was now bald and pitifully faded, Comrade Neil Castle. The others were Jews and they all looked as though their faces had been squeezed, actually and physically squeezed by an inner malice, by a strange tormenting discomfort that had dictated not only their views of things, but had ended by definitely shaping their bodies. Drinks were ordered, mostly tea or chocolate, and the rather feeble discussion turned about the protest meeting of which Sonya had spoken. Miss Bradley, who had been in the Near East many years ago, was to address it. She outlined the stale, foolish arguments and the false statistics that she was going to use, and everybody at that table agreed with her and it was impossible for Gabriel to say that she was obviously a rancorous anti-Semite who, being for some inner reason ashamed and inhibited as such, was employing a pseudo-revolutionary technique for voiding her venom. Castle was evidently not that. He was a kindly still rather noisy man who had fallen in with Marxian friends and formulæ in his youth and whose development had been arrested at some frozen point. He laughed and agreed and said: "Splendid, just splendid!" His clothes were obviously the work of a good tailor and he drank brandy out of a tumbler.

Gabriel listened and an immense forlornness came over him. He had never seen or listened to people like this before. All that they said, all that they thought, all that they wanted or seemed to want of life and man and society appeared to him of a supreme bleakness, of an immedicable unattractiveness. The world they dreamed about and had been nursing in their dreams and had been building in their imagination, the world which according to them—and Gabriel was willing to believe them—had been for many years now a reality in the Soviet Union, was a horrible undifferentiated sort of world, a homeless, blank, featureless world like a plain, an endless, endless plain with no sun over it but rather some infinitely fierce artificial light that glared intolerably by night and by day. On that plain, under that light, stood workers' committees criticizing factory technique, criticizing the technique of the war, calling that purely technical criticism liberty, but having long ago forgotten the meaning of liberty and the meaning of love and the meaning of God. A terror took hold of Gabriel. He remembered a saying of Ezekiel Frosch's, a deeply pessimistic saying: "The trouble is that the German and Italian barbarians are not meeting the resistance of free men. They may break through and break civilization in the end because slaves are fighting slaves, and the Fascist slaves are fiercer and hungrier and more desperate." With a start Gabriel awoke from the revery into which he had fallen in that close crowded, noisy place. "Splendid, just splendid!" said Comrade Neil Castle to something that had been said.

Sonya, who was beside him and had evidently been watching him, said to Gabriel: "You weren't listening. Max and Miss Bradley are both sure that the Liberty Leaguers will seize the government if the next election goes against them."

He felt himself tearing his eyes wide open.

"And the man calls that splendid?"

"Why, yes; it will hasten the real revolution. Things can't go on this way much longer."

"You do want chaos, don't you—one kind or another?"

She did not answer. Under the reddish tablecloth her two rather dry hands clasped his right hand which he had been holding on his knee. He saw her full bosom heave. She whispered to him.

"You're awfully young and foolish. But you're sweet. Come and spend the night with me."

He was stricken with a touch of icy fever. He turned from her eyes in which flickered perversities that frightened and scorched him at the same time. Slowly he withdrew his hand and looked at Max Kantor and saw on Max Kantor's face a stricken smile of irony and self-irony and self-torment. Things he had vaguely heard and words of psychologists that he had coldly read came to him suddenly. He saw. He saw that Max Kantor lived with Sonya and had been living with her for years and had a morbidly tenacious passion for her and that she quite openly betrayed him with other men whenever the impulse came to her, and that he suffered from these betrayals, but that he also courted this situation and its attendant suffering because it had become a vice and an opiate to him. How right his teachers and masters were! Fascists by and large were sadists; Communists by and large were masochists. By and large. . . . Sonya's lips almost touched his ear. "We'll just slip out together a little later. . . ."

There was a stir in the back of the room. Voices were raised in greeting. Gabriel turned. He saw a tall old man with a long beard striding through the room. The old man came toward the table at which Gabriel was sitting and surveyed the people at it with handsome fiery eyes in which there was a look of humorous appraisal. They greeted him rather vociferously and introduced Gabriel to him. The magnificent old man, Dr. Pressburg, came over and peered at Gabriel and waved his hand at Sonya, who moved aside. He drew up a chair with one hand, still regarding Gabriel, and sat down beside him.

"Gabriel Weiss? You live somewhere out West? Aha! you are the son of Dr. Kurt Weiss?"

"Yes," Gabriel said, quite simply.

Dr. Pressburg nodded his head vigorously.

"It was one of the crucial stories—one of the highly symbolical stories I had from Jehuda Brenner. Have you heard that name?"

"Certainly."

Dr. Pressburg put his hand on Gabriel's shoulder.

"What are you doing here?"

"I'm just on a visit to New York. Mr. Kantor knows friends of mine."

"Good. You don't belong to this crowd of fossils?"

They all laughed at that table. That laughter, too, was old and worn and habitual.

"I'm preparing myself to teach at our Junior Jewish Unit College."

Dr. Pressburg ordered a small brandy.

"I thought you were too young to be either a communist or an atheist or a sex radical or any of those decadent things. I am, thank God, too old ever to have been that and too sensible. Now your generation and mine meet. But we meet in darkness, my boy; we meet in a great darkness."

Again the others laughed that worn and used-up laugh.

"I come here now and then," said Dr. Pressburg, "partly out of habit and partly to watch this petrifaction of minds. There you have a picture of the world-masses. The Fascists have abandoned mind; they've become jungle-beasts. The Communists have taken the shallowest errors of the nineteenth century and turned them and their minds into stone. You and I and those like us must die fighting. But I'm afraid we will die."

"Surely not," Gabriel protested.

"Other civilizations have perished. Why not this?"

"You see," said Kantor, "the doctor is bound to believe that and so are you because you shut your eyes to the new civilization and the new world that are in the making."

Dr. Pressburg again laid a hand on Gabriel's shoulder. "I'd like to hear your comment on that."

"The new world they talk about fills me with horror. Nothing that I care about is present in it."

"That's because you're a normal civilized human being. As I am. Man cannot live by pills, even if the pills contain all the necessary elements of nourishment. Chemistry is not enough. Economic technique is not enough, however excellent. Copulation is not enough. So soon as a man has food and shelter and a woman he wants to pray. I speak in symbols. If he cannot pray his food will turn to poison, his shelter into a prison, his woman into a whore."

The people at the table snickered. Miss Bradley said: "Isn't he amusing!" Comrade Neil Castle, having half emptied his second tumbler of brandy, woke with a snort from a kind of stupor and said: "Splendid! Splendid!" Max Kantor looked more sorely hurt and disappointed than ever. He looked as if he were going to cry. Sonya was sombre. Her metallic black eyes were fixed hungrily on Gabriel.

Gabriel's eyes burned in the smoke-filled air. In spite of Dr. Pressburg he seemed to be alienated here from all he was and wanted, from all hope and health. It occurred to him that that was a good definition of hell—to be estranged from one's soul and one's world. In his nostalgia for himself he turned to the doctor.

"Why are you so pessimistic? So much is being done, after all?"

Pressburg sipped at his brandy.

"There is much goodness and soundness in America. That was proven a good many years ago when the people swept Franklin Roosevelt back into office, despite the press and the haters and the original Liberty Leaguers and the liars and the anti-Semites. And it is, as you must know, because they did so that all the reforms amid which you have grown up could be accomplished. But America is not isolated; it cannot be isolated. And as the darkness deepens the shadow falls on us."

For once they were all silent. Gabriel pressed his hands to his forehead. "What is it?" he asked, slowly. "What is that darkness? What?"

The old man lowered his heavy head.

"It began with the first World War. It began with a sudden release of aggressive instincts. In former ages these instincts had spears and catapults. Now they have tanks and airplanes. So the hunger for destruction and self-destruction could grow and grow and become monstrous and satanic and an end in itself. Then came the so-called peace—a peace of terror and revenge and hate and aggressiveness. And hate unleashes hate and terror terror and revenge revenge. And while man, first in Germany, next in other lands, lapsed back into the pack-beast of the jungle, his weapons and machines, almost self-proliferating by a process once set in motion, became more dreadful and more deadly. And the cry went up after more machines and more devices and more inventions and never after the one thing needful—remorse and expiation. Do you know what I believe?"

Amid the silence Gabriel shook his head.

"I believe that if anywhere on any of those fields of battle, if anywhere between those lines of trenches a group of men—Germans or Italians or Yugo-Slavs or Russians—were to cast away their arms and were to go forth to their so-called enemies and kneel before them, yes, kneel down before them in the mud and stench and beg their forgiveness for God's sake, for their Christ's sake, for having been weak and foolish and wicked enough to let themselves be lashed to murder—I say that if such a thing were to happen once, just once, all men everywhere would on the instant feel an intolerable pang of remorse in their hearts and would see that they had been walking in darkness and would pray God to give them the light of love and peace."

There was silence. Gabriel's lids were wet.

The old man raised his arms.

"But will it happen? Will it ever happen? Will a *Yom Kippur*, will a Day of Atonement, come over all the world and into all the hearts of men?" His voice rose almost to a cry: "Will the Lord become God again and the wound in the universe close and be healed?"

Max Kantor, though his face had been working, forced it to wear his withered, mocking smile.

"What reactionary obscurantism!"

A noise between a violent eructation and a cough came from Comrade Neil Castle. "Splendid! Splendid!"

Dr. Pressburg took Gabriel's hand in both of his:

"That is *their* answer . . ."

VI

NOT time but fate was counted now by what in remote days, days small, sweet, pastoral, as seen in this immense perspective, the poet Walt Whitman had called Presidentiads. It seemed unimaginable that "Leaves of Grass" had been first published less than a century ago. Time had been accelerated and fate raced onward with resistless speed. No one who thought, no one who felt, doubted any longer the relativity of Time. Watches ticked on a thousand million wrists, clocks chimed in innumerable places, and though they ticked or chimed in different parts of earth at times called by the names of disagreeing numbers, yet their equal timing was timed by hands moving for each unit of time through a precisely equal unit of space. What did it matter? What did it mean? Man had through certain ages slowly and laboriously, as he had done before in history, made his way up the side of a mountain, the loftiest peak yet mastered of all the peaks in that cosmic mountain-range of his fate. The ascent had been slow. Upon the summit he had stood flooded with sunlight, himself the source of a radiance that seemed to meet the sun. Dizziness had come upon him there; black clouds had risen from some underworld of the primordial; within himself old blood lusts of a forgotten jungle had leaped up. He swayed on that peak fronting the morning star and the risen sun. He faltered. With forehead suddenly wrinkled like a beast's, with back suddenly curved like a bow or a baboon's, with wolfish slaver at the edges of bared fangs, he gazed past the downward slope to the abyss below where boiled a sea of blood and mud and lava, where seethed the chaos untouched by God's creative word.

He plunged—this creature godlike but Godless only one of eternity's hours before. He plunged. The lust for death seized him as with an irresistible fury. He raced. Time raced. Not all the blare and thunder of all the machines that hurtled with him down the slope could deaden the iron music of the whirring of the wings of Time.

1948. The French Republic had fallen. Fascist hordes had crossed the passes of the Maritime Alps from Italy and the open passes of the Pyrenees from Spain. The French reactionaries had themselves been frightened. For by now the dislocation of the processes of civilization was so complete that policies were forgotten and even the maddest ideologies, though still mouthed by the slave-drivers, had fallen into decay. Invasions were now hunger invasions. All the great cities had been bombed so often that rebuilding seemed futile since there was no hope of peace. A great migration to the open country took place. But the money of the city people was of no value to the men and women who tilled the land. They refused to take it in exchange for food. They could still have subsisted had they been let alone with the deliberately diminished number of their young. Thus civil wars of sheer hunger raged in Italy and Germany and Spain and the Balkans. If the peasants were defeated, they sullenly consumed seed-grain and the potatoes left for planting, and hoarded remnants and refused to sow and left the earth barren and untilled. If the peasants won under the mystic dervish leaders that arose everywhere with the great cry that the corrupt and Godless cities had brought mankind to this unendurable pass, then were the city people driven back into the ruined cities, and princes sat in Roman palaces, offering at times the fabulous treasures of antiquity which no one wanted, which men had unlearned even to prize, for a dead dog or a brace of rats.

Hitherto France had remained almost untouched and unharmed. Her vineyards and her grain-fields, the lemon-

orchards of Var and the olive-orchards of Provence bloomed
and bore fruitage as of old. The women of Arles still wore
serenely their white peaked caps; on terraces people still ate
coquille St.-Jacques and snow-white sausage-shaped goat
cheeses and drank fragrant wines, the "small" ones and the
"great" ones of the *vignobles* of their land. The *Croix de Feu*
people had long grown subdued; even the powerful industrialists and bankers had not too brutally resisted the moderate Socialist state. They knew about those princes in
Rome; they saw the half-depopulated cities of the Rhine.
They travelled secretly and by night to the extreme north-
east of their land to inspect the hidden chain of deep-sunk
fortifications that stretched from the Swiss frontier to that
of Luxembourg, and of which the purpose was no more to
keep out the glittering armies of the Germans. Martial glitter was no more. A few dark mechanized units with mobile
tanks and super-*Feuerwerfer* waited inactive in the Rhine-
land. Otherwise the province was stripped of all males between seventeen and fifty. These were far away, plunged in
interminable battle in Poland and in Russia, seizing some
piece of territory to cultivate and plunder. Hunger and desolation being behind them, these armies dared not now turn
back. Victory and defeat had become empty words. What
the French gentlemen saw, peering across the frontier, was
mere famine and mere ruin and they were told that the
deep-sunk forts were needed now to keep out unarmed
hordes of hungry old men and women and children who
might some day, like locusts, swarm into France.

But the Fascist fighting forces of Spain and Italy, though
great parts of these were also bogged in endless battles in
Africa and elsewhere, were still numerous enough to pour
over the mountain passes into France. They had begun at
once to live on the land. The gallant French fought stub-
bornly, defending their beautiful land inch by inch. But
those others had sunk into mere barbarism. They did not

despise death. They were indifferent. If only they could fill their bellies once more. And so stricken with blindness by fate itself were the French Fascists that, though they knew what the totalitarian states had come to, they conspired against the hard-pressed Republic and brought about its fall. Heart went out of the soldiers of the Republic. For they wanted to rebel and go back to Paris, once the city of light, and bomb the dictator out of the Elysée Palace and tear up the great lamp-posts on the Place de la Concorde and batter their way into the chamber of that false Senate that had betrayed the cause of the French people and of the world. They could not; they dared not. Here too the hordes, like the locusts of the East, would have stripped the land till there was no leaf on any tree, nor seed left for planting, nor cow nor sheep nor goat. . . . And Britain sent no help. That was a bitter thing and a thing of doom. But the French had long known that no expeditionary forces would cross the Channel. England, though not at open war, was pressed to the utmost. A great fleet and air force had to protect the Australian continent from Japan, else had the empire begun to crumble. Armies and air fleets stationed in Palestine from the Sinai desert to the Lake of Tiberias kept at bay a second invasion of Christendom by the followers of the Prophet, who were whetting swords for the hands of the innumerable black millions whom their *imams* and *dervishes* had won for the fierce faith of Mohammed. From the equator to Zanzibar and the Red Sea a ringing cry that the time was ripe would have summoned the innumerable legions of the Negro world, childlike men willing, nay, eager to die for the immediate sharing of the Prophet's paradise of temperate streams and rustling groves and milk-white virgins. . . . And in the Mediterranean to guard one route of both food and empire and in the Atlantic, to guard the other route around the Cape of Good Hope, rose and briefly glittered the periscopes of the fleets of British submarines and no man knew, except a few in the innermost councils in London, what it cost Britain in gold and human lives to keep at full and necessary strength these desperately precarious fleets which guarded not only the bread of the children of England, but the fainting liberties and decencies of mankind. . . .

1948. The dislocation of world trade and the desperate breakdown of the civilizations of the Old World had narrowed the economy of the country. Beginning with the insurgent nationalists in Brazil, neo-barbarians had smashed the fragile enough structure of civilization from Panama to Cape Horn. At Panama the United States stood guard to keep that the frontier of savagery. Except for an occasional trickle of the remnant of the Jewish communities, once eight-hundred thousand strong, who had been dispersed and literally cut to pieces by the jungle-men and whom now their brethren in the United States ransomed as they had always had to ransom their captives and their fugitives—except for these the frontier was kept closed as against a pestilence. And there was literally that other danger. For the bubonic plague, still kept within limits even in the hunger-ravaged districts of Europe by new and powerful serums, manufactured in England, Holland, and the Scandinavian countries and sent freely in charity and as a self-protective measure to Germany, Italy, Spain, the Balkans, had come to Rio de Janeiro and to Buenos Aires with hordes of lice-infected rats which had scurried into hinterland and jungle and monstrously bred there and come into village and city by night. Across the gap in the Panama frontier we imported a few Jews and exported the serums. But the serums were captured by dictators and sold at exorbitant prices, and so the plague raged on.

We and the British Empire and a few small remaining civilized countries like Sweden and Holland constituted an isolated and tottering world economy within a surrounding chaos. Internal colonization, nation-wide coöperatives, the unit system, the necessity for immense armies and navies which had now to be recognized even by pacifists as frontier guards, had solved the problem of unemployment. A diminishing birth-rate was a tragic enough safeguard against its probable recurrence. But though all men had food and shelter and raiment, yet the economic level was not so high as men not yet old remembered it to have been. Trade in luxuries fell off. Radio sets were fewer; beauty parlors were fewer; expensive sports and the industries attendant on them were in full decay. Cars were plentiful. But one rarely saw any but the slow, light, tiny Langengarts at three hundred dollars. To the philosophic mind or the Judæo-Christian temper this state of things seemed good and hopeful. All were fed, sheltered, instructed. But a turbulence gathered once again among the masses of the people which was more menacing than the subdued discontent of the moderately impoverished rich. Gunther Hicks, of Mississippi, active for years now in shirt-sleeves on an improvised platform of boards in Southern towns and villages and lately a man from Minnesota named Cornelius Faithful Prout, declared to their growing followings that opportunity was gone from free America, that a caste system, worse than that of India, had been established here. No man could rise from the ranks any more. Governmental regimentation had slammed the door of opportunity in the face of the freemen of America. We were living under an Oriental despotism. This monstrous confusion between liberty and the licenses of jungle economic competition, with the devil taking the hindmost, was greedily lapped up by those vast numbers of inferior men who substitute wishful revery and rancor for ability and character. . . . Hell! Prout was right. What chance had a man any more? Sure, you had work and accident and old age insurance. Sure. But how about getting ahead? It didn't matter no more how smart a fellow was. Naw! You were stuck. Stuck—that was the word. Your name was mud. Hell! . . . To this murmur the Liberty

Leaguers listened. In their heart of hearts they were frightened. They had seen the fate of the Fascist states. They, too, knew about the Roman princes and the diet of rats; they, too, knew that the palaces of the Krupps and the Thyssens and the Hugenbergs were crumbling into ruin and decay. They deluded themselves into believing that here in America the trend of fate was unique. So, so, if they could recover the rights of mere jungle competition and pay no industrial insurance and no minimum wage and have company unions back and labor spies and thugs and break the back of the new economic order, they were willing to risk giving a dole to new armies of the unemployed and to put down hunger insurrections with machine-guns. Thus money poured into the coffers of Gunther Hicks and Cornelius Faithful Prout, as money had once poured into those of Hitler, and a million radio voices in a million cottages shrilled out the promise of a new age of golden opportunity for the common man of America if only he would cast off the yoke of the stalled oxen and become, like the Rockefellers and Goulds and Carnegies and Schwabs and Fords of the imperial days, a hero and a conqueror. . . .

1948. For a year now Gabriel Weiss had been teaching English in the Jewish Junior College Unit of Ozark City. Elizabeth Warner, somewhere in the East or in Europe, had become to him like a figure in a legend. Yet he made a point of avoiding her house. Once, in autumn, on his way to congratulate old Mrs. Jacoby on her birthday, long after the Warner house had been sold to a near-by country club, he had, half-dreamily, half deliberately, gone out of his way to stand before it. Only a very few years had passed since they had stood for the last time in Elizabeth's small sitting-room upstairs. Her trunks had been packed; her ticket to Cherbourg was in her bag. She was crisp and casual, though her green eyes filmed over now and then. His throat had been

hot and dry and constricted. At last the words came, the
wrong inevitable words:

"Don't go, Elizabeth, don't go!"

She had been slipping some last object into an open suit-
case. She turned to him with that rhythmic motion of hers.

"How sweet of you, Gabriel! How lovely it is for us to
part while I can feel how sincerely you want me not to go.
Think, dear, if I had outstayed my period and had seen in
your eyes, while out of pity you protested, your weariness
and your relief?"

He had wanted to say that that could never be. He had
opened his lips and she had put her cool hands over them.

"No, don't say that. Don't let there be any falseness. You
don't know how rare that is—a deep human relation without
any falseness."

"Are we to be strangers for the rest of life?" he had asked,
impatiently.

"How can we ever be strangers? I shall see you again when
the right time comes."

"When will that be?"

"I don't know. The signs by which I shall know it, Gabriel,
are my small secret. But when the signs are fulfilled and I
do come back, they and their meaning will be perfectly clear
to you."

Standing before her house on the autumn day of that later
year he had relived that scene and heard again her bright
brave voice. There had come over him a sharp nostalgia for
that first youth of his of which she had been the most beautiful part. With his mind, which had matured early, he had
known of the world's woe. How could he not have? Had he
not almost been cradled in tragedy? But he had known or,
rather, he had let himself know in those days only with his
mind. His emotions and his will had brimmed with hope
and with a creative onward impulse. In spite of all! In spite
of all! Somehow, sometime—was it tomorrow—peace and

goodness must prevail and wisdom rule and men come home to their better selves. He had written a long poem, which he now rejected, in spite of lines both resonant and terse because of a tumultuous excess, on the prophetic text which had then summed up all that he felt, hoped, needed to believe and so believed. "And an highway shall be there, and a way . . . fools shall not err therein . . . but the redeemed shall walk there." He had called the poem "The Holy Way" (*Derech ha'kodesh*) and had woven into it as its chief theme to rise again and again from the context like cry answering cry the phrase "and there shall walk the redeemed" (*v'halechu geulim*). He had pictured the road; he had pictured the redeemed; he had seen in his boyish vision a human caravan in which each was himself and no man desired his human brother to be aught but what he was, aught but what God had made him; he had seen a humanity in which groups had not desired any to be subject to another or to become another, but in which each had loved the other as it was.

Now, though that glow had not altogether faded in his breast, it was surrounded by an edge of darkness. That edge, at first a thin black line, had broadened. The central glow was a mere spark. And he had become aware of that widening and mounting darkness within him as he had stood on that day for a last time for ever before Elizabeth's house and had looked at the red berries of the barberry bushes and at spots of rust on a cedar hedge and at the two tall Norway spruces that were inured to winter.

It was autumn again and the electoral campaign was raging. President Whyte's health had failed, so that he was not a candidate. The federation of liberal parties had, of course, a considerable number of able, eloquent, and powerful personalities in its ranks. Since 1936 more and more intellectuals had entered politics. Service of the country had become, as in Britain, a manifest duty. Yet a tremor of nervousness went through the liberal ranks. For it was recognized by now that appeals to the electorate on the grounds of truth, of fact, of enlightened self-interest even, were not so powerful as appeals to obscure inner wishes, frustrated impulses of aggression, fear, and greed. In brief, when dealing with human masses, the most powerful methods are those that reach the Freudian *id*, the barbaric subconscious, and not those that seek to guide the conscious *ego* or induce men to act according to the dictates of the super-ego, that is to say, honour, goodness, humanity. Hope was still drawn, as it had been for twelve years now from that magnificent popular vindication of freedom which had swept Franklin Roosevelt back into office. On that victory had been based the new economics and the new cultural tolerances that had saved civilization in America. But now Cornelius Faithful Prout thundered to awaken the slumbering impulses of reckless adventurousness, of lust for death, of greed for dominance, of mere destructiveness, too, which he and his followers raised to the heat of group-fevers. And somehow the knowledge, sparse among the masses, but precise enough in character, of how those fevers had burned the marrow out of Europe, seemed not to frighten but to excite millions of common men. It was as though people, watching a burning house, were impelled not to bring water to put out the conflagration or else run to save their own dwellings, but were darkly urged on by sick primordial instincts to take axes and hew down the roofs over their children's heads and light torches by the fire that was burning and fling these torches into their ruined homes.

Gabriel came from a fairly heavy day's work. His mother, quieter than ever, white-haired, though she was barely forty-five, but smooth of skin and lithe as in youth, was laying the table for dinner. She looked up, a fork in her hand.

"Tired?"

"Not from working, Mummie. We live in such a horrible world. Everything seems in danger. If Prout wins even by the narrowest margin, we're at the beginning of the end here and will go the way of Europe."

She drew herself up.

"I don't believe he will," she said, slowly. "Remember that Hitler was supported in part at least by the facts of starvation and humiliation. What are the latest plans?"

"Mr. Roosevelt is going on the radio every other day. He'll be heard; he'll be seen. Of course he's sixty-seven now, but his strength seems to be all there."

"But the candidate?"

"It will have to be Senator Hardie Carlisle of Wisconsin. He's one of the coarsest-fibred men on our side. But we dare not take a higher type. That's what makes it so beastly and so tragic."

When they had sat down and were eating and Gabriel was less tense, Gina said:

"I got a letter today which is like a voice from the past, almost from the dead."

"From whom?"

"Jehuda Brenner."

Gabriel looked up. He brightened.

"I suppose it's just personal?"

"Yes. But he's coming here. He s once more on tour. He's sponsored this time by the Judæo-Christian Association. That was Peter Lang's doing, of course. I suspect from something in his note—I'll show it to you in a minute—that the Colonial Office wouldn't mind seeing a renewal of interest in the Pro-Palestine Christian movement in this country."

Gabriel breathed deep.

"It's like a gleam of light. We'll be able to work for something fresher and more definite again. And I feel, too, that I've all these years wanted to see Brenner again. How old do you suppose he is?"

"It's fourteen years ago." Gina spoke slowly. "He was

rather a young man then in spite of his black beard. He's in his early fifties now, I suppose."

Gabriel could not work that evening. His mind and the listening substance of his mind and the very pores of his body were tense, alert, were open, were waiting to receive and hear and absorb some unhoped-for and redeeming word. He dreamed that night of an unfathomable, unplumbed abyss in which writhed indistinguishably in snake-like coils and oily intertwinings a multitude of men and women—dark, naked, and opaque. From time to time a dim light fell obliquely on them from an unseen source and then there arose brief glints of the whites of eyes, of the enamel of teeth, of the crimson of gums. From far away, from very far away a trumpet cried out a long-drawn and a dolorous cry. . . . That cry wakened him. And he could sleep no more because in his dream that cry of the trumpet, though inarticulate, had had a meaning and he had known that meaning and now the meaning was gone and only the echo of that crying dolorous blast dwelt faintly in his ears. . . .

The morning wind refreshed him. He taught his classes not impatiently but inwardly straining forward. When he came home for luncheon Jehuda Brenner was sitting with his mother. Though the meetings of those two had been so few and brief and long ago, they were to each other like old and familiar friends. They had met at a moment, in an hour of fate and of decision, and their souls had opened each to the other. Brenner was still slender and Gabriel noticed his strong yet delicate hands. The once black beard was very grey, but the brown eyes were brilliant and the lines in his face few. He took Gabriel's hand and held it.

"Your mother has been telling me about you. We must talk over the function of the Youth Units in the Judæo-Christian movement."

"I'm so glad," Gabriel said. "There's been a stagnancy here. Of course we're all working to defeat Prout. But even if we do—and I think we will—I have a feeling that that will be only respite and neither peace nor progress."

Brenner lit a cigarette.

"You're quite right. But I don't want you to promise yourself from this work of mine more than it can accomplish."

"You used rather quietly to wave a flag of hope, Jehuda," Gina said.

"I did. Though even then I had doubts. Now we must work without hope because we have the double duty to strive and also to see clear."

"That's hard." Gabriel shook his head.

"Especially for youth," Brenner agreed. "But you know the world situation as well as I do. If your country and Britain and a few others stood entirely four-square to resist chaos there would be more than hope. There would be certainty. But you people are using up your energy to resist Cornelius Faithful Prout. The same story can be told of every other civilized country. We are all besieged. Some day our munitions, so to speak, will give out."

There was a silence.

Slowly Brenner spoke.

"Men will not do the one thing needful. God has hardened their hearts as a punishment for the hardness of their hearts."

Gabriel frowned.

"I don't quite follow you there. Forgive me. Isn't that a rather crude and anthropomorphic notion of God?"

Jehuda Brenner clasped his hands.

"A sound hypothesis, Gabriel, is a theory that explains all the facts, isn't it?"

"It is."

"The human race had come in the early years of this century near to dominating nature, curbing disease, lengthening the span of life, creating a large and well-grounded hope of peace and of social justice. Why is the world then in chaos?

Why are things as they are? Think! No knowledge was lost. No research or inventiveness was crippled. There was no reason for this most dreadful downfall either in the world of things or in the world of the intelligence. Was there? Tell me, was there?"

"I do not see that there was."

"Then the cause lies deeper. Call its seat the heart, call it man's moral nature, call it what you will. When I said that God had hardened man's heart I was merely trying to grasp in some human way that which is at once absolutely certain and yet wholly inscrutable. We can do no better."

"Perhaps we can do no better in the world of thought. But what of the world of action?"

"We are doing all we can. And we must go on. But we shall accomplish not even the little we might unless we know." Slowly he repeated. "Unless we know."

His speech was, as it were, poised. Gina said, "Yes, and ——"

Brenner smiled.

"When I was a very young man I was sent to a Lithuanian village to draw the people into the Zionist movement. They were gathered in the little wooden *shul*. An old, old man came to me, an old man in a soiled caftan over which streamed his long beard. He said: 'My son, don't bother with Zionism. It's unpractical. Tell them to keep the Sabbath.' 'What?' I cried, laughing. 'Zionism unpractical? What nonsense! It's the only practical thing in Jewish life.' The old man shook his head. 'Zionism is practical. Yes. But your method is unpractical. Our sages tell us that if all the people in all the world would keep perfectly two successive Sabbaths—*zwee Shabosim, nor zwee*—perfectly, and no soul on earth commit a *chillul shabbas* [breach of the Sabbath] on either, then would the Messiah come. *Nu,* when the Messiah comes, what will he do? He will soften the hearts of the world's peoples to give us Eretz Yisrael as a gift and he will change the hearts of the Jews so that all Jews will arise and go to Eretz Yisrael. Will *you* accomplish this double purpose with your talk? No, you're unpractical. Tell them to keep the Sabbath. The rest will follow.' "

Brenner lit a fresh cigarette.

"If we could get mankind to keep one Sabbath—just one, and that one imperfectly . . ."

"Yes," Gabriel assented, "you are right. We would have an entirely new start. Everything good could be accomplished through a humanity capable of one such action."

"Strike this civilization that remains at any point—at any, Gabriel, and anywhere and you end with the truth, the hopeless, everlasting truth in the story of the two Sabbaths. . . . Test it and see!"

VII

HE WAS, suddenly, unexpectedly to make such a test as Brenner had spoken of. He was to strike his civilization at a given point; he was in the apparently quiet course of things to see the earth open, as it were, and have vision of a depth at which he saw and for ever remembered the immedicableness of the world's moral ills. He did not even thank God that the experience was vicarious, that it was not his own. For he lived through it with the intensity of both a poet and a Jew—with the imagination that makes itself at one with the thing it sees and with the thrice forged will never inwardly to consent to injustice, even though it reign unimpaired and unassailed.

From their early adolescence on he and Alan Jones had been friends. The Youth Unit movements had brought them together; early and later meetings, when they were approaching manhood, at Elizabeth Warner's house, had given a glow of memory to their friendship. Alan's father, moreover, the minister of the First Congregational Church of Ozark City, had long ago been called by Ezekiel Frosh the "Christian *Zaddik*"—the wholly righteous man among the Christians. The name had stuck. Dr. Jones rejoiced in it and used it humorously himself. He had begun his more than local activities many years before through the Federal Council of the Churches of Christ; he had fought for two decades for the way of life according to which men were to love and serve each other as God had made them and not according to proportions of mass and therefore of power. He was now a very active worker in the Judæo-Christian movement and a correspondent and friend of Peter Lang's.

His son, Alan, a year older than Gabriel, shared all his father's convictions, but with more edge of temperament and militant fierceness. Dr. Jones was a tall, stoutish man with a faintly rosy face and mild eyes. Alan, like his mother, was smaller, lean, dark, mobile. His beliefs were all like passions of the blood. He was capable of great refusals; he chided Gabriel for being a dreamer. "Granted that you're a good poet, how dare you be a mere poet in this age?" On this theme there had been long debates. Gershon Frosch, since Gabriel was too shy to use this argument in his own behalf, had maintained that nothing in history had been so powerful as some creative word. To which Alan had replied that this creative word had been the word of lawgivers and redeemers. Now Gershon and Gabriel were sure they had him. For these lawgivers and redeemers, this Moses, let us say, and this Jesus, what had we of them in actual fact but the record of the creative speakers who wrote the five books of the Torah and the four Gospels? Behind those books we had no way of going. The books were for us the men. All we do know is that these books exist, that therefore they were spoken or written by men; therefore of the reality of *these* men we were sure—and of nothing else. Poetry, then, *is* the highest reality we know. And whether Gotamo the Buddha spoke the discourses attributed to him is of less import than these discourses themselves. We have them whether the redactors remembered or invented them. But though Alan admitted the force of this argument he was not satisfied. Great figures and mighty experiences must, he contended, have preceded speech and record. "Find a Moses, a Jesus, a Gotamo first, Gabriel! Or else go to work!"

He, at all events, embodied his own convictions in action. He went to work. He had completed his studies many months before. But he put off his ordination. He wanted to minister to men. He could not conceive of himself as doing anything else. He hesitated to stand in a pulpit and speak. Into such public speaking, he said, there entered almost necessarily an element of vanity, artfulness, self-satisfaction. But to go from man to man, from woman to woman, to search in individual souls the reasons which kept them from being redeemed from selfishness, from cruelty, from greed, and to seek to root out those reasons and destroy those barriers between the soul and good—that method, he thought, might have some meaning and some effectualness. He lived a stripped ascetic life on a small income which his mother, who had inherited a considerable interest in an Ozark City traction company, was glad to give him. He gave away most of this income in contributions to the causes he had at heart. His mother watched over him unobtrusively to see to it that he had warm food and comfortable clothes.

He had spent the last summer at one of the group of villages of the Inner Colonization Projects near a small town named Ridgeville in the western part of the state. He had come back suddenly and had dropped in to see Gabriel. Gina's eyes had grown wide. She had caught herself. Alan had always been lean. Now he was emaciated. His very lips, once a sharp vermilion, were the colour of raw young veal. His cheeks looked as though, child-like, he had sucked them in. His earnest, steady, intelligent dark eyes flickered uneasily from point to point. He kept swallowing his spittle as though to ease a drought in his throat. Gabriel did not perceive so deeply as his mother his friend's broken condition. He thought of it as an ailment of the body.

"You don't look as though your summer had done you much good."

Alan looked at his friends from under wrinkled brows.

"No, not much."

Gina could not hold back.

"My dear boy, either you're very ill or something dreadful has happened to you. I mustn't try to influence your judgement. But I've known you since you were a little boy. Have you told your father?"

Alan shook his head.

"Why not?"

He pushed out the words slowly, painfully, one by one.

"The evil in the world is so deep that I'm afraid that even Father will not see through it, because even he is implicated with it. The evil has made laws for itself. And who doesn't respect the law? Oh, I'm guilty, too. I took guilt upon myself. But between that guilt and the law there is no relation. None. Will Father see that?"

"Good Lord!" Gabriel burst out, "you talk, Alan, as though you'd killed some one or, at the least, stolen silver spoons. And of course you haven't. And so do be plain and sane."

Alan shook his head. He breathed deep. He closed his eyes for a moment.

"Not yet, Gabriel. It may not be necessary. I must say that to myself a little longer. What troubles me most is that such things can be."

They let him go, though reluctantly. Gina wondered if quietly she should go to see Mrs. Jones. Gabriel vetoed that.

"His mother must see. If she doesn't ask or if he won't tell! But I'll get it out of him, whatever it is. He must have help."

Three days after the coming of Jehuda Brenner on a rainy night Alan Jones came to Gabriel. Dripping, he brushed past and hurried into Gabriel's small study. He dropped into a chair. He beat his fists together. He did not speak.

Quietly Gabriel said:

"Take off your overcoat. I'll hang it in the hall."

Alan looked up with eyes that were frightened, that not only flickered, but winced. He stood up unsteadily and dropped his overcoat and stooped and picked it up and gave it to Gabriel.

When Gabriel came back from the hall Alan was leaning forward with his hands on his knees.

"I picked you instinctively, Gabriel, to tell you about my trouble. You don't mind, do you?"

"Don't be foolish. Both Mummie and I have been worried about you. I can't imagine ——"

"You can't. And maybe it'll seem trivial to you. But the evil, the evil, Gabriel!"

"Just what evil?"

"If there were an embodied principle of evil, if there were Satan, do you know what he would be?"

"What?"

"He would be a maker of laws, Gabriel—of rigid laws like measuring-rods of steel that are applied without any regard for the ethical values or for the people involved. He would let souls die; he would let the whole world be smothered in filth and go on measuring with those rods of steel."

Gabriel did not speak. He saw that Alan had probably wandered about for hours if not for days in a throttling silence and that the moment of release through speech had come. With a touch of horror he watched Alan throw up his arms in a grotesquely unaccustomed gesture.

"They don't see it. They are like stones. And their stoniness robs me of speech. If people are blind and don't know that they are blind and you must make clear to them the difference between black and white and must kill yourself unless you can make clear the difference to them—what then, Gabriel, what then?"

"You must give me some concrete facts to go on, Alan."

A sob shook Alan's body.

"I'm so ashamed, too, Gabriel, so frightfully ashamed. It withers me, that shame. Ashamed of my lechery and still more of my folly, my blindness, my confusion."

He drew a deep breath. He wrung his hands. His whole

body struggled tensely now toward the act of expression
that had to be accomplished.

"All last summer the quota in the Colonies was full.
Every room was occupied, so that the instructors and min-
isters and visiting artists were lodged in Ridgeville. You've
heard of it—a town of about eleven thousand, a common
town full of common people, many of them out of sympathy
with Internal Colonization. There are three or four Prout
groups in the town. Photographs of Cornelius Faithful Prout
are in many houses. Do you know the kind?"

Gabriel shook his head.

"They are full of a dumb malice, of a stealthy enmity that
existed in them before it had any object. An enmity against
life, somehow, against light. But I think, Gabriel, I think
now that it was first of all an enmity, a deep obscure hatred, directed against themselves, against themselves for
being what they are. Somewhere in their clotted souls they
know that they are dark and unredeemed. But they have no
will toward good. So, in order to affirm their darkness they
must murder light—in order to be free to be themselves they
must murder us. It's the Fascist state of mind. It's the Nazi
state of mind. I understand now at last what has been bringing Western civilization to ruin. Dark masses were threatened with light. They could not bear it; they could not live
in it; they were dazzled and wanted darkness. They murder
the light. And the insanest part of it is that very often, as
in this case, they take *their* stand on so-called moral
grounds."

A little flame of vicarious fear and horror began to glow
in Gabriel. His throat went dry, too. He found himself
clasping and unclasping his hands, too.

"I was lodged," Alan went on, more quietly now, "on the
outskirts of Ridgeville with people named Hirst, a farmer of
about sixty, a raw-boned, gnarled, blear-eyed, silent man, a
miser, I was told, a man of a brutal and purposeless tenac-

ity. There was his wife, a very fat woman who wore loud-patterned dresses and small hats, which she thought stylish in a citified way. She left her spoon in her teacup but when she lifted it by the handle, the spoon rattling from side to side in it, she stretched out her little finger as far as it would go and smirked at her own elegance of gesture."

"That's both amusing and dreadful," Gabriel said.

Alan bent his head. His eyes were hidden.

"Then there was the daughter, Kate Hirst, a woman of thirty. She has a cast in one eye and dry hair and is beginning, if you know what I mean, to wither at the edges. But she has a good figure."

He fell into a gulf of despairing silence.

"Go on, Alan," Gabriel pleaded, "please go on."

"I suppose you know that I've lived what people call a pure life. I've suffered, of course, and I can't say that I didn't have doubts and rebellions. But for a fellow like me what alternative is there? You're afraid of loose women. You wouldn't know where to find them. If you knew some one of whom you suspected that he knew, you'd shrink from the coarseness of asking. I heard vaguely of affairs in junior college. You did, too. They usually ended in marriage. Nothing like that happened to me. I'm a rather unsightly creature, too."

"Utterly ridiculous," Gabriel said. "I never dreamed you had a feeling of physical inferiority. You've got no reason for it."

Alan's mouth twitched. He had tried to smile and could not.

"Then there was the hired man at the Hirst house," he said, abruptly. "Only he wasn't in a sense the genuine article. In winter he clerked in a drygoods store in Ridgeville. Now in summer he helped on the farm and went about in overalls. But his overalls were too neat and he sat around the house more than he worked out-of-doors. I know now, though I haven't the proof even yet, that Carlsen, the hired man, is a paid spy and organizer for Prout. If these people can 'get anything,' especially of a so-called moral delinquency kind, on a liberal of any shading, they're triumphant. Then they can wreak their foulness. And so Kate Hirst and Carlsen determined to destroy me. And not only me. Father, too. Then Prout could raise the cry in this state: 'There you have the liberals and pacifists and unit people—there!' "

Gabriel began to understand.

"You were utterly unsuspicious, of course."

"What chance had I to be suspicious? Kate made small surreptitious overtures to me. I pretended not to understand. I fixed my attention on the cast in her eye and on her stringy hair because I didn't want to be inflamed by anyone like her. But I had been so damned pure, Gabriel. Little by little, in dusk or dark, she roused me until I trembled literally like a man in the grip of a chilling and searing fever. Then one fine night she simply walked naked into my room and got in bed with me. I was no more my own master in that situation than is a man who is led to the gallows in chains. Was I, Gabriel—tell me that! Was I?"

Gabriel was grave.

"You were not, Alan, you were not. But afterwards! But the next day!"

Alan Jones drooped in his chair. He bowed his head. One by one his limbs seemed to melt in the completeness of his humiliation. Slowly he lifted his hands to his head and held it.

"I told you I was guilty, too—guilty as hell. I packed my bag. But I didn't go. I tried to fool myself by saying it won't happen again. All the while I was burning that it should. I said to myself all I've got to do is to lock my door. Then I found—maybe I'd known it subconsciously all the time—that my door didn't lock securely. There were only two loose screws left in the lock. You gave the door a push and it was open. I pretended to myself that I'd get a screw-driver. I didn't. And Kate did a terribly astute thing. She didn't come the next night, nor the next, and by day she gave no sign that anything had happened between us—not by so much as a glance. And I, I was one conflagration."

He took down his hands. He seemed to gather himself together.

"Why are we made so, Gabriel? Why cannot we govern that instinct better, or else, if we cannot, why is it not blame-less and guiltless? How have you gotten along?"

"I had a great good fortune when I was just a boy. That made everything easier. Yet what happened to you might easily have happened to me. God knows it might have. There does seem to be some stupid element of mere chance in the world."

Alan looked up. Gabriel was smitten by the humility of his friend's glance.

"Thank you for saying that, Gabriel."

"What happened next?"

"She came again. Every two or three nights. And by day she gave no sign. I tried to reason that I was secure, that she wanted the thing to be known no more than I. Yet I had moments and even hours of sudden apprehensiveness that sickened me to the marrow. She took to staying longer. She took to sleeping at my side. But when I woke, even though it was dawn, she wasn't there any longer."

"What did she say? Didn't you talk?"

"She said very little. She told me she was tired of the rough people around. She said she liked me because I was different. She said her father had plenty of money but was cruel in his miserliness. She worked like a slave and got none of the things that other girls got. It sounded natural and truthful enough. There may have been some nature and some truth in it—one side of her. Who knows? Maybe I'm a worse fool than anyone. But this whole business has taken me by surprise. I mean I couldn't imagine people capable of such things. If I read of moral evil, Gabriel, it sounded to me like a legend. I never could make it seem true, although I know, of course, how especially in our time people have become brutal and cruel again. So it didn't occur to me that Kate was lying and was treacherous and was the tool of Carlsen and his gang. I know it now. I don't understand it yet. Neither it nor those people. And that's our weakness, Gabriel. That's the weakness and perhaps the doom of civilization. We don't understand. Then the brutes come and overwhelm us."

"That was exactly the situation of my father and his whole group in Germany. They couldn't believe the threats that were uttered. They couldn't believe because they couldn't imagine men capable of such things. Realization had to be burned into them by slow torture and by frightful death. And then they didn't understand."

"It helps me to think of that," Alan said, slowly. "What's happening to me is trivial in comparison. But it's the same kind of thing. Exactly the same kind. Because one morning I was awakened by the sense of something strange and sinister. I sat up. There was Kate beside me, stark naked, and in the dusk of the room stood Carlsen booted and in overalls. He grinned, a broad unnatural grin of thin dry lips which showed his blackish teeth. 'Well, I'll be god-damned!' he said. 'So I'm engaged to be married to a whore. I thought somethin' was goin' on here.' Kate pretended to be ashamed. She hid herself in the bedclothes. She tried to sob. But even in my shame and terror I noted the hollowness of the pretence. Then the trap was sprung. Carlsen, with that rigid grin on his face, said: 'I guess Kate ain't so much to blame. She's a country girl and don't know much. She's been brought up strict. It takes a city slicker, a minister's son, too, to corrupt our women—the kind o' guy we get in these here movements that goes with Reds and Kikes.

That's the ticket. Well, Mr. Jones, what the hell do you think you're going to do about it?' I didn't say anything, Gabriel. What was there to say? Could I have said: She sought me out. She's an immoral woman. Could I have? Well, I didn't. Words died in me. My voice died in me. Carlsen said: 'Well, I guess I'll call Pa and Ma Hirst and let 'em see this here sight. Seeduction and illicit intercourse is crimes in this state. Maybe we'd better send Mr. Jones to jail first off.' Then Kate took the blanket from her face. 'Please don't do that, Fred. Don't ruin me. You used to love me. I just couldn't resist him. He's a gentleman. He'll do the right thing.' A cold horror came over me. It crept over my entire body. It seemed to paralyze me, too. My sweat was literally like ice. All I knew was that I had to get away, somehow, at any cost. I cried out, desperately, 'I'm going!' Carlsen said—and now his face was a lyncher's, greenish with hate and blood lust: 'You c'n go to hell, for all I care, but you got to take the disgrace away from this woman. Ain't you man enough to want to do that?' He sat down at a little table. He had a piece of paper with him and took a fountain pen from the pockets of his overalls. He scrawled slowly, after the manner of the illiterate. He told me to get up and see what he had written. It was a statement that I had persuaded Kate Hirst to have illicit sexual relations with me under a promise of marriage. 'Sign that an' you can go!' I refused. 'All right,' he said, standing between the chair that had my clothes on it and me, 'I'll call Pa Hirst an' he'll phone the sheriff and the sheriff can see you both and you can go to jail.' I signed, Gabriel. I signed and slipped into my clothes and packed and fled. Now they're threatening a suit for breach of promise. A Ridgeville lawyer named Grant pursues me. The papers are ready to be served. They want seventy-five thousand dollars. Hadn't I better marry her and then kill myself? Wouldn't that be less disgrace and grief for Father?"

VIII

LONG past midnight Gabriel had taken Alan home. The next day, being Saturday, Gabriel was free and had promised Alan to find some one to defend him against the man Grant who was torturing him by letters, by telephone calls from Ridgeville, by constant threats of a lurid scandal. Gabriel had slept little. This matter of his friend filled him with horror, with a loathing of life. There was a complete unrelatedness between Alan's character and what had happened to him. It was exactly as though a cancer had suddenly developed in the cells of his body. Yet that would have been more tolerable. For we expect no consonance between the spirit of man and these degenerative processes of matter. Hence there is neither shame nor darkness. Such help as man has devised is used. A good fight is fought. The spirit may remain erect. But in the realm of moral evil the corruption leaves no one and nothing clean and so profoundly implicated is man with man that the innocent are contaminated by the guilt of the guilty and the clean by the foulness of the foul.

Gabriel got up early and gave his mother a brief notion of the trouble. At her advice he telephoned Ezekiel Frosch. By ten o'clock he had Alan Jones in the office of Frosch's attorney, Henry Rosenberg, a stout, middle-aged man with an impassive manner and melancholy eyes. He listened to the story, interrupted now and then by telephone calls which he answered in a tired voice. Each time he said to Alan: "Go on. I'm listening." When Alan was through he summoned his secretary. "Get me the office of Grant and Trueman in

Ridgeville." Then he lit a cigar and turned to Alan and Gabriel.

"It's a fairly common sort of case. You boys wouldn't, of course, know that. And as in all such cases they've got you on the spot, Mr. Jones, because you're not in a position, what with your father's reputation and your own future to consider, to go to trial. That's what these fellows know and that's what they count on. They'll bleed you. The best I can do is to reduce the amount."

Gabriel's whole being throbbed.

"In other words, you're going to connive in the use of the law as an instrument of blackmail."

The telephone rang. Rosenberg took up the receiver.

"Mr. Grant? Good-morning. This is Henry Rosenberg. You remember we met in the Drummond case. . . . You're right, that was some case. Well, listen: I've got Mr. Alan Jones in my office here. . . .Yes. . . .Well, that was just his inexperience. He realizes that he's got to do something about it. I suggest that you leave him personally out of the picture till we've had a conference. . . . No, I don't know what I'm going to advise him to do till you and I have had a talk. . . . Yes, we'll take care of any expense due to a delay in service. . . . Yes, I make myself personally liable. . . . Tuesday? Suits me fine. At ten? . . . Good. All right. Good-bye."

He leaned back in his swivel chair and relit his cigar and looked at Gabriel.

"I heard what you said. Let's look at the alternative to what you call conniving. We go to trial. Ridgeville is pretty much Black Legion. Dr. Jones is a liberal religious leader, a progressive, and a pacifist. His son comes to Ridgeville, working with the so-called 'reds' of the Colonies. He's taken into an old-fashioned American home and seduces the daughter—and he does so under written promise of marriage. The scandal will be a Fascist international scandal. Dr. Jones will have to resign because his usefulness will be at an end; Alan here will have no future. The jury will soak you twenty-five to thirty thousand dollars' damages. Or say, since these people haven't large notions even in their greed, fifteen thousand. But in that case you escape nothing. By settling out of court you escape everything. Am I right?"

Alan was leaning motionlessly forward, his face hidden in his hands.

"But it was a put-up job," Gabriel cried. "No innocent woman would have done what that woman did. Couldn't it be proved that the woman is a slut and that the signature was wrung from Alan under threats of immediate scandal and disgrace by the connivance of that woman and her paramour?"

Rosenberg's voice was a shade wearier still.

"Probably. After a fashion. Though it wouldn't be easy. But the jury, even if there were men on it who knew these contentions to be true, would regard them as 'red' or Jewish aspersions upon what they call the 'purity of their womanhood' and the 'sanctity' of their homes. You can't put on a trial like that in the void, you know. You've got people and places and political atmosphere to contend with. They've got us on the spot and they know it. Now the thing to do is to settle for a moderate sum. That's all."

Alan raised his head.

"Now that you explain, Mr. Rosenberg, it semes to me I knew all that in a way. That's the reason I said to Gabriel, if there were Satan, he would be a maker of laws."

Rosenberg got up heavily. He stood at the window.

"A lawyer," he said, "cannot sit in judgement on the law. What do you boys want?"

"In all the struggles of the years since Franklin Roosevelt," Gabriel said, "our parties have evidently forgotten the legal system and left it as vile and barbarous as ever."

Rosenberg uttered a sound between a growl and a hum.

"You're a bright kid. I've heard that, too, from Ezekiel. There is an element of truth in what you say. All laws touching on so-called illicit relations of any kind should have been abolished long ago. They, as well as other laws, are regularly made the instruments of blackmail. I suppose we have had more urgent problems both in the country and in the world. This seems urgent only to the few who are hard hit. But it's not a major problem."

"Is any outrage upon justice less than a major problem, Mr. Rosenberg?" Gabriel asked.

The tall, heavy man sat down again.

"I'm a lawyer. I have to do the best I can for my clients within the framework of the existing laws." He was suddenly irritated. He chewed at his cigar and growled. "It seems to me I've been saying that over and over again."

Alan rose slowly. His face was the hue of paper.

"I'll disappear. If they find me I'll kill myself."

Rosenberg shook his head.

"They'll find you unless you break all ties and stop communicating even with your parents. What kind of a life would that be? And they'd raise the scandal, anyhow. Let's get down to business. In my judgement Grant would have taken a different method if he hadn't smelled money. *Is* there any in your family?"

Alan had sat down again.

"My mother inherited traction stock ——"

"To be sure, she's the daughter of the late Theodore Hall. Well, then, we can settle."

"But I haven't told either my father or my mother. I'm ashamed of what I did. But that's the least of it. A sin of the flesh, if you like. It's the awful sordidness, the spiritual filth. The stench of those people, of that lawyer."

"Hum." Rosenberg seemed unimpressed. Gabriel watched him closely and saw that the man no longer knew the meaning of spiritual contamination. "E-ach," Rosenberg half-groaned. "Grant isn't such a bad fellow, everything considered. Does your father take as unrealistic a view of life as you do?"

Alan choked. He retched. He put his handkerchief to his mouth.

Gabriel said: "Dr. Jones won't understand, any more than Alan does, I'm afraid, your supineness and indifference. I can see how right you are practically. But don't you see, don't you see the moral loathsomeness of it all? Don't you feel defiled?"

Rosenberg grew a little red. He wheezed softly.

"I can't waste all day." He turned to Alan. "Listen to me, young man. I'll get in touch with your father. Today is Saturday. Very well, I'll see him on Monday. Grant is coming here on Tuesday. We'll try to get rid of this matter promptly. Then we'll forget about it. Could your mother, do you suppose, spare ten thousand dollars without impoverishing the family?"

Alan nodded.

Rosenberg got up.

"Then there won't be the slightest difficulty. You can stop worrying right here and now."

Alan and Gabriel went out into the sunlight, which seemed to them both at this moment like an ugly artifice. Gabriel tried to think of his father; he tried to fix his mind on the innumerable murders that had for years past filled the world and were filling it now; of the German armies slaughtering the inhabitants, men, women and children, of conquered territory in order to possess the food the land was wont to yield; of all the executions and exterminations of faction by faction which had darkened the world during the last fifteen years. He told Alan of his thoughts. "This thing is nothing," he said, "nothing at all."

Alan stopped and turned to him.

"It is everything, Gabriel, and you know it. It's exactly

all that you've been thinking about and that I've tried to think about, too, to comfort myself a little. It's the same cancer eating away our civilization that has eaten the heart out of others. From this thing it is not even a step to torture and execution; it's only a difference in immediate technique. And no one resists. Look at the man Rosenberg. He defends Grant. He sees nothing extraordinary in using a stupid law as an instrument of blackmail."

"I don't think he would do it himself," Gabriel said. "That's something."

"It isn't enough. I know that he's powerless. I see that now. If he summoned the leaders of the bar of the state, they would laugh at him. The law is the law. If it is foul and foully used, try to get out from under by bribing those who use it so. If you fail in that, let lives be broken and souls be murdered. Rosenberg's powerlessness is the measure of the spiritual corruption of this society."

Gabriel was silent. They resumed their walk. Alan went on.

"Mother can spare the money. It won't make any particular difference. So that isn't it. But suppose she couldn't. Suppose we had nothing but father's salary. Then my father —and you know what his life and work and influence have been—would be publicly crucified because of a whore's trick. And he would be crucified because the rabble wants to crucify him and all like him out of the shame of what it is and will not alter. The unredeemed would wreak on him the misery of their estate. And our groups—yours and mine —would they storm the courtroom, would they appeal against the outrage to judges, legislators, to the governor of the state? Would the moral values involved be weighed? Would the press consent for the sake of those moral values to omit the appeal of salaciousness in the case? Can't you see the headlines: 'Son of Outstanding Christian Leader Accused of Seduction and Breach of Promise'? Can you or can't you, Gabriel? So what is the last word on the subject? I'm thinking very clearly now."

"What?"

"That in this society a whore's trick is stronger than Christ, that the Christ principle is nothing and a whore's trick everything."

Gabriel sighed.

"Do you remember the line in Faust: 'You have destroyed it, the beautiful world'?"

Alan's voice was hard.

"Am I right or not?"

"You are right," Gabriel said. "And yet. Look, Alan, to a Jew things aren't so final. If we had let them be, how could we have lived? How could we live now? You and your good father know more about my people than many Jews. If we let *any* given injustice, however frightful, murder our hope for justice, we would long ago, long ago, have thrown ourselves as a people into the sea where it is deepest. When you're through with this thing you must work harder than ever to make the Christ principle prevail."

"No." Alan rapped out the word. "The Jewish people is a strange mixture of softness and hardness, of yieldingness and stubbornness. We're evidently more brittle. I don't think I can go on."

"You will. You must. Wait till it's all over. Wait."

They parted. Alan promised to be heard from. His face was white and rigid. Gabriel watched him as he walked away. The slender body was slightly bent, as though under an actual burden.

Gabriel too was weary. One thing after another had come to wrench him out of the concentration which he needed. He had been stringently revising the manuscript of what was later to be his first volume, "Moses in Egypt and Other Poems." But for months there had been an inner drought. There had been, too, a wavering of even

the small measure of faith that had once been his. Not quite
for the somewhat fanatical reason that Alan Jones had
given. No, a poet was more needed than ever if only men
felt the need of him. But did they? And what men? If a
poet was not felt gradually to be speaking for a group or a
people, what was his function? Without an ardent and compact audience, however small to begin with, the poet must
fall silent, unless he had a Miltonic faith in the future of his
genius. And that faith could not be entertained by one who
had not an anterior faith in the greatness and permanent-
ness of his nation and its spirit which would on an appointed
and triumphant day incorporate within itself the poet and
his work. For whom could a young man named Gabriel
Weiss be writing poetry in 1948 and 1949? For the American people? That, he and his generation knew, was a very
faint hope. The American people had crystallized about several centres—not about any that would include him. Oh, the
liberal reviewers would be friendly. They would, in all
likelihood, be quite sincere. The trouble was that they had
not even yet at the end of the many years learned that
essentially Freudian lesson concerning the oneness of men
and of the man speaking or singing or prophesying and the
necessary closeness of the inter-relation between audience
and speaker at a great depth of the subconscious. For whom
then was a poet, however humble, named Gabriel Weiss
to speak? For the Jewish people? In English? Today English was the language of all the free Jews in the world.
It was also their second language in Palestine. Hence they
were profoundly identified with it. But who could control
the great wheel of history? Arabic had once been the tongue
in which Jews created; for over a century in recent history
they had been incomparably productive in German. The
wheel of fate had turned. Gabriel had once met an eminent
American Jewish man of letters, a man who, whatever the
ultimate importance of his works, had written both pro-

foundly American books and had also married Jewish matter to English speech as none other had done. And this man, having read and relished certain poems of Gabriel's, had put his arm about the youth's shoulders and said, quietly: "It comforts me that my few best books—better than the others, anyhow—have been published in Hebrew translation in Tel-Aviv."

A deeper discomfort of the spirit than any he had yet felt now overcame Gabriel through the misadventure of his friend. It is, he found, one thing to read of barbarism and war, of cruelty and terror far away or in some depth of history, even of one's own short life so looked upon; it is another matter to see the worm gnawing at the root of civilization under one's very eyes. The strongest trembling of the spirit he had felt so far in his life had come at the news of repeated Arab uprisings in Palestine. They had been put down; temporary reconciliations had been effected. The Jews had again and again performed miracles of self-restraint and generosity. And in these examples of ethical civilization offered to the world he and his friends had found solace and healing. The pang he felt now was the raw pang of personal and immediate fear. No, not for himself alone, though for himself, too. But for the few last refuges of man—for America, then, where from a suddenly opened depth could rise that horror which was destroying the world. What is it, exactly, he asked himself; what is it, he cried out to Jehuda Brenner, to whom on a quiet evening he told the story. And Brenner answered: "It is simple. It is a falling away from good. It is the loss of the desire for goodness. It is, symbolically speaking, Sodom and Gomorrah once again. Many inventions do not help. Look at the Germans. New economic techniques do not help. Look at the Russians. Righteousness and the thirst for righteousness are dying. Men are no longer even paying lip worship to the command that they be brothers and love one another.

We are very near an end. Mark you, I did not say *the* end."

"And what are we to do and how are we to live?" Gabriel asked.

"We are to see to it that there be in every city the ten righteous men for whose sake God would have spared the Cities of the Plain when our father Abraham pleaded with the Eternal, so that from these groups of tens and from their seed humanity may some day be replenished and upraised."

IX

ALAN JONES had told his story to his father and mother
before Henry Rosenberg's interview with Dr. Jones
on Monday morning. He said to Gabriel: "I wasn't going
to add the self-reproach of cowardice to my other miseries.
I took a drink quite deliberately and assumed more reckless-
ness than I felt and told them Sunday night."

"How did they take it?"

Alan, who was looking much restored, laughed.

"They didn't see what we see at all. Not even as much
as Rosenberg sees. Father got pale. He said: 'I've known
for many years that we're not entitled to any margin of
moral error—not our kind, anyhow.' Mother was disgusted.
She said: 'How could you, Alan? They must be dreadful
people.' They both agreed at once that the matter must be
hushed up. So I asked Father why, on his principle of no
margin of error, it must be hushed up. He said very truly
and sincerely that I had suffered and was suffering a sufficient punishment and that a scandalous trial which would
ruin my future would be like executing a man for petty
theft. He said that if I felt that I would be eased by an
additional expiation I might well consider that my inheritance
would be diminished by whatever sum Mother would sacrifice. What do you say, Gabriel?"

"You know, Alan, how I love and respect your father.
But to me all that is insufficient; it's all on the wrong plane.
It's all compromise. *Had* the girl been innocent and had
you seduced her because she had come to love you, you
should have married her. But she being what she is and
things having happened as they did the very pillars of the

Temple should be torn down before any penalty is permitted to be inflicted. That's my, I suppose, intensely Jewish feeling. But you seem to share it."

"I do. Only after I'd talked to Father and Mother there
seemed to me to be a certain exorbitance in it. And then
again I saw quite clearly that the world is sliding to the
devil for the very lack of that exorbitance of moral demand
on the part of all the liberals. And then Mother came to
my room late to tuck me in as she used to do when I was
a small boy. She said, 'Bless you, my boy; money is only
money.' She was relieved, Gabriel, that it wasn't a nice
girl who would take me away from home and her. Was I
right, do you think, or was that only imagination?"

Gabriel nodded. This aspect of the matter amused him.

"Mummie feels quite that way about me. It's not simple
to be an only son."

"So," Alan said, "my mind is relieved, of course. Yet in
a way I despise myself for that, too, since the matter remains just what it was."

They were silent. Then in a grey, desolate voice Alan
added: "The big conference is on Thursday afternoon.
Rosenberg doesn't mind you're being there. D'you mind?
I need some one to talk to about it. It appears that this
fellow Grant has hired an Ozark City lawyer named Taylor
to join him in representing the Hirsts."

"I'll be there," Gabriel promised.

He understood profoundly Alan's misery. It came from
the thought of meeting those blackmailers on polite and
equal terms. No, it was even worse. The blackmailers would
assume an attitude of moral superiority over Dr. Jones, over
Alan, over their attorney. No, no, that wasn't possible. The
thing would assume its own unspeakable level. A bargain
would be struck—a frank but grimy bargain. He tried to
comfort Alan, as they parted, with this reflection. Dumbly
and dubiously Alan shook his head.

So soon as, unobtrusively, behind Dr. Jones and Alan he entered Henry Rosenberg's office on Thursday afternoon at three, he saw that nothing, however inconceivable in the realm of the moral imagination, would be spared his friends. Rosenberg and the two men who were with him arose; unsmiling introductions were accomplished; the two men held out hands which Dr. Jones and Alan were obliged to touch. Ramsay Taylor, the Ozark City lawyer, was a heavy grey man with a round, wrinkled head and heavy, dry, half-open lips, lips both brutal and bitter. Gabriel peered at him as he sat in the full light of a window. Something had gone subtly but violently wrong in this man's life. Frustration at the inmost core of him needed outer arrogance, demanded a front of iron to keep him erect. One could have pitied the man had he not been a menace. Grant, the Ridgeville attorney was young, apple-cheeked, grey-eyed—a fellow, Gabriel thought, capable of compunction. But there was a deliberate jauntiness in his gestures which showed that he had taken his line. His line was success. He would stay scrupulously within the letter of the law. But he would make that letter work to the utmost, regardless of consequences to man or woman, to good or God. At forty he intended to be no longer in Ridgeville, but district attorney, at least, in Ozark City and to gain that end he would—his mother's German phrase came into Gabriel's mind—stride over corpses. They were both, Taylor and Grant, respectable citizens, decent members of their professions, probably kindly to their families and friends. And they were both souls dead and damned.

Taylor began. He was ponderous. He addressed himself to Dr. Jones.

"We've consented to come to this conference, Doctor, out of respect for you and out of courtesy to Mr. Rosenberg. But there's really nothing to confer about. The case is clear. The sooner we go to trial the better."

Dr. Jones drooped. Then suddenly he drew himself up. In all his years he had not been spoken to in that tone of vulgar patronage. Rosenberg motioned to him gently not to reply.

"I don't know, Taylor, that the case is so damned clear. I know that Alan was fool enough to sign that paper. But we can show that he signed it under duress."

Grant snapped in a voice he tried to make like a lash.

"Do you think any jury of decent men and women would regard that plea as anything but adding cowardice to lechery?"

Rosenberg nodded.

"I've tried cases in towns like Ridgeville. I know your juries. I think you're a little too sure of yourself. But that's another matter. It would seem to me that if your client cares for her reputation she would prefer a settlement out of court just as much as my client. She's thirty. I've looked up her birth certificate. Even if we can't convince a jury that the promise of marriage was obtained under pressure, since when is premarital intercourse considered a creditable thing in Ridgeville?"

Taylor and Grant exchanged glances. It was Taylor who spoke with a curious writhing of his coarse, thick, broken, bitter lips.

"You miss the point. The girl fell for the glamour of your client's education and city manners. He must have persuaded her that intercourse under the circumstances was all right. She couldn't argue with a man who has a bachelor's degree and a bachelor of divinity degree. In spite of being a few years older than he she was like putty in his hands. That's just the common sense of the situation."

The blood shot into Gabriel's head. He had met this thing before. Whenever men of the type that voted as by a summons of nature for Cornelius Faithful Prout were bent on justifying some repulsive moral lie or insidious slander or wanted to lynch or crucify, then invariably they appealed to common sense. And that appeal always succeeded with the mob. For what man, however grovelling in ignorance or moral filth, however self-condemned in the inmost recesses of his nature, but would swear that he shared common sense with his fellow men, that residuum, then, of humanity, of which nothing could rob him and by the possession of which, despite his stupidity, his feebleness of will, his stealth and self-contempt, he was still judge and lord of all things between heaven and earth? Gabriel looked at his friends. Dr. Jones had closed his eyes. He had resigned himself to the immediate suffering of the situation. Alan looked as though his skull must break the skin of his forehead. His hands were clenched.

Rosenberg offered cigars all around. They were declined. He lit one himself with slow and comfortable deliberation.

"All right, gentlemen. You think your case is so strong that a settlement out of court doesn't interest you. Of course, I foresaw that possibility. I had a little interview with my client late last night on that very subject."

Gabriel saw Alan wince and Dr. Jones suddenly sit forward in astonished attention. It was evidently true that Rosenberg had persuaded Alan, as a last resort, to take a certain stand.

"And what conclusion did you come to?" Grant barked, with ostentatious virility.

"Why, this," said Henry Rosenberg, with immense deliberation, "that Alan will redeem his promise. He'll marry the woman." He smiled sleepily. "Then there will be no cause of action and we'll all be happy."

A slight redness suffused the dry wrinkled face of Taylor.

"What assurance have we that the fellow will do as you say? Judging from his past actions ——"

Rosenberg smiled again.

"You're perfectly safe on the proposition if he doesn't.

You can bring your suit any time, can't you? The statute of limitations gives you years. But all we want is thirty days. If Alan hasn't married Miss Hirst in thirty days and if no settlement has been arrived at, either, then your case is just exactly as good as it is today. Isn't it?"

"Absolutely," barked Grant.

Taylor got up. He was a very tall man and yet gave a strangely dwarfed impression.

"Will you write us a letter embodying these alternative propostions and the time limit?"

"I'll dictate it before I leave the office this afternoon."

He got up, too. With perfunctory nods Taylor and Grant walked out. Rosenberg conducted them to the outer office. He came back into a heavy troubled silence.

Dr. Jones lifted his suffering face.

"Dear Mr. Rosenberg, do you really think it's my son's duty? Whether it is or not has, of course, been my severest problem. But Alan, who has always, it seems to me, been honourable and scrupulous, doesn't think so."

"Duty!" Rosenberg laughed. "What we've got to do is to avoid the suit and subsequent trial. It would be hideous and disgusting. It would ruin you and your son; it would inflict an irreparable wound on the cause of liberalism in this state. So much is clear. All right. Suppose the worst came to the worst and Alan had to marry the slut. He would be on the verge of a nervous breakdown. I've got a physician or two who would see to that. He'd refuse her all marital rights except a weekly stipend, which would be quite small because it would be in proportion to his earnings, not in proportion to the amount of blackmailing that Mrs. Jones could stand. But the Hirst woman doesn't want to be Alan's wife. She has quite other notions, you may be sure. She'd give him a quiet divorce for comparatively little money. Do you get it, Doctor?"

Dr. Jones clasped his hands.

"I do, Mr. Rosenberg. But isn't that, God help me, most unworthy scheming?"

Rosenberg frowned.

"Is it as unworthy as their whole vile frame-up?"

"No, no. I suppose not. But to sink to their level ——"

"That's it, Father, that's it," Alan cried. "The law forces us to sink to the level of the lowest. This society supports and countenances that. It's intolerable."

Rosenberg wheezed and grunted with impatience.

"Let's not be childish. We can't live on any level without protecting ourselves. If a man comes and holds you up with a gun you also sink to his level when you either knock it out of his hand or shoot first."

"True," said Gabriel. "But he is without the law. The horror of this business is that these men do precisely the same thing within the law."

"Listen," Rosenberg said, with a touch of tartness. "We'll discuss the moral philosophy involved at my dinner table when this business is settled. May I go on now?"

They all lowered their heads a little. No one replied.

"As a matter of fact, as I told Alan last night, there's not one chance in ten thousand of its coming to a marriage ceremony. My offering to have Alan redeem his supposed promise is not a concession but a threat. What would Taylor and Grant get out of that situation? What do they want? They want a scandal and money. Which do they want more? Money. Hence by seriously threatening them with a device that will prevent the scandal, they'll concentrate on money. Did you hear me say that they could go ahead if within thirty days there had been neither marriage nor settlement?"

"I did," said Dr. Jones.

"Well, there will be a settlement. I'll hear from them within ten days. They, of course, must make the next move.

Then the haggling will begin. Now you'd better tell me how much we can pay?"

Dr. Jones smiled.

"Money is only money, Mr. Rosenberg, and Alan is our only child. If it could be done for ten thousand dollars, it would be pleasant. But it could be more. Alan cares little for worldly things and I carry a reasonable insurance on my life."

Rosenberg made a note on a pad before him.

"I hate to give those swine a lot of money. But we may have to. At all events, in my judgement there's really nothing left to worry about."

He got up. They knew that clients were waiting in the reception-room. Dr. Jones looked at his watch.

"I have an appointment. Will you walk home with Alan, Gabriel?"

Alone in the street, Alan and Gabriel looked at each other.

"No," said Gabriel, "not one word on the real issue. Not one word on what it's all about. Just a loathsome game with human beings as the pawns. Rosenberg is quietly proud of his counter-move. And it is clever and effective and I thank God for it for your and your father's sake. But it's qualitatively of a piece with their moves. He consents to their game and plays it. And that is how so-called justice is arrived at in this society. I never knew it before. Did you, Alan?"

"No, I didn't know it. But it seems to me that before this experience I knew nothing of any kind. I knew things on paper. I hated things on paper. I fought things on paper. Now I know lust and treachery and how justice is not even thought upon. That's it. They don't think of it or reckon with it. And one fine day, if not this year, the Taylors and the Grants will elect some Cornelius Faithful Prout. The Rosenbergs will try to pretend to themselves

not to see the full horror of it; they will pretend to themselves that the brutes of the jungle can be cajoled into re-
straining their utmost ferocity. And then this country will
follow the other countries to destruction, to utter ruin. What
are we going to do, Gabriel?"

Gabriel told Alan how he had asked the same question
of Jehuda Brenner and what Brenner's answer had been.

Alan laughed.

"To be one of the ten to save the city. What an exorbitant
demand to make of a fellow. At present, do you know what
my most burning trouble is?"

"Tell me."

"That woman awakened my senses." He turned his face
away. "I burn."

"There are two points of view in regard to that," said
Gabriel, "the Christian point of view that it is better to
marry than to burn, which is the thing I like least about
Christianity. And there's our point of view: that it is our
duty to serve God even with the *yetzer hara*, the evil impulse. Some of us go farther and hold that the flesh, like
all earthly things, can be entirely sanctified and redeemed."

"How about yourself, Gabriel?"

Gabriel suddenly knew that he had come to a conclusion
within, which hitherto he had not admitted even to himself.

"I'm getting a raise in salary next year. In addition Mummie can let me have an extra thousand a year without mind-
ing it. I'm going to get married."

Alan looked up.

"To whom?"

"I think I have come to the conclusion that it's better to
look about and determine and to let one's judgement have
something to do with the matter. I met a girl about a year
ago and my entrails began to burn. I found out that she
was stupid and bad-tempered and irreligious and worldly in

a way which would drive me crazy. Still my entrails burned. I tried to fool myself and make excuses for her. Thank God, she turned me down flat. She had other notions than marrying a poor young teacher."

"There's a great deal of truth in what you say."

"Among our orthodox people there still exists the *shadchan*, the marriage-broker. I don't think the custom so low or stupid. Isn't it rather an attractive thought to have young women, so to speak, presented to you and to pick? Or am I perverse?"

"Maybe. Maybe there's a touch of sadism in your feeling. But I dare say it's a healthy male sadism. I think I get what you mean. Of course I have no such chance. By the way, Gabriel, would you like children?"

"Yes," said Gabriel, gravely. "Very much."

"In spite of the state of the world?"

"In spite of everything. A man who has no children is no better than a man who is dead, our Talmud says. And I feel that way, Alan, beyond all reason and all practical considerations."

The two young men saw each other constantly during the next two weeks. Alan needed his friend's moral support. Taylor and Clark did make the first move, as Henry Rosenberg had predicted. But in order to increase the sum to be wrung from the case they set about harrying Alan and his father with a cold and bitter and altogether evil persistence, as though to grind them down and break them. They would seem to fall silent and disappear for days. Then, suddenly, they would, as it were, leap forth again with papers ready to serve, with the demand, as an alternative, of immediate marriage. Rosenberg stood like a rock. But he was obliged to summon Alan again and again to his office. "Torture," Alan said to him, "is evidently not abolished. Of course it's moral and not physical torture. But on the other hand it's private. These men are not even officers of the law or servants of the state." Rosenberg said that there were two answers to that observation. One was that neither Taylor nor Grant had any notion of the capacity for moral pain and humiliation which people like Alan and his father possessed. To them it was pretty much of a "deal." They expected to fight for every extra penny and expected their opponents to do the same in the same coldly brutal spirit. But, Rosenberg said, there was a second answer. Everything has to be paid for in this world. So fineness and ability and high repute had to be paid for too. If this thing had happened to obscure and poor people, however innocent and honourable, he would, as he put it, have "gone to the bat" and it would have been rather fascinating to watch the play of motives and the forces of prejudice and to speculate on the verdict. But Alan and his father would not desire the trial even if one could have guaranteed them a favourable verdict. They could not afford either the personal immersion in filth as a spiritual matter nor the ugly hue and cry as a social matter. Hence they were at an initial disadvantage. Rosenberg looked hard at Alan. "Didn't you know that except on your own plane, which is not the world's, people like you are always at a disadvantage?"

"I know it now," Alan answered, "and it explains many things."

Before the thirty days were quite over a settlement was made. Taylor and Grant received the money with unconcealed satisfaction. They had the audacity to offer their hands in congratulation to Dr. Jones and Alan on the satisfactory termination of the matter. Dr. Jones touched the proffered hands. Alan drew back. Then he laughed into the unconscious and surprised faces of the impenetrable rogues.

CORNELIUS FAITHFUL PROUT had not been elected to the Presidency in 1948. But twenty-five millions of men and women had voted for him. Hence since the population of the United States had not increased markedly since the earlier 'forties of the century the combined liberal parties had won by a majority of not quite six millions. Prout declared that he had the alternative between waiting four more years to walk into the White House or seizing the government at once with his legions. He refrained from the second alternative because it was not his opponents who were upholding the ancient democratic tradition of America but himself. He added, however, that he and his millions were waiting and watching. Circumstances of such national shame might arise that he would be forced for the sake of the "fair" fame of America itself to march on Washington.

Everyone knew what circumstance he meant. During the past decade the Chinese had been forced out of their wise and elegant pacifism. They had learned the hard lesson of organization and efficiency from their Japanese conquerors; they had trained and armed millions; they were slowly, steadily, relentlessly pushing the Japanese into the Yellow Sea. With them the people of Manchukuo and of Mongolia had risen; the Soviets had done an immense trade in arms; the swollen Japanese armies were coming home and at home there was neither work nor bread. Now the choice for the Japanese had lain between pouring into Eastern Siberia, which the Russians had practically abandoned, or finding land and rice to the South. They chose the South. They

seized the Philippines. And it was this circumstance which
Prout considered a national shame. The liberals pointed
out that a new era, however belated, had arisen in world
politics, that Britain had deliberately ceded North Borneo
to the Japanese in the interests of the world's health and
peace, and that the United States had no duty in the matter
except to seek to mitigate the severities to which the Japanese conquerors might be tempted. Prout and his followers
raised the old cry of the Yellow Peril and the dominance
of the white man. And the vast mob of the inferior yelled
with him. As always and everywhere, it seized upon an easy
alternative to its difficult duty of becoming civilized. It
gloried in its whiteness; it lynched a few Japanese of long
American ancestry; it harried the Negroes; it boycotted
Jewish merchants. To be white was enough. To be white was
a substitute for discipline, humility, righteousness, even for
the plain virtues of industry and common honesty. Prout
was the leader of the Great White Race in America. War
against Japan should be declared at once. It was the same
cosmic farce over again that had devastated nation after
nation; it was the same savage substitution of murder for
self-improvement, self-searching, self-discipline. To provide
self-esteem for those German masses who had none and did
not desire to reacquire it by work and ethical action, Jews
and freemen had been exterminated and a great civilization
had been stamped out in blood and dirt. In order to provide
the illiterate Russian masses with an unearned glorying
in themselves, millions of men and women had been driven
into death. The liberals of America saw the monstrous and
evil omen. Gabriel heard again and again, as though they
were being spoken to him now, those final words of Jehuda
Brenner who was gone long ago, who had a little cottage
now on the slopes of Mount Carmel overlooking the great
city and harbor of Haifa, who would go wayfaring no more,
but help to man that Palestinian promontory of justice

and goodness which jutted out into a world of raging savagery. Brenner's words had constituted the spiritual apprehension of the world's central disease. One could define that disease scientifically as the substitution of brutality to others for inner change, and of violent action for the taking of thought. But that was precisely the falling away from good and God. That was it. And it was apparently irresistible. And so it came about that as the years went on many men of various faiths in England and America, many men and women travelling to the same goal on different but parallel paths, withdrew more and more from direct participation in political and active life and addressed themselves to the task of striving after an inner perfection which might, they hoped, shine out upon a world riven and disgraced and help to save it. Books and pamphlets appeared with these teachings. A new mysticism arose. It began to be understood why at certain other times in history men had become anchorites and why the contemplative religious orders had arisen. Evil may become so strong and so pervasive that all action and reaction partakes of its nature. Thus only he who refrains from action can hope by that very fact to diminish the evil that floods the earth.

A small book in this vein, written by Peter Lang, was brought to Gabriel by Alan Jones.

"Your friend, too, has come to this conclusion."

"I'm sorry," Gabriel said. "I sympathize fully; I see the reasonableness of it. I know that we are fighting without hope. But I shall in my small way go on."

"You see the evil leaped out at me from ambush. I know it face to face."

"True. But I was, so to speak, born into it. Don't forget my father's fate."

"Where do you get your stubbornness from?"

Gabriel laughed.

"We're a stiff-necked people; I've told you before. Maybe *this* is the meaning and purpose of it, that when all despair and have a right to despair there shall be some who, despite despair, still strive."

"Perhaps."

"Practically, Alan, what are you going to do?"

"I've been offered a small congregation in a suburb of Saint Louis. I'll give the salary away. If I can get a few people to live reasonably close to the Christ principle, I'll stay. Otherwise not. And you, Gabriel?"

"Well, since we're here in 1950 and our American world still stands and I still have my job, even though we're being pushed into a Japanese war, I'm going to sanctify life, according to our religion by getting married."

A sudden melancholy suffused Alan's whole being.

"I wish I had your courage and your cleanliness. I find that love has been soiled for me; if I married the finest girl—Oh precisely then—I couldn't be with her without identifying sex with that Hirst creature. That would degrade both the girl and me. No." He drew himself desperately up. He tightened all his muscles as though to be more compact for a hopeless fray. "I must go my way alone."

"What will you do if we're pushed into the war and you're conscripted?"

Alan brightened.

"Refuse military servitude, of course. That would be a cause worth suffering for. And you?"

"Since 1940 Jews have been given the right, like Quakers, of exemption from active military service for conscience' sake. Haven't you ever read the foul reproaches to which we're subjected on that account?"

Alan looked vague.

"I don't read *their* press. Never have. What's the use? From now on I shall read even less. No papers at all. Few books. If the Gospel is to be *lived*, not messed round with theologically, but lived—it will take all my strength."

He turned to go. His eyes were wistful.

"You have met a girl, of course?"

Gabriel nodded. He was defensively casual.

"Eve is a younger friend of Ge' ulah Frosch's. I met her through Gershon. She's graduating from college this year. We'll be married in the summer."

Alan was silent. He took Gabriel's hand and pressed it. Then he went his way.

Gabriel had met Eve Israel many months ago. The Ezekiel Frosch children had given a party. It was during *Chanukah*, the celebration of the lights of the Temple and of the Maccabean revolt against Rome. Frosch, though near sixty now, still had his old energy and glow. His was a festive nature. From the very wrecks of time he could draw triumph. The young people were all discouraged. They spoke of horrors that assumed an almost mythic nature. The age of rockets was approaching. The thousand experiments were culminating in that final result of man's ingenuity in destruction. No more would it be necessary, as had hitherto been done by Germans and Italians and Japanese, to send forth squadrons of planes whose pilots had been given injections of the new intoxicating drugs, so that in a pseudo-orgasmic spasm of hours' duration they could rise and hurl themselves down and, careless of their own destruction, became living torches wherewith to set in flames what still remained of the cities of mankind. Now in a dark huge tower an engineer would measure distance and the aerial arc above the straight line of that distance, and turn three levers and set the hands on three dials, and at last press a button. Then from that dark tower open to the sky would emerge the rocket, in form like the torpedo propelled from submarines, only immense, glittering, monstrous, and would soar upward with unimaginable speed, beginning from the start to describe its accurately

measured arc in heaven and would crash with a tumult far
beyond thunder upon its destined goal. One engineer and two
assistants could now destroy cities three hundred miles away.
There was no refuge left.

But there were other circumstances that troubled the
younger people at the house of Ezekiel Frosch more deeply.
Despite the close watch kept in our coastal cities and along
our two frontiers new small bands of emissaries were filter-
ing into the country, none knew precisely from where, none
knew precisely who had sent them. Dimly it was rumoured
that somewhere between the Black and the Caspian Seas
Fascist and Communist armies had met and made a truce.
From Koenigsberg, whither the German government had
now withdrawn, and from Moscow, chiefs of the Fascist
and Communist internationals had flown to a general council in Kharkov, where the question had been raised whether
the totalitarian states, the great dictatorships, were not
stupidly lacerating and destroying each other. Would it not
be better to divide and to rule the world? And two powers
stood in the way of that consummation: Britain and the
United States. These must be undermined; these must be destroyed; these must first be ideologically attacked. In them
the parties that favoured war and force must be supported
and the Communist remnants must either be reactivated or
persuaded to make common cause with the Fascists on the
plea that democracy and the religions of Moses and Christ
and old-fashioned capitalism, however changed in the details of its technique, were the chief obstacles to the rise
and power of the dark compact masses of mankind under
whatever slogan or by whomever led.

Such were the rumours. And they fitted the facts. For
these new secret emissaries from overseas, who were said to
be directed by a chief named Andrew Saracen, were to be
found in Fundamentalist meeting-houses in the South and
in miners' towns in Pennsylvania; they urged the whites to

expel the Negro from his growing participation in the economic structure of the country, and the Negro proletarian to rise in Spartacide revolts. Everywhere they declared the present polity to be the essence of oppression and disorder; everywhere they carried their flaming slogans that Christianity, a hideous Oriental slave-religion foisted upon the world by Jews, was the opiate of the people. Subtly they changed the applications of the slogan. Among Fascists they attacked Christianity for its doctrine of brotherhood and its intolerable neglect of biological values and the consequent mongrelizing of the great races; among workers they laughed to scorn the God of the capitalists and the Christ of expensive churches and asked how long the proletariat would be contented with the sops that had in recent years been flung as one flings bones to dogs? They sought to deindividualize men, to weld them into masses, to fire these masses with a common fury. Mass-fury was their aim and end. . . .

Of these things the young men and women spoke and of the defensive measures that were to be taken. Then Ezekiel Frosch arose and stood with his back to the fireplace.

"Listen, children," he said. "You know that I was in Palestine last winter and spring. I want you to think of that and draw hope and courage from it. Not because it's ours, but because it is what it is. You've read and heard how once the Arabs feared and hated us? They don't any longer. In the long run they were convinced by the rightness of our intent. We struck no blow. We never retaliated. We went on doing good. It worked. In the long run it worked. Goodness works. Justice works. I'm not saying that Palestine is safe. Wars may sweep over it and destroy it once again. But not before, thank God, we've been able to prove what a commonwealth can be. There are no Fascists in Eretz Yisrael; there are no Communists; there is neither hunger nor ignorance, neither rivalry nor hatred. And if one group of people has found the way once, may not other groups find it on some other day?"

It had been while Ezekiel Frosch was speaking that Gabriel had first truly seen Eve Israel. He had seen her before, as he told her later, with the eyes of the body, and he had even seen her loveliness. Perhaps something within him had fled from dwelling on the sight of her, because we are never ready for the decisive, the ultimate, and prefer to dwell in the moderate twilight of the habitual. He had, moreover, made up his mind that he would marry sensibly. He carried this determination about with him. Perhaps that, too, had veiled his vision. Now that he saw her fully at last he remembered that Gershon had cursorily introduced them to each other one day. He had evidently pushed out of consciousness what now came back so clearly to him—the knowledge of her hands, of her perfect hands, not morbidly slender, as so many beautiful hands are, nor with fingers pointed to excess, nor yet too flexible like the hands of a dancer, but as precisely and profoundly articulated beneath a sufficient covering of white flesh as a syllogism or a sonnet. . . . He now saw these hands folded beneath her chin, as Eve looked up from a low seat at Ezekiel Frosch. He saw the hands and recognized them and saw the head they supported, the heavy strands of dark hair drawn back across the sides of the head from a white central line and loosely knotted at the nape of the neck, the immemorial way of a beautiful woman wearing her hair—right as the iambics of Milton, rhythmic as the hexameter. He saw the not too high forehead, the long-lashed lids and eyes of golden brown, the delicate but not trivial nose, the full but not too heavy lips, the cup-like curve of the chin.

He rose as Ezekiel Frosch fell silent and the conversation became general, and went over to her and sat down on the floor beside her low seat.

"Do you remember our meeting before?" he asked.

She took down her hands and let them sink to her lap.

"Yes. Because I'd just read a poem of yours in the *Menorah Journal.*"

"Was that the only reason?"

She smiled a tranquil smile. It was like the smile of Gina's girlhood. Gabriel did not know that, but the smile made him feel like one who after bleak wandering comes home.

"What do you want me to say?"

"Nothing. I don't know that I want you to say anything. It seems to me that I want you just to be."

"Is that poetry or truth—*Dichtung* or *Wahrheit?*" she asked.

"Both." His tone was grave as his glance. "At the right level there is no distinction. The two are one."

They were drawn into the conversation. They made the right answers. By and by Eve went to help Mrs. Frosch and Ge' ulah pass round plates and cups and glasses. But all the while, Gabriel thought, they were dwelling together in a privacy of their own, in a deep seclusion from the world, in a brooding sense of the uniqueness of what was happening to them, both aware of its eternal recurrence, yet both rightly convinced, too, of its miraculous uniqueness even as each human countenance, though possessing the same universal features, is unique among all the innumerable myriad faces of the dead, the living, and the yet unborn.

From the day of that meeting on these two had felt one and at one. Together they watched the spring come and leaned their hearts, despite the storms of time and the raging of the heathen, upon the faithfulness of the eternal processes. Whatever happened within his history, God desired man to be. They had to go back, these two, to that stark last justification of their love and of all the instincts which that love brought into play. They jested, too, yet the substance of their jest was their faith and sure reliance. Was not Eve, Chavah, the name of life itself because the woman was to be the mother of all life? And had not Adam, the earth-man called her so? And was it not God's will that the earth be replenished even though war and sin diminished and destroyed? And were not seed-time and harvest sure?

They drew courage from tight bud and shy blossom; they stood beneath a wide-spreading plum tree in full white innumerable bloom; they watched sunsets over the low Western hills and saw the bands of orange and purple fade into mauve and black and waited for star-rise and leaning back their heads lost themselves, hand in hand, in the liquid brilliance of the great wheeling constellations. Nor were they afraid of the high pulse of mutual passion in their blood. By this, too, by this not least was life, according to their faith and knowledge, to be sanctified. If they abstained from each other until a cottage was found and furnished and friends and kinsmen had witnessed the ancient rites, it was only to give the consummation of their love a day, a date, a festive setting, a memoried beauty in the world.

XI

THE world went on its clamorous, its bloody and disastrous way. But in the garden of the small house in
which Eve and Gabriel lived there stood, slanting from the
prevailing winds, a group of white birches. These Gabriel
contemplated with a new absorption. He learned from them.
He learned from Eve. From her beauty he learned and from
her unformulated faith, a faith like the faith of the birches
that, so long as the earth gave food the eternal cycle would
not be broken.

It was not that Eve was indifferent to the tragic direction of things, nor that she was less instructed than he. But
she was bent upon a graver and more enduring business.
Unconsciously she was, as her name said, the giver and
conserver of life. He often blanched at the news in the morning's paper. The last French provinces had fallen into Fascist hands; the rumoured junction of the hordes of the
neo-barbarians between the Black and Caspian Seas was confirmed; Washington sent an ultimatum to Tokyo. Eve said:
"We have each other; we have our people; we have our
work. Stop fretting."

"For how long?" he asked.

"It's beyond our control. We must live as though for always, it seems to me."

He frowned.

"It's hard."

"Stop frowning, Gabriel, or I'll think you don't love me
any more. It isn't hard for me; it shouldn't be hard for
you."

"Why isn't it hard for you?"

She lifted her head and in her gesture there was an air of triumph.

"There have been other evil ages. More evil than this. They used, as the historians say, to put to the sword the men and the women and the children of conquered cities. Yet some escaped, Gabriel. And those who did carried on life. We're better off than that. Even in Europe they're still a little better off than that. Always there must have been people like you and me who still had a chance to be happy and took it and so did a better thing for the world than those who fretted or fought."

"How lovely you are when you say that! And you're right, of course. But there's another thing. Ever since I went through Alan Jones' trouble with him, I have a sense of danger lurking here—even here; of things in ambush."

She came over to him and put her arms about his shoulders.

"No Paradise without a snake. The snake belongs to Paradise." She laughed. "Darling, we'll scotch the snake, anyhow, if we can't kill it."

He kissed her throat and shoulder. It was true. She gave him Paradise. He used the word not in the silly, derivative, sentimental sense. No, this was their *gan Eden,* their garden of Eden in which once again God walked *l'ruach hayom,* in the "breathing of the day." Nor did they need to hide themselves from Him amid the trees of the garden. For the guilt of origin had long been accomplished and had been expiated through the ages by the guilt-feeling at the core of every human soul. But the great fruits of that eating of the one fatal fruit had been love and wisdom and art and vision. Love like theirs, neither afraid nor sterile; love that was begetting whether of child or work or both; love which, whether it issued in child or work or both, was conquest over time and wrong and death and in itself triumph and immortality. It glowed and flamed, as Gabriel came to see, under Eve's less subtle guidance, all the more dazzlingly in a world in which death celebrated daily its thousand orgies. Men had become beset by self-hatred and the death-wish. These they transformed into aggressiveness and then sought to give reasons for the wars they waged by mythic hates and fantasms of invented dangers. Or else they fled from their appointed places within life and avoided the actions that are life-giving, like the Jews who deserted their people, like the Christians who betrayed their Christ, and so though passive made common cause with the fomenters of hate and war. *Amor vincit omnia* (love conquers all things). The pagan poet had spoken more profoundly than he knew. Love creates. Love saves. And Gabriel came to know that his and Eve's love of one another's souls and bodies, that their impassioned blending and oneness, were of good, of life, of God, were like the green of spring and the rising of the faithful stars, amid a world of death and moral darkness.

From these passionate thoughts and actions and gestures there came to him another revelation, a revelation not so rare as it had been in the days of his parents, but even now not frequent. It was the revelation of recurrence. It was the revelation of the venerableness of the eternal gesture. It was fundamentally divided by every quality from the mass-frenzies of the age. It was not plunging into servility or un-differentiation. It was a fathomless sense of alliance with the good and luminous spirits whose cognitions and actions bound to each other the cosmic ages and constituted them the company of the seekers after redemption. Even as Eve and he were living a Paradise upon a bitter and unparadised earth, so had other lovers from century to century defeated death by the enchantment and the fruits of their unitedness. Some of these lovers were known by name among their own and other peoples, from Joseph ben Akiba and the daughter of Kalba Sabua to John Donne and Anne More. But myriads

were nameless. Yet it was they who had passed on the torch
of love and life from age to age and had made beautiful the
blood-soaked and unconsecrated world. They had defeated
the death-wish which, turned outward, was transformed into
aggression and from time to time had devastated the innocent and peaceful earth. To this cognition Gabriel clung,
as the surges of the sea of evil rolled farther inland upon
every human shore. He and Eve were not stealing their
happiness from a world in agony. Their happiness was in
itself healing and redemption.

It was now that after the lapse of years Elizabeth Warner
revisited Ozark City. She had telephoned Gina and came
casually to Gina's house one day when Gabriel was there.

"I told you I would know the moment when I might safely
come back?"

He looked at her closely. She had aged markedly. She
had let herself age. But she was gallant and full of life.
He understood. Now that he was so absorbed and sheltered
he could look upon her without sorrow or regret. He could
see her with untroubled gratitude and affection.

"You're quite happy, aren't you, Gabriel?"

"As happy as it is possible to be. And you, Elizabeth?"

She threw back her head with a bright little laugh. His
mother sat tranquilly her long hands holding her head. It
seemed to him for an instant as though time had stood still.

"For a woman who never had anything but broken shards,
pretty jagged at that, from the beginning, I haven't done so
badly. Of course, I have no child. Eve and you must have
children, Gabriel!"

"We will," he said, quietly.

"But first and last," Elizabeth went on, "I've helped toward the begetting of a little freedom and a little work. A
poor substitute. But something."

He took her hand and pressed it. He wanted to kiss it, but
shrank from the artifice of the gesture.

"You did, Elizabeth. But did you always understand that?"

"More or less. So did your mother after the very first."

He looked at his mother. With closed eyes she quoted from her old favourite Rilke:

> "Nur wer mit Toten vom Mohn
> ass, von dem ihren,
> wird nicht den leisesten Ton
> wieder verlieren."

Elizabeth got up.

"You are right, Gina. I always felt that about you. You have been at home with the dead and shared their poppy with them and have heard, a little sooner or later, all the overtones. Gabriel, you must have Eve invite me. We can all be friends now, can't we?"

"We must be friends."

"And isn't the volume coming out at last?"

"Yes," he said in a sharp, clear way that precluded discussion. "In a few weeks."

He pleaded that he had to meet a class almost at once, and hurried off alone. What he said had been exact. He was now twenty-six. His scattered poems had slowly made for him a small but definite reputation. Two publishers, not unwilling during highly successful seasons to spend a little on poetry, had offered to print his first volume. The prices of books had long been reduced. But from about 1940 on new processes of manufacture and the willingness of an ever widening public to accept substitutes for the old cloth bindings and to do without the useless and expensive dustjackets, had still left the publishing business in America a not unprofitable one. Hence Gabriel had finally not been able to escape publication and, after many delays, the volume, *Moses in Egypt and Other Poems,* was about to appear.

Eve had urged it upon him, too. She had at first not

understood the reasons for his reluctance. He was not sure
that he always understood it himself. It was not, he believed, the not uncommon hesitation of the artist, disguised
in an hundred fashions, to give his work to the world in order
to be transformed by the world—even, nay, especially in the
event of a certain acceptance by it—into something other
than he had either said or meant. The major teachings of
Freud had long been accepted now by the really intelligent
minority among men. Writers knew that their audiences
must transform the work of art into the image of those audiences' inner needs. The work that goes forth is seed. In the
womb of man it germinates once more. Acceptance means
what the artist as an individual must call misunderstanding.

What troubled Gabriel was that other matter which had
been in his mind for years. Who was going to accept him?
He remembered as a subtle fact that a single Hebrew word
means world and universe and eternity and public, and that
another single Hebrew word means labour and worship.
He pondered upon *olam* and *avodah*. Oh yes, a publisher
would publish his verses. Reviewers would review them.
Five to seven hundred copies would be bought, a few by
isolated lovers of verse, the rest by members of his political
and religious groups and the libraries controlled by them.
But art, he knew, should be worship, such worship as the
public, *a* public, a people, a large group, a nation, a coherent
section of mankind, needed to confirm and illuminate its
relations to the world and to eternity. It must be work that
binds men closer to each other and to God. All great work,
all good work, had sooner or later done that. It was not a
question of success or of sales. Books might have an enormous circulation and remain quite outside of that realm of
the fundamental needs of man. And again a small anonymous
pamphlet—say, like the Book of Ruth or the Song of Songs—
or a fragment of a woman's body moulded by an unknown
sculptor, might become and remain part of the everlasting

legend by which men learn from age to age to understand, to endure and to transcend their fate.

Had his verses any chance of being so much as tested for acceptance in that sense? It was not arrogance that made him meditate on this matter again and again. It was humility; it was, if you like, a chastity of the spirit. He had been from his childhood on acquainted with the terrors of fate. To write little books for mere self-affirmation through the chatter of friends and find them at long last in one's old age on bookstalls—that seemed to him a thing too trivial and too wasteful. If one had any power of doing useful work, were it as a teacher or as a carpenter, one should do that with all one's might rather than go through the empty gestures of those people of the age of self-worship who had lost all gods and had lost God and had nothing left to worship but themselves and so ended in a triviality of corruption comparable to that of a withered bawd who all day long before a mirror persuades herself that vestiges of youth and beauty still remain. No, art that is not worship is baser than dust. But it must be worship that persuades. Whom, Gabriel asked, could he persuade?

Had he a people whose voice he could become, provided he were worthy? The question had, of course, haunted him since early youth. His isolated poems had been read and loved by men and women of various kinds. So much was certain. But this pleasure in his work of which he feared that it was often but an abstract and literary pleasure, though it might be transferred by a few men and women from the isolated poem to the volume, ah, this was hardly the projection and saving of the poet's self through a people's life that the poet, that the artist craved. He found it in his heart to envy the men of an even recent past who had not been disturbed in their self-worship and had lived in the illusion that from the mere romantic worship of the artist self, briefly communicated to others, great art could grow. Now in the nineteen-fifties it was understood that the age of the mere virtuoso in any art was over. Not even operatic female stars were any more called *diva*. As for the divine poet whom the renaissance had invented, he was quite simply an archaism. But there had, on the other hand, been as yet no return to such masters as those who had designed the cathedrals of Europe—men so fulfilled by the metaphysical function of art that they were well content to place no emphasis upon their names and personalities. Twilight was upon earth. Twilight was upon art. When would a morning dawn?

Meanwhile Gabriel knew that what was called success or failure by the world as applied to his little volume or to whatever he might hereafter do could hardly trouble him. From the beginning all the cultural devices of man had had but one aim—to conquer death. The very death-wish that was again destroying civilization was but the rage of an intolerable despair over the failure to defeat death and win upon some terms an immortality. From that unfathomable passion to conquer death had grown the incest fear; from its depth men had built tombs and temples. A terror lest biological immortality might fail or even defeat its end by giving the soul of the father to the child had perhaps first led men to seek to conquer death through art and fame and oneness with a group and that group's memories. But those old fears of progeny were gone and long forgotten. Vestiges of them still survived at times in the neurotic pseudo-artist in his perishing Bohemian guise. Among Jews those fears were almost unknown within historic time. To them children were immortality and strength and hope and the immortality of art, if it came to any, a by-product.

He did his work with a peculiar ardour on this day. His students were aware of a glow within him that shed its ray on them. The way of life, he had been saying to himself, is not communicated from brain to brain; it is not often communicated from book to soul; it is communicated directly

from soul to soul. Both art and teaching must be by-products
of practice. Practice, life, the finding of immortality within
life by teaching and begetting—by both spiritual and biological fatherhood—these had been the values emphasized by
the wise and saintly of his race and faith in dark far ages,
in ages which the world, according to its folly, had often
called dark. Amid the surgings of a world unimaginable to
those sages that wisdom of theirs came to the aid of him in
his American classroom in the nineteen hundred and fifties,
when his country was about to be driven into war with
Japan, when the earth was being cleft asunder in Europe and
practice-shooting with fully-loaded war rockets was being
tried between two islands of the Arctic sea.

It was Friday evening. He went home and ushered in the
Sabbath according to its immemorial rite. And later he and
Eve celebrated a rite still more immemorial and no less
sacred, and Gabriel had the sure conviction that long before
his little book appeared the earnest of a better immortality
according to the flesh from which the soul could never be
divided would be Eve's and his.

XII

IT WAS in the spring of the second year of the life of David ben-Zion, the small son of Eve and Gabriel Weiss. Months had passed since these two had, except by a glance or a fleeting allusion, spoken of the state of the world and the tendency of its events. They dared not. They feared presage and omen of what was coming. They hoarded their beautiful days in the small house with the child in it and the group of white birches at the door. Gina was now often with them, white-haired but otherwise changed little from her lithe tranquil self. More tranquil than ever, in truth, as though she had penetrated to a depth of the inner life where agitations cease.

But gradually the rumours from afar came to their very door and to their ears. They came in a strange, almost archaic form. For many years now there had been a settlement of primitive mystic Christians in southern Missouri, not very far from Ozark City, people who shared their worldly goods and "spoke in tongues" and practised prophesying and peace. These people had thriven quietly and had made no noise in the world. But now they said that an angel was troubling the waters of their spirits, for it was, according to them, superabundantly clear that the last days had come and that all the prophecies that were written in the Book of the Revelation of St. John were about to be fulfilled. They therefore sent out messengers to arouse a Godless and forgetful world. One of these, a fiery-eyed old man, with long grey hair falling over his collar and long grey beard, named Ebenezer Gadsden, came to Ozark City.

He preached in churches and tabernacles; he asked permission to speak in the synagogues. In the latter he confined himself to interpreting the sixteenth chapter of the Apocalypse. Were not the rockets, he asked, shedding "that great hail out of heaven, every stone about the weight of a talent"? Had not the Germans and the Russians now for more than a quarter of a century "shed the blood of saints and prophets," both of the followers of Christ and of the house of Israel? Was not each of the seven great angels literally pouring out his "vial upon the earth"? And were not the armies of God and of the Adversary of God—in the churches he said, of course, of Christ and Anti-Christ—about to be locked in a battle which would decide for no man knew how long the destinies of mankind? With uplifted head and outstretched beseeching arms Ebenezer Gadsden thundered out the words of prophetic doom: "And he gathered them together into a place called in the Hebrew tongue Armageddon." And Gabriel clasped the hand of Eve in the pew beside him and whispered to her: *"Har Megiddo."* She nodded. The hill of Megiddo in the *Emek Yezreel,* in the great populous agricultural valley of the pioneers.

Slowly they walked home in the mild spring night.

"But of course it's all nonsense," Eve said, suddenly. "Those texts have always been juggled."

Gabriel was silent. Eve turned to him.

"You don't believe that God spoke to John on Patmos, Gabriel. You don't even believe that God literally spoke to Moses on Horeb, do you?"

"I'll tell you, darling, what I believe. It's simply this: there have been moments in history in which definite personalities have had a sudden illuminating insight into the character and trend of human destiny. The insight is overlaid, especially in this case, by layers of Hellenistic pseudo-mysticism. But it's there safe enough."

"Oh, Gabriel!" she protested.

He laughed an embarrassed little laugh.

"Think of the facts, Eve. Just think of the facts. Call it accidental that another Salamis on a gigantic scale will probably be fought within the next year at Megiddo. Call it accidental *that* our resettlement of Eretz Yisrael since the first World War has contributed toward making Palestine the pivotal point of defence of Britain and *that* Britain today represents the last defence of freedom and of good—both Jewish and Christian—and *that* the adversaries of freedom, the Fascists and Communists now joined together, have both relentlessly persecuted both Jews and Christians and the entire Judæo-Christian view of life. Good God! call it all accidental. I don't mind, darling. But then look closely at that word and concept accidental. What have you?"

"Nothing," she admitted. "Just a word in place of an explanation."

"Well then?"

"But my mind, Gabriel, is so made that I can't accept the mystical explanation as it stands. You don't agree with Gadsden?"

"Of course I don't—not as he puts it. My mind is made like yours. The human mind isn't powerful or subtle enough to grasp the meaning of the processes of human history. Nevertheless ——"

"What? What?"

Gabriel laughed.

" 'There's a divinity that shapes our ends!' That's the minimum. And the Shakespeare of the plays couldn't be called a very religious person. Or else, rudely put it this way: Mankind gets what it deserves; certain kinds of action have certain kinds of consequences because the universe is made that way and, historically speaking, these facts and trends are symbolized over and over again by the specific fate of certain historic groups, such as the Jewish people."

"What will become of our people? What will be the fate of Palestine now? We stand or fall by that!"

"Of course we do. But so does the world. And that makes it easier for us. If England, with all her sins and faults, loses the battle at Armageddon this autumn or next spring—nothing will matter for a thousand years. If she wins, we win and the human spirit wins."

He was grave. He said no more. They were within sight of their house. Eve grasped his arm.

"Gabriel, Gabriel!"

"Not yet, my heart," he said, softly. "Not yet."

They entered. Gina had been staying with little David ben-Zion, who had long been asleep upstairs. They found her reading at a table, her head bent, her hair still falling a little forward as of old. She looked up. She closed her book. She rose.

"David hasn't cried once," she said. "He's a better baby than his father was." She peered at Eve. "You look lovely, dear, but troubled."

Eve shook her head.

"Not really." She smiled. "Gabriel has half-convinced me of all kinds of strange and menacing things that I'd rather not believe."

"I'd rather not believe them either, Eve," Gabriel said. "Wait and see."

They had not very long to wait. Gadsden and his group of preachers were only the beginning of things. And they represented a crude beginning. A fire like a prairie or a forest fire had been lit in America. Not only the liberals and the religious people flared one after the other, one after the other, like torches, like beacons. The dark masses, the followers in farthest villages of Cornelius Faithful Prout, caught sparks from the same central fire. Long racial and cultural memories stirred within them as England, sore beset by land and sea, her shipping menaced, her foothold on the rock of Gibraltar more and more precarious between the Fascists of Spain and the Moors and Germans of Tangier, landed

every division she could spare at Haifa at the foot of
Mount Carmel. There was no lack of men to fight in her
armies. For the fire that burned in America now at this late
date had begun to burn long before in the ruined and enslaved lands of the Continent; it had burned with an even
fiercer flame in those small countries which, from year to
difficult year, had maintained themselves in outer and inner
freedom amid the colossal slave-states which spilt over their
borders the diseases, miseries, contaminations of their own
decay. Thus from all the ends of Europe men flocked alone
or by twos and threes, by small groups and whole battalions,
foot-sore along the broken roads, begging a bite and shelter
in a sagging barn, to join the armies of England in her ultimate struggle against the Fascist-Communist hordes. From
France came volunteers by the thousand; with bloody border
forays Germans broke out of the reeking, hunger-riven prison
that was now their country; from Denmark and from Scandinavia men set out in small boats, in unseaworthy ships,
seeking to make the port of Inverness or else an outer island
of the Shetland group. From Switzerland, old home of freedom, they came. From Holland and Belgium, natives of those
lands; but also in their maritime cities gathered those who
from farthest Poland and the long devastated countrysides
of the Czechs esteemed it better to seek to strike one last
blow for human liberty and human civilization than to rot
and starve under the heavy, stupid, ape-like dictatorships
of the Centre and the East of Europe. Many of these men
perished on the roads; thousands were lost at sea; hunger
and disease ravaged many more before they reached their
goal of some English port. Nor would England have had the
wherewithal to clothe and feed and arm these slowly gathering hosts had not the Dominions of Canada and of South
Africa sent under convoy fleets charged with cloth and wheat
and chemicals and steel openly smuggled across the frontier
from the United States. Meanwhile the Australians, with

South African help, had built a navy and, though sustaining heavy losses from Japanese cruisers and submarines, had made their way to the Persian Gulf and landed troops at Basra. But this army, though receiving aid from small swift motor-ships running out of Bombay, was sore beset. There was no bread or shade in Iraq; the Arabs harried the Australians from the west; the Persians, inflamed with religious zeal and terror by Sovietized Turkmen from the Caspian shore, harried them from the east.

Perhaps it was that famous tragic march of the Australians which, more than any other circumstance, fired the imagination of America. And now with imagination afire and hearts in which old sympathies blended with vicarious dread at last aflame, the people of these States were no more willing to be contented with their own remote security. They heard; they saw; they studied maps; they accepted the vision and the menace as their own. The vast Russo-German armies, innumerable hosts, had long crossed both the Caucasus Mountains and the Dardanelles. The Turks had long built them roads and railroads from Scutari over Smyrna to Beirut and from Tiflis in Georgia to Damascus. The armed nations of the slaves of the dictatorships were pouring irresistibly toward Palestine and Suez, whence, with the aid of the treacherous Arabs and feeble Egyptians, they would seize the entire eastern littoral of the Mediterranean Sea. Then, like Alexander of old, they could march east. India would be theirs. All the Indies, the British and the Dutch, would be theirs. They and the Japanese would rule the world. Chaos and old Night would reign. Suddenly the last free men of the Far West saw the measure of the unheard-of menace. For behind the slave-armies were the granaries of Russia and from the Dodecanese Islands and long-conquered Greece issued forth the small wasp-like torpedo boats of the Italians whose pilots were drugged, like the German and the Soviet air-men, and dedicated to death, a well-bought death, if their single torpedo could shatter a troop-ship or a food-ship of the British defenders of mankind.

The mystics and the sooth-sayers and the speakers of "tongues" were heard no more. Hard men and practical men in America took up the cry of Armageddon. Somewhere in northern Palestine—so much was clear to the dullest—would be fought the most crucial battle of the ages which would decide for no man knew how many centuries the destiny of the race. There was no declaration of war. Many years ago Germany and Italy and Russia had closed their embassies and consulates and had let them fall into decay or be sold, and withdrawn from the usages of civilization. There was no breach, therefore, of diplomatic relations. There was little direct governmental action. The nation arose and silently swept aside the old neutrality laws. There was no bartering with Britain. Armaments were made; ships, tanks, airplanes and torpedoes were built. The great denominational and cultural and economic units—churches and co-operatives with one accord—opened stations where volunteers could report for training and equipment. There was one fear and one only, the fear lest the Americans should come too late.

Gabriel sat at table between his wife and his mother. The two women had recently drawn very close to one another. Thus may one see under black skies, the forked lightning already leaping from cloud to cloud but not yet from cloud to earth, doves at the door of their cotes huddled together for warmth and a little comfort, lightless and colourless of plumage, against the onslaught of the storm. Before Gabriel lay open a small Testament in the original tongue. "Pharaonechoh, King of Egypt, wanted to attack the Assyrian empire on the shores of the Euphrates." He spoke slowly, almost dreamily. "Our King Josiah seems to have regarded that as what later ages called a breach of neutrality. It was like the German march through Belgium in the first World War.

So Josiah sought to stop the Egyptian armies in the valley of Megiddo. But he was defeated. The archers of Egypt shot at him. His servants carried him in a chariot dead from Megiddo, and brought him to Jerusalem and buried him in his own sepulchre." The heads of the two women were bent a little lower. "But once"—Gabriel lifted his voice—"once there was a great victory won over the dark forces of the world at *Har Megiddo*. Deborah, the prophetess chanted that triumph:

> 'The kings came and fought;
> then fought the kings of Cana'an
> in Taanach by the waters of Megiddo.'

There Sisera, the captain of the hosts of the kings of Cana'an was defeated—he who had nine hundred chariots of iron and twenty years had mightily oppressed the children of Israel. But Israel attributed no victory to its own virtue or valour. *Min-shamayim nilchamu*—out of heaven they fought! *Ha'khochbim mi'mesilotham nilchamu im Sisera*—the stars from out of their courses fought against Sisera.'"

Eve looked up, white and stricken.

"You are going too, Gabriel?"

"Three quarters of a million volunteers have already registered in our country. Among them are eighty-thousand young Jews who are forming the battalions of Zion in the defence of Eretz Yisrael and of mankind. Because of you, darling, and David and my being Mummie's only son they are making me go as a member of the Y. M. H. A. staff. But if the danger becomes too great, none of us can stand back."

Eve's beautiful dark head sank slowly down upon her arms that rested on the table. Her face was hidden. Then Gina rose and quietly drew herself up to her full height. Her voice was tranquil. But Gabriel heard in it the vibration of an old woe and of an agony never wholly assuaged. Lightly Gina laid her slender hand on Eve's hair.

"Let him go, my daughter. It is more than twenty years now since his father died. And I know that retribution belongs to God. But perhaps Gabriel and the many thousands like him are being forged by God into the instrument of his justice. Let him go, Eve. Let him help strike the blow. It may be that then our little David will never have to strike any blow. It may be that then *his* world will be a world of peace."

ℂ THE EPILOGUE

Nous voyons maintenant que l'abîme de l'His-
toire est assez grand pour tout le monde. Nous
sentons qu'une civilisation a la même fragilité
qu'une vie. Les circonstances qui enverraient les
œuvres de Keats et celles de Baudelaire rejoindre
les œuvres de Ménandre ne sont plus du tout in-
concevables: elles sont dans les journaux.

PAUL VALÉRY

(We have come to see that the abyss of history is deep enough for all. We have come to
feel that a civilization is as fragile as a single
life. Circumstances which may well send the
works of Keats and Baudelaire to join those
of Menander in oblivion are no more inconceivable at all. We read of them in our daily
papers.)

THE EPILOGUE

I

LONG long ago the year two thousand had sunk back into the mists of time. How long ago? The people who lived in the old concrete-and-steel catacombs which had been built during the third world war under all the cities and all the lands of the continent of Europe did not know. Nor did the peasants know who here and there, where disease was no more virulent nor the soil for ever ruined, scratched shallow furrows in the earth and brought forth meagre crops. How were they to know—either the dwellers in the catacombs, troglodytes of a late age, or the peasants or even those who housed themselves in the ruined walls, repaired and roofed with the trunks of stripped trees, of the Cathedral of Chartres and the Hradshin and St. Peter's and the Kremlin and the thousand other fallen monuments of the age of the giants who, according to all stories now told, had had all wisdom and all knowledge and all strength and had in mighty and many battles destroyed all that the gods had given them the grace to build? How were those poor men to know?

They were hard put to it to live at all. They had neither the hardihood nor the inventiveness of primitive men. Their hand-looms and few tools were awkward and fragile. They could not have survived at all had they not before the memory of any now living followed the sun. Forests and swamps once more covered all the north. In milder regions, in what had been called Provence and the Apennine country, in the Crimea and in Sicily, the population was less sparse. Here, too, flocks and herds flourished best and a mild pastoral culture of song and legend feebly and fitfully arose. But of knowledge of either the past or of the processes of nature there was little. Always there were born men, not looked upon too trustfully by their fellows, who scratched in the ruins of the giants' age, and bringing forth books from under the great piles of refuse that had once been the world's great libraries, pored by the light of torch or candle over stained and tattered volumes. But since these books were books of many ages, now seeming, in the immense perspective of time to be all one age, and since they were in many languages, of which the use and knowledge were now lost, the eager readers gained from their reading but a vast inchoate jumble of science and fable, mistaking poetry for fact and dreams for history, and thus becoming mere stargazers and necromancers and healers with herbs and simples. Snatches of great verse and prophecy, half dimly understood, they unearthed, as well as statues and torn canvases with still the glow of flesh and gold and blue and crimson upon them and deeming a Greek bust and an El Greco saint aspiring flame-like to an unseen object and a nude of Renoir in whose skin the sunshine had been captured to be all of one age and of the meaning of one age, they built themselves a dream-world of the gods and ideals of those ancients the children of whom they knew themselves to be. Once more, as in times utterly lost to memory, they began to scratch their imaginings in a contorted Latin script upon the prepared skins of sheep and goats. Once more they entered groves and fallen monuments by night to commune with powers beyond themselves. Once more they sought in myth and legend to tell whence man comes and whither he goes.

They were a shy and fearful folk. But the objects of their fears were other things than man had ever feared before. Neither torrent in flood nor fire nor thunder scared them.

But though they did not know the past by any process that can be called knowledge, its tremendous teaching had entered into the current of their blood and become an instinct as sure as that of the migrating birds. They feared the things once called law and order by law and the power in specific men, no other or better than themselves, to hold themselves the instruments of law and the executioners of justice. They dwelt in simple small communities; if any man stole the elders, having consulted the community, drove him into exile; if any killed, he, too, was driven into the wilderness or on a small boat and with a three days' ration exposed to the mercies of the sea. Again and again there came forward those who said there should be rule and law and regulation. These were often slain by the sudden flaring fury of all the men and even women of these mild tribes and groups. Though all were poor, yet some were less so than others. Yet none envied any man his greater possessions. It was only if such an one sought by means of his greater possessions to enslave another or bend or break his will that there arose from the simple people about, whether weavers or smiths or peasants or herdsmen, that sudden flame of anger and revolt.

On the great roads built aforetime and kept here and there in tolerable repair by the men who lived, as most men did, along them, there was not a little wandering on foot or horseback or in carts. The purpose of some of this wandering was traffic. They were better weavers toward the north and better breeders of sheep toward the south; vintners sent forth their wines to exchange for cloth and corn. There were sly men who sought to introduce tokens of gold from the ruins of former ages as a medium of exchange. Against them no less than against the proponents of law and order arose the instinctive rebellion of men. It was a wicked thing and a thing against nature—thus they rationalized the monitions of their blood and genes—to assign value to baubles of no value and to say that clots of yellow metal, oozed doubtless by some disease of earth, were an equivalent of the warmth of garments or the ecstasy of wine.

But much of the wandering along the ancient highways was for the mere joy of wandering and of society. For the people of this time were inveterate tellers of tales and seekers of friendship. In harvest seasons, more especially, young men and women would wander about to help the peasants bring in their crops for no wage but food and wine and lodging and free evenings in brightly lit barns where those who could sing songs and tell tales were well received and praised and loved above any other kind of men. For all the tales were held to be true. Or, rather, the antique distinction between truth to fact and truth to the soul of man had either been lost or was held foolish or negligible. If a tale convinced it was believed. If it was believed it was true. If it stirred the passions of love or of freedom or the desire for beauty, which are, as everyone knew, the three great passions of man, into visible life and new activity, was it not far, far truer than some trivial unstirring thing that had happened to such an one on such a day in such a place?

II

THE tales and legends told in farmsteads and villages and under the shade of the ruins of old cities and by the shores of the wine-dark sea were often tales of far lands spoken and told from mouth to ear and again from mouth to ear across the many-leagued earth and gathering both force and truth and reality from the many tellers who had made the tale their own as delight, as sombreness, as warning. And one of the tales of universal currency to which always and over and over again men were glad to listen for its terror and its pity and its warning and its truth—knowing not and caring less whether it was fact or fable, history or apologue, yet distinguishing not between the two—ran in the form told especially in what had once been called Provence as follows:

Far in the East—some said on this slope of the Ural Mountains and some said on the Asian slope, and others averred not there at all but in an Ultima Thule on an ice-choked sea—there dwelt a people who had kept the ways of the giants and city-builders of old. They were a people of slaves ruled by a man who was called a god and held himself to be a god. But it was not always clear whether the god-ruler was a man or an idol with eyes of agate and crown of bronze. But whether man or idol the people bent their backs and their hearts to his bidding. To this far country came a pastoral folk, much like the people who in Provence or Sicily told the tale, whose pastures had gradually turned into desert, a free mild people dreaming that they were led, as in truth why not, by an invisible God. They were in search of new pastures and desired nothing better than to share the wool of their sheep and the milk of their ewes and the flesh of their lambs with the new neighbours in the new pastures that they might find. And so for a period matters stood. But the idol god-ruler was not contented thus. He must rule. He must lay his lash upon the backs of men. Such was his evil nature. So he said to a councillor or else, if he was an idol with agate eyes, the councillor said in his name: "These strangers increase. They grow strong. They will not be contented with their present pastures. They will desire to rob and rule us. They must be crushed before that day comes." Listeners to this tale by camp fires or in huge farm kitchens or in summer in the shade of the old walls of Avignon strangely preserved, would softly ululate, since they too of all things most feared force and rule and felt the inner dread of that pastoral folk which in the tale was about to be enslaved. And what, they asked, was the name of that wicked king or king's minion or idol's mouth. And some said the name was Pare'oh and others said it was Saracen. But most tellers said it was both of these, though the name of Saracen was more often spoken. He, the tale went on, drove those good settlers from their pastures. He drove them out into the fierce sunlight to toil at making huge rectangular slabs of mud which, held together by straw mixed in with them and thereafter dried in the sun, became the building-stones, as it were, of huge-walled cities in which were to be imprisoned as many of the land's people as possible to be forced to trade and war. Over the strange defenceless toilers Saracen set overseers with seven-tailed, seven-toothed lashes. Men and women toiled and sweated and lamented. They sighed for their old free, peaceful life. There they had known God. Now they almost lost the memory of Him. For God dies wherever men, deeming themselves gods, become devils. This sentence was the refrain of the tale. Whoever told it came to the point where these words were spoken. Whoever listened waited for this saying. And then there were often those who would cry, "Let not God die among us!"

Sorer and bitterer became the servitude of the once free folk under Pare'oh and Saracen, who was described as a dark ugly angry man with cold black eyes and lips that never smiled. And some tellers of the tale averred that when he had no slaves over whom to bid his men swing the lash, that then in a secret chamber at the top of a high tower he lashed and castigated his own nakedness. Now he had the defenceless pastoral folk and there was a dreadful quietude about his hard mouth. But at last, at long, long last, there arose among the enslaved people a strong man and a liberator. Who was he? Some said he was a man of the Pare'oh people. Others disputed this. He was a son of the oppressed. But he was among the few who had not forgotten the name of God and he had watched the Pare'oh people and had read the future of them and of his people both in the stars and in his heart. What was his name? There were many answers given by various tellers of the tale. Zur, they said was his name. Arech or Aroch, said others. Men coming from the banks of the Seine River called him Pierre Le Grand. Still others said that he was one Christos, the son of Moshe. This latter was the opinion of men from the islands of the Great Middle Sea. But all the tellers knew all the names and pronounced them with both awe and relish, as though the very uttering of the names would help and protect them.

Now this Zur saw the suffering and servitude of his people and heard their cries. But he bided his time until one day Saracen himself came out to the mud yards on the banks of a broad shallow river. The overseers swung their lashes on the naked backs of men and women that soon flashed in the dazzling sun with streamers of blood. Then did this man Zur run, his long robe flying wing-like behind him, out from among the ranks of the enslaved and with a huge staff he slew Saracen, and in the silence that fell cried to his brethren in a great voice and they arose, as though from the dead, and gathered about him and followed him, taking time only to gather up a few goods and their little children. Into the Eastern desert he led them. And Pare'oh and the oppressors thought they would perish there. But these people, having regained their freedom, remembered the name of God. And God fed them, for the free shall not know want. And God brought them to the foot of a mountain in the Eastern desert and on the top of that mountain He spoke to Zur Arech, He spoke to Christos, the son of Moshe—at this point all the tellers of the tale, this being long use and custom, called the man by all his names—and God said: It is better for men to obey my law than the law of man. To this the people, having known the hardship of human servitude, consented. And the man who was their leader and prophet brought them God's law from the top of the mountain, from the midst of a fire that burned on the top of the mountain and seemed with the tip of its ultimate flame to be aspiring to the very heart of heaven. The people received the law and wept with joy. They knew that, having God's law, they would never, save for the hardness and wickedness of their own hearts, be forced again to bow to the law of man.

III

O F ALL the tales told among the people of plain and mountain, of riverbank and seashore, this was the first to be written down. It was written down in various places by men who spoke diverse tongues. One version was written in Arles in a broken Romance dialect and one by a man on the island of Malta in an Oriental tongue now spoken by but few and said to have been called Arabic aforetime. This version was by many deemed the truest, for the versions differed greatly each from the other. But others swore the best was one that came from a far island of the Western seas. Copies multiplied and new tellings were based upon those three oldest ones and in market-places from the Rhine to the Rhone and from the Seine to the fabled straits by the ruins of Istamboul men stood on certain days and read this tale to the many who could not read.

As times grew worse this tale came closer and closer to the hearts of men. They no longer told it as tale, but as truth. It was so true to their souls and their souls' needs that they believed it as fact. It was so deeply borne out by all of life as they knew the life of man to be that they could doubt no jot or tittle of the tale, even though the versions they had differed each from the other. For all the things that happened in the story were beginning once more, as the years and the ages passed, to happen to them. In spite of all their inborn horror of rule and force and their sure knowledge of this one thing, if of no other, that the giants of olden times who had built the great cities and the great roads and the unimaginable tunnels and bridges and had written the thousand, thousand books, now buried under ruins—that these giants had destroyed all they had built by wars among each other growing out of the oppression and rule of man over man; in spite of their deep knowledge of this thing, it began to happen in the selfsame way among them, too. Here and there the strong and the subtle banded them together and persuaded weaker and simpler souls under promise of warmth and wine and women to make common cause with them. But the common cause soon faded and the rewards were nowise forthcoming and once again there were rulers and ruled and oppressors and oppressed and once again, if only of the stone and steel of the ruins of the ages of the giants, fortresses began to be built and prisons and even barracks. And once again—and this was a thing most dreadful and confusing—strong men once subtle but now made stupid by their very strength began to tell the oppressed what speech they should speak, what things believe, what roads to travel, what garb to wear. Thus small fierce kingdoms were set up using the giants' fortresses as capitals, bending the huge remains of the giants' iron and steel into rude spears and shields, such as were seen depicted upon antique paintings, digging deeper and deeper into the ruins of former times for gold and gauds wherewith to bedizen the new rulers and their women. In all these kingdoms, in that of Perpignan, in that of Florence, in that of Lombardy, in that of the Tyrol, in that of the Meuse, and in that of the Mouths of the Rhine one thing that none had foreseen, that none seemed consciously to have brought about, was nevertheless done. And it was this, that messengers and minions of the new brutal rulers sought out all copies of the Book of Zur, as that favourite legend and evangel had now long been called, and destroyed them and hunted and hounded men who sought to tell the tale again by word of mouth or to rewrite it from memory or to bring in copies written in the still free lands of the free people.

Once more dark shadows clouded the souls of men. The

joyous life of the roads dwindled. The kings promised huge rewards to men who, reading more accurately in the books of the ancients, would recover those various and victorious kinds of magic by which those ancient giants had been enabled to build their mighty works and wage their Cyclopean wars. And the king of the realm of the Mouths of the Rhine, a huge, white-skinned, shock-headed man with the bones of an ox and the forehead of an ape declared that he and his men, better and braver than any on earth, would fare southward and conquer all the other kingdoms, nay, all the shores of all the rivers and of the great Middle Sea itself and introduce right rule and strict order where there were now but sloth and arbitrariness and unmanly pleasure. He stood, shouting this threat before his men on a dais of rude wood, shaking in his muscular arm a spear made of giants' steel, when there came before him a small, lithe, dark-bearded man who held in his hands a parchment scroll of the Book of Zur. And the small man said: "It is written, 'God dies wherever men, deeming themselves gods, become devils.'" The king's face grew scarlet. His brain was not big enough to take in the saying that was written. But his muscle worked well. He drove his spear clean though the belly of the small dark man. It came out far through the back, so that the corpse could neither stand nor fall. And the king's blond warriors bellowed with laughter.

IV

THROUGH all the fields and forests ran, carried by
men, by women, and even by little children, the story
of the first martyr. In the villages of all the countrysides
that were still free of the rule of the new kings the people
gathered in fear and agitation. "Pare'oh is back," they said;
"Saracen is back. Soon we, too, shall be ruled and oppressed
and be driven like cattle and be no more men and no more
free men. We must band together and also scratch among
the mountains of broken steel which the giants left for
spears to protect us against the kings and the makers of
slaves. Unless the man Zur come again, unless he who wrote
the evangel come again and lead us into the wilderness to
the foot of a mountain where we too can receive that law of
God which will set us free of the law of man. But Zur tarries
and we do not know the law of God and have no way of finding it out."

It is not related how long it took for the news of the first
martyr and for the consequent waiting for Zur and the learning of the law of God to take hold of the hearts of men.
Years passed. Perhaps decades. It is also known that the
kings of the north and of the south found resistance when
they sought to extend their boundaries into the free lands.
There were people who fought. But there were more who fled
into forest and mountain, destroying first their wheat-fields
and their vineyards. For they had lost the use of arms and
the habit of killing men as though they were animals. Dis-
may and terror spread gradually over the earth and the
Book of Zur, read in caverns by torchlight, spoken of under
stars, was the only hope and comfort of the helpless free

342

and good men who were diminishing in numbers and whose lands were being narrowed by the killers of the kings.

Zur, for whom they prayed, did not come. But a woman came from Africa. She came on a boat with two companions, a girl and an aged man, first to Malta in a boat with a golden-coloured sail and thence to Sicily. She was dark and tall. Her eyes were soft but her forehead majestic. Her name was Malkha and her people had been driven almost into the Middle Sea by a king who had set up his kingdom in the passes of the Atlas Mountains and whose Berbers made forays into the plain. But she herself, it was rumoured, came from a very far country on the eastern edge of the great desert where men were mild and wise and read the stars as other men can read the letters of a scroll.

Malkha came to the free people who still dwelt in Europe. But she came not to the men. Quietly she went to the women and spoke to them by day and whispered to them by night. Men asked their wives and daughters what Malkha said; for some of their wives and daughters, persuaded by her, left home and made their way into the kingdoms to speak to the women there who were even sorer oppressed than the men. And the women told their men of Malkha and her message. The people of Zur, who had fled from Pare'oh and slain Saracen, who had the secret of freedom which was God's law, were not all dead and gone. Their name aforetime was Yehudim, as some said, and as others said Bnei' Yisrael, Children of Israel. And somewhere—but they did not know whether Malkha knew where—some of them still lived and knew the law of God that freed men from obedience to other men and from war. But they must be sought out and a question must be asked them and a prayer addressed to them. But what that question was or what that prayer none knew but Malkha. Only she told them it was a woman's matter. Men had no part in it, though men would be redeemed too if the miracle came to pass.

Malkha's hair was white before she accomplished her purpose, before the women of the broad lands, old and young, with their little children whom they dared not leave in carts and on asses, thousands upon thousands of them, a long, long pilgrims' train, set out toward the East. Wherever they came, avoiding the new kingdoms, people fed and housed them and bade them rest, and many women in many places joined them. And there were those among them who played timbrels and those who played flutes and there were many who sang verses drawn from the Book of Zur in their various tongues.

In earliest springtime they had set out, and now it was the misty autumn season. But the land to which they had come was a warm land this side of the Caucasus Mountains, a land by a blue sea, which had been of old called Crimea. In this land, toward the sunset of an early October day, Malkha and her closest companions at the head of that long train of the women of all lands, stopped at the small sound of the chanting of men in a tongue none knew or had ever heard. In a soft hollow of the hills they beheld a group of men, white-capped and clad in white, surrounded by a semicircle of women. The men and women were dark, with brown eyes and small hands. The men chanted their prayers from books like the books of ancient ages. And in their midst stood one tall, slender, bearded, whom Malkha recognized as one Jehuda of whom she had heard sayings and tales in farthest Africa, the leader and the teacher of these people. He stood erect. He put to his lips a great curved ram's horn and blew upon it. Thrice did he blow. And first the sound was sudden and like a cry—*T'Kiah!* And next he blew a sound soft and tremulous and beseeching in which trembled all the sorrows of the heart of man—*Sh'varim*. And lastly he blew a blast that was at once a summons and a warning and a prophecy —*T'ruah!* And all the women from the four corners of the earth heard the blast of the ram's horn. But Malkha turned to her companions and spoke: "It is the end of the Day of Atonement. He has blown the ram's horn, the Trumpet of the Jubilee. Now is the hour." And she lifted up her voice and cried aloud: "We would have peace and know God's law. Bear us the Christ again!"

The pilgrim women took up the cry. From rank to rank it passed. It sounded in voices deep or shrill, clear or broken, triumphant or tear-choked. It became at times a wail and then swelled to a chorus, and then sighed like the sighing of winds as the sun sank behind the mountains and the first stars glittered above their rim: "Bear us the Christ again!"

THE END